DAUGHTER OF EXILE

Daughter of Exile

ISABEL GLASS

A TOM DOHERTY ASSOCIATES BOOK

NEW YORK

DAUGHTER OF EXILE

A Tor Book
Published by Tom Doherty Associates, LLC
175 Fifth Avenue
New York, NY 10010

www.tor.com

Tor® is a registered trademark of Tom Doherty Associates, LLC.

Library of Congress Cataloging-in-Publication Data

Glass, Isabel.
    Daughter of exile / Isabel Glass—1st ed.
        p. cm.
    "A Tom Doherty Associates book."
    ISBN 0-765-30745-6 (acid-free paper)
    1. Young women—Fiction. 2. Fathers—Death—Fiction. 3. Exiles—fiction. I.
Title.

PS3607.L369D38 2004
813'.54—dc22

                                                          2003061493

First Edition: March 2004

Printed in the United States of America

0 9 8 7 6 5 4 3 2 1

ACKNOWLEDGMENTS

For that spark of inspiration,
thanks to the Harry Gomez
writers Retreat

Daughter of Exile

ONE

It had been fourteen years since Lord Challo Hashan was banished from court, but as the years passed he did not grow resigned. Instead he turned bitter in his exile: his once-thin frame became gaunt, lines of discontent etched themselves in his face, his mouth turned downward in a permanent sneer of unhappiness. His golden hair developed strands of gray, turning it a strange rusted color, and grew unkempt to his shoulders. His beard, completely white, fell to his chest.

From court he and his four-year-old daughter, Angarred, had gone to his manor house, Hashan Hall. Once there, though, he neglected his lands, and more and more of them had to be sold off to pay his debts. He spent long hours in his study, poring over histories and genealogies, trying to understand where he had gone wrong, trying to plot a way back to power. After a while his thoughts would stray from his books and he would remember the long candle-lit halls where he had danced, or the king's great feasts of twenty courses. As if torturing him, his mind would present each scene perfectly, the straight lines of the dancers as they bowed and curtsied toward each other on the checkered marble floor, the delicious smells of food mingling in the air.

Angarred frequently discovered him bent over one or another

leather-bound tome, the fat candles guttering in the drafty air of the study. With her father distracted Angarred grew wild, roaming the fields and forests in her ragged finery. She ran with Lord Hashan's packs of dogs or swam in the lake or visited the people who lived on his lands, some of whom had been there for years without his permission, or even his knowledge. She was tall for her age, like her father, but big-boned, more substantial, with thick red-gold hair that fell in tangles down her back.

Hashan could afford only three servants, all of them hired from the village near the manor: Rushlag the housekeeper, Elenin the cook and a steward they rarely saw. Rushlag would sometimes catch Angarred before she set out and try to bind her hair in plaits or mend the holes in her clothes, but when Angarred came home in the evening she would have lost the hair-ribbons and torn and dirtied the dresses, and Rushlag, catching sight of her, would moan and wring her hands.

Angarred did not live in complete isolation, though. Lord Hashan received many visitors: other exiles, malcontents, bankrupt merchants, pirates, indolent younger sons and daughters of nobility. They sat up late around the scarred oak table in the dining hall, drinking and plotting and laughing, taking notes and scrawling maps on scraps of parchment. As they became drunker they would clink their mugs together and swear to Hashan's innocence and vow to clear his name. Once one of them had looked up at her from under a broad-brimmed leather hat; she had held his eye for a time without flinching and then turned and ran to her room, where she pulled the covers over her and shivered, unable to get to sleep.

As she grew older she was expected to help Elenin the cook on these occasions, fetching food from the kitchen and going into the cellar for the dusty bottles of wine that Hashan's father and grandfather had laid down, bottles that were fast disappearing under the demands of the thirsty guests.

When Angarred was seventeen she heard a new note come into the plotters' voices. There was talk of a stone, or maybe a Stone; she could hear the capital letter when they said the word. The Stone had come from the country of Takeke and was supposed to have great magical power; the king wanted it to help Queen

Cherenin produce an heir, although she was far past childbearing age. Several plotters made bawdy suggestions about the queen, growing loud in their hilarity.

Nothing came of this news; nothing ever came of the bits and trifles of gossip from the capital. It was over a year before Angarred learned what happened next, when several new conspirators joined them, men fresh from Pergodi.

"King Tezue made a banquet to honor the envoy from Takeke," one of them said. Most of the men and women around the table listened eagerly. "One of his famous twenty-course banquets, with boar and eels and pheasant. He displayed the Stone there in the middle of the room, in full sight of everyone, but somehow it was stolen. And not only that. The next day we learned that a good many magicians had disappeared from the capital as well."

"I can't believe you folks haven't heard this," another man said. "It happened a year ago, or more."

The man was facing away from Hashan, and so he did not see the look of longing that passed over the lord's face. But Angarred saw, and turned away, her heart filled with fury and helplessness and pity. She left the men and women to their talk and paced angrily through the corridors of the manor house.

A while later, in a room far from the conspirators, she came upon another of the men from Pergodi. He had his back to her; she could see only that he was a little taller than she and broad shouldered, with long wheat-colored hair bound in a leather tie.

"Who are you?" she asked.

He turned quickly. He had been trying to light a fire, she realized. "You'll never get that fireplace working," she said. "There's a nest of swallows in the chimney."

He laughed. "We are far from court, I see," he said. He brushed at his hair, though none of it had come loose from the tie. He had wide-set blue-gray eyes. He bowed to her; there was something mocking in it. "My name is Mathewar," he said. "And I have the pleasure of meeting—"

"Angarred," she said curtly, seeing no reason to return his bow.

"My lady Angarred," he said. "Is there somewhere I can light a fire?"

"This way."

He picked up a battered leather knapsack and followed her outside and down a chilly hallway. He drew his cloak closely around him. Cold moonlight came in through a high leaded window and he looked around with quick, penetrating glances, undoubtedly taking note of the dust, the fallen masonry, the sounds of mice scrabbling in the walls. She showed him to a room and continued on.

"My thanks, Lady Angarred," he called after her.

She said nothing, but went into the next room. Here ivy had made its way in through a broken window and grew up thickly along one of the walls. Something rustled within it; the Godkings knew what kind of animals had set up home there.

She went to the opposite wall. There was a hole between two stones; she never knew if it had been placed there intentionally or, more likely, was part of the slow disintegration of the manor house. She put her eye to it and watched.

Mathewar made a pile of the small amount of kindling in the fireplace, then glanced nervously around him. He spotted a broken chair lying on its side and picked it up, then raised it and smashed it against the mantelpiece. He added the chair to the fireplace, building up the pile with small, neat motions.

He stepped back. She expected him to take out a flint, but instead he spoke a few words and the fire blazed into light. She gasped, then put her hand to her mouth, but he had not heard her; he was too intent on the fire.

A magician. Did her father know? The conspirators had just been gossiping about magicians: they had disappeared or were disappearing from the capital. Was he one of those? What spell did he intend to speak? Would he burn the entire house down around them?

He took some objects out of his knapsack and squatted by the fire. He began to murmur to himself; she could not make out the words.

He set a small silver cup by the fire; she saw the red flames reflecting in its rounded surface. Then he lifted a bottle of hard smoked leather. His nervousness had increased; he was trembling badly now and his movements were no longer as economical. He poured the contents of the bottle into the cup—it looked syrupy, red, like blood—and pushed the cup with shaking hands closer to the fire.

A long moment passed. Mathewar rocked back and forth, still muttering. Finally he reached out and lifted the cup, splashing several drops on the floor in his eagerness.

He took a few sips and then sat back and sighed. He drank again, upending the cup. His shaking stilled. He stared into the fire; even through the wall, in the dim light, Angarred thought she could see his eyes grow large and glazed. He rubbed at the drops he had spilled and then licked his fingers. A slow smile spread over his face.

Angarred made her way back to the kitchen, trembling slightly at what she had just witnessed, unable to put a name to what she felt. Elenin bustled back and forth between the kitchen and the dining hall, carrying mugs and empty wine bottles. "There you are," she said. "I don't know why you can't stay and help me serve like your father asks you—"

"Do people drink blood?" Angarred asked.

"What?" Elenin put down the mugs and stared at her.

Angarred returned her gaze. "Are there people who drink blood?"

"No, of course not. Where do you get these ideas?"

"I just saw someone. One of Father's visitors."

"You couldn't have. Who?"

"He said his name was Mathewar."

"That one." Elenin glanced around carefully to make sure no one could hear her and then said, "He drinks something, you're right about that. Rushlag saw it in his room. Something fashionable at court, no doubt." Her last words were scornful; she had a countrywoman's distrust of the capital.

The next time Mathewar left the dining hall she hurried through a maze of corridors and confronted him before he reached the room with the fireplace. "Does Father know you're a magician?" she asked.

"Yes. Does he know you've been spying on me?"

His hands were trembling again, but his voice was patient, almost amused. Despite his eagerness for his drink he seemed willing to stand and bandy words with her for hours.

"He wouldn't care if he did," she said. "He lets me do whatever I want."

He leaned against the wall and crossed his arms. "Ah. And do you want to marry Prince Norue?"

Earlier one of the plotters had drunkenly suggested that she marry the prince, the king's nephew, that Hashan return to power that way. She flushed with embarrassment for her father and his ridiculous friends. "Don't be stupid. I can't marry Norue. Father knows that."

"Fortunately for you. Norue's a terrible man, cold and evil-hearted."

Did he know Norue? Had he been one of the king's magicians, back in Pergodi? Hoping to regain the advantage she asked, "Does Father know why you leave the table each night?"

"You seem to know a great deal about me. May I ask why you're so interested?"

"I'm not interested!" she said, suddenly angry. "I'm worried about my father, that's all. He lets all sorts of questionable people take advantage of his hospitality."

"Ah, I'm questionable, am I? Well then, to answer your question, no he doesn't. You may tell him, if you like."

She wouldn't; she almost never spoke to him. Mathewar probably knew that. "What is it you drink? Is it something that magicians need?"

He laughed softly at that, as if she had made a joke. "Sometimes," he said. "Sometimes we do. It goes by many names—the bloodred rose, the inexhaustible jewel, the red wound. Your father would probably know it as sattery. And now—" He brushed past her before she had time to react. "—I'm afraid I must leave you. I trust I've answered all your questions, and am questionable no more." He strode down the hallway before she could think of a reply.

A few days later Lord Hashan decided to lead his guests on a hunt. Angarred hated these occasions, times when her father pretended that he was back at court and riding with all the pomp of the king. Compared to King Tezue's retinue, though, Hashan's following was thin and ragged, just eight people, their shabby clothes and hard faces looking strange in the new morning. Some of the dogs coursed at the horses' feet, more out of curiosity than to help with the hunt.

They picked their way through the forest. The sun had just topped the horizon but the light was murky, the high peaks of the firs lost in darkness. Fog drifted by in clumps, like soft herds of sheep, when the wind blew. They rode in silence, their breath coming white in the cold air. The forest smelled of aromatic needles and mold.

"King Tezue—now there was a hunter," Hashan said. "The trumpeter would announce us, and the dogs would be surging around us, barking, and the king's bearer would bring back the animal's scat, and then we'd be off, riding hard through the forest—"

Angarred had heard all her father's stories about the court before. She dropped back. Something flew past her, buzzing, and Hashan screamed.

Everything seemed to slow down. She saw the arrow jutting from Hashan's chest. "After him!" Mathewar shouted. Several men galloped off; others surrounded Hashan and helped him from his horse.

She dismounted and ran to her father. He lay on the ground, his eyes glazed, staring at nothing. He struggled to rise. "Is he . . . ?" she asked.

"Very nearly, milady," someone said.

"Father?" she said, kneeling by him. Could he speak? Would he finally talk to her, would he leave all his plots and counterplots behind, would he see her as herself and not just a piece in the game he played? A rattle sounded deep in his chest, a noise like a chain being drawn up from a well, and he fell back.

"I'm sorry, milady," someone said.

Angarred sat back, wondering what she felt, if she felt anything at all. She heard loud noises from farther in the forest, horses neighing, men calling out. Suddenly the others burst through a gap in the trees.

"We got him, milady," one of them said, and she saw a man slung over one of the saddles. Several arrows pierced him, at his thigh, his upper arm, his throat.

The men threw him roughly to the ground in front of her, and he cried out. "Careful," Angarred said, standing. "I want him alive. Why did you shoot my father?"

"Hunting, milady," the man said, his voice low and raw. The worst wound was the one at his throat; blood from it pattered on the leaves below, turning them red. "Apologies."

"You killed a lord, do you know that? You killed my father."

"Accident."

"I don't think so. I think someone hired you. Why else would you kill the most important man here?"

The man said nothing.

"Who hired you?"

"Accident," the man said again. "Truly."

Mathewar stepped forward. "Let me try," he said. He gazed down at the wounded man. "Speak," he commanded, his voice strong. "What happened here?"

Angarred shivered. She found herself wanting to answer him, to tell him everything, even that she was not sure how she felt about her father's death. Others seemed about to speak as well.

"Hunting," the man said. He bit down hard, but his mouth seemed to open of its own volition. "Hunting him. Reward."

"Who promised you a reward?"

"Can't say."

"Were you hunting anyone else?"

"Yes."

"Who?"

Blood showed at his mouth; he had bitten his tongue in his effort not to speak. "Not just him."

"Who else?"

The man fell back. Mathewar felt at his neck for a pulse, then straightened. "He's dead, milady. I'm sorry I couldn't get more from him."

"That's—that's all right," she said. There were too many things to think about—her father's death, the man who had killed him, Mathewar's transformation.

"No, it isn't," Mathewar said. "I'd like to know who else he was paid to kill. I think it might have been me."

"You! Why?"

"Did your father have any enemies?"

"I don't know," she said, annoyed at his change of subject. "He thought he did, certainly. He said that jealous factions had banished him from court, that he was innocent of the crimes he had been exiled for."

"What crimes were those?"

"I don't know."

Mathewar raised his eyebrows in surprise. "Didn't he tell you?"

"He talked about it, but I—well, I was never interested enough to find out what he meant. He said a lot of things, a lot of nonsense, mostly. But you were at court, weren't you? You probably know what happened there better than I do."

"I came to court eight years ago, when I was twenty. Lord Hashan was banished—when? Fourteen years ago, I think he said. I did hear about some kind of plot or conspiracy around then, but there were only rumors—no one wanted to talk about it. Tezue had been on the throne for two years, and there was a rebellion or assassination attempt . . ."

"Assassination! But that would be treason!"

Mathewar looked at her keenly. "And you don't think your father could have been a traitor?"

"No—he always said he was innocent . . ." Mathewar's expression didn't change, and she felt stupid, a rustic country child. Of course her father would protest his innocence. She seized on another argument. "Traitors are put to death, aren't they? He was just exiled. He couldn't have plotted treason."

"Well, then, I'm afraid I don't know. People are exiled for all sorts of things—writing scurrilous poetry, wearing clothing more sumptuous than the king's . . ." He looked out at the men and women gathered around the fallen lord. If any of them knew what Hashan's crime was, Angarred thought, they would surely be compelled to speak by that fierce gaze, but no one said anything.

"Could the killer have been after me?" she asked. "I moved back just before he shot the arrow—could I be the one he was aiming at?"

"Who would want to kill you?"

He was mocking her again. "I don't know. But I felt something, some hostility—"

"Have you ever been off your father's lands?"

"Not since I was four."

"Well, then. I doubt you've made any enemies." He bowed to her and mounted his horse. "I'll have to bid you good day, milady. I'm off to pack."

"Pack? Where are you going?"

"I can't stay here. I might be a danger to you."

"But where are you going? Can't you answer one question, by the Orator?"

His mouth quirked in the beginning of a smile. "To Pergodi, milady."

She had a wild desire to ask him to take her along. Someone had wanted to kill her, she was sure of it. And what would she do here? She knew nothing about managing an estate.

A few of the dogs were nuzzling at Hashan's body. Someone shouted at them and they slunk away. Several men stayed to load the body onto a horse and carry it back to the manor house; the rest mounted and rode away.

The day after Lord Hashan's death Angarred rode to the nearest town to ask the religious to help her bury her father. Neither the plotters nor Hashan's tenants came to the funeral; only Angarred, Rushlag and Elenin stood by the grave in the manor cemetery as the religious prayed to the Bearer to bring Hashan safely ashore, and to the other Godkings to receive his soul.

Was her father at peace now? she wondered. Would he reunite with her mother at the Celestial Court, where everyone found his or her true companion, and everything went by twos? How high would he rise in the Court, he who had pored over his genealogy and had traced his ancestors back to an ancient forgotten king? For a moment she wished she believed in the Godkings, but she had never seen any evidence that they existed.

Rushlag cried, and between tears glared at Angarred for remaining dry-eyed, but Angarred thought she would go to the Others before she pretended to an emotion she didn't feel.

Then finally it was over, and she returned to the manor exhausted. The plotters still sat around the scarred oak table in the dining hall, eating and drinking and murmuring softly among themselves.

She stood a moment, studying them. Gradually, one by one, they looked up to see her and fell silent.

"I want you out of here," she said. "All of you."

"Don't you want to return to the capital?" one of them asked. "We can find you a good marriage—it's said that Prince Norue wants to marry—"

She had as good a chance of marrying the king's nephew as he did, and she knew it. "Out," she said. "I'll give you three days to pack up, and then I'm calling the bailiff."

"But why, milady?" someone else asked.

She said nothing; she was not obligated to give them her reasons. She stood still, waiting. Elenin came to the kitchen door and peered out timidly, wiping her hands on her apron.

For a moment Angarred feared they would defy her. They were a gang of rough men and women ranged against one defenseless girl, after all. Several of them wore swords or daggers, though that was affectation; she could not remember anyone at Hashan Hall needing to confront enemies on a battlefield.

Then they stood and pushed past her, heading for their rooms or the stables. Some lifted their hats as they went; one even thanked her for her hospitality.

Finally the last of them had gone. Elenin came into the dining room, eying her with new respect. Angarred sank into one of the chairs the plotters had vacated and took a deep breath to steady herself.

She looked for the steward the next day and found him in the library, sitting at her father's desk and going over the account books. He stood when he saw her. "Good day, milady."

"Good day. I need to know all about the manor—the fields, the orchards, the cows and pigs, the barns and tools, anything you can tell me."

For a brief moment the steward looked surprised at how swiftly she had moved to take over the estate. Then he turned back to his books and the expression was gone, so quickly she might have imagined it.

"I'm afraid we're not doing very well, milady," he said. "Lord Hashan was not terribly interested in the manor, and whenever he needed money he sold some of his land to his neighbor. I'm afraid—well, there's very little left. Just the manor house and a few tenants, and even these might have to be sold to pay milord's debts."

The ground seemed to fall away beneath her. "What? But it can't—but we have dozens of tenants, people whose families have lived here and been loyal to us for hundreds of years."

"And they still live here, milady. But the land no longer belongs to us."

Something scuttled overhead in the attic. "Let me see the books," she said.

The steward hesitated before turning the book around, and in that hesitation she understood a good deal. He had taken advantage of Hashan's negligence, had stolen as much as he could while Hashan spent his days plotting and nursing his grievances. The expression she had seen earlier had not been surprise but fear of discovery.

She glanced down at the books and saw columns of numbers, each one ending in a negative. "You'll need me to explain the entries, milady," the steward said. "I used my own system of—"

"I'll study it on my own," she said. She gestured to dismiss him.

When he left she took her place behind Hashan's desk, her elbows planted to either side of the huge book. A strong smell of mildew rose from the pages. She had become her father now, she thought, poring over old books, the fat candles wavering around her. And she could make as little sense of her books as Lord Hashan had made of his.

But after a while she saw patterns forming, the same transactions repeating every few months. Here Hashan had sold a pig, there a plow. Here he sold the apple orchard; she had passed the orchard nearly every day on her way to the lake, and had never known it no longer belonged to them.

Several weeks after that Hashan sold another pig, this one for less than the first one. The steward had taken the difference; she was certain of it but knew she could never prove anything. The same thing happened with another few acres of land, with some cows, with more pigs. And on the other side of the ledger things began to cost far more; the steward had paid inflated sums for candles, nails, parchment, salt.

Some time later she became aware that the shuffling sounds overhead had stopped. Something screeched in pain; wings fluttered. Owls, hunting mice in the attic at night. It was far later than she thought.

She stood. The room seemed to sway around her, and she gripped the edge of Hashan's desk. She had eaten nothing since breakfast, she realized. She went down to the kitchen and found the remains of yesterday's meat pie.

She woke the next day reluctant to study the ledgers again. Without thinking about it she headed to her mother's room, something she had done many times as a child when she needed cheering or comfort.

She opened the wardrobe. Once it had held at least a dozen dresses. Over the years, though, she had destroyed them one by one, wearing them out to the lake or while working on a household chore, until they had become fit for nothing but rags.

Four remained; she chose a white embroidered dress that had turned a sickly yellow over the years. It smelled of mold, but under that she thought she could still make out the perfume that had once been so strong, the scent that was now her most powerful memory of her mother. She put the dress on and studied herself in the wavy looking glass, moving by habit to the spot that gave her the least distorted view.

Her mother, Verret, had died of a fever when she was four, shortly before Hashan's exile and their move to the country. Angarred remembered her as a strong-featured woman who had had little time for her daughter, always rushing off to court or a feast at some noble's house. She had wondered many times why her mother's clothes had ended up in Hashan Hall if she had died in Pergodi; she had asked her father once when he had not seemed so distracted and he muttered something about needing to remember her. But when she pressed him for more details about her mother Lord Hashan waved her off impatiently.

For a while after that, whenever she tried on the dresses she slipped into a fantasy, taking two parts, Lady Verret and herself. She would stand in front of the glass and talk to her mother, and her mother would answer, giving her advice, assuring her of her undying love. Now she scowled at her face in the glass; she had not done anything so childish in years. Still, she did not take the dress off.

She went to the library and continued where she had left off. The steward had been right, she saw, though it had taken her a while to accept it: they owned very little, and were in debt to a number of tradesmen. There was nothing for her to do here but follow the progress of her father's decline.

She brushed back a strand of her unruly hair and turned a page. Someone had drawn a grotesque face in one of the margins, an old man with hollow cheeks, a vacant expression and an open drooling mouth. The word *Snoppish* was written under it.

Who had done this? The writing looked like her father's. And who was Snoppish, was he Hashan's enemy at court? In the drawing the man looked senile, unable to harm anyone. Even his name sounded faintly ridiculous.

She put aside the ledger and picked up another book. Hashan had covered the pages of this one with vague plans and third-hand gossip from court. "No child yet from Cherenin," he wrote. "Norue will take the throne." Under this was a drawing headed *Lady Snoppish,* an old woman with a leering, stupidly lustful look.

She found other drawings, of Snoppish, of his wife, of Jerret and Arys, who must be their son and daughter. Why had her father hated them so much? She tried to remember if she had ever heard of them from any of the plotters, but there had been so many visitors to the manor, and all the names had blurred together . . .

There were lists of lords and ladies; at the top Hashan had written *For* and *Against.* The names moved from one group to another as she paged through the book, as Hashan changed his mind about who his friends and enemies were.

At one point she was startled to read own her name. Across from it her father had written other names, lords and knights, people he had thought to marry her to, probably. Anger rose within her at his presumption, at the way he had considered her just another piece to be traded for advancement. Then she remembered that he was dead, that he could no longer harm her, and the anger left her.

As she turned the pages she began to form a plan. She could go to Pergodi and ask the king for justice for her father's killer. Surely Tezue was sworn to protect his lords.

She stood and took down Hashan's book of maps. She found Pergodi immediately, a great blotch of ink on the coast. Lake Sar, the lake near Hashan Hall, was harder to spot, and when she finally did find it she was amazed to see how small it was.

She would have to travel west. A marked road started a short distance from Lake Sar; she could follow it all the way to Pergodi.

She stood and began to pace, excited now. She had never seen the ocean; at least, she did not remember seeing it.

But the king had sent Hashan into exile, she remembered. Wouldn't it be dangerous for her to speak to him? If her father's enemies were noblemen, if they attended upon the king at court, she would be delivering herself up to them, walking wide-eyed into a web of treachery and deceit.

She sat. A great wrong had been done her, and there was nowhere she could go for justice, no one to make it right. She was all alone. She began to cry, for herself, for her dead father, for her mother who had died so long ago. Then she wiped her cheek roughly and turned back to the ledgers, following the slow disintegration of her inheritance.

She read in the ledgers until midday, when she started to feel hungry. She stood and went down to the kitchen, names and pictures and numbers swirling through her head.

Rushlag and Elenin sat at the kitchen table, eating dinner. She had asked them earlier if they knew why Hashan had been banished, but they were from the countryside and could tell her nothing about court. Now she took a chair and asked, "Have you ever heard of anyone named Snoppish? Lord Snoppish?"

They shook their heads. "Why do you ask?" Rushlag said.

"I've been going over the account books," she said. She looked at the housekeeper and cook. How to break the news to her father's old servants? "We—we're destitute, it seems. My father spent everything he had."

Elenin put her hand to her mouth. Rushlag said, briskly, "You'll have to go to Pergodi and find a husband then. Trade your name for a fortune—it's done all the time. You're good-looking enough to find someone."

"Sell myself to the highest bidder, you mean?" Angarred said bitterly. "That's what my father wanted."

"There you are, milady. He knew what was right for you."

"He had no idea! He squandered his entire fortune trying to get back into the king's good graces. No, if I go to Pergodi it will be to see justice done. To tell King Tezue about my father's death, and to find the man who killed him. Snoppish, or whoever it was."

"I knew someone who went to Pergodi once," Rushlag said. "She wanted to petition for justice, just like you. She said that the king only hears petitioners once a month—they stand in long lines and most of them never even get in to talk to him. They have to come back the next month, and the month after that. She finally gave it up and returned home."

Angarred looked around the table, feeling defeated, holding back tears. She would not cry in front of them. She picked at a spill of hardened wax on the table. "What should I do, then?" she asked, and was horrified to hear her voice sound small and broken.

"Get yourself a husband, like I said," Rushlag said.

"No," she said.

TWO

Gedren rose early as always, got dressed and went through the house to the bakery, where she fired the ovens while still half asleep. Her sons, Labren and Borgarrad, soon joined her, and the family worked in silence, mixing flour and yeast and water, kneading bread, heading down to the storeroom for more ingredients and wood.

The sun rose over Pergodi, slanting gold in through the open shutters of the shop. Soon Gedren and her sons wore a light sheen of sweat, warmed by the sun, the heat of the ovens, and the heavy work. They were all plump—not, as most people thought, from the food they turned out but from family resemblance—and all had a faintly harried expression. Dalesio had been plump as well, but his smile could sweeten the sourest of customers.

A knock came at the door. Gedren scowled; they were not close to being ready. The people of Pergodi were the rudest in the world, she thought, and then remembered how Dalesio had charmed them. But it did not do to think of Dalesio too often.

The knock sounded again. "Open up!" someone shouted. She heard the hollow noise of a staff hitting wood. "King's militia!"

Perhaps they brought word of Dalesio, she thought, her heart beating faster. She hurried to open the door. A man in the midnight blue of the militia pushed his way into the shop, followed by three men in coats of buffed ox-hide.

"Have you—have you heard anything?" she asked. Her sons, Labren and Borgarrad, stopped work and came to stand protectively behind her. "Do you know what happened to my husband?"

"Your husband disappeared a year ago," the blue-cloaked man said.

It was a statement, not a question, but she chose to answer it. "That's right," she said. He had gone to serve cakes and pies at one of the king's banquets and had never come home. She remembered waiting for him the next day, losing hope as the hours passed, and then the terrible ride in a neighbor's cart all the way up to the castle.

Pergodi had been decked out for some reason she didn't remember: the paving stones shone from all the washing, the wooden bridges had been repainted, banners and flags flew from every corner. Singers and acrobats, rope-walkers and fire-swallowers entertained the populace on street corners, and the midnight blue cloaks of the king's militia were everywhere, rousting drunks and thieves and prostitutes. She had watched it from the cart bitterly, the only person in Pergodi not caught up in celebration.

When they reached the castle she had not been allowed past the wall. The blue-cloaks stopped her at the guardhouse, and one of them told her to go home, that they had more important things to concern themselves with. "Husbands stray," the blue-cloak said. "No doubt he'll be back tomorrow." In desperation she had left her name and the quarter she lived in, but no one had ever called.

And here they were a year later. Did they have news?

"Do you know what else happened the night he disappeared?" the man asked.

She had heard rumors, of course—everyone had. But the stories were jumbled and changed from person to person. Something had been stolen, someone else had disappeared . . . "No," she said, hoping to learn more.

"There was a banquet for an envoy from Takeke that night," the man said. "He was coming to Karededin with—with something King Tezue wanted. The king displayed it at the banquet and it was stolen out from under his nose. A good many people disappeared that night—magicians, most of them. Was your husband a magician?"

She didn't follow most of this; she knew nothing about politics, or countries outside Karededin. But she understood that the man thought her husband a magician, and she began to laugh.

"A magician? He's a baker! Look around you, man—does this look like a magician's workshop? We transform flour and water into bread—that's the only magic we do here."

"It's not a joking matter," the man said sternly. "If he stole the Stone he'll be hanged, and probably you along with him. Think again. Was there anything uncanny about him? Have you ever seen him do anything out of the ordinary, anything you couldn't explain?"

He stayed cheerful in the face of terrible provocation from his customers, she thought. He'd probably talk cheerfully to you as well. I can't explain that.

"No," she said. "He was a baker. A good man. Have you heard from him, or did you just come to ask me questions?"

"Do you know what he did before he married you?"

"He was a baker. His father was a baker, and his grandfather before him. Dalesio Baker, that's his name, and I'm Gedren Baker. No one ever called him Dalesio Tobrin, at least not in my hearing." Magicians were given the last name of Tobrin after the founder of the College.

"Very well," the man said. "We may have to take you to the castle later and question you there. For now just think about what I've asked you, and let me know if you remember anything."

She couldn't let them go without getting some answers. "Why are you asking me this now? Have you found out something new?"

The blue-cloak said nothing for a long moment. "We've had more important matters to take care of," he said finally. "There's nothing terribly urgent about a man who probably ran off with his mistress."

"He didn't—" Gedren started, but the blue-cloak was headed out the door, his three men following him.

She thought she knew why they had visited her only now,

though. It had taken a year for someone to put together her note at the guardhouse and the disappearing magicians. Her complaint might even have been lost for a while; after all, as the blue-cloak said, they had more important matters.

All day, while she set out loaves of bread to cool and bargained with customers and gave cookies to children, she thought about the soldiers' visit. She remembered now that Dalesio had said something about an envoy from Takeke. And her neighbor Mashak Cobbler, the shoemaker who had taken her up to the castle, had come back later to tell her something, some story, but she couldn't remember what it was. And what was the stone the man had mentioned? She had the idea he hadn't intended to say that, that the word had slipped out by accident.

During a lull in the afternoon she told her sons to continue working and went next door to talk to Mashak. He was a short, dark man, his face tanned like the leather he worked with, his expression a permanent scowl.

"Hello, Gedren," he said, his face softening into something like a smile. Because of his harsh expression she had avoided him for years. Then Dalesio had vanished and he had offered to help in any way he could, and she had seen how kind he was. "What brings you here?"

"A blue-cloak came to visit me," she said. "He thinks Dalesio's a magician, if you can believe that."

"A magician!"

"Tell me again what happened that night. You heard some stories, you said—"

Mashak sighed and turned away from his last. "I heard a number of stories. I *think* the envoy was bringing the king the Stone, the Stone of Tobrin—"

"What's that?"

"It has something to do with magic, I'm not sure what. When the king learned that Takeke had the Stone he bargained for a loan of it, promising them—I don't remember. A good deal of money, probably. And the envoy brought it over, and it was stolen."

"And the magicians disappeared that night?"

"Yes, that's another story I heard."

"Could he—do you think Dalesio could be a magician?"

Mashak shrugged. "You would know that better than I."

He couldn't. He couldn't be. She would have known . . . She brushed flour from her apron absently. "Well, thank you. Let me know if you hear anything else."

"Of course."

She got back to the bakery as her sons were closing up. She made supper for them and then, when they had finished, took out her pipe and sat down to think. Dalesio used to complain, only half-jokingly, about the herbal mixture she used. "It smells like old rope!" he would say. "How can you smoke that?"

At first, when he hadn't returned home, she had expected him every day. Now, though, after a year with no word, she was forced to consider other possibilities. He had gone away on an errand (but then why hadn't he told her?); he had been kidnapped; he was hurt somewhere; he was dead.

And yet even this wasn't the worst that could have befallen him. She had managed to keep the thought at bay for a year, but now she wondered if he had been taken by the Others.

The Others were not human; that was nearly all anyone knew about them. It could be said that they had been banished to their own land and were rarely able to leave it—but even this would not be precisely true, since their land existed somewhere other than the human realm, and a man or woman could wander into it from anywhere.

The Others sent out enchantments and dreams and fantasies— men and women of a beauty surpassing anything seen in human lands; skirling, pounding music; strange and powerful visions. Those trapped in such enticements, or those who had strayed from sanity by themselves, would sometimes follow their madness and wander into the land of the Others, or come close enough that the Others could ensorcel them entirely. Irrational themselves, the Others drew the irrational to them. In places where enough people succumbed the borders would grow porous, and finally the Others would break through and wreak chaos around them.

Wild-eyed madmen, despairing lovers, dreamers whose gaze turned to something other than the life around them—these people would vanish one day and never return. Gedren had even heard that the Others started wars and fires and famines once they had gotten free of their realm, hoping to drive folks to insanity and despair.

Dalesio was the sanest of men—and yet she had caught him staring at nothing for long minutes, like a cat, or listening to her talk without the faintest idea what she had said. He lived very much in his own world, a world where all people were sweet and gentle, like him, where a good meal could fix all problems. This didn't seem enough to summon the Others, she had to admit. But she had run out of ideas.

She finished her pipe and stood. She had gone through Dalesio's things after he left, of course, but she had not known then what to look for. Now that the blue-cloak had made his astonishing suggestion she thought she might find something she had missed, some connection to magicians or the College or even that Stone they had mentioned.

She took a candle and climbed up to the attic, then made her way around old furniture, a stack of broken pans that Dalesio had never gotten around to mending, the trunk she had brought from her parents' house. Finally she reached an old wooden box of Dalesio's, knelt before it and raised the lid.

At first she saw ancient clothing, suitable only for rags. A smell rose from them, yeast and sweat and that elusive scent that was his alone. The smell brought him back so strongly she had to sit back and swallow hard to keep from crying.

Everything goes by twos, she thought, the dull ache of his absence flaring suddenly into a sharp pain. She had not been the same since he had gone.

Twenty years ago she had gone into his bakery on an errand from her mother and had fallen in love almost immediately with Dalesio's laughing eyes, his wonderful smile. For the next week or so she found excuses to visit the bakery. She had thought that no one in her family noticed, that she had her own secret to hug to herself, though as it turned out everyone had known and had discussed it every time she left.

Only Dalesio had not seemed to know why she kept visiting the bakery. She even thought she would have to make the first move herself—and then finally, with a great deal of diffidence, he had asked her if she wanted to go walking with him in the square of the Craftsman's Quarter.

She lifted the clothing out. Underneath was an old leather-bound book, the one Dalesio had used to teach her her letters. He had worked from it as a boy, when the religious had taught him and the other boys to read. Dust rose as she took it out, more dust and crumbling paper as she opened it and saw his familiar handwriting. She brought the candle closer and paged through it. Her handwriting followed his, at first rounded and childish and then growing more assured. She worked her way to the end of the book, but nothing in it seemed significant.

And that was it; there was nothing left in the box but the carved horse Labren had had as a child, two of its legs broken off, a drawing of the family Borgarrad had done when he was six or seven, and an old scrap of parchment. She remembered trying to read it, but the lettering was too faded to make out anything but a few words: *leave tomorrow* and *keep watch* and *Pergodi,* and a signature at the bottom that looked like *Narinye.*

She sat back on her heels and stared at the paper. The candle flickered, and bulky shadows shifted around the attic. She had not been able to make any sense of the letter the first time she had seen it, and over the intervening months she had forgotten all about it. Now, though, after what the blue-cloak had told her, she found all sorts of sinister meanings in those few words. Leave where? Keep watch on what? Who was Narinye, was he another magician? Dalesio had never mentioned him, yet he had thought his letter worth saving, no matter that it was unreadable.

Had she known her husband as well as she thought? Did his disappearance have anything to do with Narinye's instructions? Was it the Stone that Narinye wanted him to "keep watch" over?

She began to pile everything back in the box. She should go to the king's militia with what she had discovered, she knew. But they had been rude and uncaring, and they would certainly not share what they had learned with her. And if Dalesio had stolen the Stone he would be hanged, or so the man had said.

She could not believe he had taken the Stone. Still, he had kept secrets from her, had perhaps meddled in the king's politics. She needed to find out what had happened to him, if he was safe or in danger, if he had run afoul of the blue-cloaks. She closed the lid of the box, a plan beginning to form.

She spoke to her sons at breakfast the next day. She would give them the running of the bakery, she said. Borgarrad was eighteen, Labren sixteen—they were old enough to take it over now. She would hire herself out as a servant at the castle, would listen and learn, and see if anyone had heard anything of Dalesio, or the Stone.

THREE

Angarred relieved the steward of his duties and spent long hours in the study, picking over her ledgers in the light of the mouse-eaten candles. There had to be a way to make the estate work again; it was the only thing she had left. She sold furniture and tapestries and old silver and even the dogs, hesitating only over her mother's jewelry, one of the few things she had to remember her. In the end, sighing, she had put the jewels back.

Late one night she stood, yawning, and pushed the ledger away. She picked up the candle and let herself out of the study. The house echoed strangely as she walked through it; she had sold off nearly everything of worth. She went down to the kitchen for something to eat, then started up the stairs to her room.

A rustling noise came from the top of the stairs. She was used to the animals that found their way in through gaps in the stones, and she continued on. Still, she felt uneasy. She held her hand before the candleflame; its strange shadows wavered as she climbed. As she neared the top she sensed something—someone—standing in the dark. She saw two shining eyes staring out from dark hollows, from nothing, and she thrust her candle toward them.

A man screamed. Angarred screamed too, for a moment too terrified to press her advantage. The man came closer, reaching for her, and she shoved the candle at him again. The man roared and grappled with her, too maddened to fear the flame. They fell down the stairs together, each clawing and hitting out in the darkness. She smelled burning flesh.

Rushlag and Elenin ran out of their rooms, calling out to her. She had landed on top of him, and without thinking about what she was doing she grabbed hold of his hair and hit his head against the floor again and again. The man pushed her away roughly and ran for the door.

"What is it?" Rushlag said. "What's happening?"

She groped for the candle, her hands shaking, but she had lost it somewhere in the fight. "Did you see him?" she asked, sitting up.

"Who?" Rushlag said.

"That man. He tried to kill me."

"What? What man?"

She felt a chill from the door; he hadn't closed it as he left. "Someone came here to kill me, just like my father. I was right— I'm their target too." She shivered and hugged herself tightly. "Close the door, someone. Please."

Elenin went to the door. "Can I have your candle, Rushlag?" Angarred asked.

"Why?"

Angarred wanted to shout in frustration. Everyone seemed so slow tonight, and she had to hurry, had to move quickly before the man came back. "I have to pack."

"Pack? Where do you think you're going?"

"Pergodi. I have to find Mathewar. He said I wasn't in danger, but I am. They want to kill me too, whoever they are."

"You can't leave tonight. It's far too dark, and you need to sleep. It can wait until tomorrow."

"No it can't. He might come back."

"It's much more dangerous out there than it is in here. Go to sleep. You can leave in the morning."

"Give me the candle," she said, pitching her voice to sound like Mathewar's when he had ordered her father's killer to speak.

To her surprise it worked. Rushlag gave her the candle, but

then, instead of following Elenin to bed, she climbed the stairs after Angarred.

Angarred went down the hall to Hashan's old room and brought out a large leather traveling bag. The bag probably hadn't been used since Hashan came from Pergodi, she realized. Then she continued down the hallway.

"Where are you going?" Rushlag said.

She went into her mother's room and opened the wardrobe, then reached for the dresses.

"What are you doing?"

"Packing. I told you. I have to find good clothes to wear for the capital."

"These are fifteen years out of date."

"Fourteen. Do you have a better idea?"

"Yes. Wait until tomorrow. I can try to make them over—"

"What in the name of the Spinner do you know about court fashion? And how long will it take you to fix them all?"

"A few days, that's all."

Angarred paid no attention to Rushlag's answer. She held up each of the clothes in turn to the light, rejecting the white embroidered dress and stuffing the rest into the bag. When she was done she knelt to a carved wooden box in the corner of the wardrobe and pulled out her mother's jewelry, a tangle of pearls and tarnished silver. A ruby charm spun downward on its chain like a spider.

She stood and hurried along the corridor to her room, stuffing the jewelry in the bag as she went. Once there she took out more clothes, and the small leather bag of coins she had received from selling the things in the manor house, everything that had not gone to paying her father's debts.

"What will we do?" Rushlag asked. "Elenin and I?"

Angarred thrust some coins at her. "Here, this should keep you for a while. And you're sure to find work at some other house."

"You're really going, then?"

"I said I was."

She hurried downstairs, putting on her cloak as she went, Rushlag still following her. They stopped at the front door and she embraced the housekeeper awkwardly. "The Navigator protect you," Rushlag said.

"Good-bye," Angarred said.

She closed the door and headed for the stable. The night was colder than she expected, and only a small sliver of moon lit her way. Her bag felt heavy and unwieldy. At the stable she saddled her horse—the only one she had left—tied the bag on behind, and mounted up.

There was only one path leading away from the manor house; the horse followed it in the dark without difficulty. After a while her eyes adjusted to the moonlight, though there was nothing to see but weeds, some of them as high as her horse. They were passing through fields she knew, land that had lain fallow and untenanted for years.

Sometime later she made out the dim bulk of the great oak tree that had once marked the end of their property. She could not remember ever riding past it, though of course she had come this way when Hashan had been exiled from the capital fourteen years ago. Then she set her face resolutely to the west, toward Pergodi.

She woke to feel the sun on her shoulders. She jerked in the saddle, panicked. Where had the horse carried her? She could have gone back to the stables for all she knew.

But the path here was better than the ones on the estate, and she noted with relief that the sun had risen behind her; at least she was still going west. Broad farmland lay on either side, and to her left, beyond the cleared land, the trees of the great forest marched into the distance. She saw no one save the farmers working their land, too far away to hail.

By midday she started to grow hungry, and she cursed herself for not remembering to bring food. Her shoulders hurt from the fall she had taken. She twisted in the saddle, trying to get comfortable, but the ache did not go away.

A while later the path she was on joined up with another, larger road, and she began to pass villages and pastures, Godhouses and great manors. Several times she had to cross the broad meandering river that flowed down to Pergodi and into the sea, and sometimes she saw mill wheels turning out over the river, creaking as they ground the grain. The forest still kept pace with her, far in the distance.

At the end of the day she saw a lit inn ahead of her, and she urged her horse forward. She reached the stables quickly and settled the horse, then went inside. Noise and light and heat hit her in one powerful blow, and she realized how alone she had been, how used she had grown to the silence around her.

Groups of people sat at the trestle tables in the common room, merchants and farmers and others whose occupation she could not guess. She started toward them, eager for conversation, and then stopped. She could not trust anyone; whoever had attacked her at the top of the stairs might be traveling this road as well, waiting to try again. She sat at a table in the shadows and ordered her first meal of the day.

She continued on the next morning, feeling better after breakfast and a good night's sleep. Most of the people at the inn were traveling to Pergodi, and they grouped together on the road, telling stories, complaining about the weather, talking about where they were from and what their business was in the capital.

One of them counted the group and saw that there were nine of them, an odd number, an unlucky number. He beckoned to her to join them. She spurred her horse ahead, giving in to her strong desire for company. But when they asked why she was going to Pergodi she said only that she was visiting a friend, and she was careful to say little after that.

They reached another inn in the evening. When their horses were settled they went into the common room, the loudest among them calling for food and ale. One of the loud men sat next to her, and after they had been served their supper he turned to her and asked, "Who are you going to visit in the capital?"

Why had he remembered her out of all the travelers? She stirred her porridge without eating. "A friend," she said uneasily.

"So you said. Yet it's unusual to see a woman alone on the road. He must be quite a friend, to make you come all this distance."

"I don't want to talk about my business," she said, and he turned away and said nothing to her for the rest of the evening.

But her fear of two nights ago, of the man in the dark, had returned, and she retired to her room after supper instead of staying for conversation. A number of men watched her as she climbed the stairs, and she knew they were wondering what it would take to get her to their rooms, kind words or drink or threats. Or were they thinking about her death instead? She could trust no one in this company.

She was so deep in thoughts about the travelers, especially the man who had asked her all the questions, that she did not see the shape at the top of the stairs. A shadow fell across the landing and she screamed loudly, then screamed again. Below her she heard the scrape of benches being shoved back, and then footsteps as men ran up the stairs.

"I—I'm sorry, milady," a maid was saying. "I didn't mean to frighten you."

"What?"

"I'm sorry—"

The men reached the top of the stairs. "What's going on here?" one of them asked.

Angarred took a deep breath. "I was startled by the maid," she said. "I saw a shadow and I thought—I thought I was about to be robbed."

"We hire no robbers here, milady," the innkeeper said.

"I know. I'm sorry. I—I'm not feeling well. Good night."

More people joined them on the road the next day; in addition to the merchants and farmers there were craftsmen and beggars, and a group of religious in their drab brown robes. Once she saw a lord with a great retinue; they rode up to an inn and hung their standard on the wall to indicate they were staying there. She studied it as her party went past, headed for another inn down the road, this one smaller and less welcoming.

She went to her room after supper once again, knowing but not caring that the travelers would gossip and speculate about her. She lay on her pallet for a long time, listening to the loud and bawdy conversations in the common rooms, feeling lonely.

She had guessed from Hashan's map that her journey would take three or four days, yet a week later they were still on the road. She was heartily sick of the dust and boredom, of the fleas and uncomfortable beds and bad food at the inns. And she felt apprehensive about the rest of the travelers, and strange to be among so many people, far more than she was used to seeing at once. Judging by their numbers Pergodi must be bigger than she had realized; the blotch on the map, about the size of her thumbprint, must cover more territory than she thought.

One day she saw a wall appear in the distance. She studied it as she rode, but it seemed to grow no closer. After a while she realized that it must be farther away than she thought, and far larger than she had first thought as well. "Is that Pergodi?" she asked the rider next to her.

"No," he said. He was a farmer, hauling his cabbages and beans to the capital. He still smelled of his labors, a powerful odor. "That's the Giants' Wall. Pergodi is another three days' ride, two if we push ourselves."

"What giants? Who were the giants?" Angarred asked.

"I don't know, really," the farmer said. "That's just what it's called."

They passed a tavern called The Giant's Head. Another hour of riding brought them to the wall, which stretched away on their left. It was a brilliant, sunlit white, broken in places. There were more ruins to the left, dozens of buildings, tall green grass springing up around them and smoothing their contours. Houses lay spilt across the plain like huge broken blocks, with whole roofs or walls gone. Perfectly straight roads made of enormous stones met at right angles; other paths were nearly obliterated by the grass. Many of the ruins faced a great square, now gone to grass as well. And everything was built of the same massive white stones, almost blinding to look upon.

Birds flew low over the square, squawking, landing to peck at seeds and insects. She squinted up at the wall, higher than anything she had ever seen. No human could have quarried these stones and transported them and piled them so exactly on top of each other. But if they were giants, how had such a great people been defeated?

She pressed on. The group rode faster, encouraged at passing the wall, hoping to reach Pergodi in only two days.

The villages grew larger and closer together. The land sloped upward, the road broadened. More and more people joined them on the road the next day, until she found herself part of a makeshift caravan of travelers, many of them speaking languages and dialects she didn't recognize. She smelled unwashed bodies, and horse dung, and cinnamon from the cart in front of her. She felt covered with dust from head to foot.

Another wall rose in front of her, this one smaller than the Giants' Wall and made of gray irregular stones stained green with moss. Battlements peered down from the top but she saw no one in them, and no guards challenged her as she passed with the caravan through a vaulted gate.

A city huge beyond anything she had ever imagined spread out in front of her. She dropped her reins; her horse, unguided, sidled away from the caravan, and she reined it in sharply.

She stood on a slight rise. Houses sloped down before her, so many there seemed no end to them. Some were even built right up against the city wall, like barnacles clinging to the hull of a ship. Steeples and towers rose up over the roofs, and far off she thought she saw something massive squatting on a hill, the castle, possibly. People crowded the roads; vendors called to them from rickety booths, selling pies, ale, other food she had never heard of. Carts squealed, bells rang, dogs barked at one another.

How in the name of the Navigator would she ever find Mathewar here? She cursed herself for her foolishness. She was a simple girl from the countryside who knew nothing about the outside world; if she did she would have never come here.

"Welcome to Pergodi, the City of Seven Bridges," one of the travelers said next to her.

It would grow dark soon; she needed to find a place to stay. "Do you know of a cheap inn nearby?"

"The Spiderweb Inn is fairly good. Go down that road, turn left, and cross the Spiderweb Bridge."

She thanked him and continued on. A short while later she came to a bridge made of strands of delicate iron; it looked as if it would blow away in the next puff of wind. She rode cautiously over the spiderweb tracery, wondering if it would hold both horse and rider. It was solid enough, though—and there, on the other side, was the Spiderweb Inn.

She left her horse in the stable and went inside. She decided to get a room for one night and make plans in the morning. But when the innkeeper told her the price of a room she nearly gasped at the expense; at those rates she would run out of money in a month. Everything she had owned, all of Hashan Hall, amounted to mere weeks in Pergodi.

She went to her room and tried to sleep, but her fears kept her awake. Pergodi was full of unfamiliar noises, even at night, people laughing and singing, carts rumbling, bells marking the hours. She dozed a little, then woke as the sun shone through her window at dawn.

FOUR

ngarred felt slightly better in the morning. She called for water for a bath, her first in weeks, and then went downstairs to the common room for breakfast. Perhaps, she thought, she would run into Mathewar on the streets, or find someone who knew him.

No, what was she thinking? She couldn't afford to sit here and wait; every day in Pergodi cost her what it took to keep the estate going for a month. But she couldn't go back to the shell of the manor house either.

An idea came to her. She still had her mother's dresses and jewelry. Why not go to the castle and pretend to be a noblewoman? She could see the king, demand justice for her father, get protection from the killer who stalked her. No, not pretend—she really was a noblewoman, though of a family no one had heard from in fourteen years. She stood and went back upstairs to change.

An hour later she left the inn, wearing a green silk dress with only a few tears, her mother's pearls at her neck and her hair pinned back as tidily as she could manage it. At the stables she realized she had never ridden while wearing a dress, and she mounted awkwardly, hiking her skirt up over her knees.

Once outside she saw the castle immediately; it loomed over the city, sitting on its hill like some malevolent toad. She headed toward it, passing a bewildering succession of neighborhoods. There was a crowded outdoor market, with folks shouting out praises of their lemons, their fish, their baskets; a sad grouping of broken-down hovels, where men sat lethargically in the street and barefoot children swarmed her horse begging for food or money; a foul-smelling tannery; a street of crooked chimneys where every-one seemed to play a musical instrument. Once she came across a group of people from Takeke, looking wildly exotic in their color-ful clothes and tall cylindrical hats.

She crossed a bridge, much larger than the one by her inn. Water on either side lapped at the houses, leaving dirty high tide marks on the walls. On the other side she saw a statue of a woman, bent and grieving over some tragedy, and she wondered if this was the Cry-ing Madwoman Bridge someone had mentioned at breakfast.

For the first time she wondered why Pergodi had seven bridges. Even numbers were lucky: every Godking had a wife, everyone was expected to marry, and every person arranged their tasks to fall into patterns of two or four or six. Seven bridges seemed a bad omen.

The dusty lanes gave way to cobbled streets and the houses grew larger, more elaborate, ornamented with tile and gargoyles and wrought iron and copper roofs and squat turrets like mushrooms. A procession of religious marched two by two in their drab brown robes, droning through their noses about eternity.

Finally she came to the hill and followed the winding dirt road up to the castle. There were no houses here, just great boulders and groups of trees—the only trees, she realized, that she had seen so far in the city. Halfway to the summit she looked down and saw a spill of houses and streets and towers and banners, and roofs of all col-ors, gray slate and red brick and yellow thatch. Beyond them spread flat silver-gray water, looking for all the world like one of the tar-nished silver plates she had sold. So that was the ocean; she stared in amazement. A ship sailed between the arms of a port; she could barely make out the men on the deck, and the masts were the size of needles.

Near the top of the hill the road went over a small rise and came to the outer wall of the castle. A guard stood by the great arched entrance. The iron gates were open; she could see a little way into the dusty courtyard. "I'm expected at court," she told the guard.

He studied her, and for a moment that seemed to go on forever she worried that her clothes were wrong, or her hair, that Rushlag had been right and she was fourteen years out of date. Finally he stood aside to let her pass.

Groups of people headed though the courtyard on castle business: sweating knights attended by their squires, two noblemen talking in low voices, women carrying laundry baskets, another woman sweeping away clucking chickens. An ostler came to take her horse.

She dismounted, then looked out over the courtyard, uncertain where to go. A man in richly colored, tight-fitting jacket and trousers hurried past her toward the castle entrance, and she followed him inside.

The man walked without hesitation through the vaulted halls and corridors. She caught glimpses of rooms on either side, great canopied beds, rows of books, a fire in a hearth, a man sitting alone at a desk, writing. A woman carrying dust-rags and a broom hurried though the hall without giving her a glance.

Suddenly the man turned, and she found herself in a vast hall, a vaulted ceiling far overhead. Standing statues lined the walls, each as tall as two or three men, kings to the right and queens to the left. In their hands they each held an object representing their works on earth; their faces gazed down with holy indifference, and at their feet red torches burned.

Even she, growing up so far from the castle, had heard of this place, the Hall of the Standing Kings. When a king died a statue was made of him, and his name was changed slightly to indicate his transformation into a Godking. Then his body was carried through the hall, the first leg of his journey to the Celestial Court, where all the Godkings lived in harmony under the First King and First Queen. And there they were at the beginning of the rows, Marfan and Mathona, the father and mother, the sun and moon.

She glanced up and saw the man far ahead of her. She hurried forward in time to see him stop at a closed door and knock. An old man in sumptuous clothes and hung all over with jewels came to the door. She could not remember seeing anyone so grand; surely he must be a wealthy nobleman, maybe even the king himself.

"Lord Enlandin," the man she had followed said.

The other man bowed and walked with Enlandin through a small hallway, where he shouted, "Lord Enlandin!" The lord passed through into the room beyond.

The old man must be—Angarred strained to remember the word. Her father had mentioned it a few times, talking about the castle. A chamberlain, that was it. Thank the Orator she had not bowed to him and addressed him as the king.

The chamberlain came back. "Lady Angarred Hashan," she said, as haughtily as she could manage.

He hesitated, studying her as the guard had done. Then he bowed and walked toward the second door. "Lady Hashan!" he shouted.

Just before she entered she reminded herself that one or more of these magnificently dressed people might have plotted against her father, might have even killed him, might have nearly killed her. She took a deep breath and stepped inside.

She stood in a vast room glittering with light and color. A burning room, she thought at first, her eyes unused to brightness after the dim corridors. The place was a confusion of patterns, few matching any other, created from a blaze of colors, emerald, scarlet, indigo, topaz. Every inch of the walls was covered in tapestries, carvings, mosaics, paintings, as if each king had added to what his predecessor had done without regard to style or fitness. A painted round sun and moon looked down from the high vaulted ceiling, a shoal of silver stars between them. Light came from long windows set under the ceiling, and from candles whose colors added to the dazzling hues, red, blue, gold.

The courtiers themselves wore clothes as bright as jewels, made of silk or velvet or Emindal cloth. More jewels hung from their necks and ears and waists, the facets glinting in the light. Some of the courtiers had swords or daggers as well, but the weapons looked useless, engraved and decorated with so many gems they seemed just another ornament. They stood together in groups and factions or walked back and forth across the black-and-gold checkered

floor. The room echoed with talk, men and women hailing each
other, lowering their voices to whispers, laughing loudly.

Angarred stood in the shadows in the corner, feeling foolish.
She couldn't even pick out the king, assuming he was in this room
at all.

"You're old Challo Hashan's daughter, aren't you?" a woman
asked. She looked Angarred up and down slowly, from head to feet
and back again, not bothering to hide her curiosity at this new
arrival at court. "How is your father? We don't see much of him
these days."

"He was exiled," Angarred said. "Milady," she said, and curtsied
belatedly.

"Of course—how foolish of me. That old business."

"What business? What happened to him? That's why—"

"Enlandin!" the woman called. "Come meet this sweet young
child. Hashan's daughter, if you can believe it."

Lord Enlandin strode over to where Angarred stood, a number
of courtiers following in his wake. "Yes. Yes, you're right,
Karanin—I do see a resemblance."

"Is she like him in other things as well, I wonder?" another man
asked dryly. He was tall and thin, with tangled blond hair hanging
limply to his shoulders. His face looked knobby, his cheekbones
and chin bony protuberances. He had slate-colored eyes, curiously
blank, and no eyelashes. "Lord Hashan did not leave us under the
best of circumstances."

"My lord, could you tell me—"

"I'm sure you must find the court very odd," the first woman—
Lady Karanin—said. "You were raised away from it, weren't you?
In the country somewhere?"

"Yes," Angarred said. Clearly they were not going to answer her
questions; she would have to play along until they tired of their
game and she could ask again. "It does seem strange to me. My
father died, you see, and—"

"Died! Oh, I'm so sorry to hear that."

Then why didn't you visit him once in his exile? Angarred
thought. But she knew the answer as clearly as if the other woman

had spoken aloud. Lady Karanin was lying; she did not care about her father in the slightest.

"What do you find the strangest?" Enlandin asked.

Don't they want to know how my father died? She shrugged, determined to play this bitter game to the end. "Everything, milord. This room, for example. I've never seen anything so rich, so bright."

The courtiers laughed. They must be very bored, she thought grimly, if they need me to provide amusement for them. "The mosaics, the tapestries," she went on. "Tapestries even on the floor—"

They laughed again, much louder this time. "What did she say?" a woman asked from across the hall.

"My dear, you won't believe it," Enlandin said, calling to her. "She said there were tapestries on the floor."

The woman walked slowly over to him. Her blond hair was piled in elaborate curls, and she looked even more bored than the others, if that was possible. "Oh, she is quaint, isn't she?" the woman said, drawling her words. "From the country, I assume."

"She's Hashan's daughter, Dorilde," Lady Karanin said. "He raised her on his estate, out in the middle of nowhere, poor child."

Angarred's face grew hot with anger. "If I'm such a poor child, someone might explain to me what I said that was so amusing."

Silence fell among them. She had confused them with her directness; she didn't know whether to call it a victory or not. Finally Lady Karanin said, "They're carpets, my dear. Not tapestries. Have you truly lived your entire life with only rushes on the floor?"

She had thought at first that the woman was being kind, but then she heard the mockery in her voice. "Yes, indeed," Angarred said. "And with no one to tell me to be ashamed of them, either."

The courtiers formed their groups and circles again, excluding her. She caught a few fragments of their conversation; she suspected she was meant to. ". . . rude as well . . ." "Hashan is really to blame, I suppose . . ." "Not surprising when you know his history . . ."

She stood and watched them, determined not to say a word to anyone until she met the king. Could one of these people have ordered her father killed? They seemed to fight with other weapons, arrogance and mockery.

A few of them were always at the center of the knots of people, and the others seemed to defer to them, to hang on to their every word. The man with the lank blond hair was one of these; he seemed to have some power over the rest of them.

She felt a sudden strong desire to be one of those important people, to hold the fates of these horrid men and women in her hands. She'd show them then. They wouldn't be so quick to laugh at her, not if she could exile them for it. That fish-face Dorilde, and simpering Lady Karanin . . .

"Hello, Lady Angarred," a man said, bowing to her. "I hope you weren't too offended by them—they don't take to strangers easily, I'm afraid. Where are you from?"

The man was older than her by ten or fifteen years, thin and of medium height, with straight brown hair that fell across his forehead. His dark brown eyes seemed to gaze at her with kindness and concern, but the spite of the courtiers had made her suspicious. Was he about to ridicule her too?

"I don't think the place has a name, my lord," she said. She had forgotten to curtsy. Well, it was too late now. "It's to the east, near Lake Sar. I'm afraid I don't know your name."

"Jerret, milady. Jerret Snoppish."

Snoppish! She backed away. Here was her father's enemy, the man who had sent him into exile.

"What's wrong?" he asked. "There's no need to be frightened of me."

"I'm not frightened. You—my father thought you caused his exile."

Jerret laughed.

"What's so amusing, by the Orator? I'm not the court fool, despite what everyone seems to think."

"I wasn't laughing at you, milady. Oh, maybe a little. But I'm far too young to have done anything to any father of yours."

"Oh," she said. Of course. She had made an ass of herself again. "Your father, perhaps? Has he ever spoken about Lord Challo Hashan?"

"Not that I remember."

There was nothing here for her, Angarred thought, nothing that explained her father's long hatred. But Jerret was saying something; she forced herself to pay attention. "Why does your father think we caused his exile?"

"I don't know."

"Could you ask him? If we hurt him in any way we should make amends."

"He died, milord."

"I'm sorry to hear that," he said. He looked truly sympathetic, nothing like the silly men and women she had spoken to earlier. "How did it happen?"

"He was killed by an assassin while out hunting."

"But that's horrible, milady. Do you know who killed him?"

"No, I—"

The rest of her words were drowned out by a commotion in the hall. Most of the courtiers turned toward the door, some of them laughing loudly.

Angarred turned as well, relieved they had decided to mock something other than her. A woman in tattered gray clothes came into the room, walking on her hands, her skirts over her head and her underclothes showing. She tumbled over, seemed about to fall, then caught herself, flipped again and stood up. She laughed, an idiot's cackle that went on far too long.

A nurse hurried after her. The nurse was young and fit but she was panting hard, seeming exhausted by the struggle to keep up with her charge.

"Come, child," the nurse said, though the woman was no child but older than her keeper. The woman ignored her. "Princess Rodarren!" the nurse said.

Rodarren? Angarred thought. Now she remembered her father saying that the king's niece had lost her wits, but she had not known that it was as bad as this. What had happened to her?

Rodarren stopped laughing. She stood and looked at them, eyes wide as a child's, sucking on one finger. A scar slashed down one side of her face, leaving her eye milky white, like a gob of spit. Her clothes were ragged and dirty, layer piled atop layer, all of them shades of gray.

"Hello, Rodarren," the man with the flat gray eyes said.

"Why, where are you going, Cousin?" Rodarren said, speaking around the finger in her mouth.

Cousin? The man must be Prince Norue, then, Angarred thought, pleased to be able to attach a name to a face.

"Going?" Norue asked. "Nowhere."

"Yes you are, Cousin. You are going away . . . away . . . away. A long way away. Bye-bye. Oh! You'll never get there. Your ship is lost, your horses lamed, your traveling companions dead, all your pretty things gone. May the Others protect you!"

A few courtiers rapped on the walls twice, a gesture meant to avert evil, to restore balance by using even numbers. "You're talking nonsense, Cousin," Norue said evenly.

"It doesn't do to speak to her, milord," the nurse said. "She doesn't know what she's saying."

"Doesn't she?" Norue said.

Rodarren skipped toward the door, the nurse hurrying after her.

Jerret turned to Angarred. "That was Princess Rodarren, the king's niece," he said, speaking quietly.

"I gathered that. What happened to her?"

He glanced around to see if anyone was listening. "She and her cousin Norue and some other children were on an excursion outside the walls of Pergodi."

"Children? How long has she been like this?"

"Thirty years, I think. They were surrounded by nurses and servants and tutors, but somehow Rodarren and Norue managed to slip away. No one missed them until Norue came running back screaming that his cousin had been attacked by a bear. They found her curled up on the ground, her face covered in blood. She lost the eye, of course. And there are two fingers missing from her left hand as well."

"And the Others haven't taken her?" Angarred asked.

Jerret looked back toward the door. "It was a terrible tragedy," he said, shaking his head. "And her so beautiful, too."

Beautiful? she thought. She hadn't noticed, all her attention focused on Rodarren's dreadful scar and strange behavior.

A man carrying a great horn walked into the room. He lifted it and blew four loud notes. Some of the courtiers began moving toward the door. "That's the signal for dinner," Jerret said. "I'm afraid you can only dine with the king if you've been invited."

"I was about to leave anyway," Angarred said, relieved at the thought of escaping the castle.

"Will you come back tomorrow?"

"I suppose. I still don't know if I'm allowed to be here."

"No one challenged you, did they? And the chamberlain announced you?" She nodded. "Don't worry, then. You're one of us now."

She didn't know whether to be pleased at that or not. "Thank you for all your help," she said. "I might see you tomorrow."

She left the castle, got her horse and rode back through the city to her inn.

FIVE

She went back the next day, noticing more about the city as she rode. Unlike her father the men here were almost all clean-shaven, and she remembered one of the plotters commenting on Hashan's beard, saying that he would be terribly unfashionable in Pergodi. Her father replied that of course he would shave before he returned to the city, and then said scornfully that most of the Pergodek could not grow much of a beard anyway. Thinking about the plotters and the men in the Great Hall Angarred realized that that was true. Mathewar, for example, had always been clean-shaven; perhaps if he grew a beard it would be sparse as well.

At the castle she stopped for a while in the Hall of the Standing Kings. She stared up at the vast stone figures, red-tinged from the torches at their feet, their attributes familiar to her even if she could not remember their names. Here was the Navigator, the king who had explored far beyond Karededin, holding a small ship in his hands. There was the Spinner with her spindle, and the Balance with his scales, the king who had collected and codified Karededin's code of justice. Far down the row, at Marfan the First King, a servant had climbed a ladder and was dusting the sun held between the king's great hands.

All of them standing two by two, she thought, all of them said by the religious to have been happily married. She wondered how many of the kings had had mistresses, or had loved men, or had grown to hate the wives they had married for political reasons. And how many had been cruel or merely stupid, and how had the religious decided on attributes for them? What would Tezue's attribute be, and Norue's after him?

The courtiers ignored her as she entered the Great Hall. She stood awhile and watched as they moved from one group to another, talking about things and people she had never heard of.

Jerret Snoppish, at least, seemed pleased to see her. "Lady Angarred!" he said, coming over to her and bowing. "You decided to come back."

"For now," she said, smiling and curtsying to him.

She and Jerret talked about Jerret's father, very old but still alert, about his many sisters and their families, about Angarred's journey to the capital. I'm a courtier now, Angarred thought wryly, but she knew that she was enjoying Jerret's easy talk far more than any of the courtiers enjoyed their own brittle conversations.

"Does the king ever visit the courtiers here?" she asked.

Once again Jerret hesitated and glanced around before he spoke. "The king is ill, milady."

"Ill?" she said. She thought of the rumors that Queen Cherenin was ill as well, and of Rodarren's performance the day before. "Is there anyone in the royal family who isn't?"

"Hush," Jerret said. "Please, you must say things like that quietly. Prince Norue is well, praise the Healer."

She looked over at Norue, surrounded by his flatterers and wearing his usual expression of disinterest. She didn't think his continuing health was a matter for praise, and, if she knew Jerret at all, he probably didn't think so either. She would have to learn the artifice of the court, to lie when necessary. "Praise the Healer," she said dryly, and Jerret grinned.

A week later she was still going to court, wearing one of her mother's three dresses with each visit. Only Jerret spoke to her; the others had lost interest, or scorned her for her pathetic wardrobe. The king had not yet visited his Great Hall, and it did not seem as if he ever would. Nothing had happened as she had planned; she was no closer to solving the mystery behind her father's exile and death.

She got her horse and headed back to the inn. Some people, nobles mostly, stared after her as she rode. It had taken her a while to realize that noblewomen did not risk their clothes by riding astride as she did but used an uncomfortable-looking contraption called a sidesaddle. She scowled at the nobles' amused smiles and tried to convince herself she did not care what they thought.

Everything was so different here; it seemed impossible to learn all the customs and rituals she needed to know. Perhaps, she thought for what seemed like the hundredth time, she should just admit her failure and return home.

A group of people blocked the narrow street in front of her. From her vantage point on horseback she could see a man at the center of the crowd; below him, at about half his height, two odd-looking people capered and sang.

The little people were made of wood, she saw, and were attached to the man's hands by a multitude of strings. When he moved his fingers they appeared to dance, and when he made their mouths open they seemed to talk and sing, though the voice was his own. The crowd around them laughed and gasped at their antics.

She sat awhile, captivated; she had never seen anything like it. Then a movement at the edge of the crowd caught her eye. A man stood there, a familiar man. Her heart jumped, then beat very fast. Mathewar?

No, of course it wasn't. This man's hair was dull, not Mathewar's shining wheat color. And he was smaller, too—or did he only seem that way because he stooped? She dismounted and made her way around the crowd to where he stood. "Mathewar?" she said.

The man didn't turn around. But it was him—she was nearly certain of it now. "Mathewar—it *is* you!"

"Hush," Mathewar said.

"You look so different—I almost didn't recognize you."

"I meant to. And can you speak more quietly, please? I don't want my name bandied about on the streets of Pergodi."

"Why not?"

He sighed. "I suppose I'd better take you back to my inn, or you'll be shouting my business to every passerby," he said. "Follow me—it's just a few streets away."

She walked her horse alongside him. He *did* look different, she thought, stealing glimpses of him as they went. His face seemed older, more lined, and even his eyes were a different color: the blue appeared leached out, leaving a dull, stolid gray. He wore the plain brown workman's clothes she remembered from Hashan Hall, trousers and a shirt of rough cotton.

When they reached his inn, the King's Head, he seemed to shift back into the man she knew; his hair became silky, his walk straighter. She had imagined this meeting so often that it felt terribly strange to be here with him now. So many things about him were different, or remembered wrongly; still, he seemed far more solid, more authentic, than anyone else in the city. She watched him as he walked, looking at his stained boots of heavy leather: she had not remembered them, and yet there they were, a real thing.

The sign over the inn's door showed a ruddy, powerful-looking face with piercing blue eyes. "Is that King Tezue?" she asked.

"Yes."

"I thought he was ill."

"He is."

Mathewar showed her the stables, then led her upstairs to his room. It looked like hers, like rooms all over the city, she supposed—a pallet, a chair, a chest and a washbasin. It also had a hearth, which hers lacked. He sat on the pallet, leaning against the wall and stretching his legs out in front of him.

As she took the chair she suddenly saw herself from the outside, a young woman alone in a room with a man. She had lain with the coachman of one of the plotters, and more recently had spent several pleasant afternoons with one of her father's tenants—but this was different somehow, though she couldn't say how. For one thing, she thought, Mathewar was far less civil than those men, almost as rude as the courtiers had been.

"Why are you here in disguise?" she asked.

"Are you usually this blunt?" he said.

"I'm usually much worse. You should have heard me at court."

"Really? What did you say?"

"I asked them why they had tapestries on the floor."

"Oh, holy Godkings—they must have loved that," he said, laughing. She had never seen him so amused, his eyes alight.

"Well, what was I supposed to say? I don't have a gift for mindless talk." She put on the affected drawl of the courtiers. "And how did you enjoy the dolls in the street, my good sir?"

He laughed again. "They're called puppets." She looked at him suspiciously, searching for his old mockery, but he seemed genuinely to want to teach her, to keep her from making more mistakes. "Let's start with what you're doing at court. Or why you're in the city, come to that."

"I'm here because someone tried to kill me," she said. "You were wrong about the attack—it wasn't only meant for my father." She told him about the man at the top of the stairs.

He watched her closely as she spoke. "I still don't understand. Why did you come here?"

To ask for your help, she thought—but now that she had finally caught up with him she saw how foolish that idea had been. She couldn't face it if he refused. "I'm going to ask King Tezue to avenge my father's death."

He frowned, and she went on quickly: "And don't tell me how little I know, and why my plan won't work. It's the only thing I can think of to do."

"But what if the person behind these attacks is someone at court? If it's someone you talk to every day?"

"I thought of that, of course. No one's attacked me yet, though. And why would anyone at court care about me?"

"I don't know. Someone cares about you, that's clear enough."

"Who?"

"I don't know. Has anyone shown an interest in you? Talked to you a good deal?"

"The only person who talks to me at all is Jerret Snoppish. Do you think . . . Oh, holy Godkings. My father hated the Snoppishes—do you think they killed him?"

"Jerret Snoppish. No one in that family is much interested in court politics. Jerret's the only one who even goes to court, isn't he? It doesn't seem likely."

"No, it doesn't. But really, I don't know anyone else. They're all too high and mighty to talk to me." She thought of her father's drawings of the Snoppishes, then thrust them out of her mind.

There was silence for a while, and then Mathewar asked, "Have you seen a man named Alkarren at court?"

"No. Who is he?"

"The king's magician. He's the one who stole the Stone. Do you know about the Stone of Tobrin?"

"Only that the king borrowed it from somewhere, and it disappeared. And you think Alkarren stole it?"

"I know he did. And the Stone is very powerful—it holds more magic than exists in all the lands put together. Eight hundred years ago, every strong magician in the land tried to gain power for himself, to triumph over his rivals. The land was shaken over and over again by magical storms, by fires, plagues, ravening beasts, by other, more terrible things that people have mercifully forgotten. Cities were devastated, crops withered in the ground, whole peoples left their homes and wandered the roads, looking for safe havens. Finally a few of the magicians saw that the lands would be utterly destroyed if the wars went on, and they banded together to vanquish the others. Then, with most of the magicians dead or powerless, Tobrin bound what magic he could into the Stone. And so no magician has ever become strong enough to wield that sort of power again. The Stone was stolen from the College around four hundred years ago and somehow came to Takeke—no one knows how."

"Why does the king still keep Alkarren, then? If he took the Stone?"

"The king doesn't know."

"Well, why don't you tell him?"

Mathewar laughed. "It's not as simple as that. The Stone makes Alkarren more powerful than any magician alone or with others. That's why the magicians left. That's how frightened they are of him."

"But you didn't, did you?" Angarred said, remembering how Mathewar had brought news from Pergodi, how her father had listened eagerly. "You stayed at court for a while after the Stone disappeared. Why did you do that?"

"I was very foolish. Many people were endangered by my actions, and some of them—some of them died."

"What happened?"

Mathewar seemed not to hear her. He looked lost within himself, abstracted. She tried another question: "Is Alkarren dangerous to me? Should I be careful of him?"

"Alkarren?" He brought his attention back to her. "I don't know. But if he's the one behind your father's death you should leave this city and never come back."

"And go where? I had to sell everything in the manor house to come here."

Mathewar shrugged. "To relatives, perhaps. What about your mother's people?"

"My mother didn't have any people. None that my father told me about, anyway."

"Well." He paused. "I doubt that Alkarren killed your father. Why would he, after all? And he rarely comes to court—the king has to come to him, in his tower. But if he shows any interest in you at all you should run away as fast and far as you can."

"What about my father?"

"What about him?"

"I can't let his death go unavenged."

"Oh, yes, you can. Don't make the mistake of thinking you can stand up to Alkarren." He hesitated again, and then said, "He's the reason I'm here in disguise."

"He is? Why? What did he do to you?"

"The less you know about this business the better. Just remember what I told you."

"Very well."

"If you hear anything about him I'd appreciate it if you came and told me. But don't approach him if he comes to court. And don't tell anyone what I've said about the Stone."

"Of course not."

As soon as she had gone Mathewar hurried to the hearth and started a fire. His thoughts had started to jangle, to rub against one another painfully, like broken bones, and he had had to give

Angarred a useless task to get rid of her. Well, at least if she visited to tell him minor court gossip he could keep an eye on her, make sure she stayed out of trouble. He would not see another person come to harm because of him.

But why in the name of the Spinner had she come to Pergodi? If Alkarren was behind the attack on Lord Hashan there was no place more dangerous for her, and yet here she was, wanting to avenge her father. To avenge him! She was far too innocent, and that and her beauty, her long, tangled red-golden hair and dark blue eyes, would attract just those courtiers she should be most anxious to avoid. Poor sheltered girl, she did not even know what the king looked like.

Well, he was long past thinking about women, however beautiful; his lover was sattery, a red wench dressed in silver, who was always willing and always kept her promises. He poured the red liquid and pushed the cup toward the fire, his hands trembling.

He thought he had been so careful, that he had gone somewhere no one would ever find him. He had met one of Hashan's plotters on the road and they had gotten to talking, and he had seen immediately that Hashan's manor house would be the perfect place to hide. No one remembered old Hashan, no one had bothered him for fourteen long years. No one until now.

He lifted the cup and drank. Almost immediately he felt the tangle in his mind smooth out. Everything seemed lighter, softer, more amusing; all the dark thoughts disappeared. The wonderful thing about sattery was that it made any sort of thinking difficult. Angarred was . . . she was . . .

He couldn't remember. He got back to the pallet and flung himself on it, feeling a languorous warmth in every part of his body. The warmth would wear off, he knew, and he would fall asleep, be carried out over the black ocean to the place where the evil dreams waited. But for now he didn't care.

Angarred began to explore the vast castle, turning off into side corridors and hallways before heading toward the Great Hall. It had been built over centuries, and as in the Great Hall no section perfectly matched any of the others. She found towers, battlements, spiral stairways, abandoned rooms, courtyards that had been enclosed as the great work of building encroached upon them and now served as living quarters, fountains and all.

She was telling Jerret some of this when the trumpeter came into the Great Hall and played four loud notes on his horn. She prepared to leave, but Jerret held up his hand to stay her. "That's the king's signature," he whispered.

All around her courtiers were bowing or curtsying. She dropped into a curtsy as well. The trumpeter blew another two notes and everyone straightened, their brocades and silks and Emindal cloth rustling.

King Tezue stood in the center of the room, followed by soldiers and guards and body servants. Angarred put a hand to her mouth but managed not to gasp. She had known the king was ill, but she had not been prepared for the sight before her. His face was lined; the flesh hung from his jowls; the gnarled hands trembled with palsy. His bright blue eyes were vacant and threaded with red veins, and he sagged under the weight of his wine-red fur robe and his gold-and-ruby crown.

A tall man stood behind him and a little to the side, and Angarred knew immediately that this was Alkarren. He had white hair that fell to his shoulders, a white beard and piercing black eyes with overgrown black eyebrows. He held a staff in his right hand but seemed strong enough not to need it. His clothes were the equal of any in the hall, brightly colored and glittering with jewels.

The magician glanced around the room. She moved quickly to stand behind several courtiers but his eyes passed over her without a flicker of interest. The others surged forward to crowd around the king.

Tezue looked around him vaguely, as if he had forgotten what he wanted from the courtiers, and then waved his hand and ushered his party back out. Angarred glanced at Jerret. He frowned back at her; apparently no one was allowed to show the slightest reaction to the king's appearance.

Conversation started again, at first softly and then growing louder. "He looks terrible," Angarred whispered. "No wonder he wanted the Stone."

Jerret nodded, still unwilling to say anything. People began to cluster around Norue; clearly the king's visit had reminded them how close the prince stood to the throne.

Someone stood outside the door, waiting in the shadows of the hallway. Angarred tried to make the figure out, wondering if the king had come back. It was a woman, some sort of servant, beckoning to her.

Angarred pointed to herself. The woman nodded emphatically, then pointed to Jerret. "Someone wants to talk to us," Angarred said.

Jerret turned and saw the woman. A few other courtiers had noticed her as well. Lady Karanin and Lord Enlandin were laughing; no doubt they found it amusing that a serving-woman had come looking for Jerret. Angarred headed toward the woman, impatient with the courtiers' games, and was pleased when Jerret followed her.

The servant curtsied. "Are you Lord Snoppish?" she asked quietly. She was plump, with fair hair, and carried several dust-rags in her hands.

"Lord Snoppish is my father," Jerret said. "I'm Jerret Snoppish."

"Yes, well, your family's in danger, milord. I just overheard that magician, Alkarren. He's ordered the blue-cloaks to search your house."

S I X

It had not been hard for Gedren to find a place in the castle. Hundreds of people worked there, as cooks and laundresses and grooms, in storehouses and treasure-rooms and stables. Because she was new she was assigned tasks no one else wanted, dusting the rooms, sweeping or mopping the floors, emptying the chamber pots twice a day.

For the first several weeks she learned nothing. No one mentioned Dalesio in her hearing, and she thought more and more that he might be dead. Then she made her discovery, and all thoughts of leaving the castle vanished.

She had been ordered to clean a rarely used room. A thin layer of dust covered everything but the room was otherwise fairly clean; this would be an easy task compared to some. She gathered the rushes, swept the floor, swept the ashes from the fireplace. As she straightened she hit her back on the mantel. Someone groaned behind her.

She turned quickly. The groaning continued, but there was no one in the room. Then she noticed that a section of the wall had rolled away, leading to a darkened hallway.

She took a candle from the outside corridor and ventured a few steps inside. The flickering light showed the beginning of a passageway; the rest was lost in darkness. Suddenly something creaked behind her: the door closing, about to trap her within the walls. She hurried back to the room and continued cleaning.

In the days that followed she returned to the fireplace and the hidden door whenever she had a spare moment. She grew bolder, taking longer journeys down the hallway, at first propping the door open and then learning how to work the closing mechanism from the inside.

She discovered that the corridor had been built to spy on the occupants of the castle. Small holes had been placed at eye level along the hallway, offering glimpses of rooms beyond. She listened in on the king and his council, observed Princess Rodarren in her rooms, watched Norue and Alkarren and various courtiers and body servants. No one said anything about Dalesio, but there had been tantalizing mentions of the Stone, of magicians and lost power.

One day she noticed light shining out into the hallway in a place she had never seen it before. She set her candle down and put her eye carefully to the wall.

The room beyond was smaller than most in the castle. She saw King Tezue first, lolling back in a chair, his eyes nearly closed. Alkarren paced back and forth in front of him, muttering angrily.

"It's useless, completely useless," Alkarren said. "This has to be a counterfeit—it's nowhere as powerful as legend has it. There has to be another Stone. Why don't you speak, by the Orator! You must know where it is. You can't have been king for nearly twenty years without learning something, hearing some rumor . . ."

"I thought you knew," Tezue said. He opened his eyes and blinked, looking puzzled as a child. "You know everything, don't you?"

"Quiet!" Alkarren said. Gedren breathed in sharply to hear him speak so rudely to the king, but fortunately neither man heard her. "I need to think. You're no help, no help at all." He turned to Tezue, a naked look of cunning on his face. "Perhaps I do know. Why don't you tell me what you think, and I'll tell you if you're right or wrong. A sort of guessing game."

"Tell me, did the Snoppishes fix their roof? That was a terrible thing, when their roof collapsed."

Alkarren took a step closer to the king, his hand pulled back. For a moment Gedren feared he was about to hit him. "The Snoppishes' roof fell years ago, fifteen years at least. Concentrate on what I'm saying, you fool."

Alkarren paced a moment, then slowed. "Wait. You're a fool, and fools speak in riddles. And you're answering my own riddle, aren't you? The Snoppishes have the other Stone, don't they?"

"Lord Snoppish has always been very kind to me."

"That's it! The Snoppishes have it. Eshtold! Eshtold, come here."

A man in a blue cloak came into the room, followed by three men in ox-hide coats. Gedren nearly gasped again. It was the blue-cloak and the three soldiers who had visited her house, the ones who had asked her if Dalesio was a magician.

"Eshtold, take your crew and go to Lord Snoppish's house. Do you know where that is?" Eshtold nodded. "Turn it upside down. Search it from top to bottom. I don't want anything overlooked. You're looking for a Stone, a small green-and-black Stone. If anyone gives you trouble tell them you're on the king's business. Do you understand?"

"Yes, milord," Eshtold said.

"Help me up," King Tezue said. "Help me. I want to—I want to see my court."

Eshtold looked at Alkarren, confused about which order to obey. "Oh, very well," Alkarren said. "Take him to court. He won't stay there long anyway—he never does. And after that I want you to pay old Snoppish a visit."

Gedren left the secret corridor and headed toward the Great Hall, pretending to dust whenever anyone came into view. She hung back as King Tezue and his retinue went into the Great Hall and watched them leave again, then moved past the chamberlain to the entrance. The chamberlain tried to stop her but she ignored him and polished a candlestick until he went away. She had learned her first day that no one paid much attention to servants.

She had seen the man they called Snoppish many times in the castle. Once he had helped her carry some rushes and had wished her good day, and she had stared after him, amazed at how little like a courtier he seemed. When she heard about the danger to his family she had not stopped to think but had hurried to warn him. Now she wondered if he would receive her or if, like everyone else, he would scorn to talk to servants.

Jerret saw the chamberlain straining to hear their conversation. "We can't talk here," he said quietly. "Come with me—I know a room . . . This is Lady Angarred, by the way. You can trust her with anything you tell me. And you are—"

"Gedren Serving-maid, my lord," the woman said, dropping into another curtsy.

He led them into a private room. "Searching my house, you said?" he asked. "But why?"

"They're looking for the Stone. Alkarren thinks your family has it."

"He does? How do you know all this?"

"I overheard him, I told you. But you'd better hurry—they're heading toward your house right now."

Jerret turned to leave, thanking Gedren quickly as he went. "I'm going too," Angarred said. He looked at her, surprised, then saw her stubborn expression and shrugged. She could do as she liked, he supposed.

He and Angarred hurried to the stables. He mounted his horse and left, not waiting for Angarred.

She caught up with him as he left the courtyard. "We have to get a friend of mine," she said. "He knows a good deal about Alkarren."

"We can't stop," Jerret said impatiently. He urged his horse faster, pushing through the crush of carts and people on the street. Angarred dropped behind, halted by a vendor selling fruit.

He reached the river, then crossed it over the Two Sisters Bridge, passing a statue of a sister at each end. A short time later he came to his family's manor house. A man stood guard at the front door, but Jerret barely had time to notice him as he rode past and into the stables. He dismounted and ran to the rear of the house.

Another man stood before the rear door. "Hold," the guard said. "What do you want here?"

"What do I want here? This is my house!" Jerret said, brushing past him.

He took a few steps down the hallway and stopped. Noise and chaos surrounded him: soldiers shouting, smashing open chests, tearing apart stools and chairs, slicing through tapestries with their swords. Angarred had come up beside him, her eyes wide as she watched the soldiers carry out their destruction. Arys's young son Tomsin picked a piece of the wood out of the ruins and hit the walls with it, screaming in imitation of the soldiers. "Tomsin, stop that!" Jerret called, but either Tomsin hadn't heard him or he pretended not to.

The men wore ox-hide coats, all save one who stood to the side wrapped in a midnight blue cloak. "What is this?" Jerret asked the blue-cloak, shouting to be heard over the din. "What are you doing in my house?"

Lord Snoppish came out of his study, leaning heavily on his cane, looking bewildered. He started toward the blue-cloak, but Jerret waved him back.

"We're to search the house," the blue-cloak said. "Orders from King Tezue."

"Then by all means search it," Jerret said. "We're loyal servants of the king. But there's no need to destroy all our possessions."

"King's orders," the blue-cloak said again, and strode away to talk to the soldiers.

Arys came out into the hall, grabbed Tomsin by the hand and held him tightly as he squirmed to get away. "Oh, Jerret. Did they—"

Jerret shook his head and nodded toward Angarred, indicating that Arys should not speak of family business in front of strangers. His sister nodded back. Angarred glared at him with a mixture of fury and betrayal, then stalked off down the hall. He felt moved with pity for her, but his family's secrets were not his to give.

Finally, after what seemed like hours, the noise stopped and the blue-cloak ordered his soldiers outside. Jerret closed the door carefully behind them; to his mild surprise the latch still worked.

"Where's Mother?" he asked.

"Upstairs," Arys said. "And Father?"

"I thought he was here. Maybe he's gone back to his study."

To Jerret's vast relief they found Lord Snoppish in the study. Books had been pulled out at random and lay scattered across the floor like fallen men on a battlefield. Lord Snoppish seemed not to notice; he stood in the middle of the wreckage and showed Angarred a picture in an old volume. Jerret smiled at her, pleased that she had managed to distract him, and she nodded back grudgingly.

"Why does Alkarren think your family has the Stone?" she asked.

"I have no idea," he said. He was not good at lying, he knew, and he picked up one of the books on the floor to hide his expression.

Angarred bent to help him. "I think you do. I think you know far more than you're saying."

"Everyone has secrets, you know that. Or you should have learned that by now. Here, you don't have to do that," he said, taking a book from her hand.

"I thought you were different from all those others. I thought I could trust you."

"You can."

"I can? When you're hiding something from me?"

"She looks trustworthy enough," Lord Snoppish said. "Go ahead—tell her what you like."

Jerret smiled fondly at his father. "You think everyone looks trustworthy."

Angarred faced Lord Snoppish. "My father hated you, you know," she said. "And he was assassinated, killed coldly and deliberately while he was out hunting. If you had a hand in that you should tell me now."

Jerret stared, amazed all over again at her directness. "No, my dear," Lord Snoppish said mildly. "We had nothing to do with that. But your father . . . Oh, dear. It's a story you should hear in better surroundings than this. Can you stay to supper?"

Whatever Snoppish wanted to tell her, Angarred thought, it would have to wait a while, until there was a lull in the conversation. The Snoppishes all talked at once at supper, Jerret explaining how he had known about the soldiers' raid, Lady Snoppish lamenting the state of her crockery and trying to find unbroken dishes, the children arguing.

Finally the food was cleared away, and silence fell over the table. "Can you tell me about my father now, Lord Snoppish?" Angarred asked.

"Lord Hashan, yes," Snoppish said. "He—well, there's no good way to tell you, I'm afraid. He was part of a conspiracy to kill the king."

"What?"

"Fourteen years ago, this was. King Tezue had just come to the throne a few years earlier, and he'd made some unfortunate decisions. And there was a drought, and many of the crops failed . . . Well, a number of people, your father included, thought the time was right to depose him."

She sat still, trying to take in what Snoppish was telling her. Her father was a traitor after all; he had lied, it had all been lies. She remembered that Mathewar had tried to warn her the day Hashan had died, and remembered, too, her certainty that he was wrong.

There were too many questions she wanted to ask. "Who would they have put on the throne instead?"

"Prince Norue."

"Norue? He'd be a terrible king."

"Yes he would, my dear, but that's not something you should say, even in the most trusted company. He will take the throne when Tezue goes to the Celestial Court, whether we like it or not."

"But why did my father want to make him king?"

"I'm afraid you've got the question backwards. Prince Norue wanted the throne—your father was only one of the people who joined his cause. Some of them seemed sincere, seemed to think that Norue would truly make a better king, but some of them simply saw a chance to grab riches and power and lands."

"And my father wanted the riches and power, I suppose."

Snoppish nodded. He seemed relieved that she had not forced him to say it.

"But—but I still don't understand," Angarred said. "If Norue plotted against King Tezue, why wasn't he sent into exile as well? Why wasn't he killed?"

"He'd been very careful—very little of the plot had been written down, and there was nothing to show that he was the leader of the conspiracy. All the documents pointed to other people, Lord Hashan among them. And even these didn't completely prove that there was a conspiracy—that's why your father was only exiled and not killed. Besides, the king was reluctant to believe his own blood would plot against him. He'd known even then, I think, that Norue might be his only heir."

"But if there was so little in writing how did the king find out about the conspiracy?"

"Ah," Lord Snoppish said. "I'm afraid this is the reason your father hates—hated—me. I was the one who told him."

"Well, how did you find out?"

Snoppish waved his hand vaguely. "Oh, you know," he said. "People talk, rumors travel . . ."

Angarred frowned. Snoppish had not been vague about anything before. "Who told you, then?"

"Oh, I don't remember. It was so long ago. And your mother—"

"My *mother?*"

"What do you know about her?"

"Only that she died when I was four."

Snoppish looked at her in surprise. "No, she didn't, my dear. As far as I know she's still alive."

"What!"

"She'd joined the conspiracy too, though I don't know how big a part she played. Afterward she left Pergodi and never returned. There were rumors that she had taken refuge in a Godhouse, that she had become a godwife in penance. Did your father tell you she was dead?"

Angarred nodded. It was too much to take in: her father a traitor, her mother still alive . . .

"That was cruel of him," Jerret said. "I suppose he hated her for leaving, for not standing by him."

She barely heard him. All her questions had reduced themselves to one, the most urgent: why had her mother left her? Why hadn't she rescued her from her half-mad father and his decaying house? Had Lady Verret not loved her enough to take her along?

Jerret was speaking. She tried to concentrate. "We still don't know why Hashan was killed," he said. "It couldn't have anything to do with the plot against Tezue—that was far too long ago."

Angarred put her hand to her mouth in alarm. "Why not?" she said. "Could Prince Norue be the one who killed him, could Norue be worried that my father would tell the king who the real leader of the plot was?"

"Your father had already told King Tezue about Norue," Lord Snoppish said. "He and the other conspirators tried to excuse themselves by pointing to Norue fourteen years ago, but the king didn't believe them. Surely Norue must know that your father poses no threat to him now."

"Anyway, why would Norue want to kill me?" Angarred said. "Unless he thought that my father had told me about the conspiracy—"

"Someone tried to kill you?" Jerret said, looking concerned.

"Oh, yes. A man tried to push me down a flight of stairs."

"But that's terrible!" Jerret said.

Lord Snoppish was also saying something, expressing his horror, but another dreadful thought occurred to her. She tried to remember what she had said to Norue, if she had said anything at all. Was he watching her, biding his time, waiting for the best moment to pitch her down the stairs? No, Lord Snoppish had to be right. Why would Norue concern himself with her family, so long after her father's exile? If he wanted to kill Hashan, why hadn't he done it fourteen years ago, after Hashan left Pergodi for his estate?

"It's getting late, far too late for you to go your inn," Jerret said. "Would you like to stay here for the night?"

"Yes, very much," Angarred said. "That is, if I won't be a bother."

"An inn?" Lord Snoppish asked. "What in the name of the Godkings are you doing in an inn?"

Angarred looked at him, unsure what to say. He had been accepted as a nobleman all his life; he had no idea what it was like to come to a strange, friendless city . . . But Jerret was answering for her. "What do you mean, Father?"

"The Hashans have always had perfectly good apartments in the castle," Lord Snoppish said. "Didn't anyone tell you?"

It was another surprise in an evening of surprises. "No," she managed to say.

"Who keeps the apartments these days?" Snoppish asked Jerret.

"Prince Norue. Ah, that explains it. He probably doesn't want you in the castle."

"Will I have to—to ask him about them?" Angarred said.

"I'm afraid so, my dear," Snoppish said. "But those rooms are yours by right, probably given to your family long ago. He has to let you live there. Your father couldn't use them, of course, but any other member of your family can stay there when they come to Pergodi."

"Thank you," she said. "I—"

"Too many revelations for one day, eh?"

She grinned at the old man. "Very much so," she said.

They left the table soon after, and she and Jerret and Arys managed to clear some of the devastation. Then Lord Snoppish led her upstairs and down a hallway to a room, leaning heavily on his cane. "There you go, my dear," he said, opening a door.

The cold of the stone room hit her almost immediately. "I'm afraid this room has no hearth," Snoppish said. "But there are a good many blankets, and I can get you more, if you like."

"No, it looks fine," Angarred said. I've slept in worse places, she thought, but the tact she had learned in the court kept her from saying it. "Thank you very much."

She picked up the blankets from where the soldiers had flung them. Then she relieved herself in the chamber pot, blew out the candle and settled in bed. This house was like her own, she thought. There was a shabbiness here beyond what had been caused by the soldiers' destruction; as at Hashan Hall things had been used and reused until they were nearly beyond repair. And yet the Snoppishs' house appeared far livelier, for she had avoided her father and his plotters and treated her house as if no one lived there.

She could not go to sleep. Questions and answers chased themselves in her mind, the small along with the great. Could she find out at a Godhouse which order of godwives her mother had joined? Did she want to—or would her mother simply reject her again? She knew now why Lady Verret's clothing was at Hashan Hall—her mother, about to don the rough brown robes of a religious, had had no need for it, and her father, never one to accept reverses, had kept it in the hope that she might come back.

Who would want to kill her father fourteen years after his treachery? Who would want to kill her, for that matter? What were the Snoppishes hiding, should she follow her instincts and trust them? And a new question presented itself—why would Alkarren search the Snoppishs' house for the Stone if, as Mathewar said, he had the Stone himself?

Her last thought was of Mathewar—she would have to tell him about Alkarren's search. She pulled the blankets closer around her and fell asleep to the sounds of Arys's children, too excited to sleep, running up and down in the hallway.

SEVEN

She sought out Prince Norue immediately the next morning: better to get it over with, she thought. The prince dismissed her with a gesture into the care of one of his flatterers, and a while later she stood at the door to her apartments, holding her own key.

After her closet-sized room at the inn the apartment seemed amazingly grand, though in reality it had only three rooms. One held a table and some chairs and the second a bed, a chest and more chairs.

She opened the door to the third room, and to her great delight she discovered a copper-plated tub. After having to share a bath with an entire floor at the inn this seemed almost unimaginable luxury.

She walked through the apartments slowly. The furniture was a little worn, the floor a little scuffed. Still, she saw no dust or cob-webs; though no one had lived here for fourteen years the serving-maids had apparently kept the rooms clean all that time. She looked carefully on the table and in the chest and under the mattress, searching for signs of her lost mother or her ancestors, but nothing yielded any clues.

She left the castle and went to the inn, to tell the innkeeper she was leaving and to pick up her meager belongings. Then she decided to visit Mathewar; it was more auspicious to have two errands rather than one.

He did not seem to think the news she brought was important. "Alkarren wouldn't search for the Stone," he said. "Not when he already has it."

"That's what the servant said, though," she said.

"She must have misheard then," he said. "They must have been searching for something else."

She talked to him some more, about her new apartments and what Snoppish had said about her mother and father, but he seemed distracted and said little.

She returned to the castle after noon and carried her belongings up to her rooms. After she had put everything away she realized she was very hungry. She had seen servants bringing up meals to other apartments, and when someone knocked at a door down the hall-way she went outside, wondering who she could ask about the possibility of food.

A tall solid woman in black turned away from a door and came down the hall toward her, walking so gracefully she seemed almost to glide. Keys and scissors and knives and other odd implements dangled from her belt. Angarred had seen women dressed like this before and recognized her as one of the housekeepers.

"Excuse me," she said.

The woman stopped and nodded regally. If not for her clothes, Angarred thought, she could be one of the courtiers.

"How can I get something to eat?" Angarred asked.

"How?" the housekeeper said. "I suppose you could go down to the kitchens."

"No—I mean I'd like some food brought up to my apartments."

"Yes, well, the midday meal ended an hour ago. You have to tell me what you want in the morning, to give the kitchens time to make it. Didn't you know that?"

"No, I didn't. Do you mean I can't get anything now?"

"Yes."

"Very well," Angarred said, willing herself not to become angry. "Where are the kitchens?"

The woman gave her complicated directions and glided away. As she went Angarred heard her laugh, no doubt enjoying the idea of a noblewoman forced to forage in the kitchens. Wonderful, she thought. I've become the court fool once again. She'll tell the rest of the servants, and none of them will ever take me seriously.

She tried to convince herself that it didn't matter, that she didn't care what servants thought. She didn't quite believe it, though; Rushlag and even Elenin had been large terrifying figures for much of her childhood.

She squared her shoulders and headed downstairs. But either the housekeeper had given her the wrong directions or she had misheard them; she spent a long confusing time in basements and underbasements searching for the kitchens. Finally she found several overheated rooms, their floors slippery with water and vegetable peelings and plucked feathers. Cooks bustled back and forth, apprentices hunched over ovens, servants ran for plates or scrubbrushes or forgotten ingredients, everyone seeming far too busy to stop for her.

She finally got the attention of an assistant cook, who heaped a plate full of cold food and gave it to her. But when she turned to leave she heard more laughter; even cooks and servants, it seemed, felt superior to a courtier who had to seek out her own meals.

She returned to her apartments and stayed there for the rest of the day. Her sense of pride in having her own rooms, in moving up in the hierarchy of the court, had disappeared. Someday she would gain power, she thought grimly. Someday they would be sorry for mocking her. Especially that housekeeper.

When she went to the Great Hall the next day, though, she found that she had gotten a bit more status along with her new rooms. A few of the minor courtiers started to speak to her, some even flirting with her, and she learned more court gossip.

Prince Norue, they told her, was the son of Tezue's brother, and Princess Rodarren the daughter of his sister—and since Rodarren was older than Norue, and her mother older than Norue's father, there had been talk in her childhood that she would inherit the throne. Karededin had had a queen in the ancient past, some said. But the religious considered the very idea blasphemy; it was King Marfan, not Queen Mathona, who ruled in the Celestial Court, and Norue who had descended through the male line. After the princess's accident, though, no one thought her capable of governing, and Norue's faction grew in importance.

It was good that she found people to talk to, because Jerret had other business. A few days after she had gotten her rooms the chamberlain announced a herald, and a man came into the Great Hall carrying a blue flag emblazoned with a silver circle. Jerret and some others—among them Lord Enlandin and Lady Karanin—followed him as he left. The herald wore his shoes on the wrong feet.

Her new acquaintances told her that the flag called the councillors to the King's Council, that they were trying somehow to govern during the king's illness. The herald wore his shoes that way to indicate that the council was impartial, they explained, that those serving the king should not favor either the left or the right. In the cynical manner of the courtiers, though, they went on to say that the custom had probably started when a herald had put his shoes on too quickly. She shook her head, marveling at how much there was to know about court customs, and how little of them she had learned so far.

Jerret was gone for several days. When he returned she asked him about it, but he shook his head and smiled and said only, "It was chaos." By then, though, everyone at court knew that Norue had tried to get himself appointed regent, and that Jerret, worried that the prince might have enough votes on his side, had managed to postpone the decision.

The day after she talked to Jerret she saw Gedren; the servant was on her hands and knees, polishing the slate floor. She hurried toward her. "I have to talk to you," she said.

Gedren rose slowly, looking alarmed. "What's the matter, milady?" she asked.

"Nothing," Angarred said. "Don't you remember me? I was with Jerret—Lord Jerret—when you told him his house was being searched. My name is Lady Angarred."

"That's right." Gedren glanced around her. "We can't talk here, milady. Come, I'll take you somewhere private."

Gedren led her to an empty room and walked over to the unlit hearth. "How did you know Alkarren would send soldiers to Jerret's house?" Angarred said.

"I told you. I overheard him."

"Come now. Magicians never allow themselves to be overheard."

"They do, though." Gedren hesitated a moment, then seemed to come to a decision. "Watch."

She reached inside the fireplace and pressed. A section of the wall swung outward.

"Come with me," Gedren said. She took a candle and headed into the dark space beyond. Angarred followed eagerly.

"See these holes?" Gedren whispered, shielding the candle with her hand. "They look out onto different rooms in the castle."

"How did you find this?"

"Hush. By accident. Look—these are Princess Rodarren's rooms."

Angarred put her eye to the hole. "Prince Norue's there," she whispered.

"Yes. He often visits her."

"Don't stare at me like that," Norue was saying. He wore his usual haughty expression, but he sounded angry. "Listen to me."

"I visited the Others yesterday," Rodarren said. Her voice was low and pleasant, far different from her crazy shouts in the Great Hall.

Norue looked alarmed; it was the first sign of emotion from him that Angarred had ever seen. He rapped twice on a nearby table. "Never mind that. You know old Tezue doesn't have long now. And then I'm taking the throne, by the Balance, and you won't challenge me in any way."

"The Others say you'll be going on a voyage. That you'll be leaving soon."

"No, Cousin, not a voyage. A coronation, that's where I'm going. And you'll be there to see me."

"And the Others. They'll be watching you too. They're watching you now, in fact."

"You understand everything I say, don't you?" Norue said, his voice louder. "I can see it in your eyes—your eye. All of this is just mummery, to convince everyone you're a mere fool. But I'm not convinced, Cousin. You'll challenge me for the throne, I know you will."

"Mummery, flummery. Plummery, plum. Frumenty."

"You can't hide from me forever, you know. You'll make a mistake, and then I'll catch you. And then I'll put you to death, so help me."

"Yes, death! That's where they say you're going. To the Land of Death. Perhaps you should get ready now—I hear it's a long journey, and very difficult."

Norue strode from the room, his face set in anger. Angarred watched for a while longer, wondering if he had been right, if Rodarren understood more than she seemed to. The princess sat unmoving, her one good eye unfocused.

Jerret was right, Angarred thought, she is beautiful. She had a long face which appeared longer because of the straight dark hair that fell to her shoulders. Her good eye was the same color as her hair, deep brown like polished wood. There were gray hollows under her eyes, but even these added to her grace; she looked like a wise, sad woman from an old tale, someone trapped within an ancient enchantment.

They moved down the corridor. "So Norue thinks Rodarren understands what he's saying," Angarred said.

"Yes, he says that a lot. He stands there and screams at her sometimes."

"Does he?" Angarred said, laughing softly. "He seems so unconcerned at court."

"Yes. That's why I like to come here. You see everyone unadorned, real. They take their masks off here."

Gedren stopped at another peephole. "This is Queen Cherenin's room," Gedren whispered. "Poor woman, she isn't well."

Angarred peered inside. A woman lay on the bed, her gray hair fanned out beneath her. Her eyes were closed, the lids a dark purple, in stark contrast to the paleness of her skin. Another woman sat beside her on a chair, sewing. Cherenin stirred and moaned, and the second woman reached out and brushed the back of her hand gently down the queen's face.

"How long has she been like that?" Angarred whispered.

"A few years. She's lucid, but she's never free of the pain."

"No wonder King Tezue wanted the Stone."

"What do you know about the Stone?" Gedren said, her voice suddenly low and urgent.

How much should she tell this woman? Mathewar had told her to say nothing, after all. And she still had her old habit of secrecy, of never telling her father anything. "Very little. I just arrived at court, after all. What do you know about it?"

Their candle burned low, and they headed back down the corridor. When they reached the deserted room Gedren pressed the section of the mantel that rolled the wall back into place.

Gedren said nothing for a while. "My husband—my husband disappeared," she said finally. "The same night all the magicians except Alkarren vanished."

"Is he a magician?"

Gedren's mouth twisted. "That's what they asked me, those blue-cloaks. And they said something about a Stone too. But I think if he was a magician I'd know it—we've been married for twenty years. I just don't know. I'm even starting to think that he left me, that he grew tired of living with his family. Or that he's dead, or taken by the Others."

Angarred rapped the wall twice, quietly, just as Norue had done. "I wish I could help. I have no power here, though, and I need help myself. My father was killed, attacked by an assassin. I've come to ask the king for justice. Though it's all worse than I imagined—the king's lost his wits, and his wife is ill, and his niece has gone mad . . ."

"And that cold fish Prince Norue will take the throne," Gedren finished. "And then all the Godkings help us."

"I do know someone," Angarred said, thinking of Mathewar. If Gedren's husband was a magician Mathewar might be able to tell her. "A friend of mine. I'll see what he can do."

"I'd be grateful for that, milady. We need to stick together."

The next day Angarred heard that a group of people were planning to visit Queen Cherenin. "I'd like to come too," she said, remembering the sad figure lying in the bed.

"I don't think so," Norue said. She had not heard him come up behind her. "You'll only weary the queen with your foolishness."

She thought of the conversation at the Snoppishes', and she felt real fear of the prince. Was he keeping an eye on her? Or had he forgotten her name already, seeing her as just another of the hangers-on at court? Her fear made her angry, and she decided to confront him head-on.

"Many wise men play the fool for their own purposes, milord," she said. "And many wise women, for that matter."

She had the satisfaction of seeing him turn pale. "What do you mean?" he asked, lowering his voice.

"What do I mean? I don't know. I'm a fool, don't you remember?"

He said nothing more, and she followed the small group of courtiers to the queen's bedchamber. Norue did not come with them, she noticed, pleased.

Cherenin was awake, talking to the same lady-in-waiting Angarred had seen yesterday. "Hello," she said. She managed a smile. "Thank you all for visiting me."

They arranged themselves around her bed. "I don't know you," Cherenin said, frowning at Angarred.

"I'm Angarred Hashan, milady. My father was Lord Challo Hashan."

"Ah, Angarred." She smiled again, more deeply this time. "The one who doesn't know about carpets."

Angarred felt a flash of anger, then realized that there was warmth, not mockery, in Cherenin's voice. "That's right, milady," she said. "And I'll never be forgotten for it, not if I live a thousand years. Angarred of the Carpets, they'll call me."

Cherenin laughed. For a moment Angarred saw her as she must have looked before her illness, not beautiful but spirited, lit from within by her intelligence. "I haven't laughed like that in a long time," the queen said. "Tell me, how is Lord Hashan?"

"He died, milady."

"I'm sorry to hear that. He was always one for conspiracies, wasn't he? Did he continue plotting to the end?"

"I'm impressed you remember him so well, milady."

"I haven't lost my wits yet," Cherenin said, smiling again.

"Yes, but he left your service fourteen years ago."

"He was exiled, as I remember. How did he die?"

"He was assassinated while we were hunting in the forest."

"Assassinated?" Cherenin frowned. "Does my husband the king know about this? He should certainly be told, if he does not."

One of the courtiers, unseen by Cherenin, put her finger to her lips. Angarred understood; the queen did not know the extent of her husband's infirmity. "No, not yet," she said.

"He's been busy with state business, milady," someone said, and the talk turned to other matters.

They stayed and recounted the latest gossip for nearly an hour. Several times Angarred wondered if Gedren stood just beyond the wall, watching them. As they filed out Cherenin grasped each of them by the hand; when she came to Angarred she held on a little longer and looked into her face. "You'll come to visit me again, I hope," she said. "You're like a wind, blowing away the cobwebs."

"I'd like to, milady."

When the group left she heard two men talking behind her; one of them spoke her name. "Lady Angarred's made a conquest, it seems."

"She'd do better to befriend someone with real power at court," the other man said.

Angarred whirled around. "Is that why you think I did it?" she said. "The poor woman—don't you even care about her?"

"No one cares for anyone here, milady," the first man said mildly. But if that was true, Angarred thought, there would not have been such a crowd around the queen's bed.

On her day off from the castle Gedren went home, looking forward to seeing her sons and hearing the news from the bakery. As she made her way through the familiar twisted, crowded lanes and alleyways of the Craftsman's Quarter her heart rose, and when she came closer to her house people called out to her, asking her to stop and talk. "Where have you been?" the silversmith asked, and the wine-seller and the butcher, who had undoubtedly talked to Labren and Borgarrad, asked, "How's life in the castle?" She waved and continued on, drawn forward by the delicious smell of baking wafting out over her street.

Now she noticed several blue-cloaks in the streets, and she frowned and walked faster. What did they want in the Quarter? None of them looked like Alkarren's man—Eshtold, that was his name—but she felt anxious just the same. Finally she saw her son Labren, the impractical one, deep in conversation with a blue-cloak outside her house. The Orator only knew what he might have told them.

"Mother!" Labren said when he saw her. He stopped talking long enough to give her a hug, and then turned back proudly to the blue-cloak. "This man is from the king's militia."

"Yes," Gedren said. "I know."

"He's recruiting for soldiers, Mother. And I'm going. I'm going to be a soldier."

"Who told you that? You're not old enough, for one thing."

"Yes, I am. I turned seventeen this week."

"Well, that doesn't matter. You're not going into any army. I need you here, especially with your father missing."

"I'm afraid you have no say in it," the blue-cloak said. "I have his signature right here. If he doesn't report for duty next week he'll be thrown in prison."

"Let me see that," Gedren said, taking the blue-cloak's paper. Labren had indeed signed it; she recognized his uncertain scrawl. He had never been one for reading or writing. She spoke directly to her son, ignoring the blue-cloak at his side. "Never mind that— you're staying right here. We'll find a way to invalidate this."

"You can't," Labren said. "You heard him. I have to go."

"We'll see. And where's your brother? Why didn't he talk you out of this foolishness?"

"Someone had to take care of the bakery, Mother."

"You should be proud of him," the blue-cloak said. "He's protecting his country."

"I don't see that Karededin needs much protection," Gedren said. "Or is there an enemy somewhere I've overlooked?"

"Didn't you hear?" Labren said, excitement clear in his voice. "Takeke's declared war."

"What!"

"It's true. They're coming for the Stone—they say we stole it from them. The council's put more men on the city walls, and they've ordered the gates closed at night."

"Come inside here," Gedren said, infuriated. She gripped his ear, something she had not done for at least ten years. "We'll talk about it in the family, without this man listening to our every word." She nodded to the blue-cloak. "Good day, sir. There's no need for you to come again."

He ignored her. "Remember, Labren," he said. "We start drilling at Tornish Fields at dawn. Do you have a sword?"

"A sword!" Labren said. "No."

Gedren dragged him into the house before he could say another word.

All that day, while she ranted at Labren for signing the contract and at Borgarrad for not watching out for his brother, she thought of ways to keep her son from going to war. In the afternoon she went next door to talk to Mashak, but he had no suggestions for her. If only Dalesio were there! Everything had gone wrong since he left.

The next week, the day Labren was due to start training, she set out early for Tornish Fields. It was the first of the month, the day people came to the castle from miles around to petition the king, and she thought she would not be missed in all the confusion.

She reached Tornish Gate as the sun rose over the walls, nearly blinding her after the half-shadows of the streets. She followed a few boys through the gate, then saw to her dismay that they were heading toward the fields, that they had signed up for the army too. Children, she thought. Infants. Whose idea was it to send them to war? One of them carried an ancient rusted sword nearly as big as he was.

The fields were in chaos. An enormous number of boys wandered around, shouting and wrestling; those with swords staged mock fights, and at least one was already wounded. Mobs of others clustered around soldiers in buffed ox-hide who were passing out more swords to the clamoring crowd around them. Men drove carts up to the fields and bellowed to the boys to help them unload.

A few brightly clothed men wearing swords stood near her, officers probably, talking quietly among themselves. One of them looked like—yes, it was. Lord Jerret, Snoppish's son.

Jerret turned in her direction and glanced at her quizzically, clearly wondering where he had seen her before. "Lord Jerret," she said, going over to him. "Hello. Do you remember me? I'm Gedren, from the castle."

"Yes, of course. What brings you here?"

"My son is here somewhere."

"Which one is he?"

She spotted him at that moment, standing not far from her in a mob of unruly boys. "Labren!" she shouted. "Labren, come here."

Her son looked around, saw her and turned back to his companions.

"Labren!" she said again. "There's someone I want you to meet."

He glanced around again. This time he noticed the richly dressed men with Gedren, shrugged and started over to them. His face was bright red with embarrassment. But his expression showed curiosity about Gedren's companions as well; she took that as a good sign.

"This is Lord Jerret Snoppish," she said. "Lord Jerret, this is my son Labren."

Jerret studied Labren closely. Finally he seemed to make up his mind about something. "Would you like to join my division?" he asked.

Labren said nothing. "Yes, he would," Gedren said firmly. She could rest a little easier if her son was under Jerret's command. "Thank you very much, milord."

"Think nothing of it," Jerret said. "It's the least I can do after the help you gave me and my family. Very well—Labren, is it? Labren, take that box out of the cart there and bring it to me."

"What is it?" Labren asked.

"A soldier does not question his commander," Jerret said. He was different here, Gedren saw; he had taken on the trappings of an officer. She was almost sorry to see it. "It contains more swords, actually. When you open it you can be the first to choose one."

"Oh," Labren said, sounding thrilled. He turned to his mother.

For a brief moment she thought he was actually going to thank her, then he hurried away toward the cart.

Jerret smiled at Gedren. "I think he'll do fine," he said.

"I hope so, milord," she said.

Labren helped Lord Jerret pass out swords to the excited swarm of boys around them. As the day passed he thought of his mother and grew more and more dissatisfied; somehow she had meddled in his life again, just when he thought he was leaving his family behind for good. And this Lord Jerret fellow was not Labren's idea of a commanding officer at all. With his medium height and expensive clothes and mild expression he looked like one of the courtiers dancing attendance on King Tezue—or at least, since Labren had never actually seen the king, the way he imagined them to look.

Lord Jerret lined his troops up and had them practice thrusts and parries with their swords. They soon began to sweat; as the day grew hotter they stripped off their shirts and wiped their faces.

Finally they took a break. Jerret showed them the type of armor a Takekek soldier would be likely to wear: a heavy helmet and a padded jacket with metal rings sewn between the layers. The armor, he said, left a small space between the head and body unprotected, and he demonstrated a sword thrust to the neck that might kill them.

After the break they split into groups of two and practiced killing Takekek soldiers. Labren had to admit Jerret knew some things about sword-fighting at least, but his dislike of the other man remained. Two-names, he and his friends called the nobility— he himself was just Labren, or maybe Labren Baker. Or Labren Soldier? And Snoppish—what a ridiculous name. Perhaps he could slip away when the Two-name wasn't looking and join another division.

Gedren, meanwhile, had returned to the castle and was watching Lady Angarred and some of the other courtiers visiting the queen. "Is it true we're going to war?" one of the women asked.

"It looks like it," someone else said. "All the interesting men are away, practicing on Tornish Fields. The court's nearly deserted."

"It's not just that," a third courtier said. "Today's the first of the month, when King Tezue hears petitions. His advisors are gone too."

Gedren had seen the crowds of people waiting to get into the Audience Chamber; she had also seen King Tezue slumped on a chair in one of the smaller rooms, dressed in his nightshirt, his gray hair tangled to his shoulders. His advisors had been clustered around him, urging him to get dressed. She doubted anyone would be getting an audience today.

"Is it?" Queen Cherenin turned to Angarred. "Why aren't you out petitioning my husband about your father?"

"I'm hoping for a private audience later, milady," Angarred said. "There's too much of a crowd now."

Very tactful, Gedren thought. Obviously the queen had not seen Tezue in a while.

"I hope you get it, then," Cherenin said. "And I'll mention you to my husband, if he ever comes to see me. Poor man, he's always so busy. But I don't know why he hasn't taken notice of you before." She turned to the others. "What would you say she is? A wolf? An owl?"

This was clearly a game they had played before. Several courtiers made suggestions as to which animal Angarred reminded them of, but Cherenin shook her head at each one.

"A leopard, milady?" the lady-in-waiting said.

"Yes, of course!" Cherenin said, pleased. "Like the leopard in the menagerie. Wild and graceful and beautiful, something from outside our small safe streets and houses."

"What's a leopard?" Angarred asked.

Gedren wondered the same thing, but Cherenin seemed not to have heard her. "Isn't that the same dress you wore the last time you visited?" the queen asked.

Angarred looked down. Gedren saw her flush. "Yes, milady."

"You should go see my dressmaker," Cherenin said. "Tell her to make at least three dresses for you. Something in copper, or, no, peach . . ."

"I—I can't—"

"Nonsense, of course you can. She gets her salary from the royal treasury and she hasn't done much to earn it lately, what with me in bed, and poor Rodarren . . . And we have enough cloth around here to dress an entire town, anything you'd like. Except gray, I suppose—Rodarren's taken most of that. I'll have one of my ladies tell her to expect you, and I want to see you in a new dress the next time you come visiting."

Gedren marveled at her tact. Without coming out and saying so directly the queen had made certain Angarred knew she didn't have to pay for anything.

"Thank you, milady," Angarred said.

Cherenin's head fell back and she began to snore softly. Then, as Gedren watched with approval, Angarred drew the blanket up over the queen and smoothed it around her.

The other courtiers left quietly. The lady-in-waiting took Angarred aside; they stood a few inches from Gedren's spyhole. "Could you watch the queen for a few moments, milady?" the lady-in-waiting asked. "Her other woman should have been here half an hour ago, and I need my supper."

"Of course," Angarred said.

Gedren went back down the corridor. She passed the king, who had not moved from his chair, and returned to work. No one seemed to have missed her.

EIGHT

Angarred woke at a noise. The room was completely dark, the candles all burned down. The door opened, and light shone into the room.

She looked around frantically, fearing the worst. Were they coming to kill the queen? How had they gotten past the guards?

She stood, her back cramping painfully. She had been sleeping on a hard wooden chair, she saw. "Hello?" someone said softly, a woman's voice. "Who's there?"

"Who are you?" Angarred asked.

"Rethe," the woman said. "I'm sorry I'm late." She raised her lantern and saw that Angarred was not one of the queen's ladies-in-waiting. "Oh," she said, putting her hand to her mouth in alarm.

"It's all right," Angarred whispered. "I've been watching her until you got here."

"Thank you. How is she?" The lantern moved out over the queen sleeping on her bed. "Oh, thank all the Godkings."

Angarred took a candle and lit it from the lantern. "Cherenin's fine," she said. "She's been sleeping peacefully."

"Thank all the Godkings," Rethe said again.

They bid each other farewell, and then Angarred went out into the hall and looked around. She had never gone prowling through the castle at night before. Bright frostlike stars shone in through the high windows. She walked carefully through the stone corridor, amazed at its emptiness, her footsteps echoing back from the walls. A rat ran past her, squealing, but she had seen too many of its brethren in her own house to be frightened.

A servant tiptoed around a corner. Gedren? No, of course not—there had to be hundreds of maids here. They nodded to each other as they passed, the servant looking slightly guilty. Going to meet a lover?

Angarred came to the room with the secret hallway and went inside. What did the people here do at night? She pressed the spot on the mantel that opened the wall and ventured down the hallway, her heart pounding. Princess Rodarren's rooms were dark, and so were Prince Norue's, but a light shone out from the king's apartments. She walked on, the stone muffling her footsteps.

Alkarren stood there. His candle flickered, illuminating some of the harsh planes of his face and casting others in shadow. Light came from his hand, green shot through with black. "Get up," he said to the king.

The king stood heavily. He was barefoot, Angarred saw, and wearing a nightshirt.

"Good," Alkarren said. He fingered the thing in his hand, and the strange light shifted and grew stronger. The Stone, Angarred thought in terror. Mathewar's right—he has the Stone. "Come with me."

Alkarren left the room and turned down the corridor. Tezue followed as though sleepwalking.

Angarred ran back through the secret corridor, her candle flaring and nearly going out in her hurry. She went out into the hallway and looked around frantically. The queen's apartment lay over that way, and the king's should be close to it . . .

She saw candleflame and jumped back into the empty room and blew out her candle. Alkarren and Tezue came around a corner. She waited until they had passed and then followed them, careful not to get too close.

Alkarren led the king past the Great Hall and through the vast

Hall of the Standing Kings. The flickering torches at the statues' feet burned a deep red, and the two men's shadows danced wildly against the walls. Then they were through the door leading into the courtyard. The guards at the door saluted; if they noticed Tezue's nightshirt and bare feet they said nothing.

Angarred nodded to them, thinking frantically. Should she say something, tell them about Alkarren? But she remembered Mathewar's warning: Alkarren was dangerous; even Mathewar was afraid of him.

The guards nodded back to her, seeming to take her for one of the king's party, and her chance was lost.

Alkarren and Tezue left the courtyard, more guards saluting them, and headed down the hillside. No moon lit their way; at times Angarred thought she lost them, or mistook a bush's shadow for the magician's cloak. Fortunately only one road led down to the city, though it twisted back and forth around the trees and boulders as it went.

Pergodi lay before them. Despite the late hour people still passed through the streets: farmers coming from the countryside, their carts rumbling over the cobblestones; patrolling soldiers; drunkards reeling home. A stray dog crossed the street in front of them. Few lamps or candles shone, though; only the stars above them dazzled down, nearly bright enough to cast shadows.

No one paid attention to the king and the magician walking silently through the streets; they looked terribly ordinary, and perhaps, Angarred thought, Alkarren had put some sort of glamour on them. If they spoke Angarred did not hear it.

After a long time they came to Taelish Gate. Alkarren whispered something into Tezue's ear and then melted back into the shadows. Two blue-coats stood on either side of the closed gate; more men had been ordered to the walls since the threat of war from Takeke.

The king walked up to one of the guards. "Open the gate," he said loudly.

"What? But—"

"Don't disobey me. Do you know who I am?"

The guard who had spoken looked the king up and down, taking in the nightshirt, the naked feet. Finally he sighed and signaled to his companions, and together they lifted the heavy bar and opened the gate, then raised the portcullis.

The king stepped back quickly. Soldiers burst through the gate, dozens of them, their swords and helmets glittering like ice in the starlight. Angarred backed away from the road, tripped over a stone and lay where she fell, her heart pounding. When she was able to look out again she saw that three of the guards had been cut down, their long wounds glistening black like roads marked on a strange map. A soldier caught up with the fourth guard and stabbed at his back. The king stood by the gate, unmoving. Alkarren was nowhere to be found.

She turned down a narrow street and ran.

The city seemed to tumble around her, gates and walls and chimneys and windows. Once she climbed a flight of stairs only to find herself in a private courtyard, a dead end. Somewhere soldiers shouted, their mailed feet ringing on the cobblestones, but it seemed a long way away. Someone screamed. Dogs barked loudly, and a few people were coming out into the streets, rubbing their eyes.

She reached the King's Head at last. She ran through the front door and up the stairs and knocked loudly on Mathewar's door. No one answered. She pounded on the door again and then pushed it open.

Light bloomed in the room, cast by no lamp or candle. Mathewar sat up in the bed, his eyes dark pools, his hair falling to his shoulders. "What—"

"You were right about Alkarren. He has the Stone. He has the king under his spell somehow, he got him to open the gate, there are soldiers—"

"What?" Mathewar said again.

He's taken sattery, Angarred thought in despair. She had seen addicts of sattery in the streets, unmoving, smiling foolishly at nothing, unable to understand the simplest comment. "Alkarren has the Stone."

"Yes," Mathewar said. "I know that." His speech wasn't slurred, at least; if anything, Angarred thought, it was overprecise.

"He's ensorceled the king somehow. He made the king go to a gate and order the guards to open it, and there are soldiers in the streets, soldiers from Takeke, I think—"

"Soldiers?"

Angarred sighed. It was hopeless. "Yes."

"Then what are you doing here?" Mathewar said. "Ring the alarm bell—the city must be warned."

"What alarm bell? Where is it?"

"At the castle. To the left of the guardhouse, at the corner. Hurry."

"What about Alkarren?"

"We can't do anything about him now. Call out the militia. We'll talk about him—we'll talk about him tomorrow."

The light dimmed. Angarred left the room and went quickly down the stairs and out into the street. She had gotten her wind back; she felt as if she were moving effortlessly, all her muscles working in concert, even as she ran up the hill to the castle.

She hurried into the alarm tower and pulled on the rope to ring the bell. Even this seemed easy, though she felt the drag of the huge bell and the roughness of the rope against her palms. The bell tolled out shrilly over the city, once, twice, a third time. Far off, she heard another bell answer, and another.

Labren, asleep in the Craftsman's Quarter, woke instantly at the alarm. He fumbled at the side of his bed for his sword, then stood and began to dress.

"What?" Borgarrad said from the other bed, still asleep.

"Hush," Labren said. Where had Captain Snoppish said to meet? At Tornish Fields, but if they were held by the enemy . . . The Leaping Dog Bridge, that was it. He buckled on his belt and thrust his new sword through it, then ran downstairs and outside.

Lord Jerret also heard the bells and woke immediately. Had Takeke attacked? Had war come at last? He dressed quickly and made his way downstairs in the dark, careful not to disturb his family. He heard shouting, and someone screaming, and when he stepped outside he saw red fire hanging over the rooftops in the east.

He saddled his horse and rode to Tornish Gate. People spilled out of their houses and called to him, asking questions, but he ignored them and hurried on. Tornish Gate was closed; a man there told him they were guarding it against the enemy, who had come in by treachery through Taelish Gate. Jerret rode hard to the Leaping Dog Bridge, hoping his troops remembered and would be there to meet him.

Halfway there he met Prince Norue, his commanding officer, also riding toward the bridge. They nodded to each other briefly, Norue's face impassive. Even in the midst of war, Jerret thought, marveling, the prince was careful to let no emotion show.

High in the castle in an attic room, Gedren heard the bells as they pealed through her window. She rose and looked out; far off on the horizon she saw fire glowing like an evil sunrise. She said a prayer to the Godkings for Labren, and stood gazing out the window hopelessly until dawn.

Queen Cherenin woke abruptly, thinking she had heard a noise, and called out weakly for her lady-in-waiting. The room was plunged into darkness, all the candles out; she felt alone and vulnerable. She turned in the bed and fell back asleep, and the bells rang through her dreams, tolling out over scenes of violence and blood and death.

Mathewar, deep in the sleep of sattery, heard the distant sound of the bells and tried to remember what they meant. He had told Angarred to ring them, but why? There was something he had to do, something urgent . . . He struggled to wake, but the sattery held him fiercely in its grip.

And Alkarren led King Tezue back to the castle, taking him through tiny lanes and alleyways and places where no roads existed at all, looking at the chaos around him with profound satisfaction. Everything had happened exactly as he planned it. All the guards at the gate were dead; no one could report what he had seen. And best of all, he thought as he spirited the king into the castle through a servants' entrance, no one had noticed a thing.

A soldier ran screaming toward Labren, his sword drawn. Red torchlight reflected off his helmet, glittering like rubies, and then the soldier was on him and he remembered Snoppish's instructions. He parried the man's sword-thrust, parried again, waiting for the moment when the man would be vulnerable, when he could reach the exposed neck between the helmet and the padded jacket. Labren feinted, the soldier turned, and Labren stabbed outward, feeling the sword glance off metal and then go in.

The soldier fell to the cobblestones. Labren stabbed him through the neck again, making sure he was dead. Blood bubbled through the wound and slopped over the mail-shirt with a horrible wet sound. Rubies again, Labren thought, then ran into a ditch and threw up his supper, his family's good bread.

He wiped his mouth on his sleeve and returned to the road. A Karedek soldier stood over the dead man, removing the valuable jacket padded with metal rings.

"Labren," someone said.

Labren turned quickly, his sword at the ready. It was Snoppish. Had the officer seen him be sick? He had killed one other that night and wounded two without flinching, but he had been unable to ignore that awful sound . . . Fortunately Snoppish gave no sign of noticing.

"I want you to scout for more of the enemy," Snoppish said. "Though I think it's over—I think they're gone, for now."

"Yes, sir," Labren said.

Dawn had come without his noticing. A gray light suffused everything, the dead bodies, the wounded, the people looking out fearfully from their houses. Labren saw other soldiers stripping the dead, taking jackets, swords, helmets, rings, anything of value. Three or four men carrying buckets of water ran past him, heading for the fire in the distance; it gleamed over the rooftops, pale against the growing sunrise.

Snoppish paired him with another soldier, and together they patrolled the streets and lanes, looking for more of the enemy. Snoppish seemed to have been right, though; the Takekek soldiers had retreated for now.

"He knows what he's doing, that Snoppish," the other man said. "I'm sure glad he taught us that trick about their armor. He's all right."

"For a Two-name," Labren said.

Someone laughed on the path behind him. He turned, startled, and saw Snoppish. The officer gave him a wink and continued on.

Mathewar woke as light came through his window. His head pounded as though a stake were being driven from his left eye to his jaw, and his mouth tasted metallic, as if he had sucked on a lump of lead all night. He sat up, feeling the familiar disgust with himself. He would stop taking sattery, he thought; this would be the last time . . . He grimaced, knowing that the resolve would disappear by noon, when his craving would grow intolerable again.

He spat and headed for the basin, where he washed his face. It was only then that he remembered the bells ringing all night, sounding through his sleep. Something had happened . . . Angarred had come, that was it, telling him that soldiers were fighting in the streets of Pergodi.

And he had slept through it. The city might be occupied by now, all of them subjects of Takeke or whoever had attacked them. He went to the window and looked out, squinting in the sunlight, but he saw only the familiar scenes of the street, shops opening, carts driving past, servants out early, shopping for their families' suppers.

Now he remembered more, that it had been Angarred herself who had rung the bells. And he had told her to come back the next day; she might even be on her way right now. He ran a hand over his face, decided he didn't need to shave that day, then quickly combed his hair and tied it back.

But why was she coming? He couldn't remember. He found clean clothes and put them on. He would go to the Others before he admitted that he had forgotten what she'd said last night, that he had been deep in a sattery dream. Though why it mattered what she thought of him he didn't know.

A knock came at the door. Angarred stood there, her dress torn, hay sticking out from her tangled hair. "Did you sleep in the bell tower all night?" he asked.

She ran her fingers through her hair, dislodging some of the hay, and laughed. "Yes, I did. I was afraid to go outside, into the fighting."

"I assume we won. I didn't see any soldiers from Takeke on the streets this morning, at least."

"We pushed them back through the gates, anyway. People think they'll try to attack again, that we should settle in for a siege. But we have to talk about the king."

The king? He looked around his room, seeing it as she might—the rumpled bedclothes, the sattery cup overturned by the hearth—and felt suddenly repelled by all of it. "Let's go outside," he said. "I need some fresh air."

"What about breakfast?"

The thought of breakfast turned his stomach. "We should talk somewhere we won't be overheard."

"Oh. Of course."

They went downstairs and out into the bright sunlight. "It was terrifying," Angarred said. "Seeing King Tezue like that, completely under Alkarren's control. Seeing him let the soldiers in, something he would never do in a thousand years on his own. I thought the king had lost his wits—well, we all did—but this was much worse."

Despite the heat Mathewar shivered suddenly. Had Alkarren used the Stone? He needed to know, but what if she had already told him and he didn't remember? He had to frame his question carefully, so she would not suspect his attention had been elsewhere last night. "Did you see the Stone?" he asked.

"Yes. And everything around it turned green and black, but it was a different black from just darkness, if you know what I mean. A darker black, somehow."

Mathewar nodded. "What's wrong?" she said, catching sight of his face.

"It's worse than I thought," he said, choosing his words carefully. "Alkarren's made King Tezue into a Hollow One."

"What's—"

He went on without hearing her, barely seeing the street in front of him. "Once there were magicians who could—well, who could take over a person's thoughts and will, who could do with him whatever they liked. The person would still be aware but buried deep within himself, struggling against the sorcery, forced to do things that would horrify him ordinarily. And then he would begin to fade, and they would slowly turn him into something else . . . No one's been able to create a Hollow One for hundreds of years, not since the Stone disappeared. I knew that Alkarren could do it with the Stone, but I never dreamed he'd dare to attack the king himself. But then why—why did he force Tezue to let the soldiers in? Is he working for Takeke?"

"Can we do anything?"

He shook his head. "I can't free a Hollow One. Not without the Stone, anyway."

"How do you know? Have you ever tried?"

"I know."

"Alkarren thinks the Snoppishes have a Stone," Angarred said. "I told you about that."

The heat was making his headache worse. "Quiet," he said. "Let me think."

Finally they came to the Bridge of the Summer Stars. He leaned against it, his arms on the railing, studying the cool water rushing beneath them. "The College might know," he said. "I suppose I'll have to go there."

"I'll come with you."

He turned to look at her. "Will you now?" he asked. "Do you know where the College is?"

"No. But you do, so that doesn't matter."

He laughed. "It's a long way away. We'll have to travel through the Forest of Tiranon, an uncanny wood where no path goes the same way twice. And that's assuming we can leave Pergodi, which is not at all certain now."

Even she had heard of Tiranon. Currents of magic ran wild there, and strange things stalked the pathways, and landmarks changed slowly around you, so that you no longer knew where you were, or even who. And in the oceans bordering the forest the men and women who cast their nets brought up golden stars and coins, and fish with silver scales and jewels for eyes.

"If you can make it so can I. And I'll bet I know more about how to survive in a forest than you do—I practically lived in one while I was growing up."

"But why in the name of all the Godkings would you want to?"

He had what his master Narinye called Clear Sight: he was gifted with rare moments in which he could see what a person truly meant, or truly wanted. Now, even as he struggled against the morning glare and the pounding in his head and a growing craving for sattery, one of those moments came upon him, and he was able to call forth the truth.

"I don't have anywhere else to go," Angarred said, her voice quieter now. "I sold everything I had from the estate but the money's all gone . . . And it was folly to come here—no one's interested in justice for a minor lord, and they've all forgotten him anyway. Maybe—well, maybe I can help save the king. If we free him he'll be able to talk to me, won't he? Maybe he'll even reward me."

He saw her desperation, saw, too, how she tried to hide it from him. He even understood that she had another reason for wanting to come with him: she craved power at court, enough power to triumph over all the lords and ladies who had mocked her. That was the trouble with the Clear Sight, he thought—you learned so many things you never wanted to.

He sighed. It was good to have a companion on the road—at least, so they said at the College. "A companion is better than wine or food," a magician he knew used to say.

"Very well," he said. He raised his hand. "But even if we come back in triumph, able to free King Tezue, you should not hope for very much. His decisions were always eccentric, even before Alkarren got hold of him."

Suddenly bells began to toll, not the high shrilling of the alarm bells but a deeper, more somber sound. "Someone's dead," Mathewar said. "I wonder who it is."

"Not the king, I hope."

"Let's go back to the inn," Mathewar said. "Innkeepers are always the first to know everything."

By the time they reached the King's Head the common room was filled with the news: Queen Cherenin had died that morning.

"Oh, no," Angarred said. "And I said I hoped it wasn't the king—I didn't even think of her."

"No one ever did, milady," a man sitting at a trestle table said. "She deserved better."

"She did," Angarred said. To Mathewar's surprise he saw that she was crying. "She was a good woman. Did she die alone, do you know?"

"No, thank the Godkings," the man said. "Her ladies-in-waiting were getting her ready for the morning, sitting her up and brushing her hair . . . They said she died very peacefully, just one minute there and gone the next."

"May the Bearer bring her safely to shore," Angarred said, wiping her face roughly.

The man bowed his head in respect. "I'm sure he will, milady. She'll reach the Celestial Court soon, and she'll change her name like the rest of the kings and queens. Queen Chelenin, we'll have to call her."

"Poor woman," Angarred said. "She never seemed very happy."

"Were you close to her?" Mathewar asked.

"As close as I ever got to anyone at court." She tried to smile. "Now I'll have to go with you. There's no one left who can help me there."

They made plans to meet after Cherenin's First Journey and said good-bye. He could almost find it amusing, he thought, watching her leave the inn. He had not taken action for so long, had hidden in out of the way places to keep from coming to anyone's attention—and his latest attempt at running away had brought him, step by step, straight to Hashan and Angarred and their plots. And now he was going to the one place in all the lands he had worked so hard to avoid. But he had to save the king, or at least warn the College; he did not see how he could get out of it this time. It was Fate, perhaps, the Spinner working out his destiny. But he did not believe in the Spinner, or any of the Godkings.

Cherenin would make her First Journey a week after she died; it took that long for the carvers to fashion her statue from the rough red stone. Angarred was impatient to be off, but she felt strongly that she had to stay and say good-bye to one of her few friends in the castle.

The week passed slowly. In the Great Hall the courtiers talked about war, troop strength, Takeke; Cherenin might not have lived and died for all the courtiers cared. The housekeepers and servants found new ways to humiliate Angarred: they neglected to tell her what time they brought the hot water for her baths, so that she arrived to find the copper tub stone cold; they cleaned her rooms haphazardly; they forgot to take her clothes to the castle laundry or brought them back with new stains.

Worst of all, she had seen a man following her several times. He was a spy, that much was certain, but for who? Norue, Alkarren, someone she didn't know who had a grudge against her? Perhaps she had done exactly what Norue wanted when she moved into the castle; here in his own domain it would be much easier to have her watched.

Finally the week ended, and the nobles gathered in the courtyard before the castle for Cherenin's First Journey. They wore the two colors of mourning, of course; they would not miss a chance to commission new clothing. The two colors were a reminder that everything went by twos throughout eternity, that one day Tezue would join his queen in the Celestial Court.

Angarred saw green and gold, red and orange, gray and purple. She herself wore black and dove gray, but she meant her clothes to be a tribute to the queen. Cherenin had said she wanted to see her in a new dress the next time she visited.

The religious chanted the liturgy, the names and attributes of all the Godkings and queens starting with Marfan and Mathona, and at the end they sang out "Chelenin," the queen's new name and the first indication that she was changed utterly from her earthly form.

Then came her attribute. A few people listened closely, curious what the religious had decided after a week of debate, but most seemed not to care. "The Artist," the religious chanted in their droning voices.

Artist? Well, the queen had known a good deal about colors and fabrics, but that was certainly not the attribute Angarred would have chosen. Something to indicate how kind she was, how good to a friendless woman from the countryside . . .

The pallbearers lifted the bier and carried Chelenin toward the castle. As they passed Angarred saw the queen's pale face, and her white hair spread out on the litter; she looked peaceful at last.

Tezue was one of the pallbearers, of course. He seemed puzzled but resigned, as if forced to bear a heavy burden without understanding why. Norue had the place across from him. Angarred scowled, knowing the scorn Norue had felt for the queen.

The pallbearers climbed up the stairs to the castle. The religious followed, and then the other mourners. At the Hall of the Standing Kings the bearers lowered the queen to the floor. The religious went to the statue of Chelenin, placed against the wall only that morning, and lit the torch at her feet.

When the torch burned as red as the others, the religious picked up the bier and carried it out of the hall on the next step in its journey. Only they were allowed to perform the burial rituals in the graveyard at the back of the castle; then they would return and continue their chant, stating that the Bearer had come for Chelenin, and that she was on her way to the Celestial Court.

Angarred had learned this from Jerret; she had been worried she would make a mistake at the funeral. No one, he said, actually thought the religious saw the Bearer take the body, but the ritual was so ancient they all went through the motions of belief. And he explained that while the religious dug the grave and spoke the correct words the people in the hall would talk about the queen, praising her works on earth.

To Angarred, though, it seemed like another day with the courtiers in the Great Hall. Noblemen and women stood around talking to one another in their usual groups and factions, their voices sounding bored. Chelenin's serving-women formed a knot in the corner; only they seemed genuinely upset.

Tezue stood apart from the others, surrounded by his guards and body servants. Angarred heard his name murmured several times, though; people wondered why he hadn't stopped the Takekek forces before they got to Pergodi, and whether he was competent to lead the country if they did go to war.

Angarred looked around for Jerret. To her shock she saw Norue heading toward her. "I suppose you came here to see if her promise still held, if you could still use her dressmaker," Norue said. "I shouldn't worry—an order from royalty continues beyond death."

His presumption made her furious. "I—I—of course I thought no such thing," she said.

He smiled, though his eyes remained expressionless. "Didn't you?" he said. "I notice you're wearing new clothes right now, something you could never have afforded on your own. And you've got those rooms as well. Moving up in the world, aren't we?"

He walked away before she could answer him. Once again she remembered Cherenin—Chelenin—and how the queen had wanted to see her in a new dress, and the room became blurred with her tears.

She wiped her eyes with her sleeve and looked for Norue, finally finding him in a circle with his usual flatterers around him. He knew who she was, then. He even knew—had made it his business to know—that the queen had offered her her dressmaker. The man following her must be his, then. But why? What interest could he possibly have in her?

She could not find Jerret, though she knew he had wanted to pay his respects to the queen. Probably he had been delayed by his troops or state business. She had been looking forward to seeing him before she left. Mathewar had warned her to say nothing about their journey, though, and perhaps it would be easier to go without saying good-bye to him, easier to keep her secret to herself.

All around her people gossiped and talked about the war; even the pretense of First Journey rites had disappeared. The red smoke stung her eyes. She decided to leave before the religious returned; Chelenin's arrival in the Celestial Court had never really been in doubt.

She took one last look at Chelenin's statue, three times her height, holding its brush to signify its attribute. The queen had ascended to godhood, at least according to the religious; she had become entirely changed. But Angarred could not imagine her as a Godqueen. If they ever met again beyond this life Chelenin would be as kind and soft-spoken as always, changed only in that she would be finally free of her pain.

Angarred headed down the rows of kings and queens on her

way to her apartments. Something—a face?—peered out from between the first few statues at the beginning of the row. She hurried toward the front of the line and studied the space between Mathona and the next Godqueen, the Teacher, looking for a crack or one of the levers Gedren had shown her. There was nothing there but smooth wall, shadowed by the red light from the torches. She went a little ways back up the row; the same blank wall looked back at her. She must have imagined it; the smoke was addling her brain. She turned and went to her rooms to prepare for her journey.

NINE

L abren could not recall ever feeling so uncomfortable. Lord Jerret had brought him to a small room in the castle for a midday meal, and now, confronted with a shop's worth of linen and silver and crystal, he felt clumsy and massive and terrified of moving. Worse yet, he could not help but worry about his mother. It would be just his luck if, in the course of her duties, she came in to clean up after them.

But Lord Jerret was saying something. "What did you think of your first battle?" he asked.

"I—fine. It was fine," Labren said. He adjusted his sword, trying to get comfortable in the chair.

"Was it?"

Jerret was watching him closely. Labren remembered his revulsion after killing the last soldier, and his sense at the time that Jerret had seen everything. Now that feeling became a certainty; the lord had undoubtedly noticed a good many things about his troops during the battle.

"Well, I—there were some things I didn't enjoy, if that's what you mean. That last man, for example, the one that was so hard to kill."

"Good." Jerret poured wine for both of them, then took a sip from his glass. Labren followed him. The crystal was so thin he feared he would shatter it without noticing, and he barely tasted the wine. "You're not supposed to enjoy it. Sometimes we have to kill, but we have to keep in mind that those we are killing are people just like us. And at the same time we have to ignore that fact and see them as an enemy, as a helmet and a jacket of mail. Do you understand?"

Labren took another sip of the wine. Now that he was able to concentrate he realized it was the best he had ever tasted, and he forced himself to drink more slowly. "I'm sorry, sir, but I don't. Those are two different things you just said."

"Yes, and that's the point. You have to be able to think a thing and its opposite at the same time. Well, never mind. You'll either learn how to do it or you won't."

"Do I have to? Learn, that is?"

"Do you want to be a professional soldier?"

"I think so. It's exciting, isn't it? My father was a baker, and believe me, that's not very interesting."

Jerret frowned. "I thought your mother was a servant at the castle."

"She is," Labren said quickly. "She began working there after my father left. My brother's in charge of the bakery now."

If Jerret wondered why his mother had given up a perfectly good craft to go work in the castle he didn't say so. He leaned back in his chair and began to tell stories, about fighting a skirmish in Takeke, about the time his nephew Tomsin had tried to ride a cow. Labren drank more of the wine and started on the dinner, which was also excellent. Finally he had relaxed enough to ask the question that had been bothering him all during the meal.

"Why did you bring me here, milord?"

Jerret looked at him, startled. "I'm an idiot. I thought I told you. I wanted to commend you for your part in the battle, nothing more. By the Orator, I hope you weren't sitting there all this time waiting for some dreadful ax to fall."

Labren, who had been doing just that, shook his head quickly. "Oh, no, milord. And thank you for the dinner—it was wonderful."

The mistake made him feel better about Jerret. Jerret was

human after all, and not some godlike commander or inaccessible Two-name. He leaned back in his chair like the other man and they continued talking.

Suddenly Jerret stood as someone else came into the room. "Prince Norue," Jerret said, nodding.

All of Labren's discomfort returned immediately. He stood just as Jerret said, "Prince Norue, I want you to meet one of my best men. This is Labren Baker."

"How—how do you do, sir? My lord."

"One of your best, you say?" Norue said. "I might have some use for him. I'm putting together a group of good fighting men, an elite division. Would your young man like to join me, do you think?"

"You'll have to ask him that," Jerret said.

Norue turned his lashless unemotional eyes on Labren. "Yes, milord, I would," Labren said.

"Well, we'll see," the prince said. "Good day."

When he had gone Labren dropped into his chair and let out his breath. "If that isn't just like him," Jerret said. "He asks you if you want something and then, just as you say yes, he pretends he hasn't offered it to you in the first place."

Labren barely heard him. "Was that all right, sir? To say I wanted to join his division? I know I can learn a lot from you, but—"

"But the opportunities will be much greater with the prince. Don't worry, I understand. I'll even put in another good word for you, if you like."

"Thank you, sir. Thank you very much."

Labren left the meal feeling expansive, larger than when he had come in. His mind on deeds of bravery, on steady promotion through the ranks, he collided with one of the workmen in the Hall of the Standing Kings. "Watch where you're going, you dolt!" the man called after him.

They were there to continue work on the statue of Queen Chelenin, which had just been installed the other day. Now that was a sad thing, the queen's death. But even that couldn't quell his mood, and he ran nearly all the way home.

Angarred met Mathewar at the door to his inn, holding her horse's reins and carrying her battered leather bag over her shoulder. They were both wearing clothes suitable for a journey, shirts and trousers and leather boots. "How are we going to get outside Pergodi?" she asked.

The Takekek soldiers still controlled the gates, letting no one in or out. They had marched through the Karedek countryside, burning and looting as they went, leaving a corridor open to Takeke for troops and supplies. King Tezue had apparently heard about their progress from his spies but had done nothing; his incompetence continued to be the most talked-about subject at court.

Except for the soldiers in the streets, though, little had changed in the city. Pergodek still went about their business, barely remembering from hour to hour that troops were camped outside the walls. The two sides were fighting a pitched battle out at sea to keep the port open, but some ships bringing supplies managed to slip past the fighting and Pergodi had stockpiled enough food for months.

Mathewar headed to the stables for his horse. "The gates are easy," he said. "The difficult thing will be hiding from the soldiers once we're out. Follow me."

He mounted and they headed south, through neighborhoods Angarred had never seen. They passed a Craftsman's Quarter and came to a two-towered Godwife House; the House was closed, the women asleep until nightfall, when they rose to worship Mathona the Moon. She thought about her mother again and then put her resolutely out of her mind, concentrating on the city around her. They crossed several bridges over the meandering Pergodi River; she wondered if she had seen all seven and had begun to count them when she realized they had come to the city walls.

Mathewar reined in his horse and turned to her. "There's a way out of the city through that house there," he said, nodding to it. "As we go through I'll put a glamour over us to make us look like soldiers from Takeke—though obviously we'll have to try to keep away from the real soldiers."

He dismounted and knocked at the house. An old man opened the door. "Mathewar!" he said, pleased. "When didst come to the city?"

"Not very long ago," Mathewar said. "And now I must leave again. May we use thy house?"

"Of course, of course!" He went on in his strange archaic accent, and to Angarred's surprise Mathewar answered in kind. Soon they were speaking so fast she couldn't follow them.

The man studied the streets carefully and then beckoned them through. First Mathewar and then Angarred led their horses over the threshold. Inside there were no rooms at all, just a hollowed out house leading to a door at the other end. Light shone from high, slitted windows and fretted the unpainted walls, the packed dirt floor.

Halfway through the passageway Mathewar stopped her and began to speak slowly. This was the glamour he had mentioned, she thought, and to her alarm she felt herself changing. Her sense of balance shifted and her body seemed thicker, stronger; horrible thoughts of fighting and blood flickered through her mind. She looked down and, dizzied, saw someone she didn't recognize, a soldier in a heavy padded jacket with a sword at his hip.

"All of this is illusion, of course," Mathewar said. "But it is very strong, and some come to believe the illusion and take on more than just the outward show. You must hold hard to your true self, or it will be difficult for me to change you back."

She nodded, her throat dry. They continued on. Her steps were weightier, and she nearly fell before she discovered how to carry her new body and the burden of the mailed jacket. The horse bobbed his head a few times, nervously.

When they came to the far door Mathewar looked out through a small window. "Mount up," he said, opening the door, and they rode through.

She blinked in the strong sunlight. She had expected the wall here to look like the outside of Tornish Gate, where she had entered the city, but she saw only fields and untilled lands. Takekek soldiers on horseback patrolled in the distance.

Mathewar seemed unconcerned about the soldiers, though he must have seen them. He found a small farmer's path and they continued south.

Suddenly one of the soldiers motioned to his fellows and the

Takekek headed toward them. Angarred, terrified, nearly drove her heels into the horse's side. "Don't," Mathewar said urgently, as if he had guessed her thoughts. "Wait until they come, and then salute them."

"How do I—" she began, but she realized that she knew how to salute, that the information came to her as if she had always known it.

The men rode closer. Her horse, sensing her fear, began to shy away, and she tried to calm herself. The soldier in front—the leader, she guessed—said something to her and Mathewar. Her new, strange body seemed almost to understand him, and in her terror she nearly turned and fled, thinking of nothing but running flat out across the fields. She forced herself to concentrate and saluted, lifting one huge ungainly hand to her forehead and then to her heart. The leader said something and the soldiers rode away.

Now that it was over her heart pounded uncontrollably, so that she barely saw the fields around her. Her salute seemed to drive her deeper into her masquerade; she began to think that it had not been pretense at all but something terribly real, that she would not be able to find her way back to her real self. Sounds of battle clamored within her: horses neighing, swords clashing on shields, men screaming. They rode a while, the confused roaring in her head making conversation impossible, until finally Mathewar stopped her for the spell of unbinding.

They dismounted and Mathewar began to speak. She looked down at the heavy jacket and saw, overlaid with it, her familiar scuffed traveling clothes. Then the picture wavered and broke, and she was back in the armor of the Takekek soldier. Mathewar spoke again, louder this time. Thoughts of fighting and killing grew stronger, crowding into her mind so that she could nearly smell the battlefield, blood and horse dung, iron and smoke and sweat. Far away Mathewar was saying something, but it didn't seem important.

"Angarred!" he said, his commanding voice cutting through her daze. "Remember yourself! Remember your father, and King Tezue!"

She blinked. Mathewar stood in front of her. She felt suddenly lighter, and she saw that the armor had gone.

"Oh, holy Godkings," she said. A breeze blew, its coolness wonderful on her bare arms and face. "Thank you. I thought I was a Takekek soldier—the Others take me if I didn't."

"Angarred," he said. His blue-gray eyes, nearly the same height as her darker blue ones, gazed directly at her, into her; he looked more serious than she had ever seen him. "We are about to travel through a strange wood, a place like nowhere you have ever been. The Others are very real there. You must not mention them, or anything uncanny. Do you understand?"

"Of course I understand," she said, trying not to become angry. Would he ever think of her as anything more than an idiot, an encumbrance?

They mounted and rode on. In the silence her thoughts turned over and over again to her near escape, to her possession by the heavy, harsh soldier, and she began to long for conversation. "Everyone at Chelenin's First Journey was talking about the king, wondering why he hadn't stopped the Takekek before they got to Pergodi," she said. "No one seemed to care about Chelenin at all. I didn't talk to anyone, though. No one at court knows I was planning to leave, not even Lord Jerret."

That roused him. "Good," he said.

"I wanted to," she said. "But he has secrets he keeps from me, and I still wonder if the Snoppishes had anything to do with my father's death. They seem so friendly, but sometimes I wonder if Lord Snoppish told me the whole truth about my father's exile."

"Why shouldn't he?"

"I don't know. You didn't see the pictures my father drew. They were so—so *hateful*. Would sending someone into exile account for that much hate?"

"I'd imagine so, yes."

Now she heard the trace of an accent in his voice, the same intonation as that of the man he had talked to earlier. His sentences had a different cadence, rising and falling almost like music; he sounded unlike anyone she had ever known.

"And I'm certain that Jerret likes me—I can't be that mistaken about someone."

He said nothing to that, and they continued in silence for a while. To her relief there were no more soldiers; they all seemed to be camped outside the gates. Tilled fields lay before them like blankets covering the earth, deep green, straw yellow, occasional ordered rows of trees bearing ripe fruit.

She had forgotten the round of the seasons in the stone-filled city. It was getting to be autumn; already she saw men and women in the fields, helping with the harvest. She stirred uneasily. The Takekek might come through at any time, taking what they wanted and burning the rest; even she knew that a good many sieges started in autumn, when the advancing soldiers could loot the harvest for themselves and keep it from those in the city.

"Where are you from?" she asked.

"The Forest of Tiranon," he said. He nodded toward the flat land ahead of them; she could just make out a dark blur on the horizon. "We'll reach it soon, tomorrow, probably."

She remembered what he had said about the forest and wondered what it would be like to grow up in such a place, if it was even possible to live there at all. "They say a good many magicians come from Tiranon," she said, remembering stories she had heard.

He said nothing.

"Is that where Alkarren is from?" she asked.

"No."

"Then how do you know him?"

"He was a teacher of mine, at the College."

"Oh." She thought that over for a while. "Was he a good teacher?"

"I didn't think so," he said. "Others disagreed with me, though."

"Why wasn't he?"

"Well, he wasn't a good magician. You can't teach what you don't know."

"Are you a good magician?"

He laughed at that. "I think so, yes."

"Why was Alkarren teaching at the College, then? If he wasn't a good magician?"

He laughed again. "That's an excellent question. Because he claimed other people's work as his own, because he flattered the right people . . . He wants power desperately, wants to control others. And he was very envious of those who didn't need to work as hard as he did, those to whom the study of magic came easier."

"Did you ever want to be a teacher?"

"Yes, eventually. The College sends you out into the world first, though, before you can come back to teach." He was silent a while, and then said, "And I wanted to see Pergodi, to see the king, and the court. Like you, I suppose."

He smiled, and at that moment she thought that he might not be as bad a traveling companion as she had feared. "You do ask a great many questions," he said.

"I wouldn't have to if you told me more about yourself," she said.

"That's fair enough, I suppose," he said, and they continued on, speaking sometimes and turning silent, comfortably, when the conversation flagged.

As evening came on, though, he grew taciturn and distant once more. The land was not as cultivated here; stands of trees broke the monotonous flat horizon, harbingers of the great forest ahead.

They decided to camp near a stream. They led the horses down through trees and dried grass and bracken to the water, where they all drank thirstily. Then she and Mathewar built a fire and ate the first meal of the journey, dried meat and apples, while the horses grazed nearby.

The sun set to their right, throwing the shadows of the trees before them. Shining stars lit the sky one by one. Their fire burned down; sparks cracked and showered brief golden fire. Mathewar moved to gather more wood and build it up again.

He drew a familiar bottle from his knapsack and poured the red liquid—black in the dimming light—into the cup, then set the cup carefully near the fire, his hands trembling. Of course, Angarred thought. No wonder he hadn't spoken for the past hour.

He drank the sattery quickly. He spread out his blankets, his motions slow and overprecise, his darkened eyes focused on his own interior world. "Good night," he said. He pulled off his boots and settled into the blankets.

She felt annoyed, though she was not sure why. Because he

would be unable to help if they were attacked; because he should not waste his gifts as he did; because he had gone away from her? "When will we reach the forest?" she asked, hoping to irritate him.

"Tomorrow," he said.

"And how long will it take to get through it?"

But he said nothing this time, and soon his steady breathing told her he was asleep.

She came awake abruptly in the middle of the night. She knew immediately where she was: south of Pergodi, near the Forest of Tiranon. The fire had burned down, but the smell of woodsmoke lingered. A noise had woken her, and she remembered her earlier thought, that Mathewar would be useless in an attack.

"No," Mathewar said. He thrashed restlessly inside his blankets. "No, oh Godkings, no!" He was silent a moment and then screamed aloud, a call of pure horror.

A bad dream. Should she wake him? As she sat, uncertain, his movements quieted and finally stilled, and his breathing grew calm once more.

Mathewar said nothing when he woke, still struggling against the grip of sattery. Angarred ate breakfast alone, and then they packed up and continued on.

At midday they saw more trees, at first in ones and twos and then more and more, clustering together. They rode through dappled shade and then sunlight and shade again, until finally the trees surrounded them, ash and oak and pine. Their path was strewn with grass and fern and fallen leaves. Somewhere a creek murmured as water poured over stone; birds cawed and chittered around them and lifted heavily off their branches.

She began to see footprints she recognized, mostly the slots of deer. Twice she spotted bear tracks, paws that looked almost like human feet save for the great talons, and she resolved to stay on her guard.

The forest grew dimmer, darker; dull gold shafts of light thrust like swords between distant trees. By late afternoon the trees stood so close together they blotted out the sun. Sounds became muffled and finally ceased altogether, until she could hear only the beat of their horses' hooves and the ring of their bridles. "Be careful here," Mathewar said. "Don't step off the path."

They rode cautiously through a shadowy corridor, the trees arching over them like a vaulted ceiling, barely able to see the next turn in front of them. Odd-looking yellow mushrooms clustered at the base of the trees but nothing else grew on the uneven path; only mushrooms could survive in that gloom.

"Don't eat—" Mathewar said.

"—the mushrooms," Angarred said. "Yes, I could guess that."

The forest smelled musty. The leaves had started to curl and would soon fall, but for now the trees seemed to have stood like this forever, an eternal world that would never decay. Occasionally, through the smell of dust, she caught the sharp scent of pine. There was no wind, and no leaves rattled, and the forest was hotter than the land outside, as if centuries of air lay trapped within it. Her long hair clung to her cheeks and neck, making her sweat.

Every so often she would see, or thought she saw, a pale globe of light bobbing at the edge of her vision. She would turn quickly, straining to catch it, but it vanished as soon as she focused on it.

"What are those lights?" she asked.

"No one knows. Some folks tell the story of men who captured the moon, and carry it about in their lanterns. You can't ever see them clearly."

As they rode deeper into the forest the trees grew stranger, or perhaps she only began to notice their strangeness. She saw trees with five-fingered leaves like hands, each hand stained a bloody red; and another cluster with grotesque faces on their trunks, faces contorted into sly and malignant expressions that seemed to change as she passed them.

Even the sunset was different here; night appeared to spread outward from the trees' reaching hands until finally everything was covered in darkness. The air cooled quickly, much to her relief. They stopped and built up a fire, careful to use only fallen wood. She climbed a tree and hung her pack from one of the branches.

"What are you doing?" Mathewar asked, forcing his gaze away from the fire and his cup of sattery.

"Keeping the food out of reach of bears," she said.

He said nothing, but stood and hung his pack next to hers. Then he drank his sattery and they spread out their blankets; and if he had bad dreams during the night she did not hear them.

The next day they passed sights even more odd. Once she saw a clearing, and in the clearing a gray tower, wound round with choking roses. Another glimpse through the trees showed a meadow with a thatched hut taller than the castle in Pergodi.

These things seemed so improbable she found herself asking Mathewar if they were real, and each time he assured her that they were.

Near midday Mathewar suddenly halted his horse. An instant later a heavy branch crashed down to the path before them. He dismounted and studied the branch carefully, looking worried for the first time since they had entered the forest.

"What is it?" she asked.

"Magic, maybe," he said, straightening. "Well, maybe not. We'll have to watch carefully, see if something like this happens again."

"My father was killed in a forest."

"Yes, well, so were other people." He seemed to realize how abrupt he had been. "I'm sorry—I meant only that I don't think this has anything to do with your father. It comes from the forest itself, or from the people here."

"How can people live here?"

"There are huge clearings, places with whole villages in them. I grew up in a town like that, a community of farmers."

"Farmers? Here?"

"Oh, yes. We'll probably see some of them."

"I hope we get to a clearing soon. I don't know if I can stand much more of this gloom."

So he had come from farmers, she thought. Mathewar Farmer—it sounded odd. Still, she was glad he had told her something about himself. He had seen her father and Hashan Hall and could probably piece together her entire life from that, if he wanted to; she felt at a disadvantage with him.

A while later—it could have been a few minutes or several hours; she had no way of telling time in the forest—they passed two rows of golden trees leading off to the side, standing like the pillars of a great building long fallen into ruin. The path between the rows looked like green marble, inlaid with gold filigree, and far down she saw a tantalizing play of colors: lavender, apple green, silver. She felt a pull toward the end of the path and the enchantment she was sure would lie there; but then she remembered her possession by the soldier and remembered, too, how Mathewar had called her back to her true self.

"Don't step off the path," Mathewar said.

"I wasn't going to," she said. Her hair stuck to her face in the humid air, and she brushed it away angrily. "I've had enough of illusions for the time being. What is it?"

"The Others."

His voice was so low she did not understand what he had said at first. "You mean—you mean they're real? They live here?"

Far down at the end of the pillars the colors had brightened and were pulsing quickly, dancing to some music she felt she almost knew. "Let's go," Mathewar said harshly, urging his horse along the path.

She remembered one of her father's plotters, a man who had lost an important post when loyalties at the court changed. One evening he had said loudly, "I'll go to the Others then, see if I don't!" and the next day he was gone, with his horse still in the stables—and no one, not her father or Rushlag or Elenin, would tell her where he went.

She learned as she grew older that the Others summoned dreamers and lunatics and malcontents, that they enchanted them, made them leave their homes and families without a second thought, and changed them utterly. But she had heard that their realm existed somewhere else, that they did not dwell together with humans.

She thought Mathewar was not going to answer her, but when they had gone a good distance away he said, "They exist here, and in other places—though they aren't truly alive, not in the way we are. You know how they summon people, and how dangerous they are. Well, when they've called enough people in one place then that place begins to fall apart in a confusion of dreams, of madness and upheavals, and ordered life breaks down. And then, because chaos is their element, because that's what they desire above all, they can leave their realm and come here."

She suddenly thought of Gedren and her missing husband. Had the Others come for him? She had never remembered to ask Mathewar about him and she could not bring him up now, not with the Others so close. She would have to do it later, when they finally reached one of the towns Mathewar spoke of.

"But they're trapped in their realm otherwise, aren't they?" she asked.

Mathewar nodded. "Tobrin tried to bind them eight hundred years ago with the Stone. He wasn't entirely successful, but at least they're no longer free to come and go as they please, the way they did during the Sorcerers' Wars."

She shivered, though the air was hot under the trees. What could it have been like to live in such an age?

She woke again that night, hearing Mathewar cry out. She nearly went to wake him but was too exhausted to move, and she fell back into an uneasy sleep.

The next day they came to the first fork in the road. Mathewar dismounted and studied the two branching paths. "Which one should we take?" she asked. "Do you know?"

"That one," he said, pointing unhesitatingly to the right. "This other was made by magic, though. Someone wants us to wander lost in the forest."

"Who?"

"I don't know," he said. He got back on his horse and they turned down the right-hand path. "Whoever it is was not trained at the College—I can tell that much. It's probably one of the forest people."

"But that's good, isn't it? That means it's not Alkarren."

"Good and bad. Wild magic is usually weak, but sometimes an untrained magician can be dangerous."

She had a vague memory of a time when she was very young, when two magicians came to her father's estate and talked to some of the people living there. "Isn't everyone who can do magic taken to the College?" she asked.

"It's supposed to work that way, yes. Teachers from the College travel all over Karededin, looking for boys who show promise. If they know things before they happen, or they can find lost objects without thinking—"

"Boys?" she asked. She remembered now that the magicians had not talked to her, but she had thought that was because she hadn't the talent to go to the College. "Aren't there any woman magicians?"

"No—they don't seem to have the ability."

"But—but surely they do. There's a woman I used to talk to on my father's lands who could work magic—I saw her. And when my father was killed I dropped back before the arrow could hit me . . ."

"You can ask the masters about this if you like. They'll tell you the same thing, though—that women haven't worked magic in over eight hundred years, for as long as the College has stood."

She wanted to ask him other questions—how he could be so certain there were no women magicians among the forest people, for example—but she felt put off by his arrogance and kept silent.

They saw nothing untoward for the rest of the day, but several times they heard something moving within the trees, something that kept pace with them. And once, as the light was draining from the forest, Mathewar squinted into the shadows and said, "I don't like that crow sitting there. I saw it a few miles back, or one that looked exactly like it."

She followed his gaze and saw the crow on a branch of one of the trees, glossy black against the gray-black leaves. It gave a sharp caw and flew off.

As night came they stopped and made camp, then ate and set- tled down inside their blankets. She could not get to sleep, think- ing of the crow and the person or animal that had followed them through the forest. Perhaps it was there now, just outside the circle of light, watching them . . . She strained to hear over the crackling of the fire.

Suddenly Mathewar shouted: "No, please, no!" She jumped, ter- rified. What had he seen? Even when she realized that he was having another dream her heart continued to beat wildly. "Embre! Embre, no!" he said.

He sat up suddenly, breathing hard, his hair loose and tangled with sweat. He wiped his eyes with the back of his arm. "What . . ." he said.

"You had a bad dream," Angarred said. "What was it?"

"All my dreams are bad," he said.

"Who's Embre?"

"Did I say her name? My wife."

"Your *wife?* You might have told me you had a wife. Where is she?"

"She's dead."

"Oh. I'm sorry, I didn't know." She hesitated. "How did she die?"

He was silent a moment. "That is not a tale for the night, or for these haunted woods," he said. He lay back down, and for once Angarred asked no more questions.

TEN

Things moved much more quickly than Labren had ever expected, and the day after he had spoken to Prince Norue he was transferred from Jerret's company to the prince's elite troops. And these troops, Norue informed them, were going to Takeke, where the prince would try to negotiate an end to the war.

They left Pergodi through the Tornish Gate. Norue rode at the front, slightly ahead of his two standard-bearers: one carried the flag of truce, blue with a golden knot symbolizing unity and friendship, and the other Norue's colors, gold and purple.

Labren tried not to stare at the Takekek camp spread outside the gate. It had reached the size of a small village, with flour mills and smithies and great satin pavilions erected for the officers. Men carrying papers or arrows or helmets marched purposefully through the lanes between the tents and booths, and washerwomen knelt by Pergodi River, scrubbing at brightly colored clothing. A train of carts rode up, bringing supplies. Soldiers taunted Norue and the others in a strange language as they rode past, but no one challenged their flag.

A few miles outside of Pergodi they saw the destruction worked by the Takekek army: torched fields and farmhouses, stolen harvests, deserted roads. Then they moved away from the Takekek's corridor, and Labren, who had never traveled outside Pergodi, began to look around him eagerly.

There was little to see, only tilled fields and villages so small they didn't even have a Godhouse. After long days of this they passed across the border into Takeke, but he only knew it when Norue told them; the land still looked the same.

Almost immediately, though, columns of soldiers rode toward them. Norue's drummer moved to the front and played the rhythm that signified a truce, and the two standard-bearers waved their flags, and the Takekek soldiers saluted and turned away.

The next day they left the cultivated fields behind; the land became rugged, and the teeth of a mountain range loomed ahead. By afternoon they reached a defile between the mountains. Labren looked up and saw a great fortress perched on a cliffside. Who guarded the gate in the mountains? Would they pour out of the fortress and attack before they saw Norue's flag of truce?

He pointed it out to the man next to him, and soon everyone slowed and began to mutter to each other. It seemed ominous, shadowed by trees and the higher mountains.

Norue turned back. "Get moving, you dolts!" he said. "It's deserted!"

They started up again reluctantly. As they turned a bend in the path Labren saw that the prince was right: one side of the mountain fastness lay in ruins. "But what is it, sir?" someone asked. "Who built it?"

"What does it matter?" Norue said. "It's not going to bother us—that's all you need to know."

Another man said quietly, so Norue wouldn't hear: "It belonged to a magician, during the great Sorcerers' Wars. He had his own fiefdom here, and made raids into Karededin and Takeke from these mountains. His coat of arms is over the door—you can just barely see it, those two swans there."

Labren nodded. Swans were sacred to the Godkings because they mated for life. "What was his name?" someone asked, and another soldier said, "How do you know all this?"

"I know it because that time interests me—I've read a good deal about it," the man said. "I don't know his name, though—Tobrin defeated him in the wars and no one remembers him now. But I can tell you this much—you don't want to go up there. There's wild magic and power all around the place."

Labren glanced up one last time. A huge bird preened on the branches of a bare tree, not a swan but some sort of carrion eater. Labren shuddered.

A few days later they left the shadows of the defile and turned north. The villages were larger here, and more people thronged the roads. They passed men in the strange costumes of Takeke: long vests and shirts, loose trousers, and tall cylindrical hats, each piece of clothing a different bright color, red or green or yellow. Every so often soldiers rode toward them and then turned away when the drummer pounded out his rhythm of peace.

They saw more ruins from the age of the Sorcerers' Wars, huge half-fallen forts and castles that could not have been built by any natural agency. Some people even lived in the ruins, using wood and stone to patch up the gaping holes.

There were still no Godhouses, and Norue said that the Takekek worshipped different gods. The idea shocked Labren, who had grown up praying to Marfan and Mathona. But the villagers danced with the last sheaf of wheat they harvested, just as folks in Karededin did, and gave it to the person who had cut it, to put above his or her doorway for luck in the coming year.

Finally one evening they came to a walled city. "We'll rest here," Norue said, "and enter the capital in the morning."

After the men had built their fires and eaten supper Norue called them around him for instructions. "These people are very different from us," he said, his pale face serious. "There won't be much that's the same, not their clothing, or their language, or their food. They take a great many words to say very little, and they bow a good deal. I want you to remember, though, that they're excellent fighting men, and that they should be respected for it. I don't want to see any soldier laughing at anything they do, or hear any insults or boasts about how much better you Karedek are. Watch me and see what I do, and if you're still uncertain, bow."

A few of the men laughed, but Norue had not been joking; Labren had already noticed that the prince had no sense of humor.

He seemed even more serious than usual, though; these negotiations must be very important to him.

In the morning they knocked at a gate to the capital, which Norue had told them was called Nebokbok. A gatekeeper wearing a padded jacket came out and spoke in a low sonorous language; it had a good many *r*s and *n*s and another consonant that sounded like someone getting ready to spit. They waited while someone sent for a translator, and when he arrived Norue and the gatekeeper exchanged bows and elaborate compliments for what seemed like a very long time. Finally the gatekeeper motioned them inside.

They marched through the city, passing a good many people dressed in the exotic clothes and cylindrical hats of Takeke. "What, has the New Year come already?" one of the soldiers said, referring to the great New Year's masquerade parties in Karededin. Several other soldiers laughed.

Norue turned quickly. "I said no insults," he said to the man who had spoken. "You—you're dismissed. Go back to Pergodi."

"But—but I'll be killed without the flag of truce," the man said.

Norue said nothing. The man dropped out of his place in line and slowly turned to go. The other soldiers, too ashamed to watch him, continued to march. They all knew that what he said was true, that a Karedek soldier wandering alone, not under a flag of truce, would almost certainly be killed.

A while later Norue ordered them to halt. In front of them stood a great wooden building that had been added on to a tumbling ruin. The wood was painted the same bright colors as the Takekek's clothing; there was even a tall golden turret that looked a bit like one of their hats. Another translator waited at the door, along with someone Labren took to be a chamberlain; apparently word of their coming had preceded them.

Norue bowed and said, "I and my men beg the honor of a mere glimpse of your gracious and mighty king, known throughout the lands for his splendor and majesty."

The translator said something to the chamberlain. The chamberlain spoke, and then the translator again. "No, it is we who are honored by your presence. We have heard of the glory of the men of Karededin, but the rumor has fallen far short of the truth, as the light of the moon falls short of the bright light of the sun. Surely we see before us the greatest company of fighting men in the world."

Norue made as if to reply, but the chamberlain was not yet finished. Labren's attention wandered. None of these words had meaning; they were all empty. It was like eating air.

Finally the chamberlain motioned the men forward into the castle and down a long hallway with many turnings. They came to a great room with a table stretching nearly its entire length. Men sat around it, eating and talking and singing. There were rows of lighted torches on the two longer walls, and a huge ox roasted within a hearth. Slender, elegant dogs roamed up and down looking for scraps, or lay curled up under the table. The room smelled of cooked meat and clean rushes.

A boy of about three ran back and forth atop the table, stopping to take food from various plates. Suddenly he picked up a cup of ale and poured it over a man's head. The man roared in anger but did nothing to the boy; the boy laughed so hard he fell backwards in a heap on the table, and everyone except the man drenched in ale chuckled softly along with him.

In a convoluted speech filled with superlatives the chamberlain explained that this boy was the king. The king took no notice of them; it seemed that he was allowed to do whatever he wanted.

The chamberlain led them to the man at the head of the table, and another long exchange of compliments followed. After a good many minutes Labren gathered that this man was the king's uncle, and that his name was Dindin. This seemed so ridiculous that Labren nearly laughed, and he stamped on his foot with the heel of his other boot to stop himself. A few of the others seemed to be having trouble as well.

Dindin was a big man, with a wide, crazed grin. He wore a yellow shirt, green vest and blue trousers but no hat; apparently the men took them off while eating. Strands of his brown hair and beard had been plaited into braids and tied off with beaded gems that winked in the torchlight. He spoke to Norue in badly accented Karedek and Norue turned to the company. "We're to join them at their feast," Norue said.

The Takekek made room for them along the benches, and serving men put meat and ale in front of them. Labren waited for Norue to eat and then took a tentative bite. The food tasted strange, with several spices he couldn't identify. He felt a sudden homesickness for the bakery and his family's simple bread.

The prince spoke intently to Dindin, ignoring his troops. The translator stood behind them, leaning forward to help when he was needed.

Suddenly the king ran toward Labren on the table. Labren shoved back on the bench, terrified of the little brat and what he might do. The king shouted something in a shrill voice and the other men took up the call, pounding the table with their mugs.

High bells rang out from somewhere, and someone began to sing. The Takekek quieted at once. The song reached every corner of the room, uncanny and poignant and at the same time triumphant. Labren understood none of it but it didn't matter; it was as if he had moved to another realm, one purer and finer than this one. At the end the Takekek pounded the table again, and Labren found that he had been holding his breath.

Prince Dindin rose. He clapped his hands and said something, and the translator informed them, using a good many words, that the dinner was over and they would now be shown to their lodgings.

Angarred woke to see the sun pouring through the branches, lighting the dust motes and turning them golden. She had breakfast and she and Mathewar packed up and mounted.

As they rode she noticed what the dusk had hidden last night, that the trees here were farther apart and not as massive. And they were not the strange growths of the past few days but varieties familiar to her from her father's woods. Birds sang back and forth.

"It looks like we might be coming to a clearing," she said.

Mathewar said nothing. She had thought, when Mathewar had spoken of his wife's death, that they might have drawn closer, as people do when they share a secret. Now she saw that he was as distant as ever. Very well, she thought as they rode along in silence. She didn't have to talk either.

In the middle of the afternoon she looked up and spotted a crow flying along with them, balancing on a drift of wind. She said nothing to Mathewar; presumably he had seen it too.

The crow flew off. They rode around an outcropping of trees and came upon three paths branching outward. Mathewar took the middle, but this time he did not seem as certain.

More choices led from that path, and more beyond, like a branching tree. Suddenly she saw a sailing ship cutting through blue waters ahead of them. It seemed as real as anything around her, as if the sea began a few yards from where she stood, and yet the trees appeared again where the picture ended.

She couldn't see Mathewar; he was hidden by the illusion. She called his name, panicked.

He didn't answer. More illusions appeared, some of them overlapping the sea and blotting it out: a vast golden city thronged with people; a caravan made up of green carts; a woman and child imprisoned in a tower, red roses breaking through their only window. The trees around them vanished utterly; scenes unrolled like living tapestries behind and before them, one on top of the other.

She put out her hand; it touched one of the people in the city as he hurried past, and she pulled it back again sharply. The horse turned and turned, trying to get his bearings.

Where was Mathewar? Had he chosen the wrong path? Would she wander lost among these illusions forever, surrounded by this vivid life but unable to enter it?

The colors came faster and faster, so quickly she barely had time to understand what she was seeing. A new scene laid itself over the others: a path leading off through the forest. Was it real? Should she follow it, or would it only take her deeper into the haunted forest, toward the Others perhaps?

Far away, she heard Mathewar speak in the commanding tone he had used the day her father died. The scenes faded; the forest showed through the illusions like an old painting appearing beneath a newer one. The path in front of her disappeared. Somewhere a woman shouted.

The shout came again, closer this time. "Peace!"

"Of course they want peace," Mathewar said softly, appearing beside her. "Now." He rubbed his forehead and called out, "Show yourselves!"

"Stop thy magics!" the woman called.

"I have," he said.

After a long moment two people stepped out from between the trees and stood on the path in front of them. They looked almost identical, thin and small and young, their hair the color of polished wood, with silver circlets bound around their foreheads. They wore rough brown cloaks that nearly hid them within the colors of the forest, and they carried tall black staffs that were bound and tipped with silver.

"Who art thou?" Mathewar asked. "Why didst attack us unprovoked?"

"Hast no right to come through Tiranon," one of them said, the woman who had shouted. As they came closer along the path Angarred saw that her companion was a man. "Art an outsider."

"I have as much right as anyone," Mathewar said. "I am no outsider but grew up in this forest."

Their eyes widened at this. "Canst not pass, nonetheless," the woman said.

"Why not?"

"I heard thee speak. Sayest that women cannot be magicians."

"They cannot. It is none of my doing, but—"

The woman became a crow. It happened so fast Angarred nearly missed it. One minute the woman stood in the road arguing with Mathewar, and the next there was a crow in the same spot, cocking her head and studying them with a bright black eye. Her staff fell loudly to the ground.

The crow spread her great wings and flew upward. She cawed, a sound like a rusty door opening, and settled on a branch overhead.

"Very well," Mathewar said, pitching his voice to be heard in the tree above him. "Hast some magics, I agree."

The crow flew down to the path. She made a show of folding back her wings and then shifted back into the woman. "Good," she said. "I am Rone, and this is Torren."

Mathewar introduced himself and Angarred, but Rone only nodded; she had probably overheard their names in the forest. "Come along with us, to our village," she said.

"Why?" Angarred asked. "You tried to get us lost in the forest."

"I tried only to steer thee away from our village," Rone said.

"How do we know you're not going to trick us?"

"Wilt have to trust us."

Angarred shrugged. Mathewar nodded to her and they continued along the path, slowing their horses so as not to overtake the walking forest people. As they rode the light grew brighter, dappling the ground beneath them, and Angarred saw grasses and weeds and wildflowers she recognized. The air here was cooler, not as close. From somewhere came the sound of a falling stream.

"What would your masters say about Rone?" Angarred asked.

Mathewar said nothing.

"You have to admit there are some things your masters don't know. There are things you don't know, for that matter." His silence began to wear on her. "What—do you think that if you ignore her she'll go away?"

He rubbed his eyes. "My head hurts horribly," he said.

She began to laugh. "Is that why you were so silent, all these mornings?" she said.

As Mathewar watched, looking startled, she dropped from her horse and handed her reins over to him. "I suppose I can leave the path now," she said. She went a short ways into the forest, passing vivid purple and gold wildflowers, and bent to pluck several tight brown nubs.

"Here," she said when she came back. "They're called Mathona's buttons. They're good for head and stomach pains, and to lower fever. Eat one."

To her alarm he threw them all into his mouth and began to chew, wincing at the bitter taste. "Not all of them, for Mathona's sake!" she said.

"Where did you learn this?" he asked.

"From an old woman on my father's lands, Worrige. She knows a lot about the properties of herbs and flowers. And she can work magic."

Mathewar held up his hand. "Peace, in Mathona's name," he said. "Women can do some magic. I freely admit it."

She mounted up and they continued to ride. The sun shone through the leaves overhead, casting the land in green shadow. As Rone and Torren walked ahead of them their cloaks turned the pale green of a new leaf, and they seemed as much a part of the forest as any of the trees or animals.

"Why are we going along with them?" Angarred said, whispering.

"I want to learn what they know," Mathewar said.

The path widened. They stepped out into a great green meadow, hedged all about by the forest. Wooden cottages stood near the edges, looking as if they had grown there like the trees, and more cottages nested in the branches of the trees themselves. The sound of the stream was louder here.

They dismounted and tied down their horses. "Come," Rone said. "Let's have some supper."

They walked out over the grass. It was very short; goats cropped the meadow around them, their heads bent low. Some of the forest people brought a table and chairs out from somewhere and set them up on the grass. Another put a hot cauldron on the table; it smelled deliciously of stew. Angarred felt a mild surprise; she had expected a supper of acorns and spiderwebs.

They sat at the table with Rone and Torren and a few of the others. Angarred found herself opposite Rone. As the other woman looked up Angarred saw with a shock that her eyes were the same shiny black as the crow's.

The stew tasted as good as it smelled. After a while during which no one said anything Mathewar put down his spoon and asked cautiously, "How many women here do magic? And where do they learn it?"

Rone turned her bright inquisitive eyes on him. "Many here know magic. We learn from each other."

She looked down the table. Angarred followed her gaze and saw another woman. She had prominent features—thick black eyebrows, a hawk nose, wide lips—but somehow on her face they seemed in harmony. Her tangled black hair was streaked with gray.

She reminded Angarred of something—but what? Perhaps it was only that she looked so much like an eagle; Angarred could easily guess what animal shape she took. The woman had deep black eyes, eyes that looked as if they held fathomless wisdom. She could have been in her forties but for the eyes; they appeared to have seen a great deal, much of it unhappy.

"Where are they from?" Mathewar asked.

"Oh, come," Rone said. "Surely women have disappeared from thy village. Where didst think they went?"

"I thought—to their lovers, I suppose. Or to the city, or that an accident befell them. This shape-shifting—"

"Thy masters cannot teach thee this. I know. And I will not tell thee our secrets either. Why should I? Thy College does not share their knowledge with us. How didst overcome my magics? No master would ever teach us this—wouldst not tell me thyself."

"It was a simple Spell of Strengthening. I strengthened the reality of the world around us, opposed it to thine illusions. But I have never met anyone who can change a thing truly, who knows Spells of Becoming. Nothing can change into something foreign to its nature, just as I could not change myself into a crow."

They were fencing, Angarred saw, both trying to learn as much as they could while giving as little as possible away. She had already seen that Mathewar might appear to say a great deal, but that when you went over the conversation you would discover you had learned nothing after all. He would never, for example, tell Rone exactly how to cast a Spell of Strengthening.

"I can become a crow through illusion," Mathewar was saying now. "It is seeming only, though, and I could not fly. But thy magic changes thee truly, I think. Canst become other animals as well?"

Rone laughed. "I said I would not teach thee our secrets. But I will tell thee one thing. We do not work our magic by seeming. Once, long ago, the difference between people and animals was not as great as it is now. People could become animals, and animals people. And there were some who were both animal and person, and some of these still remain—wilt see a few of these in the forest, belike. Dost understand this? I do not seem to become a crow—I am a crow. Everyone can become some animal or other, even thee, or thy companion here."

Once again Rone fixed Angarred with her strange black gaze. "What is thine animal?" Rone said softly to her, and she shivered. "Who art thou?"

"Why doesn't the College know about thy people here?" Mathewar asked.

"Some do, surely. But they say naught—their precious College would change out of all recognition if they did, and they hate change above all things. And we are able to hide from most of them—our magics are stronger than theirs, or so different that they cannot penetrate them. Thy magics are strong, of course. Art from the forest, whence all great magicians come."

"Why—" Mathewar said. He stopped, then continued on. "Why didst choose those pictures? The ship, and the—the tower?"

"I took them from thee, from thy mind. Do they mean aught to thee?"

"I don't know. The tower does, or seems to, but I don't know why."

Mathewar and Rone continued to talk after the supper ended, Mathewar asking about her magic and Rone parrying his questions. Angarred grew bored and began to amuse herself by guessing which animal each of the people around them would turn into. The big shaggy-haired man next to Rone looked a little like a bear. And the woman down the table was an eagle, of course. She glanced at the woman and found that she was staring back at her, studying her intently. Their eyes met like fencing swords, dark black against blue. Angarred felt a jolt and turned away quickly to break their connection.

The sun set beyond the trees. The sky overhead turned the red of tempered steel, as though fired in a vast furnace. Then it deepened: to blood red, violet, violet black. A wind came up and Angarred shivered.

"We cannot leave tonight," Mathewar said. "May we stay for the night in thy village? We can make a fire to sleep by."

"Certainly," Rone said. "Canst not use living wood for thy fire, of course."

"Of course," Mathewar said. "We would not have survived this far had we harmed any of the trees."

Mathewar and Angarred gathered wood and stacked it near the forest, away from the smooth grass. Mathewar spoke and the fire blazed up. Rone, passing them, nodded with approval.

Mathewar took out his bottle of sattery. Rone frowned. She watched him sit cross-legged and pour it, then push the cup near the fire. "Hast been corrupted by dwelling in the city, I think," she said.

Mathewar ignored her. He drank the sattery and spread out his blankets, then pulled off his boots and prepared to sleep.

He was gone in the morning when Angarred woke but returned soon after, clean-shaven and with his hair combed and tied back. She guessed he had bathed in the stream and she went to do the same, feeling with pleasure the cold water on her skin.

She dressed and they left soon after, thanking Rone for her hospitality. "I wish she'd offered us some food," Mathewar said, after they had ridden through the meadow and gone some distance into the forest beyond. "Mine's nearly gone, and from the look of your pack you don't have much either. We'll be starving when we get to the College."

"There's a lot of food in the forest," Angarred said.

"That's right—you said you'd learned things from this woman. Porridge, or whatever her name was."

"Worrige," Angarred said, then noticed that he was smiling. He seemed more alert this morning; he must have picked some more Mathona's buttons while she'd been asleep. Well, she'd taught him that, if nothing else.

She got another chance to demonstrate her knowledge that evening when they made their camp. The stream had kept pace with them, and she got out the small net she had bought in the city and caught some trout, then searched the forest floor for herbs. Mathewar had made the fire by the time she got back, and she moved some flat stones near it to cook the fish.

"This is very good," Mathewar said, taking a first bite.

"I know," Angarred said.

He laughed. "We may be coming to the end of this forest soon, thank the Navigator. We might even reach the College tomorrow. I think I remember this part, though the forest changes each time you enter it."

"Is that why you'd never met Rone before, or seen her village? I was wondering."

"Yes—every journey you take is different."

They finished their supper. Angarred hung what little food she had left out of the reach of bears, thinking of the shaggy bearlike man in Rone's village as she did so. Could the tracks she sometimes saw belong to him? Mathewar drank his sattery and they spread their blankets.

Angarred lay back and studied the stars through the trees. She remembered, at Rone's village, thinking of the sky as burning in a vast furnace, and now she saw, sleepily, what the furnace had forged: stars, uncounted thousands, spread across the sky. She closed her eyes and slept.

They set off again the next morning. As the forest dwindled, so did its magics; they saw nothing unnatural all that day. The river joined up with other streams and became broader and wilder; they rode along its bank among the ferns and grasses, the land sloping gently upwards on either side. The river was too strong for her small net, so instead of fishing she stopped once in a while to pluck the small red berries Worrige had shown her. They were very tart, and delicious.

At dusk they left the forest completely. The land leveled out, and the river, now a strong torrent, sounded loud in the darkness. They followed it to where it plunged over a cliff into the ocean, feeling the water spray back over their hands and faces. Angarred did not see the College until Mathewar pointed it out to her on her left: a massive gray stone structure nearly indistinguishable from the cliffs around it.

No lights shone from the College. "It looks deserted," Angarred said.

"It always looks that way from here," Mathewar said. "Most people can't even see it."

They rode closer, then dismounted at the arched doorway. There were lamps on either side of the door, unlit. Mathewar knocked.

No one answered. He tried the door then knocked again, frowning. "Is there a doorward?" she asked.

He nodded, still intent on the door. He said a few words but nothing happened. "Usually. But now there's a spell here instead, barring outsiders."

"What if no one's there? What if we have to go back?"

"Someone's here. More than one person, I think. Hush—let me think about this."

He stepped back. Over the next few minutes he tried several words and combinations of words, but the door remained shut. Finally, just as Angarred was thinking that she was right, that they would have to return all that way through the forest, he laughed shortly.

"Dalesio," he said. "I might have known." He addressed the door: "Eat the meat and drink the wine, and do your work with a willing heart."

The door moved inward a few inches. He pushed it the rest of the way; it made a harsh sound, protesting, as it rasped against the floor.

At first she could see nothing; she had only a sense of distance before her, as if they were in a large empty room or hallway. Then Mathewar spoke and lamps bloomed outward in the darkness, one after the other, illuminating the way down a corridor. "Hello!" Mathewar said. His voice echoed from the stone walls, sounding hollow. "Is anyone here?"

The lights reflected back to them strangely, making giant shadows out of doors and chairs, glittering from copper lamps and doorknobs and even from the stone walls. Three men came out of the shadows toward them.

"Mathewar!" one of them said, blinking and running his hand through his scant hair. "It's good to see you!"

E L E V E N

Of the three men before them, only one looked like a magician. The man who had spoken was around sixty, with lines of worry radiating from his blue eyes; his nose curled in like a snail's shell, and his features were so unremarkable Angarred wouldn't have looked twice at him if she passed him on the street. Another was younger, plump, with unruly sandy hair that kept straying into his eyes. The third, though, commanded attention: he was tall and broad-shouldered, with a cap of thick white hair, dark gray eyes and an aquiline nose.

"Hello, Narinye," Mathewar said to the man who had spoken. He nodded to the others. "Angarred—this is First Master Narinye, and two other masters from the College, Merren and Dalesio. And this is Lady Angarred Hashan, my traveling companion."

"Go settle your horses and then let's eat," the plump one—Dalesio—said. "You have something important to tell us, or you wouldn't have made such a long journey."

They went out to the stables and then returned to the College. Dalesio led them down the hallway. The floors were deep brown wood, the walls white stone with carved wainscoting, and though they bore the marks of unnumbered students everything seemed freshly washed and polished. Dark wooden beams ran across the ceiling. Comfortable old chairs or benches stood against the walls or ranged around fireplaces, and every few yards they passed a portrait of some ancient master in archaic clothing.

They went into a room. "Are you hungry?" Dalesio said. "I'll make supper, if you like."

Someone lit a few lamps in the corner. The light spread only a few feet, but Angarred could see glimmerings and reflections from the rest of the room and realized that it was huge, probably the College dining hall. Wooden pillars reached up to the ceiling, carved and painted red and black, with glints of gold. Dark tapestries hung behind a dais at the front of the room, and carved golden letters ran along the wall and into darkness, spelling out some motto or proverb.

Mathewar said nothing. "That would be wonderful," Angarred said.

"Good, good," Dalesio said, smiling. "Please, sit down."

They sat at the corner of a massive wooden table. Mathewar's gaze followed Dalesio as he left. "That man thinks every problem can be solved by food," he said, and Angarred saw, startled, that for some reason Mathewar disliked him.

"That's unfair," Narinye said. "He's given up as much as nearly anyone."

There was an uncomfortable silence. Then Mathewar said, "Well, I suppose I'll have to wait with my news until he comes back. You're hiding because of Alkarren, I take it."

"We are," Narinye said. "I don't think any of us could stand up to him now that he has the Stone. We've stayed to protect the College against more mundane intruders—animals, and curious people from the forest. And there have been rumors that the giants are leaving their homes and marching—no one knows why."

"The giants?" Mathewar asked. "Marching? When did they start to march?"

"Some time ago, apparently. They've found a king to unite them, people say."

"But the giants have always been a peaceful people—they've never bothered us. And anyway Tobrin bound their magic into the Stone along with all the other magics."

"Nonetheless, this is what we heard. But to speak truly I have to say we're hiding, mostly, as you said. Trying to keep from coming to Alkarren's notice."

Mathewar laughed harshly. "It's ludicrous, isn't it? Once Alkarren could barely work the simplest spell. And now look at us—the most powerful men in all the realms, forced into hiding."

"I doubt he was as inept as you say," Narinye said mildly.

"No? He nearly set his classroom on fire once."

Narinye smiled, lines creasing his face. "Yes, I remember that. And you shouted a counterspell just in time." His smile faded. "Perhaps that's why he hates you so much. Even as a student you were better in some things than he was."

"He hates me because I wouldn't help him with the Stone. And there's more proof of what a poor magician he is. He's the first magician in over four hundred years to possess the Stone of Tobrin, and he scarcely knows what to do with it."

"Yes, that's strange, isn't it?" Narinye said. "We expected him to cause far more disruption than he has."

"He thinks there's another Stone somewhere," Angarred said. "That the one he has is a counterfeit."

Narinye and Merren turned to her, surprised, and she saw that they hadn't expected her to speak. "What do you mean?" Narinye said, and Merren said, "How do you know?"

"A woman I know heard him say so. He thinks a family called Snoppish have another Stone. And it's true that the Snoppishes are hiding something."

"There's no record of another Stone," Mathewar said. "He's using that story to excuse his incompetence. Anyway, he's done quite enough damage as it is."

They heard singing from the hallway, and then Dalesio came in carrying two plates piled high with food. He set them in front of Narinye and Merren and left again. On his second trip he somehow balanced three plates along his arms, and on his third he brought a bottle of wine and five mugs, each dangling from the fingers of one hand.

The food smelled wonderful—chicken, cooked along with a

mess of herbs and vegetables, and a slice of warm fresh bread. Angarred began to eat eagerly.

When she had nearly finished Mathewar said, "We should explain why we're here. Angarred, could you tell them what you saw?"

She swallowed quickly, then glanced at Mathewar. He had barely disturbed the food on his plate. "Yes, well." She took a sip of the wine Dalesio had poured for her. "I saw him use the Stone. Alkarren. He was holding it in his hand, and he ordered King Tezue to do something—to open the gates to the city. And the king did—he left the castle and went down to the gates and told his guards to open them. And then all the soldiers from Takeke who were camped outside came in and attacked us."

Narinye drew a harsh breath. Dalesio said, his voice low, "A Hollow One."

"Yes," Mathewar said. "I suppose you'll want us to kill him."

There was a bitterness in his voice that Angarred did not understand. Dalesio ignored it. "I've been looking for ways to free a Hollow One ever since I got here," he said. "I've found one spell, but it requires the Stone."

"I'd like to see it," Mathewar said. He leaned back in his chair and took a sip of wine. "And to look in the library for others."

"Of course," Narinye said. "But there's a good deal here I don't understand. How could you possibly have seen Alkarren use the Stone?"

Angarred told him about the secret corridor, and what she had overheard. Narinye smiled. "I've heard about such corridors," he said. "Kings built them long ago, to eavesdrop on their courtiers and relatives. I suppose they're all forgotten by now. But why would Alkarren want to open the gates to the enemy? That's what truly puzzles me. If Alkarren controls the king he controls Karededin. An invasion would be the last thing he would want."

"Perhaps he made an alliance with Takeke," Dalesio said.

"But then why is he mustering an army to fight them?" Angarred said. "If he controls the king as you say, then the order to raise troops must have come from him. He could have commanded the king not to fight, couldn't he?"

"There's a council, isn't there?" Dalesio said. "There was when I lived in the city, anyway. Maybe they overruled him."

"That's right," Angarred said. "My friend Jerret Snoppish is on it. I'll ask him when I get back." She turned to Mathewar, excited. "And I'll ask him about the Stone, too. I'm sure he'll help us, if the king's involved."

"But why wouldn't Alkarren just take over the councillors as well?" Narinye asked.

No one said anything. "Merren?" Narinye asked. "You haven't said what you think of all this."

Merren looked abstracted, as if he had been paying attention to a different conversation. He turned toward Narinye, concentrating with difficulty. "Maybe he isn't strong enough," he said.

"It can't be that difficult," Mathewar said. "Not if he has the Stone."

"I don't know," Narinye said heavily. "I don't understand this at all." He turned to Angarred. "I don't even know why you're here with Mathewar, for one thing."

She told the masters, briefly, about her father's death and the attack against her on the stairs. "Who do you think wants to kill you?" Narinye asked. "Norue?"

"Maybe," she said. "I don't know."

"Have you tried to read him?" Narinye asked Mathewar.

"No. I doubt anyone can—his mind is far too well guarded to allow it."

"I meant with the Clear Sight."

"No, not that either. I haven't gone to court in over a year—it's too dangerous." He was silent a moment. "I suppose I could always search through his papers," he said.

"Mathewar!" Narinye said.

Mathewar grinned crookedly, and Angarred understood that for some reason he had decided to play the rebel in front of his former teachers. Or perhaps it wasn't an act. "We read people all the time," he said. "How is that different?"

"You know very well how it's different," Narinye said. "If you don't we've wasted years of teaching."

"It's late," Dalesio said. "We should talk again in the morning, when we're fresh."

They stood. Narinye held up his hand to stop Mathewar from leaving. "You're still drinking sattery, aren't you?" he said. "I can see it on you."

"And what if I am?" Mathewar said.

"We should all be at our best, to counter this threat. You heard everyone here—we don't know what Alkarren is planning, or why."

"Don't worry about Alkarren—I'll take care of him."

"While you're besotted with this drug?"

"I can take care of him, I said. And myself."

"I'm almost more worried about you than Alkarren," Narinye said. "You were the best pupil to come through the College during my term here. I don't like to see you waste your talents like this."

"They're my talents, aren't they? I'll waste them however I like. And now," Mathewar said, looking over the others at the table, "I'm afraid I must leave you gentlemen, and lady, and go make a fire."

They gave Angarred a room on the top floor under the eaves, used, they said, by one of the masters who had gone into hiding. The soft mattress felt uncomfortable at first, after nights of sleeping on the forest floor, but the sounds of the waves below soon lulled her into drowsiness.

A loud booming woke her in the middle of the night, and she went to the window set in the slanting ceiling. The tide had come in—waves crashed against the cliff, sending their spray high in the air. She watched a few moments in wonder, stepping back as a great torrent of water reached up as far as her window, and then went back to bed.

She woke again at dawn, and after a few false starts found her way back to the dining hall. Dalesio had left her a pot of porridge and some milk, along with a note explaining that the masters would be in the library. In the daylight she could read the carving on the wall: "Eat the meat and drink the wine, and do your work with a willing heart." So that was where it had come from.

The porridge, as she expected, was delicious, mixed with spices she could not identify and served with fresh berries. When she finished she went down the hall and looked into open doorways. Most of the rooms seemed to be abandoned classrooms, containing nothing but tables and chairs. Some of the doors were locked. One was closed but opened when she tried it; the room beyond was empty except for a small table in the center. Richly embroidered gold silk covered the table, and on it stood an elaborately worked piece of gold and gems. She went closer. The gold had once held something, she saw, but whatever it had been it was gone now.

She came to the library, a room with a maze of shelves and boxes crowded full of books and scrolls and manuscripts. Merren stood near one of the shelves, looking at a single page in his hands. She could see his profile; he was frowning at something.

Mathewar came around the shelf and Merren quickly set the page on top of a row of books. "Have you found anything?" Mathewar asked.

"Nothing yet," Merren said.

They both moved behind a line of heavy black shelves. Angarred stepped quietly into the room. She took the page Merren had been reading; the words were written in an ancient style, decorated with loops and flourishes. She managed to make out one phrase— something about "the habitations of the Others"—and she put it back, shivering.

She studied the rows of leather-bound books in the case, some in languages she didn't recognize. A slim volume stood among them: *The Life of Tobrin*, it said on the spine. She checked to see if anyone was watching, then took the book and left the room.

She continued down the hall and came to a rear doorway. She opened it and went outside. A flight of rickety wooden steps led down the cliffside and met the water; probably they had once reached all the way to an ancient beach but over the long centuries the ocean had encroached on land, crumbling the cliffs. The waves were mild now, the sea billowing like a sheet in the wind. She went down the stairs to a landing and sat and opened the book.

The cry of a bird startled her and she turned back toward the College. The building came right to the edge of the cliff, its rough massive stone rearing up out of the rock. She imagined it as it would look at night, golden lights streaming from every room as the students bent over their books; imagined sailors passing and seeing the cliffside run with gold.

She looked at the book again, making an effort this time. Tobrin, like Mathewar, had been born in the Forest of Tiranon. The great Sorcerers' Wars that Mathewar had told her about had shaken the land as he grew up, and by the time he reached adulthood he had resolved to try to end them. He journeyed through many lands, from huge realms to tiny fiefdoms, and attracted likeminded followers; though others, those bent on their own rule, swore to kill him, and nearly did so several times.

Near the end of his life he retreated to the sea cliffs, where he embarked on his great study of magic. With the help of his supporters he built the College and collected many of the books now in the library. Finally he learned enough to bind most of the destructive forces into the Stone. He chose an ordinary stone he had found on his travels for the binding, hoping that no one would ever think it was worth anything. In this, though, Angarred knew he had been wrong; far too many people had learned the nature of the Stone over the years.

At an advanced age—eighty or ninety, the stories varied—he disappeared. The masters at the College thought that he had ventured into the forest and met with some magical force he did not understand; but others said that he was merely sleeping, and that he would wake and come to aid the realms in times of need.

A while later she heard footsteps heading toward her and turned. Mathewar sat next to her. He saw the book she was holding and smiled wryly. "I had to read that as a boy. It's a good choice—it might answer a lot of those questions about magic you asked me."

"I didn't know if I was allowed to take it from the library," she said.

"Probably not," he said, unconcerned. He looked around him. "Well, you're wise to come out here, anyway. It's far better than closeting yourself in a room with three musty old masters."

"Why don't you like Dalesio?" she asked.

"I don't like any of them, truth to tell."

"None of them? But Dalesio's so kind, so generous. And Merren—what has he ever done to you? He hardly says anything."

"Yes, and that's my problem with him. He looks wise, and so people take his silences for wisdom. But what is he really thinking? Half the time he isn't even paying attention, I think."

"Maybe he's senile. Or drinking sattery."

She had expected Mathewar to become angry, but he only crooked his mouth in the familiar mocking smile. "He's too young for senility. He looks older than he is—it's all that white hair. And if he drank sattery I'd know it."

"Anyway, I don't think he's hiding something—he just looks distracted. But even he is trying to help you—I saw him in the library earlier. And what about Narinye? You don't like him because of what he said about sattery, I think."

He turned and looked at her levelly. "Listen. There's something odd about those men you like so much, something they're hiding. Or one of them is hiding, anyway."

"Which one?"

"Well, they're magicians. They guard their thoughts better than anyone."

They sat for a moment in silence. Small waves lapped at the cliffs below them; the waves looked blue, though the ocean farther out was as green as jade. Seagulls screeched overhead. A cooling breeze came from the water.

Mathewar picked up a piece of rotten wood and threw it into the ocean. "It must have been hard for you at court," Angarred said, "if you can read people so well."

"It's not that easy. I can only read people who are open to it, and those courtiers hid everything, even what they had for breakfast. Sometimes I would see them with the Clear Sight . . . but you don't need Clear Sight to know that not one of them tells the truth."

"Jerret does, I think."

"Maybe—I never knew Jerret very well. He's the one who fancies you, isn't he?"

"He doesn't *fancy* me. He's the only one who's interesting to talk to, now that Chelenin died."

"You seem to have done well at court, though. Especially since no one ever taught you court etiquette."

"I don't know if you're complimenting me or not."

His mouth quirked in a smile. "Well, that depends. Are you using a magic of seeming, or one of becoming?"

"Seeming, of course! I would never become one of those—those empty-headed scheming hypocrites."

"You may have to go back to them, though. I don't know if we'll be able to free the king, not without the Stone."

"But—then our whole journey here was for nothing. Tezue can't help me if he's still a Hollow One . . ." She stopped. Surely Mathewar didn't want to hear about her troubles.

"No journey is ever truly wasted," Mathewar said, his voice surprisingly kind. "We learned some things about the forest, and the masters here will continue to look for answers after we leave . . . And maybe something will turn up for you at court."

She sighed. "Maybe I'll marry Jerret, if, as you say, he fancies me," she said, trying to sound unconcerned. "Though my father will come howling back from the Celestial Court and haunt me if I do."

He picked up another piece of wood and threw it. "Would you truly do that?"

"Well, you tell me. You're the one who reads people."

"I don't read people I know, not unless I have to. But no—I don't think you would. You're too honest for that."

"Two compliments in one day. You're spoiling me, I'm afraid." A gust of cold wind came off the water and her skin prickled. "But you know, if we fail here I think I am going to try to gain power at court. It'll be the only way left to me. You can be a courtier and remain honest—look at Jerret."

"Maybe." Mathewar stood. "I should get back to the library."

She went back to the book after he had gone. The rest of it was taken up with what Tobrin had learned in his studies. "Magic was stronger once, before we bound so much of it into the Stone," he wrote. "It was wilder, and magicians then could work all sorts of evil. They could create Hollow Ones: that is, they could take over a person's mind and force him to do their bidding, until finally they quenched that person's very being. And they made shadow people, likenesses of men and women, and they sent these copies out into the world to impersonate the original. The likenesses were not perfect, but several instances are recorded of friends and family members who were tragically deceived.

"In these latter days, fortunately, such horrors are no longer possible. Magic is weaker now, it's true, but it is also true that abominations such as these, which occurred far too often during the Sorcerers' Wars, cannot come again.

"Before the Binding of the Stone magicians could also work true transformations. This too can no longer be done today, though a good deal of nonsense is spoken about it: it is said, for example, that some folks are able to become birds and fly away, or turn invisible. But in these latter times nothing can change its nature except by illusion, and as for invisibility, no one can change himself from something to nothing.

"Many stories are told about the forest people, especially the women among them, that they can become animals, for example. This is arrant foolishness. In all my travels I have never met a woman who can work magic. Perhaps the persistence of these legends means that a very few women had this talent, perhaps one in a century. But such a woman would be very weak, her magic wild and untrained, and we will not concern ourselves with such things in the course of our studies.

"You will hear of other magics as well, and their nature should be addressed. A magician can read unguarded thoughts; most people, however, know without thinking how to guard themselves from an early age. This ability is different from the Clear Sight, which comes upon some magicians unawares and lets them look into another person or see events in the future. The Clear Sight is erratic, incapable of being called up by any spell, and may not be part of the proper study of magic at all."

Angarred stopped reading and looked out at the ocean. How could Tobrin have missed the magic of the forest people in his journeys? She had seen what they could do, and she had not traveled nearly as widely as the old magician. Perhaps they had hidden themselves from him—but if so, why had they been so open with her and Mathewar?

She read until the air became too chilly to stay, then climbed the steps up the cliffside. Autumn had come; the leaves on some trees were edged with gold or red. Moss covered the wall of the College up to the top floor, and blurred the shapes of the gargoyles on the roof.

Supper that evening was livelier than yesterday's. They talked about everything and anything: masters and pupils who had passed through the College, Norue's ambition, the death of Queen Chelenin, the woman Rone who had shown she could work magic. To this last Narinye said only, "Well, we'll look into that when Alkarren ceases to trouble us."

Angarred frowned. Rone had been right; she had known they would dismiss her. But for the most part the masters included Angarred in the conversation, and listened to her with genuine interest. She told them about going into the room with the table and the empty stand of gold, and Mathewar said, "Odd you should have found that. The table once held the Stone of Tobrin, stolen from us four hundred years ago. The masters have hoped to get it back ever since."

"And now maybe we will," Narinye said. "I hope we've been able to help you, anyway." Dalesio poured wine and began to clean up around them.

"I don't know," Mathewar said. "The spells are good, I think, and strong. But to go up against the Stone . . ."

"Are you finished here?" Angarred asked, surprised.

"For now," Mathewar said. "Other spells remain to be found, I'm certain of that. But we have to hurry back. The longer King Tezue remains a Hollow One the harder it will be to free him."

"Be careful—the Godkings know what dangers are rousing in that forest," Narinye said. "The giants are massing, for one thing."

"Yes, you mentioned them before," Mathewar said. "Are you certain, though? As I said, they've always been peaceful . . ."

"Just be careful," Narinye said again.

———

They said good-bye to the masters the next morning. Dalesio gave them a large bag filled with food, and when Angarred looked inside she saw cheese and dried beef and a wineskin and bread baked with several kinds of herbs. She hugged him in thanks.

Then they set off. The trees near the College were ordinary, familiar—tall green pines and spreading oaks with fiery red leaves. The air felt chill and held the promise of more cold to come, and huge gray clouds massed far off beyond the trees.

They came in the afternoon to the forest she remembered: the dense shade and suffocating closeness, the trees whose leaves looked like hands. Some of the leaves now lay on the ground, red as blood; as the horses passed they seemed to crush them underfoot. The sight disturbed her so much she had to keep her eyes on the road ahead.

After a while she thought the forest might have changed since the last time they had come this way; things seemed to have shifted, or moved subtly out of true. And yet whenever she tried to compare their surroundings with her memories of a few days ago she could not decide if anything was truly different. Even Mathewar, when she asked him, did not know for certain, though he guessed they had come to another part of Tiranon.

Suddenly a great roar shook the forest, sounding as though it came from all around them. "What's that?" she asked.

"I don't know," Mathewar said.

They stopped their horses and listened. The roar sounded again. The horses moved skittishly, trying to break away; they urged them into the trees and waited, making as little noise as possible. Something crashed through the forest and Angarred's muscles tensed.

A young deer bounded out onto the path. Its eyes rolled in panic, showing the whites, and the muscles at its shoulders and haunches worked desperately. Its ears stuck straight up; they were ridiculously large, as if they belonged to another animal.

Something followed the deer, knocking the branches off the trees as it came. A huge man strode along the path, a man two or three times the size of an ordinary person. He bent, reached forward, and grabbed the deer by the throat.

The deer lunged and kicked out, but the giant held it fast. He got his hands firmly around its neck and twisted; a dreadful crack sounded as the neck broke. Then the giant lifted it to his shoulders and settled it there like a scarf and walked away down the path.

"Holy Godkings," Angarred breathed.

"Yes," Mathewar said. "And those are the people Narinye said have found a king, and are massing against us."

There were no other signs of the giant that day. But as they rode Angarred saw that the forest had definitely changed around them; for one thing they had lost the stream that had kept them company all the way to the sea.

"The stream's gone," she said. "I wish we still had it—I got used to being clean."

"There's a story about a man who went to bathe in the stream," Mathewar said. "And when he got out the forest had changed around him, and his clothes were gone. They say he accosts travelers in the dark, stark naked, asking them if they've seen his clothes."

"Really?"

"No."

She looked at him. He began to laugh. She tried to scowl at him but found herself unable to hold back her own laughter, and they rode that way for a time, their mirth echoing from the trees.

The lacing of his shirt had come undone; she could see the muscles of his broad shoulders. Suddenly she realized what a handsome man he was. No, "realized" was the wrong word; she had always known it, like a song that ran below the surface of her thoughts. A wave of desire coursed through her like a river.

No, she thought. No, I am not going to fall in love with this man, with his silences, his mockery, his addiction to sattery. But another part of her thought, Who said anything about love? We spend the nights together, it would be easy enough to go to him when he has nightmares and then . . .

Then she had a terrible thought. He had learned to read people at the College, he had said. Could he see into her? Did he know what she was thinking? No, he had said he could only read people who were open to it; she would have to take care to hide her thoughts, and to hope that he wouldn't be able to see her with what Tobrin had called the Clear Sight. She blushed so strongly her face felt as if it had been singed by fire, and she turned away from him.

They stopped to make camp at dusk. She was newly awkward with him, wanting to keep her distance but at the same time trying not to seem too unfriendly. They shared some of the food from Dalesio's bag in silence. She uncorked the wineskin and drank from it, then held it out to him. He had already poured his sattery, though, and he raised the silver cup to her in a mock salute and set it down by the fire.

He drank the sattery, pulled off his boots and lay down among his blankets. Angarred, listening to him tensely, heard his breathing become regular as he fell asleep. She struggled to stay awake, tired from the journey and the wine.

She woke suddenly, hearing him cry out his wife's name. Her heart pounded. Should she go to him? What if he rejected her? She felt disgusted at her indecision; she had gone into the Great Hall in Pergodi Castle with less debate.

"Embre!" he shouted again. "Oh, Godkings, no!"

She found herself lying next to him with no memory of having gotten there. She drew him into her arms and held him, amazed and excited at her daring. Every sense felt heightened, everything exhilarating and sharp and new: the feel of his body against hers, the harsh wool of the blankets, the small rocks beneath them. She thought she could even hear his heart beating erratically. His muscles were as taut as stretched rope. "Hush," she said, moving to caress him beneath the blankets. "Hush, it's all right."

He relaxed slightly. He turned on his side and drew her close. His eyes were open, but muddy, unfocused: he was dreaming, she thought, or still in the grip of sattery. Unable to stop herself she threaded her fingers through his unbound hair; it felt wonderful, like fine silk.

"I thought . . ." he murmured. "Embre, I thought . . ."

She jerked away. He thought she was Embre! "What . . ." he said. He seemed to be trying to focus.

She backed away quickly toward her blankets. "What?" he said again, still not fully awake.

"You had a dream," she said. Her face burned with fury and embarrassment: at his mistake, at her lie, which he would not believe for a moment.

"Oh," he said. "I thought . . . I thought that she . . ." He trailed off and fell back asleep.

She could not relax enough to sleep. She rehearsed what had happened over and over, wondering what she should have done, wondering how much of the night he would remember. He made very little noise as he slept, but every soft breath, every rustle of his blankets brought fresh arousal, and fresh frustration. Dawn found her wide awake, staring up through the trees.

T W E L V E

Jerret left the council room feeling tired and disgusted. Norue had gone with his troops to Takeke, the day after Jerret and Labren had met him in the castle; in fact Labren was traveling with him, part of his elite company. The prince was supposed to discuss peace with the Takekek, though no one outside a small inner circle knew that.

With Norue gone and the king ill there were only five people at council, not enough to make any important decisions. Lady Sorle once again raised the question of making Norue regent, but Lord Enlandin came in on the side of the king's men—much to Jerret's surprise, since Enlandin was part of Prince Norue's inner circle. He wanted to ask Enlandin about his change of heart after the council meeting but the lord hurried away and he lost his chance.

Jerret sighed. It was true that Karededin needed a well king, especially now that war had broken out. But he felt strongly that Norue would be worse than Tezue. Better to have a king who did nothing than one with Norue's ambitions.

He walked aimlessly through the castle, avoiding the Great Hall. Like Norue and Labren, like everyone, it seemed, Angarred had left Pergodi. She had not said good-bye; he worried about her when he was not busy worrying about other things, and wondered if she was safe. And with her gone there was no one among the courtiers he wanted to talk to.

His steps took him toward the Hall of the Standing Kings, and he thought he might look at the statue of Queen Chelenin once again. He turned a corner and saw Princess Rodarren ahead of him.

He slowed, not wanting to meet up with her. Like all the courtiers he found her disturbing, eerie. Unlike them he thought her beautiful as well; with her moon-white eye she seemed almost a phantasm sent by the Others. He heard quick footsteps behind him and a young man passed him, hurrying. The young man took out a knife.

"Hey!" Jerret said, running after him. The man rushed forward, making for Rodarren. "Stop! Put away the knife!"

All three of them were running now, Jerret, Rodarren and the man with the knife. Jerret put his hand on the sword he wore ever since the Takekek had attacked Karededin. They entered the Hall of the Standing Kings. Rodarren ran toward the statue of Mathona and, as Jerret watched, squeezed herself between the First Queen and the Teacher and disappeared.

The young man hurried after her and peered between the two statues. Jerret grasped him by his cloak and forced him around. He drew his sword and held it lightly, ready to deflect the other man's knife. "What in the name of the Others are you doing?" he asked.

"Nothing, milord," the man said.

"It looked to me as if you were trying to kill Princess Rodarren."

"I would never—"

"What's your name?"

"Ranle Carpenter."

"Well, Ranle Carpenter, what were you doing with that knife?"

"This knife, milord?" He pulled a knife from his belt, slowly. The Others take it—he had put it away without Jerret noticing. "I use this to eat with, and for simple tasks. As I said, I'm a carpenter."

Jerret took the knife from him. "Why were you following Princess Rodarren?"

"I wasn't. I wanted—I wanted to see where she went, that's all. I never knew there was a passageway there."

Neither had Jerret. He looked past Ranle to the space between the statues but could see nowhere Rodarren could have gone. "Come with me," Jerret said.

"Where?"

"To prison."

"But—but milord! I did nothing. I'm a carpenter, milord. I was going to fix some timbers in the outer gate."

"Well, you're going to prison now. And you'll stay there until you tell me what you were doing here."

Jerret marched Ranle, protesting, down the steep drafty stairs to the prisons, then went back to the Hall of the Standing Kings. He looked between the statues as Ranle had done, and he felt around for a latch or lever that would open a doorway, but he found nothing. Finally, nearly overcome by smoke from the red torches at the statues' feet, he turned away, leaving the puzzle for later.

He walked slowly across the length of the hall to Chelenin's statue. Princess Rodarren might have found the secret passage by accident, Jerret thought, but it took some intelligence to remember it and use it again. Perhaps she had not lost her wits as everyone believed. He remembered a rumor current in the Great Hall, probably spread by Norue, that said that she had stolen the Stone.

But then why did she play the idiot? And why had she kept up the masquerade since childhood?

And who had ordered the attack? Could it have been Norue? The prince was the only true enemy Rodarren had at court, after all. But Norue was gone, still in Takeke.

The excitement of Labren's first day in the capital did not last. The company's quarters were simple wooden huts, with none of the glamour and color they had seen in the castle. Even worse, Norue had ordered them confined to quarters while he negotiated with Dindin. Their sole purpose, Labren realized, had been to impress the prince and his important councillors. They had nothing to do but talk and play games; and by the end of the week they had thrown their knives at a spot on the wall so many times they had worn a hole in the wood.

One man pointed out that they had not seen any women, and after this observation they discussed endlessly why this was, and where the women might be. Some of them even ventured outside, though Norue had strictly prohibited it. One man reported seeing a woman dressed in layers of colorful veils from head to foot, but the others were fierce in their ridicule.

"How did you know it was a woman, if it was wearing veils?" someone said.

"I could tell," the first man said, and the argument went on long into the night.

By the second week they began to fight among themselves. Quarrels flared up at the slightest provocation: someone had moved someone else's gear, someone had insulted ironmongers, or tin miners, or merchants.

Labren was writing a letter to his brother when two of the strongest men in the company, Fion and Hallen, came to blows. He quickly set the letter down and joined the others trying to pull them apart, but the brawlers were enraged now and nothing seemed to stop them. They fought like madmen, overturning chairs and trampling on pallets, roaring like animals.

The company made another attempt to force the two men away from each other, but Fion and Hallen shrugged them off as if they were children. They closed and grappled together, each seeking an advantage. Finally Fion grunted and, his arms wrapped around Hallen's thighs, he lifted the other man and threw him to the floor. Hallen fell heavily and lay still.

The room quieted in a moment. Then someone said, hesitantly, "You killed him."

"He's not dead," someone else said. "Look, he's breathing."

"He needs a doctor."

"We don't have a doctor, you idiot."

"Get him off the floor, at least."

"No—don't touch him!"

"I'll go find Prince Norue," Labren said, anxious to be outside, away from the close-packed quarters.

"No, I should do it—I'm the standard-bearer."

Norue had not put anyone in charge in his absence, but the standard-bearer was probably the closest thing to a leader they had.

Labren slipped outside quickly, before the other man could argue further, and closed the door behind him.

No one had followed him, he saw with relief. He stopped a moment to get his bearings, and then, remembering their march from the castle, he set off to the right.

Nebokbok seemed smaller, less vital than Pergodi, with fewer people on the streets. And compared to the Karedek, who wore their hair long and went clean-shaven, the Takekek men with their thick beards looked barbarous, more like animals than people. Some had plaited their beards with gems and beads and colored string, and most wore huge mustaches the size of combs which covered their mouths and made it impossible to guess their expressions, so that Labren felt obscurely that everyone he passed was laughing at him.

Once, memorably, he saw a woman carried in a litter and surrounded by soldiers. She was covered in veils of bright colors; rows of coins sewn to her veils made a jingling sound as she passed.

Norue should have appointed a leader, Labren thought—Lord Jerret would have. He had known for a while now that Jerret was a better commander than Norue, and not for the first time he wondered if he had made the right decision when he joined the prince's company. Still thinking about the two men, he looked up and saw that he had come to the castle.

The guard at the door recognized Labren's uniform and allowed him to pass. He found his way to the main hall, but the fire and torches had gone out and he could barely see in the dim light. It was deserted except for a few thin dogs, the long table strewn with plates and scraps of food.

He heard voices and headed toward them, feeling his way along the table in the gloom. A door on the far side of the room stood open and he went through it, into some sort of corridor.

The only light came from small high windows. He groped along the wall; the rock here felt smoother, almost mortarless, and he guessed he was in the older part of the castle. He stumbled into emptiness and realized he had come to a door. The voices sounded just around the corner.

"It's agreed, then," someone said. Labren recognized Prince Dindin. "Our swords will shine like stars together, and the entire world will wonder at our might."

"Our enemies' blood will run like rivers," Prince Norue said.

"Like rivers the setting sun touches," Dindin said, "turning all its torrents red."

"When should we start the invasion?" Norue asked.

"Pergodi will lie helpless before us, and we will take it as a lion leaps upon a gazelle."

"But when—" Norue said.

Labren stepped back in shock. Norue wanted to invade Pergodi! He was not here negotiating peace; he was traitorously allying himself with Prince Dindin against Pergodi instead.

He stood still. If he showed himself now he would be killed for what he had heard. But Hallen might die if he hesitated too long. He waited impatiently for the meeting to end, listening to Dindin's sonorous phrases and Norue's curt attempts to discuss strategy.

A small figure came around the corner and began to urinate against the wall. The king, Labren saw, and at that moment the boy turned toward him and began shouting loudly in Takekek.

Prince Dindin ran into the corridor, Norue following him. The two men grasped Labren by the shoulders and pulled him around the corner. Light hit him. "Labren!" Norue said. "What in the name of all the Others are you doing here? How long were you standing there, spying? I said no one was to leave their quarters."

"I wasn't—I wasn't spying, milord," Labren said. "I just got here. There's a man back at the quarters—he's hurt himself, he needs a doctor."

"Hurt himself? Someone's hurt him, more likely. Have the men been fighting?"

"I don't know, milord. I didn't see it," Labren said, knowing better than to inform on his fellow men.

"And what do you expect me to do about it? I brought no doctors on this journey, you know that."

"If the splendid prince will allow it, I will send the king's own physician to look upon your man," Prince Dindin said.

"I would be honored, my lord," Norue said.

Dindin scowled; he had probably expected far more flowery phrases. Then he grinned his mad grin and left the room, his loose blue trousers fluttering, calling for someone as he went.

"I'm not finished with you," Norue said. "I want to be certain you haven't heard anything here."

"I haven't, milord," Labren said. "I swear it."

Whenever he had time Jerret looked in on Princess Rodarren, making certain she was safe. She still spoke in riddles and idiot phrases, and Jerret wondered if he had made too much of her disappearance in the Hall of the Standing Kings, if she had been guided there by luck and not cleverness.

One afternoon after a long frustrating meeting of the council Jerret saw Rodarren quietly leave the Great Hall, and he excused himself and followed her. He expected her to go toward the Standing Kings, but instead she wandered through back corridors and passageways until she came to the servants' part of the castle.

She left by a door Jerret had never seen. Once outside she stopped so quickly that Jerret barely had time to duck back inside the castle. She put her fingers to her mouth and whistled shrilly, then whistled again.

She headed down the winding road to the city. Jerret waited, putting some distance between them, and then continued after her.

There were a good many people on the road; he slowed some more and hid among them. Ahead of him Rodarren walked purposefully; but did she have a destination or was she following some idiot whim?

Halfway down the hillside the road swerved left to avoid a great stand of trees. She had nearly gone past this when suddenly a pack of men moved out from the trees and converged on her, drawing knives and swords. There were twenty of them at least. Jerret longed with his entire body to join them, to fight for her, but he could not win out against so many, and he would be of no use to anyone dead. He watched as the men surrounded her, feeling helpless.

The men walking behind her hurried forward, joining the knot attacking her. Jerret nearly looked away, certain she was about to be killed.

The men began to fight among themselves. He heard the ring of sword on sword, sword on shield, and saw with amazement that the second group belonged to Rodarren. He drew his sword and ran to join them.

He had to call out "Rodarren!" several times before her men accepted him; then they all pushed forward, side by side, making for the princess. Rodarren had her own sword out too, landing expert blows on the sword of a man near her. Jerret worked his way toward her over the uneven ground and thrust his sword into her attacker's back.

The man fell between them; she recognized Jerret, and her good eye widened. "Behind you!" she cried, and he turned and saw an upraised sword. He parried wildly, trying to find his footing before the man came closer, then stabbed toward his attacker's heart. The man parried, and the fight began in earnest.

They fought a while, back and forth, neither one gaining the advantage. Then suddenly the other man began to step away. Jerret followed cautiously; he had done nothing to cause the man's retreat and he suspected a trap. But all around them men were withdrawing, running, making for the city below. Soon the princess's men had control of the road.

"They were probably told to avoid capture at all costs," one of the men said. "Whoever hired them does not want them questioned."

"You know who hired them," Rodarren said wearily. "My unholy cousin Norue. Even when he's out of the city he's able to do mischief."

"Especially when he's out of the city," another man said. "That way he can't be connected to any attacks on you."

A crowd had formed at a distance, people using the road who had stopped when they saw the clash of arms. Some of them pointed; others spoke among themselves, repeating the princess's name over and over.

"The Others take it," Rodarren said. "They've seen me—my masquerade is over. That's why he attacked me, you know—not to kill me but to bring me out into the open. He couldn't hurt me with so many witnesses around, but he's managed to rip away my mask, my protection." She shook her head. "I should have learned by now not to underestimate him."

"My lady Rodarren," Jerret said. "It's dangerous to stay here—they might come back, and bring more men with them. Please—my father's house is near by. I would be honored if you would stay with us for a while."

She looked at him keenly. "Lord Jerret, is it? How do I know this isn't another of my cousin's traps?"

"Because you know me, milady. You've seen me at court. You've seen more than anyone ever guessed."

"That's true enough. But you guessed, didn't you? Well, I certainly can't go back to court now. Yes, I think I will accept your invitation. Lord Jerret, the only honest man at court."

For the first time that day Jerret felt at a loss, uncertain what to reply. For an answer he gave her directions to his father's house. The company formed around her, hiding her in the center, and they continued down the road to the city. Several people in the crowd tried to follow them, but the company drew their swords and motioned them back. Jerret nodded in approval; it was best to have as few people as possible know where she was going.

He found himself next to the princess. He looked at her, still amazed at her transformation, and he felt awe at her bravery, at the way she had stood for so long, all alone, against her treacherous cousin. "These men followed you when you when you whistled, I take it."

"Yes. I knew someone in the castle was watching my movements, but I had to go into the city. I didn't really think Norue would move against me, though. As I said, he couldn't have killed me with all these witnesses. How was it that you turned up so opportunely? Were you following me?"

"What do you want in the city?"

She smiled. "I have not yet completely taken you into my confidence, Lord Jerret," she said. "I would still like to know why you were following me, for one thing."

"I saw a man try to attack you with a knife a while ago, milady. I worried about your safety." He stopped, remembering. "That man is in prison now—I can question him if you like."

She looked at him. How could she be so calm, so regal, after such a vicious attack? "I would like that very much," she said. "It would help a good deal if I could get proof of my cousin's treachery—he's usually very careful not to leave evidence of what he does. Clever man."

When they reached Lord Snoppish's house most of Rodarren's men left her; two stayed to guard the house and two followed her inside. Jerret's mother came out of the kitchen, her hands covered with flour, and he introduced them.

"Would you like something to eat or drink?" Lady Snoppish asked, showing no surprise at her royal visitor. "We have some very good ale."

"Ale would be wonderful, thank you," Rodarren said.

Jerret offered her a seat. The guards took their places behind her. For once none of his nieces or nephews or unmarried sisters seemed to be around; he said a silent prayer to the Godkings for that and sat opposite her, next to an empty fireplace. Lady Snoppish bustled in with a bottle and two mugs and poured some ale for both of them.

"You want to know why I played the idiot for so many years," Rodarren said.

Jerret blinked at her directness. "No, milady. Well, yes, but what I'd prefer to know is how. You're intelligent, accomplished—how can you stand being a fool, and having others believe you a fool?"

"I have some close trusted friends. I read a lot, I play cards, I sing. I can leave the mask of the fool behind sometimes."

"But—how many years has it been?"

"Over thirty."

"Over thirty. And without a mishap."

"Until today," Rodarren said, smiling wryly. The scar on her face twisted. "I had to do it though—he would have killed me otherwise. I was nine years old when Norue attacked me with a knife he took from the kitchen. He was eight, but strong for his age, and horribly cruel. I had never felt such pain—my eye, my face, my hand, all destroyed. I collapsed, and when I woke I found that Norue had told everyone that I had been attacked by a bear. He thought I was dead, you see—otherwise he would have continued his attack. I knew then that he would stop at nothing to be king. And I knew also that no one would listen if I told them the truth. It is far easier to believe that bears live just outside Pergodi than to accept that the heir to the throne is a monster."

"And you thought that if you were dim-witted he would dismiss you, would not see you as a threat."

"Yes, exactly." She smiled again. "And I was able to annoy him no end. I found that fools are allowed to say the most outrageous things."

Jerret sipped his ale. "What will you do now, milady?" he asked.

Rodarren put her cup to her lips. He realized that she had been waiting for him to drink, that she had thought the ale might be poisoned. He wondered what it would be like to distrust everyone except a few friends, and his amazement at her strength deepened.

"Right now I think I'd like to sleep," she said. "We can discuss my plans in the morning, if you're still interested."

"Of course I'm interested, milady," he said. He stood. "If you'll come this way I'll show you to your room. I apologize for the cold—we've never been able to heat this house properly."

"Don't worry," Rodarren said, standing with him. "Your hospitality is warmth enough."

It was a platitude common among the courtiers, but to Jerret it seemed that she meant it. As if to prove how much she trusted him, she dismissed her guards before following him down the hall. He made certain she was comfortable in her room and then went to tell his parents how they had come to play host to a princess.

THIRTEEN

It was still light outside when Jerret finished talking to his parents, and he knew the excitement of the day would keep him up for hours yet. He paced a while, looking for something to do, and then realized that he could visit the prison and interview Ranle Carpenter, the man who had attacked Rodarren.

The guard waved Jerret into the room. Ranle sat in his cage, shivering from the cold and damp of the prison despite the blanket he had wrapped around himself. His beard had grown out; it made his face look filthy.

"Who hired you to kill Princess Rodarren?" Jerret asked.

"I wasn't going to kill her," Ranle said. His voice sounded weaker, but the certainty in his tone was the same. "I already told you that. How many times do I have to say it? I wanted to see where she went, nothing more."

"Was it Prince Norue? Did Norue hire you?"

Ranle tried to laugh; the attempt made him cough for a long time. "Where would I meet Prince Norue?" he said finally.

"Where you met Rodarren. In the castle. You work here, don't you? He asked you to kill her and you agreed. How much was he paying you?"

"I wasn't hired to kill her. And I never met Prince Norue."

"You're waiting for him to come and rescue you, aren't you? He must have promised you a great deal, for you to sit there in that foul cage day after day. Unfortunately he has no idea where you are. Your best chance is to tell me everything you know about him. Maybe we can come to some agreement about the length of your stay here."

"I already told you—I don't know anything. Anyway, how could I have talked to Prince Norue? He left the city a while ago."

"Yes, but no one was supposed to know that. Where did you hear it?"

Ranle paled beneath his beard. "I—everyone's heard it. Someone in the castle knew. I remember now—the woman who cleans his rooms told me. She said he'd be gone for a while."

Jerret shook his head. He would get nothing more from this man today; Norue had probably frightened him and promised him riches in equal amounts. The prince would have brought a torturer, Jerret knew, but Jerret had never employed anyone from that disgusting profession. He would have to wait, let Ranle think about spending his life in the prison; then, when the other man had become terrified by his imaginings, he would return.

"Think about what I said," he said. "I'm your only route out of here, remember that. I want to hear the truth when I come back." He left the prisons, wishing he could bring more information back to Rodarren.

Jerret woke the next day to voices coming from the kitchen. He headed downstairs and found his mother and Rodarren talking over a breakfast of bread and ale.

"Good morning," he said, pouring himself some ale. "How did you sleep?"

"Wonderful, thank you," Rodarren said. "I feel far safer here than in the castle."

Lady Snoppish left to wake her husband. "You're welcome to stay as long as you like," Jerret said. He told her what he had learned at the prison, then asked, "Have you decided what you'll do next?"

"Yes, I have. I'm going into exile."

"What? Where?"

"Emindal. Do you know it?"

He did, but only by reputation. It was an island that had stead-fastly remained neutral during all the wars on the mainland. Most of the people there were weavers; Emindal cloth was said to be the finest in the world.

"I thought they didn't get involved in our battles," Jerret said.

"They don't, usually. But I wrote to their leader, Pentethe, and she invited me."

She, Jerret thought. Well, that made sense. "Isn't there any way you can stay here?" he asked. "If you go you'll leave the field clear for Norue—he'll take the kingship without opposition."

"I know. But now that he's seen I'm not the fool he's taken me for he'll try even harder to kill me, and this time I'm certain he'll succeed. There are so many ways to die—poison, strangling, accidents, knives . . . I can't anticipate them all. And from Emindal I might be able to gather an army and return."

"Yes, I see that. May I—would you—" He stopped; he was not normally this tongue-tied. He left his chair and knelt before her, holding out his sword hilt-first. "Milady, I would like to go with you, and serve you to the best of my ability."

She looked taken aback at first, her good eye as empty of expression as her bad one. Then she smiled. "I would like that very much. Though I should warn you that if you join me you'll be called all sorts of things—traitor will not be the worst of it. And it won't be easy—most of the people at court are loyal to Norue, and will not accept a queen in Karededin. We may never be able to come back."

"I know all this already, milady. Will you accept my service?"

"Yes." Her smile grew broader, and her one clear brown eye gazed at him levelly. Once again Jerret noticed how beautiful she was despite the ravages to her face. "But I can't knight you—you're a knight already. Stand up, please, and put your sword away."

He stood and returned to his seat. "Thank you, milady. When will you be ready to go?"

"Not for a while yet. I'll need weapons and food and ships—"

"I can help you with that."

"And I have to rally my men as well. That's something no one else can do for me—that was why I took the chance of going into the city yesterday. And I'll need to plan an escape from Pergodi—I'm afraid it may be weeks before we can leave."

"Well, let's get started now, then." Jerret stood and brought an old scraped parchment and a pot of ink over to the table. "Tell me what I can do."

Rodarren looked past him, her eyes widening in alarm. Lord Snoppish headed toward them.

"This is my father, Lord Snoppish," Jerret said, trying to sound reassuring.

"Yes, my wife told me about our distinguished guest," Snoppish said. He bowed stiffly to the princess, an old man's bow. "What are you writing there?"

"We're going to Emindal," Jerret said. "We have to get out of Prince Norue's reach, and to prepare our troops."

"We?" Snoppish asked, frowning.

"Yes. I'm in service to the princess now."

Snoppish's frown deepened. Suddenly Jerret felt like the greenest of his troops, an eager young man who knew nothing of the battlefield.

"Norue will kill her if we stay here," Jerret said. "It's the only way she can be safe."

"Yes, I understand that," Snoppish said. "But exile . . ."

"I'm sorry," Rodarren said. "I don't mean to put you in an uncomfortable position. I know Norue will make things difficult for you if he learns you're giving me shelter—"

Snoppish waved his hand. "It's not Norue I'm worried about—I've been in trouble with him before. It's just—be careful, son. Your mother and I worry."

"I will," Jerret said, returning to his parchment.

Their journey back through the forest was shorter than their journey outward had been, Mathewar thought, almost as if the forest wanted to spit them out, to get rid of them.

He turned to say this to Angarred, then stopped. Something odd had happened between them the last few days. She had become quiet, distant; along with her beauty it made her look regal, like a statue in the Hall of Standing Kings.

He didn't know why she had changed. She had withdrawn from him around the time he had had a strange dream about Embre, and he wondered if the two were connected. The dream had been very different from his usual nightly horrors, wonderfully so: in it his wife came back to him, alive again; she ran her fingers through his hair and assured him that everything would be all right. He had nearly laughed with joy. Why in the name of the Godkings had he thought she was dead when he could feel her here with him, when he held her in her arms?

He thought the woman had been taller than Embre, though, and with more tangled hair, and sometimes he had an uneasy feeling that it was Angarred who had comforted him. It frustrated him that he couldn't remember, that the events of the night were hidden behind a haze of sattery. Had he said or done anything to offend her? He was used to forgetting things; it had caused some awkward moments. But if he had transgressed in some way then why in the name of the Orator didn't she say anything?

He'd felt aroused, too, by the dream or whatever it had been. Sattery drinkers could take lovers, of course, but for the most part they didn't want to. Why strain yourself for a few minutes of pleasure when you could simply have a drink and experience hours of unfailing delight?

He hadn't minded this; he'd wanted to keep his distance from women, had not wanted to tarnish Embre's memory. No, truthfully it was more than that: he had tried to steer clear of people, to avoid the inevitable pain and disappointment they caused. Now he felt he was waking up again, moving toward others, caught in their orbits, and he didn't like it. He had worked hard to blot out the world, to keep everyone and everything at bay.

Well, none of it really mattered. He'd seen other sattery addicts and he knew that in a few years he would be taking the drink several times a day, and that a short while later he would be dead. He would not have to worry about Embre or Angarred or anyone else. His story was over; nothing more would ever happen to him.

They had gone through the wall in the early morning and were now riding through Pergodi. He glanced around him, noticing all the changes that had taken place in the past month. People looked anxious, strained. Businesses were closed, in places even boarded up; signs on taverns and market stalls announced that they were out of fish, or venison, or fruit; soldiers walked the streets; and a good many Pergodek went armed, carrying everything from ancient swords to kitchen knives.

Once they heard a loud boom and they both flinched, but no one around them seemed at all bothered. It was a catapult, Mathewar realized; the Takekek had managed to build a catapult under the city walls. Their own soldiers should have fought back, loosing arrows at the builders, but probably Alkarren had kept the king from giving that order.

Suddenly Angarred brightened and waved to a man ahead of them. She urged her horse forward and dismounted; the two hugged and then stepped back, studying each other.

"Angarred!" the man said. "Where were you, by the Navigator? We missed you at court."

"You did, maybe," Angarred said. "I'll bet no one else even noticed I was gone. This is Lord Jerret Snoppish," she added as Mathewar rode up and dismounted.

Mathewar had already guessed as much. As he studied him he realized how he and Angarred must look to this fancy courtier, their faces filthy, their clothes grimy and torn from a week and a half of hard travel.

"And Jerret, this is—" Angarred hesitated.

Mathewar tried to read Jerret, but like all courtiers his mind was too well guarded. He took in Jerret's open, hospitable expression, unfazed by their appearance. The only honest man at court, Angarred had called him. Well, he would have to trust her judgment.

"Mathewar Tobrin," he said. He held out his hand and they shook.

"Good to meet you," Jerret said. "Did you travel with Angarred? You look as if you've been on a journey, but how did you escape the siege? What—I don't even know what questions to ask!"

"Let's go to your house," Angarred said. "We'll talk about it there. We have some things to ask you as well."

Jerret hesitated. Good, Mathewar thought. He has secrets too. To listen to Angarred the man never put a foot wrong, never let anyone down. "All right," Jerret said finally.

They made their way to Jerret's father's house and settled their horses in the stable. "I should tell you—" Jerret began as they headed toward the back door. "I—we have a visitor. Princess Rodarren."

"Rodarren!" Angarred said.

"Yes. She's not as she seems."

They went inside and headed toward a private room. Rodarren sat by an empty fireplace, her eyes closed. She opened them at the sound of footsteps and half-stood, looking with alarm at Jerret's two companions.

"Don't worry," Jerret said. "These are friends."

Another round of introductions began. The three of them sat in the Snoppishes' old comfortable chairs, Mathewar realizing only then how tired he was from the journey.

They told each other their stories, leaving little out. Rodarren described Norue's attack on her when she was nine years old, and how she had disguised herself ever since. Angarred related her tale of seeing Alkarren control King Tezue, and Mathewar told them about the College and the masters' advice.

For the first time in over a year Mathewar felt a part of something larger than himself. The others felt it as well; he didn't need the Clear Sight to see that. In just a few hours they had become a group, a company, companions facing dangers together. The sense of excitement among them was palpable, almost a fifth presence in the room. It was another form of awakening for him, but one he didn't mind. It had nothing to do with him; he had no stake in the outcome.

Bells rang in the street at midafternoon. Finally Angarred reached the point of their visit. "I think you have the Stone, the one Alkarren was looking for," she said, blunt as always. "We need it to free the king."

And Jerret faced her with the same forthrightness. "We do," he said. "Let me get it."

He returned carrying a wooden box and passed it to Mathewar. "Be careful," he said.

Mathewar took out a rough green-and-black stone small enough to fit in his palm. There was something odd about it, almost sickening; he felt nauseated, as if he had gone without sattery for a while. But at the same time he saw its power, saw how it radiated outward, touching everything, connecting everything in its path. He understood how Alkarren had been tempted: the Stone could give him the power and mastery he coveted, all he ever wanted. And he, Mathewar, he could use it to take his revenge on Alkarren, as he had come to Pergodi to do.

He turned it over and over in his fingers. "Is this like the Stone you saw?" he asked Angarred.

"Yes. Almost exactly."

"But how can that be?" Jerret asked. "I never heard that there were two Stones."

"How did it come to your family?" Mathewar said.

"Our roof collapsed one night fourteen years ago," Jerret said. "There was a terrible storm, lightning and thunder—it sounded as if people were walking on our roof, those giants you spoke of. Everything in our attic came tumbling down, old furniture and boots and winter apples from our estate—and this. We have no idea how it got there."

"But how did you know what it was?"

"There was a parchment wrapped around it which told us. But I think we would have known it anyway—the thing had a power we all felt. Sometimes—sometimes when we touched it we saw pictures of things which had happened, or were about to happen. We used our knowledge to rise in court—we could never have gone this far on our own, could never have played the complicated courtiers' games." Jerret turned to Angarred. "That's how we learned about Norue's treachery, and your father's part in it."

As he spoke a picture formed before Mathewar's eyes, the scene that had haunted his dreams for so long. He put the Stone back in its box and set the box on a table, his fingers trembling slightly. "You speak of it in the past tense," he said.

"Yes. There was something wrong with it—we all felt it. We realized that we were not magicians, that we did not understand its workings. And my father was very sorry he got involved in Norue's plots and counterplots—he had liked your father, I think." He nodded to Angarred. "We all agreed never to touch it again."

"You were wise, I think," Mathewar said.

"How did you hide it from the men who searched your house that day?" Angarred asked.

Jerret laughed. "Do you remember that my mother had gone upstairs? She pretended to be ill and had gone to bed, and she took the Stone with her. Alkarren's men never suspected her, and even if they had they would have feared contagion and left her alone."

Angarred laughed with him. "And here I thought your family was so honest."

"We are, for the most part. But we know not to let the Stone fall into anyone else's hands—they would be too tempted by its power."

"We still don't know which is the true Stone," Rodarren said. "This one has power, but so does Alkarren's, or he wouldn't have been able to make Tezue into a Hollow One."

"But there's only the one Stone," Angarred said. "Isn't there?"

"It broke in two," Mathewar said. They all turned to him. "That's the only explanation. This Stone is too small to fit in the place waiting for it at the College. And if Alkarren has only half the Stone that would explain why he hasn't worked more destruction. Even he should have been able to draw more power from it."

"That's another question we had," Angarred said. "Why did Alkarren use the Stone to open the gates to the Takekek soldiers? And if he was working with them, if he wanted them to come in and conquer us, why did he let the king raise an army to fight them?"

"The council is making these decisions now," Jerret said. "We've taken over leadership of Karededin during the king's illness, and we voted to muster the army."

"That must have made Alkarren angry."

Jerret nodded. "I wonder if he took over some of the councillors, made Hollow Ones of them as well. There's a man on the council, Lord Enlandin—you might have seen him at court. He's one of the prince's men, always votes whatever way Norue tells him to. But at the last council meeting Enlandin came in on the side of the king—fortunately, because Norue wants to be regent during Tezue's illness, and with Enlandin he would be able to do it. Perhaps Alkarren's taken him over and is using him to keep Tezue in power—he would lose his control if Norue takes the throne."

"Enlandin was very rude to me, as I remember," Angarred said. "He's probably a better person as a Hollow One."

Jerret laughed. "In a way this could all work for the best. Norue and Alkarren each want power—they can frustrate each other and leave the rest of us to get the business of the council done."

"Yes, but Alkarren may take over the council as well as the king," Rodarren said. "Anyway, the realm can't be governed this way, by those who want only personal power. It needs someone who sees farther than that, who puts the good of the people first." She looked at Mathewar. "Do you think you can challenge Alkarren using this Stone?"

He remembered his boasts to the masters at the College, and he knew that a little over a year ago he would not have hesitated. He had not understood then what it was like to fail. Now it seemed as if he understood nothing else. The fear that had kept him company for so long uncoiled in his stomach. "I—I don't think so," he said. "He's had the Stone for so long, more than a year—I'm afraid he knows far more about it than I do."

Rodarren frowned, and he went on quickly. "I might be able to free the king, though."

"How?" she asked. "If the Stone broke, as you say, wouldn't you need both halves?"

"Maybe. But I also have a spell from the College. I can try, anyway."

"How will you get to him?"

"I'll go through the corridors Angarred found. That is, if she'll guide me." He turned to ask her and she looked away, more coldness.

"Yes, good idea. When do you think you'll be ready?"

"Tomorrow, perhaps. But first I need to get some sleep. It's been a very long day, and a long journey."

"Of course," Jerret said. "I'm terribly sorry—I wasn't thinking. We haven't even eaten—you must all be hungry. Would you like some supper? And you can stay the night here if you like, stay as long as you like."

"I'd prefer to go back to my inn," Mathewar said. Now it was his turn to avoid Angarred's gaze, knowing she would guess his reason: that he wanted to drink his sattery alone.

"But if you're tired—" Jerret said.

Anger nearly overcame him: would this man never let him go? Would they trade polite phrases until Marfan and Mathona established their Celestial Court here on earth? He forced himself to smile, to answer quietly. "Thank you, but no. I'll come back tomorrow—we can make our plans then."

He stood and tried to still the shaking of his hands as he lifted his pack. It would be easy to dislike Jerret, he thought as he left. Jerret was the good son in every story he had heard as a child, the perfect knight in every courtly song. And he thought he had seen something between Jerret and Angarred, though admittedly except for the Clear Sight he hadn't been at his most observant this past year.

Well, it didn't matter. Nothing mattered, save getting to his inn.

FOURTEEN

Angarred accepted Jerret's offer to stay the night. She and Jerret and Rodarren ate cold meat and drank wine, and then she took a bath, sinking into the warm water with deep pleasure, scrubbing away the dirt from the journey. When the water grew cold she dressed herself in a nightgown Jerret had found for her, left behind by one of the sisters, and went down the hall to her room.

It was the room she had stayed in on her last visit: the same soft pile of feather blankets, the same wind whistling through cracks in the wall. The noises of the city sounded loud after the silences of the forest, and she turned uncomfortably, trying to sleep. There was too much to take in from their discussion: the reason Lord Snoppish knew about her father's treachery, the attempt they would make to free a Hollow One tomorrow . . .

And she would spend another day in Mathewar's company, when she'd thought they would go their own ways at the end of their journey. A part of her felt anxious to leave him; his rejection of her still rankled, and if they never saw each other again she thought she might forget him eventually. Her desire for him had only grown stronger as they rode through the forest, after that extraordinary moment when he had held her under the trees. No wonder she'd

been so happy to see Jerret, a man who was honest and uncompli-
cated and didn't carry his dead wife around with him.

Sometime before dawn she dreamed that Mathewar gave her the
Stone; that it turned to blood, or sattery, and dripped from her fingers; that it was his heart; and she woke with a cry of terror.

To her surprise Mathewar was already eating breakfast with the
others when she came downstairs. He was fresh-shaven, his hair
tied back; he wore his usual rough serviceable clothes but they were
clean as well, probably new.

"We thought you should wear a dress of my sister Arys's," Jerret
said to her. "If someone sees you you could pretend to be returning to court."

"What if they see Mathewar, though?" she asked.

"I'll disguise myself," Mathewar said. "I'll pretend to be your
servant."

Her heart pounded. They were really going to do it, then. They
were going to match their wits and strength with the most dangerous magician in the country. A besotted magician, a one-eyed
woman, a woman who had lost everything she ever had, and half a
Stone . . .

No, she shouldn't think that way. All of them had skills, talents;
it would come right in the end. And if it didn't . . . if it didn't she
had nothing to return to anyway. Still, she could eat nothing; her
throat was dry and she couldn't swallow.

Jerret brought out Arys's dress and a heavy topaz-and-silver
necklace. The dress was dark purple velvet, with purple lace at the
neck and wrists. She went back to her room to put it on, slipped
the necklace over her head, and then tied her hair back as best she
could, in some semblance of the knot fashionable at court.

She and Mathewar went to the stable for their horses, then
headed out toward the castle. "I'm terrified," she said.

"Yes," Mathewar said.

He looked deadly serious, his mocking expression gone. He
knew what she meant, then. She was glad of that at least.

They continued on through the winding streets of Pergodi. She
tried to keep her mind on the road ahead of her, on the task they
had to do, but every so often she would glance over at him and

remember running her fingers through his hair, or see the fluid way he moved, and she would force her mind away, disgusted with herself for giving in so easily to distraction.

They said nothing the rest of the way. As they approached the outer gate Mathewar's hair grew dull and he began to stoop, and he pulled out a cap and set it low on his forehead. The guard at the outer gate remembered her and nodded as they rode inside. They settled their horses in the stable and went into the castle.

Angarred led them away from the Hall of the Standing Kings and the Great Hall, to a deserted room she had found on one of her explorations. It had a secret entrance like the one Gedren had shown her but was farther from the heart of the castle; there was less chance of their being discovered here.

Mathewar exclaimed softly as she pressed the lever within the fireplace and a door in the wall swung open. She closed it behind them and they went into the hallway beyond; he fashioned a dim light and she walked on ahead.

They came to a place where two corridors crossed and she went left, toward the king's apartments. Then there were more junctions, more choices; she continued on, guided by Mathewar's light.

Once she turned back to look at Mathewar. He was carrying the box with the Snoppishes' Stone; green and black light seeped through cracks for a few feet before being swallowed by the gloom in the corridor. It looked uncanny, somehow wrong; and as they went deeper into the corridors she thought it grew in intensity, until finally it eclipsed the light Mathewar had made.

They took one last turn. Several small lights shone out ahead of them, each one marking a spyhole. She hurried on, toward the one that led to the king's rooms.

She peered inside. The king sat there. He wore his royal robes, his gold-and-ruby crown, but his face was vacant and he seemed nearly crushed by the trappings of his office. There was no one in the room with him, no messengers to carry his orders and proclamations, no courtiers to fawn over him or make him laugh.

Mathewar took the Stone from the box. The sickly light grew. He spoke the spell the masters had given him. Then he added in his commanding voice, "King Tezue, awake! Awake and look around you, take back your kingdom!"

Tezue blinked his red-rimmed eyes and slowly turned his head, studying the room. "What—" he said. "Who—Alkarren? Alkarren, come talk to me."

His voice quavered and sounded hoarse from long disuse. No one outside the room could have possibly heard him. He stood heavily, muttering, and went to a rope and pulled it. "Alkarren!" he called, louder this time. "Where are my servants, my men? What is happening here? Come to me at once!"

Angarred looked at Mathewar, jubilant. They had done it; they had saved the king. Mathewar stood unmoving.

"What is it?" she asked softly.

He turned to her. He looked stricken, disbelieving. "It was that easy," he said. "It was that easy all along, and I never knew—"

"What? What was that easy?"

He seemed not to hear her. "Come, we'd better go," she said. "The king's men are going to be here any minute. And you should put the Stone back in the box."

They headed back down the corridor. "What was that easy?" she asked again. "Did you try to free a Hollow One before?"

"My wife," he said, only then putting the Stone away. "My wife and my daughter. When Alkarren stole the Stone every magician in Karededin vanished, terrified of what he might do. Everyone but me—I was arrogant, always so stupidly arrogant. I thought I was a match for him.

"And then—and then my wife and child, Embre and Atte, they began acting odd, different. At first it was just little things—they would say something they would never have said before, and Embre—Embre lost interest in gardening, and Atte stopped riding her horse . . . I sought out Dalesio where he was hiding then and asked his advice. He told me he thought they had become Hollow Ones. But I looked at them with the Clear Sight and I couldn't see it, and the Clear Sight had never failed me before.

"Weeks passed, and their behavior grew worse. Sometimes, briefly, I saw their eyes grow pale, colorless, or their teeth become long and black, though I tried to convince myself I imagined it.

Sometimes, in the middle of a conversation, their faces would turn vacant and they would speak gibberish.

"Finally even I couldn't ignore the changes any longer. And then I got a letter from Alkarren, telling me he would free them if I would help him master the Stone. I asked Dalesio back to our cottage, and he—and he—"

Mathewar stopped and leaned against a wall. "He had to destroy them, he said. There were no traces of them left, just empty shells. I begged him not to, I told him I was certain they weren't Hollow Ones, but he spoke the spell to show their true nature. And they turned—they turned into dreadful things, serpents and monsters, and then, at the end . . ."

He took a long breath. "At the very end they became themselves again. They pleaded with me for help, they begged me not to kill them. They told me I was making a terrible mistake. But Dalesio had gone too far with his spell—I could do nothing but watch in horror as he called up their deaths. That's what I see every night in my dreams—not monsters but my wife and child, holding their arms out to me, looking terrified, and puzzled too, wondering why I want to kill them . . ."

"Holy Godkings," Angarred breathed.

"And I still don't know. I don't know if they had become Hollow Ones or if I killed my own wife and child, if Alkarren had enchanted me in some way to make me believe they had changed . . . If only I'd gone to the College . . . but Dalesio seemed so certain . . . if I'd gotten the Snoppishes' Stone . . ."

"You didn't know. You didn't know they had a Stone. You couldn't do anything other than what you did."

"And then, when it was too late, I disappeared along with the others. I ended up at your father's house, thinking that no one would ever look for me there. But when your father died I became certain Alkarren had found me and I fled to Pergodi, determined to get revenge for my family."

"And you did. You released the king from Alkarren's grasp. He can't—"

"No," Mathewar said. He seemed to be listening for something. "Oh, no."

"What is it?"

"Run. As fast as you can."

"But what—"

He grasped her by the arm and thrust her in front of him. She began to run. "Faster," he said. "Hurry."

His light kept pace with her. She turned corner after corner, moving as quickly as she could, infected by Mathewar's urgency. The corridors all looked identical, the same narrow passages, the same rough stone walls. She stopped, trying to get her bearings.

"Move," Mathewar said.

"I don't—"

"It doesn't matter. Hurry!"

She ran. She was utterly lost now; she seemed to have gone through the same hallways several times. Once she heard water running, somewhere in the walls. Once the passageway opened out onto a courtyard and a dry fountain walled up by some king years ago, and she exclaimed in amazement.

"Go!" Mathewar said.

"I *am,*" she said. She ran past the fountain, making for the opposite wall, trying to see a door by Mathewar's light. She found one and plunged through it, and then they were back in the passageways again, turning and circling, lost. Her side hurt, and her breath came in ragged gasps.

Suddenly she saw a light up ahead. She ran toward it, hoping she had not imagined it. It was a spyhole. She looked through it and saw Rodarren's room, no one there now. She knew where she was. She hurried on, turning left and left again, then went a long straight way, panting.

Finally she reached the room they had come through earlier. She fumbled for the lever and pulled on it, and the secret door opened. She stepped out carefully.

Bright light hurt her eyes, but it was only daylight, not the lamps of guards sent to capture them. Mathewar came out after her. "What was it?" she asked.

"We can't stop now. Jerret's house. Quickly!"

They ran outside to the stable, mounted their horses and galloped down the hill. Once on the streets of Pergodi they had to slow to a walk, blocked every few feet by people and carts and stalls. Surely they were safe now, she thought, among all these people and houses. She turned to Mathewar but he shook his head, looking grim, and then studied the streets behind him carefully.

Jerret and Rodarren were waiting for them at the house. "What happened?" Rodarren asked. "Were you successful?"

"Yes," Angarred said, but at the same time Mathewar said, "I don't know."

"But we were," Angarred said. "I *saw* him—I saw the king. He stood up and called for Alkarren, for his men—"

Mathewar sat in one of the chairs. "I don't know," he said again. "As we were leaving I sensed Alkarren's presence. I don't know how long he'd been there—perhaps it was the entire time, perhaps he saw everything. Perhaps when the king seemed to break free of the spell Alkarren was still controlling him, making him act, pulling his strings—all so that we would believe that Tezue is no longer ensorceled."

"No," Angarred said. "No, Tezue looked far better, more alive—"

"Alkarren could have made him seem so—such a thing is not at all beyond him. And I know he became aware that there was magic somewhere in the castle—I felt him, though I don't know if he recognized me. And even if we were successful, if we did free the king, we still stayed far too long in the corridors, allowing Alkarren to find us. Once again I underestimated him." He shook his head. "I still think of him as a doddering schoolmaster. I still can't imagine him capable of the magic he's done with the Stone."

"But why did he make his presence known to you?" Angarred asked.

"He didn't. He made a mistake, he didn't hide himself well enough—and thank the Godkings that he's still capable of mistakes."

"What do we do now?" Rodarren said.

"I'll go to court and keep watch on King Tezue," Angarred said. "I'll see if he's changed, if he seems to make his own decisions now."

"You might not be able to tell," Mathewar said.

"Well, you can come too. You can watch from the spyholes—"

Mathewar shook his head. "I have to leave Pergodi. It's too dangerous for me here—Alkarren might be aware of me. If you don't mind, Princess—" He turned to Rodarren. "—I'd like to come with you to Emindal."

"Are you offering me your services?" Rodarren asked.

"Yes."

"Then I accept, with pleasure. I could certainly use a good magician—for one thing I'll need a diversion when I leave Pergodi. Something unmistakable, and loud."

"I can do that," Mathewar said. "I may not be able to stand against Alkarren, but I don't think I've lost my talent for explosions."

She turned to Angarred. "You can come with me too, if you like," she said. "You might not be safe at court."

Mathewar looked at her. She knew he expected her to agree; she had gone through the Forest of Tiranon on almost as thin a pretext. But she felt too uncomfortable in his company; she had to leave him and go her own way.

"No," she said. "Someone needs to watch King Tezue, as I said."

She returned to her rooms in the castle after their discussion. She couldn't sleep again that night, haunted by Mathewar's story. It explained nearly everything: his silences, his need for sattery, his dislike of Dalesio. And instead of cooling her desire for him it enflamed it. It made her pity him along with everything else; she wanted terribly to be the one to make him forget, to make him happy. And at the same time she knew that he would hate her pity more than anything in the world.

But the thing she thought of most, the thing that stayed with her as she fell into sleep, was his hand grasping her arm as he told her to run; she thought she could still feel it there, strong and urgent.

FIFTEEN

Norue said nothing more to Labren during their stay in Takeke, but several times he saw the prince's slate-colored eyes rest on him speculatively, and he knew that Norue was trying to guess how much he had heard. He entertained wild ideas of running away, of bolting headlong over the mountains and plains toward Karededin. The only thing that stopped him was the knowledge that he would be killed without the flag of truce.

The journey back to Karededin was a nightmare. The other men sang and boasted and talked about what they would do when they got home, even Hallen, who had recovered surprisingly quickly. Labren walked apart from them and thought of death or imprisonment or torture. He would not stand up to torture, he knew—he would confess everything.

After several weeks they came to Pergodi and marched through the Tornish Gate. Norue led them to the outer castle walls, then called for several blue-cloaks from the guardhouse and dismissed all the soldiers except Labren. The others looked back at him, puzzled or worried. A few were even envious, thinking Labren was about to receive a bonus or a promotion.

"I'm almost certain you heard nothing in that cursed castle," Norue said, drawing his sword, "but I can't be sure. You're going to prison, young man, and you'll get a visit from my torturer when I have the time to arrange it."

Labren felt nearly too terrified to walk. The blue-cloaks grasped him by the elbows and steered him through the courtyard and into the castle. He took a few deep breaths and forced himself to think. He could jab the guards in the gut and run—but Norue still walked behind him, his sword out.

They passed through hallways he had never seen, then went down several flights of stairs and through yet more corridors. The air grew colder as they descended. Norue stopped at a door with a guard sitting by it. "Good afternoon, Prince Norue," the guard said. At a command from the prince he led them into a huge dark chilly room.

"That one, I think," Norue said, pointing to a rusty iron cage. There were several other cages around the room, and iron rings set into the walls. A man stood in one of the cages, rattling the bars and calling out to Norue. The prince ignored him.

The guards shoved Labren into the cell, and the jailer locked him in. "I didn't hear anything," Labren said weakly. "I didn't, really."

"I'm innocent too," the other prisoner said. "Prince Norue, please . . ."

Norue glanced at the other man, then looked again, studying him through the gloom of the prison. His eyes widened. Labren had the feeling that they knew each other, but for some reason the prince did not acknowledge him.

"Milord, please . . ." the prisoner said.

Norue turned away and left with his guards. Labren sat in his cell and began to shiver.

Gedren was on her knees washing the floor when she recognized Prince Norue's richly embellished shoes. She looked up to see him walk down the corridor, followed by his usual circle. For the first time in her stay at the castle she welcomed his presence. Labren had said that he would be leaving with the prince's company; he must be back too, then. It would be wonderful to see him again. And she could make another attempt to talk him out of the army; she had

had great misgivings when she heard he had left Lord Jerret for Norue.

She hurried through her chores, eager to get home. When she finished she did not join the others for supper but headed outside and down the hillside. The autumn evenings had grown dark and chilly but her brisk walk warmed her, that and the thought that she would see Labren soon.

The lights were out in the bakery, and the front door closed. She went around to the family's quarters at the back and used her key to get inside. Borgarrad stood in the kitchen, washing dishes.

"Hello, Borgarrad," Gedren said. "Where's your brother?"

Borgarrad turned. "Labren? He's still with Prince Norue's company, as far as I know."

She felt the first prick of fear but continued on. "But—but the prince is back. I saw him today."

"I don't know, Mother," Borgarrad said, his expression softening. "All I can tell you is that he didn't come to the bakery, and I've been here all day."

She sank into a chair. Her mouth had gone completely dry. "Oh, holy Godkings," she said. "What—where could he be then? Did you hear anything about—about fighting? Norue's company fighting the Takekek, or anyone else?"

"No."

"Well," she said, trying for lightness, "he's probably still out with the company, celebrating their return."

"I'm sure that's it. Don't worry, Mother—as I said, I didn't hear anything about deaths in Norue's company."

She felt exhausted. She wished Borgarrad wasn't so blunt, but she knew he had never had much imagination; if he felt certain of a thing then that was the way it had happened.

How did the army deliver news about . . . She couldn't bring herself to even think the word. "I'll come here every day after work. I want to see him when he gets home."

"I'd like to see him back too. It's not easy here, with everyone gone. You know, last year I had a family, and now I'm the only one in the bakery all day. I'm thinking of taking on an apprentice . . ."

The fear that Gedren had been trying to banish burned through her again. Borgarrad's words—"Last year I had a family, and now I'm the only one"—sounded like a portent, some kind of evil prophecy. It still seemed impossible that their once close family had scattered, the Godkings knew where.

She tried to pay attention; her older son needed her as much as the younger one. She listened to his complaints and made a few suggestions about running the bakery, and then, exhausted, she climbed the stairs to her old bedroom.

Once alone, though, she was haunted by her missing loved ones. No, she thought, getting ready for bed. No, I won't lose another one. The Others may have gotten Dalesio, but I'm going to find out where Labren is.

She knocked twice on the headboard to avert misfortune and then climbed into bed, already dreading the long sleepless night ahead of her.

As the days passed and Labren didn't return Gedren realized that she had to ask Prince Norue what had happened. The prospect terrified her. Like everyone else in the Craftsman's Quarter she had been raised to defer to those with titles, and she knew that commoners did not start conversations with noblemen. She had defied this rule only once, with Lord Jerret; and even though what she said then had benefitted him, not her, it had been hard enough to find the courage to begin. The Orator alone knew how the prince would receive her.

She would go to Lord Jerret if she could, but these days he came to the castle only to attend council meetings; he seemed to spend the rest of his time at his family's house. The courtiers gossiped endlessly about what he was doing there: he was dallying with a woman, most of them agreed, but who?

Gedren saw Angarred through the spyholes nearly every day, but she looked anxious, as if she feared something terrible would happen. Anyway, Angarred had little power in the castle; she was certainly not the person to go to for help.

It took her three days to gather her courage to approach Norue. She watched him through a spyhole, and finally, when she saw him about to leave his room, she hurried out into the corridor to meet him. She curtsied deeply as he came toward her.

"My lord prince," she said.

He walked past her as if he hadn't seen her. She stood and stared after him, at first astonished at his rudeness and then shaking with anger; she had to bite her lips to keep from shouting at him. "A fine fellow," someone said mockingly behind her.

She turned and saw Angarred. "Oh, Lady Angarred," she said. "Maybe you can help me."

"What's wrong?"

"It's my son, Labren. He went off with the prince's company and never came back. I don't know where he is. Did you hear— did you hear anything about fighting, about soldiers—"

"No, I didn't. I hear very little, though."

"Can you ask Lord Jerret?"

"Of course. Don't worry—we'll find him."

"Thank you," Gedren said. "Thank you, milady."

That evening Jerret went back to the prisons to talk to Ranle. The guard let him in and he turned immediately to the cage. It was empty.

"Who removed the prisoner in this cage?" he asked the guard.

"I don't know, milord," the guard said.

"You don't know?" A rare anger moved through him. "Well, find out. Now."

"No, I mean no one knows. The man on duty that day died the day after."

"How did he die?"

"He was killed, milord. Stabbed on the street, and his belongings taken." The guard shook his head. "Whoever it was didn't get much, that's for certain."

Whoever it was had orders to kill him, Jerret knew. Someone had been a step ahead of them all the way.

A shape in another of the cages stirred. "Lord Jerret," the shape said, standing. "It is you, thank the Godkings. Please—I need your help—"

Jerret nearly ignored him, used to people petitioning for his aid. Something about the voice made him look closer, and to his shock he saw Labren in the cage. It was a Labren greatly changed, though: filthy, unshaven, shivering, and without his usual plumpness. He had wrapped himself in a stained blanket but it hadn't seemed to warm him.

"Labren!" Jerret said. "What are you doing here?"

"Come here, milord," he said. "Please."

Jerret went forward into the gloom of the prison. "Prince Norue put me here," Labren whispered, glancing at the guard. "I overheard something—you have to tell King Tezue—Norue made an alliance with Takeke to attack Karededin."

"What!"

"Hush. You can't trust anyone—I found that out. Tell—" A fit of shivering overtook him, and he broke off.

"You're coming with me," Jerret said. "Guard! I'm taking this man out of the prison. If anyone asks you can say it was Lord Jerret Snoppish who took him—I'm not playing any shifty underhanded games."

The guard headed toward the cage, a ring of keys in his hand. "You shouldn't have told him who you were, milord," Labren said. "It's dangerous."

"Everything's dangerous," Jerret said.

The guard unlocked the cage and Labren walked unsteadily toward Jerret. Jerret got his arm around him and together they moved toward the door. A horrible smell surrounded the boy, but Jerret tried to ignore it.

By the time they reached the stairs Labren could walk by himself. Still, he seemed to take hours climbing the two flights, and Jerret hoped fervently that Prince Norue wouldn't suddenly decide to visit his prisoner.

It was only at the top of the stairs that Jerret realized he had no place to take the other man. He couldn't go home; Rodarren was there, and she had trusted him with the secret of her whereabouts. Labren seemed harmless enough, but it was as he had said: you couldn't trust anyone.

"Where do you live?" Jerret asked.

"The Craftsman's Quarter, milord."

"Which Craftsman's Quarter?"

Labren blinked. "Is there more than one? Near the Waning Moon Bridge."

Jerret looked at him, amazed he knew so little about the city he lived in. The Waning Moon Bridge was a long way away, and when they left the castle Jerret saw that it was night out, and cold, with dark scudding clouds; they would have to hurry. He roused one of the blue-cloaks in the guardhouse and told him to ready a cart for them. Labren shivered through the entire journey, though Jerret had given him his cloak. At the Waning Moon Bridge Labren directed him through small crooked streets until they came to a bakery, its lights off and its front door shut tight against the darkness.

"Around the back," Labren said.

They left the cart and walked slowly to the back. There were no lights here either. Jerret pounded loudly on the door.

After what seemed like a long time a wavering light shone in an upstairs room. They saw the light disappear, then reappear on the ground floor and head to the door. "Who is it?" a man said.

"It's—it's Labren."

"Labren!" The door opened wide. A tall stolid man grasped Labren and held him against his chest. "Mother! Mother, Labren's here!"

A woman hurried downstairs. The room suddenly seemed full, everyone except Jerret hugging each other and exclaiming and finally dragging Labren into the kitchen.

"I don't know how to thank you, milord," the woman said to Jerret. "Sit down, please."

He knew her, he realized. Of course—Gedren, who worked at the castle and who had told him about Alkarren's plans. "It's I who should thank you, for coming to my family's aid," he said. "I'm only glad I was able to repay a little of what I owe you."

The tall man, who seemed to be named Borgarrad, had gone over to the hearth and was heating something—apple cider, it smelled like. "Well, I should be going," Jerret said. "I'm sure you have a lot to talk about. And Labren could use some sleep."

Labren shook his head. "I have to tell you," he said. "Tell you about Norue."

Jerret understood; the boy wanted immediate vengeance against the prince. But Jerret didn't think he could help; as always Norue had planned everything meticulously, careful to let nothing lead back to him. "Did you see who freed the other man in the cage?" Jerret asked, sitting with the family at the table.

"No," Labren said, taking a sip of hot cider. "I'm sorry. I was asleep. I think Norue knew the prisoner, though."

It wasn't enough as evidence, unfortunately. "Well," Jerret said. "Tell me what happened."

As Jerret listened, shocked, Labren told him the story of Norue's deceit and treachery. Jerret had seen the terrible things that people could do to one another and had heard of even worse, but even he had never guessed that Norue would be foul enough to plot with his country's enemy.

"And you—what will you do now?" Jerret asked. "Norue will be searching for you once he discovers you gone."

"I still want to fight for Karededin," Labren said. He tried to grin. "Especially now that Norue's sided with Takeke."

"What?" Gedren said. "You've just escaped the prisons, all thanks to the Godkings. You could have been killed, or—or worse. You're staying here until Norue's forgotten he ever met you."

Labren ignored her. "I'd like to rejoin your company," he said to Jerret.

"Labren," Gedren said. "It's a sign from the Spinner. You're not meant to be a soldier. Stay here, and if you don't like the bakery we can talk about it, think of something else you can do—"

"I'm a soldier, Mother," Labren said. He turned to Jerret. "What about it? Will you take me back?"

"I—I'll be going away for awhile," Jerret said. "My command will probably be taken over by someone else."

A terrible look of hurt appeared on Labren's face. "Don't tell me you're going to make an alliance with Takeke, too," he said derisively.

"No. No, of course not. But—but I can't tell anyone where I'm going."

"You'll need a guard, won't you? Someone to watch out for you?"

Jerret was silent a moment. Perhaps he should invite Labren to join Rodarren's company, to come with them to Emindal. But no—the boy wanted to fight for Karededin, for King Tezue. He might see no difference between Norue's alliance with Takeke and Rodarren's with Emindal; both would be equal treachery in his eyes. He could say nothing to Labren about his plans.

"It's a secret errand, I'm afraid," he said. "I can't take anyone with me. Anyway, your mother's right—you should probably stay away from the fighting, at least for a while. Norue will kill you if he sees you."

"What if I kill him first?" Labren's grin was stronger now. "I'm a soldier—that's what I do. I can't think of anything I'd rather be. Anyway, it's wrong what Norue's doing, isn't it? I want to stop him—I want to be on the right side, doing the right thing."

Jerret studied the boy. Had he ever been that idealistic, that certain? He had just had the same conversation with his father, but at least he understood what he would be getting into, understood what war was like. "Very well," he said. "I can recommend you to another commander. But be careful, for the Spinner's sake."

Labren looked hurt again. "I know that," he said.

SIXTEEN

Finally the day came when Rodarren and her company would leave Pergodi. Jerret and Angarred, following the plan they had made, went to the Great Hall, Angarred wearing a dress that the dressmaker had just finished. "Very nice," Lady Karanin said, looking her up and down. "Is that new?"

Jerret watched with admiration as Angarred kept her temper. "Yes it is," she said. "I'm so pleased you like it."

He hated to leave Angarred to the mercy of the courtiers but at that moment the herald walked into the hall in his mismatched shoes, carrying the banner for the council meeting. Bells in the castle rang two hours past dawn, and he and the other councillors filed out.

Once in the council chamber Norue managed to take the chair at the head, as he had done for the last several meetings. As they had planned Jerret hurried to sit beside him. Lady Karanin and Lord Enlandin took places next to each other. Jerret studied Enlandin surreptitiously. Was he truly a Hollow One? He looked and acted exactly as he always did.

When all six of the councillors had found seats the two scribes took their places discreetly at the foot of the table. Prince Norue led the council in a prayer to the Balance, invoking his aid as lawgiver, and then began the meeting. "I'm sure I don't need to tell you how precarious our position is," he said. "And I'm not just talking about the siege of Karededin—I'm afraid I have some very bad news for the council." He looked around at the councillors and scribes, even sparing a glance for the guards at the door. "Princess Rodarren is missing. I'm afraid she's gone over to the enemy."

"No!" Lady Sorle said. "How could she? She can't even make the simplest plan—"

"She's far cleverer than we ever guessed," Norue said. "She waited patiently all these years, and then betrayed us."

"Do you mean she played the fool for thirty years?" Sorle asked.

"As I said, she's clever," Norue said. "It's possible she even took the Stone herself."

"How do you know this?" Jerret said, wondering how far Norue would go with his lies.

"I have my spies," Norue said. "Well, there's nothing we can do about her now. But I urge all of you to keep an eye out. And go to the watch if you spot her—as we've seen, she can be very dangerous."

"Speaking of Takeke," Jerret said, "how did your negotiations with them go?"

"I'm afraid the Takekek refused to parley. I didn't think they would, but I wanted to give them every chance at peace before we showed them what we're capable of. But we have to move quickly. Every day the siege lasts we're forced to consume valuable food and wood. We need a plan, and someone who can put that plan into action. We need a strong, experienced man at the helm, a man who knows what to do in war. At the last meeting I attended you refused to make me regent during the king's illness, foolishly, in my view. Can I hope that one of you has finally come to your senses and changed your mind? Lord Enlandin?"

Enlandin shook his head firmly. "Come, Norue," Lord Tarkenin said. "We've already voted on this. What about our strategy against Takeke? That's what we should be talking about."

Someone outside the council chamber spoke to one of the guards. The plan's begun, Jerret thought, his heart pounding. He hoped his face, usually so easily read, gave nothing away.

The guard argued with the other man. The man persevered and was finally ushered into the chamber. He handed Jerret a piece of paper. Jerret opened it and pretended to read.

"What's that?" Norue asked, straining to look over Jerret's shoulder.

"I'm afraid I have to leave," Jerret said, standing. "I have some urgent business to take care of."

"*What* urgent business?" Norue asked.

"Nothing you need concern yourself with. Please, continue the meeting without me."

"Let me see that," Norue said, taking the note from Jerret's hand. "'Takekek attacking at Tornish Gate,'" he read. "Why didn't you want me to see this?"

"I didn't think you should waste your time. I can take care of it, as I said. You're needed here, in council."

"You wanted the glory all for yourself, more likely. Well," Norue said, standing, "it looks as if we'll have to finish this later. I'll be at Tornish Gate with my company if anyone needs me."

Jerret and Norue left together. How is Angarred doing? Jerret thought anxiously. Her part of the plan is harder than mine. I hope she's safe.

Angarred looked out over the Great Hall. Most of the noblemen had exchanged their decorative weapons for great incised scabbards they wore at their hips. Her new friends had told Angarred the lineage of some of these swords: they had been passed down through families for dozens of generations, some of them going as far back as the Sorcerers' Wars.

The courtiers' minds seemed elsewhere now, the feverish splendor of the court subdued. Many of the important players at court had gone to the council meeting; there was no one left to fawn over and flatter, or to impress with witty comments.

Finally she spotted Alkarren, standing in a corner and talking to a minor lord. She wound her way toward him past groups of people, hiding her cold hands within her skirts, trying not to look as frightened as she felt.

As she came closer he turned toward her, but there was no

recognition in his eyes. "Be very careful," Mathewar had said. "Don't approach him if he seems to know you, and for the Spinner's sake hide your thoughts from him."

"I'd like to speak to you, milord," she said.

"Would you indeed?" Alkarren said. His black eyes under their overgrown eyebrows studied her closely. "Come with me then—I need some air."

He moved past her, walking quickly for such an old man, and out into the corridor. She hurried to follow. His staff rapped against the marble floor but it was clear he didn't need it. He led her through hallways and courtyards she had never seen before. The torches on the walls broke into light as he approached and quenched themselves after he passed.

Finally he opened a door. Sunlight streamed in; she blinked at the sudden brightness, then hurried outside after him.

Dozens of cages lay spread out on a vast lawn, each one holding a different exotic animal. A lion roared, padding back and forth in its confined space. Monkeys squealed and hurled themselves against the bars of their cages. An elephant lifted its trunk and trumpeted. The rich smell of raw meat and dried grass and dusty pelts drifted out from the grounds.

She stood still, astonished. She had never seen any of these animals outside of books. Their cries grew loud and raucous as she and Alkarren began walking between the cages.

They stopped in front of a giant cat with spotted tawny fur. "Have you ever been to the menagerie before?" he asked.

"No," she said. Her heart pounded against her ribs like the monkeys beating against the bars of their cages. "I—I never even knew it was here."

"I come here when I need to get away from the court. What did you want to speak to me about?"

She faced him squarely, with no idea of what she was going to say next. "I wondered if you knew how the king is. If he seems to be recovering."

He said nothing. Her heart beat louder; it seemed impossible that he didn't hear it. "Talk to him," Mathewar had said. "Keep him occupied, keep his attention elsewhere."

"Do you know someone named Mathewar?" Alkarren asked, running his hand through his white beard.

"I—no. No, who is he?"

"Never mind. I thought I sensed him near you, but I must have been mistaken. It's terrible growing old—your mind doesn't work as well as it used to." He peered at her. "The king, yes. He does seem better. He'll be able to sit in council soon, I think, and rule again. We won't have to see that odious nephew for a while. Don't worry," he said, laughing at her sudden nervousness. "No one ever comes here—we're free to say whatever we like. Only our friend the leopard can hear us."

Who had said something about leopards? "Is that what that animal is? A leopard?"

"Yes. Look—she has the same red-gold hair as you do."

Now she remembered—Queen Chelenin had said that Angarred reminded her of a leopard. She studied the animal doubtfully. It stopped its pacing and opened its mouth in a mute snarl, its ears up.

"I feel sorry for Prince Norue, in a way," Alkarren said.

"Why?"

"He's out of his depth. He wants to be king but he has no idea what it's like to govern. If he ever does rule Karededin, which the Spinner forbid, he'll impoverish the country. Or worse."

"But he'll succeed King Tezue, won't he? Everyone knows Rodarren can't—"

He seemed not to hear her. "I know a little of what that's like—to want something and then find yourself incapable when you finally get it. The study of magic is a difficult road, very difficult. Do you know anything about the College?"

"No. Well, only that it's where people go to learn about magic."

To her surprise her voice was steady. Mathewar had shown her how to keep her thoughts hidden, and fortunately it had been a simple skill to learn; Mathewar said that most people did it without even being aware of it. But surely Alkarren could read her, could rip away her lies to get at the truth beyond. And if he had the Stone . . .

"Yes, that's right," he said. He smiled, abstracted and slightly puzzled, as if he looked into the distant past and saw something he did not fully understand. For the first time he showed his great age. "I arrived there as a boy, oh, many many years ago. And the course of study proved far harder than I expected, almost too much for me. But I persevered—I worked at it while the other boys were out playing, I studied long into the night . . . There were other students, then and later, who learned more quickly, who were praised by the masters and made much of, but they couldn't keep it up, you see. They burned out like shooting stars while my fire grew steadily brighter and brighter. That's how I became a master, and why I was chosen above everyone else to be the king's magician. And now there's no one in all the lands who can stand up to me."

He's talking about Mathewar, Angarred realized, shocked. He ruined Mathewar's life, and he's proud of it. And he really thinks he did it all himself, that he had no help from the Stone at all.

He stopped and frowned at her from under his bushy brows. "Did you tell me your name? I haven't seen you at court before, have I? You're very kind to listen to an old man reminisce, who- ever you are."

"I'm Lady Angarred Hashan, milord."

The puzzled look came over his face again; he seemed to be try- ing to remember the name. Her fear returned; she still did not know if he had had anything to do with her father.

"Ah, Lord Hashan's daughter," he said. "Why did you ask about Tezue?"

She repeated her story about her father's death. Alkarren nodded sagely as she spoke.

"Do you think you can help me, milord?" she asked when she had finished. "Could you speak to King Tezue about justice for my family?"

"I'll see what I can do," he said, stroking his beard.

She shuddered, suddenly realizing the implications of what she had asked. If he had made Tezue into a Hollow One his help would be tainted, a foul thing. She did not think he would speak to the king, though. He seemed more interested in finding out what she most desired, in case he could use it in some way.

But he was still speaking. "I hope I'm not keeping you from anything," he said.

"Oh, no," she said. "It's all been terribly interesting. Do you know the names of all these animals?"

"Yes, of course."

"I'd be honored if you'd show me around the menagerie. It's all so unfamiliar—I've never seen any of them before today."

"Certainly, my dear." For a horrid moment she thought that he was about to give her his arm, but he leaned forward on his staff and they began to walk the paths between the cages.

Mathewar stood in a high tower overlooking Tornish Gate, one hand holding Lord Snoppish's Stone. A battle raged outside the gate, a confused melee of Takekek and Karedek soldiers.

He was enjoying himself, though he would never admit that to anyone. He had created all the Karedek soldiers and sent the illusion out onto the field to clash with the Takekek, who were no doubt wondering how their enemies had managed to come through the heavily guarded gate. His mind was stretched to the utmost. He had never worked anything this complicated, not even at the College: keeping every soldier whole and solid and making certain all the shadows matched, moving the troops in response to Takekek attacks, calling up the sounds of screams and the clash of sword on sword. Even the sickening touch of the Stone barely bothered him.

Voices reached him over the dim noise of battle. Jerret and— yes, it was Norue. Jerret's plan had worked, then: the prince must have insisted on joining the battle.

Mathewar grinned and raised a soldier's sword to parry an attack. Dark green fire sparked along the sword's edge; he was relying on the Stone's power too strongly. He frowned in concentration and the fire disappeared.

The great gate opened, no longer guarded, and Karedek troops rode into battle, Jerret and Norue at their head. A Takekek soldier hurried off in the direction of Solinay Gate, no doubt to seek reinforcements.

The battle swirled around Tornish Gate. Mathewar exploded a stand of trees near some Takekek troops, and in the confusion some of Jerret's and Rodarren's men slowly retreated. Smoke and flame billowed up over the battlefield, cloaking more men and allowing them to slip back toward the gate.

After about twenty minutes the Takekek rider returned, leading a marching line of men. Solinay Gate was unguarded now. Mathewar whistled loudly. The rest of Jerret's and Rodarren's men ducked back through the gate into Pergodi, closing it behind them, leaving Norue's troops and the false soldiers to fight the Takekek alone. Mathewar's illusions dissolved into air as he ran down the tower stairs.

He mounted the horse waiting for him and rode north with Jerret and Rodarren and their men. They traveled through small back streets and alleys, their way crowded with carts and people. Everyone stepped aside for the soldiers, but even so they moved far too slowly. At any moment Norue might realize that Jerret's men were no longer there, or Alkarren might scent the tang of magic in the air and recognize Mathewar.

They reached Solinay Gate and burst through it, then followed a neglected path rough with rocks and tree roots. Finally, at dusk, they came to the ocean.

The boat was drawn up in an inlet as they had planned, tied to a tree. They gave their horses to waiting men, and then the boat rowed Rodarren, Mathewar and Jerret and some soldiers out to the ship that would take them to Emindal.

"We did it!" Jerret said, exultant. The sun laid a glittering trail before them, sinking below the horizon. "It all went perfectly, every part. I knew Norue would come with us, especially if he thought that someone else was about to gain glory. And even Alkarren stayed away—he doesn't seem to have noticed our magic."

"Let's hope not," Mathewar said. "I wonder what Angarred did to distract him."

"Can I have the Stone back?" Jerret asked.

"What? Oh, of course." Mathewar reached into the pack at his feet and gave him the wooden box. As Jerret took it Mathewar felt his dislike of the other man return—did Jerret think he was not to be trusted with the Stone? By what right did Jerret claim it, other than the fact that it had practically fallen on his head?

They reached the ship and climbed a rope ladder to get aboard. The small boat returned to shore for more people. "Where is my room, do you know?" Mathewar said.

"I thought we'd have supper, celebrate our victory," Jerret said.

The man was as bad as Dalesio, Mathewar thought. "I have a few things to do first," he said. "I'll join you later."

Jerret stared at him curiously. Mathewar had never hidden the fact that he drank sattery, had never cared what people thought of him, but something about Jerret made him decide to keep it secret from the other man.

"I suppose you can take any room you like," Jerret said. He seemed about to say more, but Mathewar hurried away.

They saw Emindal long before they reached it, a jade green island rising up out of gray water. The island's central mountain reared higher and higher above them as the days passed, and they began to see waterfalls coursing down its flanks, inlaying the green with silver. As the waterfalls roared down toward pools or the sea a great mist rose up, veiling the base of the island.

They entered the port along with gaily painted vessels flying colorful flags, and saw men and women unloading the wool and silk and cotton that would be made into the famous Emindal cloth. Several people greeted them as they stepped off the ship, delegates from Pentethe herself. "Would you see her now, or would you rest here?" one of them said in halting Karedek. "It is a great climb up the mountain."

"We'll see her now, please," Rodarren said.

The guides shrugged and led them to a wide pathway, and they began the ascent. The green they had seen from the ship turned out to be a lush growth covering the mountain: great trees, shaggy stands of bushes, wild roses and blackberry brambles near the path.

On their left they could see a waterfall, dropping from height to height but always leading down and down. The steady roar of water sounded in their ears.

They passed small cottages set into the trees; people sat at the windows looking out over the forest and worked at something with their hands. "Weavers," the Karedek speaker said.

They climbed for several hours. The day was mild but they soon grew hot, and most of the men stopped to take off layers of clothing. Gnats whined around them, sometimes landing on their skin, and were waved away with tired hands. Every so often a welcome breeze brought a spray of water from the waterfall.

Mathewar felt a dim surprise that he could keep up with the others, that he could do the climb at all. He was twenty-eight, no longer young, and had been indolent for over a year. Once, in the time he thought of as *before,* he had worked hard, speaking spells for the king and then coming home to chop wood for his family, or play with Atte, or climb to their roof to hammer in a new piece of lumber. But the strength he had gained during those times would last at most another few years.

He reminded himself that it didn't matter, that in a few years he would be dead. The thought usually brought nothing in its wake, neither joy nor sorrow; but for the first time he felt a small tendril of regret. It would be interesting to follow the story to its end, to see who triumphed, Rodarren or Norue, and whether Tezue managed to free himself from Alkarren's control, and why the giants were massing, and what Angarred did next . . . Well, there was no help for it now.

Finally they reached a clearing at the summit of the mountain. Eastward, below them, Emindal fell away to the ocean, the base of the mountain once again hidden in a haze of mist. More mountains reared their heads behind them. A good-sized village of wooden cottages lay scattered haphazardly across the clearing.

Several women came out of the cottages. The one in the lead reached Rodarren and grasped her hands. "Welcome to Emindal," she said in nearly unaccented Karedek, smiling. She was a plump woman; soft curls of light brown hair had escaped her head-covering and floated around her face. She wore a robe of Emindal cloth with a complex pattern of silver stars and moons on a dark blue background. "I'm Pentethe."

"Thank you for granting us shelter," Rodarren said.

Pentethe and her women showed them to their lodgings, light, airy rooms in several of the cottages. "Your journeying is over, for a while," she said. "Rest for an hour or so, and then we will have supper in the main house."

Once again Mathewar saw Jerret looking at him curiously. And once again, he thought, he would live up to whatever bad opinion Jerret had formed of him—he would not be present at that supper.

SEVENTEEN

More of the courtiers spoke to Angarred now, and drew her into their circles. Part of it was her apartment and new clothes; the nobility made much of appearances. But the most important reason seemed to be her apparent friendship with Alkarren; because of it she had become an important player in the court's games.

And she *had* grown closer to the magician, much to her surprise. She hadn't forgotten what he had done to Mathewar and to King Tezue, but ever since their talk in the menagerie she understood him better. He had been a lonely child, envious of the other students; it was no wonder that he sought a way to make himself stronger, to triumph over them.

Of course that did not excuse the deaths of Mathewar's wife and child. Or the control Alkarren once exercised over Tezue, control he perhaps still had.

A few weeks after Rodarren's party sailed away King Tezue came into the Great Hall, accompanied by his guards and body servants. He greeted several courtiers by name, Lady Karanin and Lord Enlandin among them, and spoke quietly to others. He looked confident, almost arrogant, though his body was still wasted by illness. The long strides he took about the hall seemed the movements of another, healthier man.

Finally he noticed Angarred. "And who is this?" he asked. "I haven't seen you here before, have I?"

"She's Lady Angarred Hashan," one of the courtiers said, eager to be of service to the king. "Lord Hashan's daughter."

"Hashan, is she?" Tezue said. "The traitor?"

"Yes, milord," Angarred said quickly. "But I am loyal to the king, and no traitor. I came to get justice for myself and my family."

Tezue turned his red-rimmed eyes on her. "How do I know that you're not a traitor? That your father didn't include you in his wretched schemes?"

"I was four years old, milord."

"Ah, but you're not four now, are you? Did he feed you on tales of King Tezue, the man unfit to rule?"

"No, not at all. He—"

"And where is he now?" The king looked around the hall with some of his old uncertainty. "He didn't come back to court, did he, after all the prohibitions I placed upon him? He wouldn't be that great a fool, would he?"

"No, milord. He's dead."

"Dead. Well. Sorry to hear it."

"He was killed with an arrow while out hunting."

"Should be more careful, shouldn't he? The man never did know how to hunt."

"He was assassinated—the killer was hired by someone. And another killer came back and threw me down the stairs."

Tezue glanced at a knot of courtiers, his attention wandering. "I want justice, milord," Angarred said desperately. "Justice for him, and for myself. No one has the right to assassinate a lord of the realm."

"Yes, well. Unfortunately I have greater affairs to attend to. The war, isn't that right?" His eyes settled on Alkarren. "I don't have time for these trifles. Maybe later . . ."

His voice trailed off. He gathered his robes together and swept out of the hall.

Angarred watched him go, her heart sinking. Was he merely senile, or under the control of someone else?

"You must know he will never take up your cause," a voice said at her shoulder. Her muscles jumped, but she schooled her face to show nothing as she turned.

Prince Norue stood there. "How do I know that, milord?" she asked, her heart pounding.

"Because your father was a traitor. And kings do not give ear to the daughters of traitors."

And so are you a traitor, she thought, remembering what Lord Snoppish had told her. "Nonetheless I must ask for justice," she said. "Lords cannot be killed with impunity, not even the least of them. If one is killed, where will it end? Who will be next?"

"Not I, that's for certain," he said. She realized to her horror that he thought she had threatened him. "Speaking of traitors, though, I wonder if you know where Lord Jerret has got to."

"No, I'm afraid not."

"Surely he said something to you. You and he were great friends, isn't that so?"

"He didn't tell me anything. I'm as puzzled as you are, milord."

"We've traced him to an inlet, a small bay. He seems to have sailed from there. We've found a few people who helped him. They haven't told us much, but we haven't had the intimate conversations yet."

She tried not to shudder at the euphemism for torture. "And if you had anything to do with his disappearance we'll talk in earnest with you as well," he said.

"I told you, milord—"

"Yes, yes, you told me. Did you know he may have taken Princess Rodarren with him? And that the princess may have stolen the Stone?"

Fury rose within her at the man's outrageous lies, and it was only with an effort that she was able to reply with a semblance of courtesy. "No, I hadn't heard that. But she's half-witted, isn't she? How could she have taken the Stone?"

"Never mind that. Do you know a magician named Mathewar?"

Here was another shock. As far as she knew Prince Norue had never had any dealings with Mathewar. "No, milord," she said.

"No? I've heard different." He stroked his bony chin. "Well, as long as you stay out of the affairs of your betters you should be safe enough. These things are far beyond the wit of a simple provincial from Lake Sar, or wherever it was you came from. It's dangerous to play the game if you don't even know the rules."

"Yes, milord," she said. To her relief he nodded to a group of courtiers across the hall and began to make his way toward them.

As soon as he left she began to tremble. She excused herself and headed for the door.

"Mathewar, is it?" someone said as she passed.

She turned quickly. A bored-looking woman stood there, her blond hair up in elaborate curls. Angarred searched her memory for the woman's name. She had met her on her first day at court . . . Lady Dorilde, that was it. Dorilde Enlandin—she had since learned that the woman was Lord Enlandin's wife.

"Lady Dorilde," she said politely. "We haven't seen much of you at court."

"Oh, I only come to look for interesting men," Dorilde said.

Angarred tried not to show her surprise. She knew, of course, about the intrigues between men and women that went on all around her, but court etiquette dictated that no one ever mentioned them, that everyone pretended to be as truly married as Marfan and Mathona. She had never heard anyone speak so openly.

"You look shocked," Dorilde said. "I suppose someone raised in the country would be unfamiliar with the way we do things here. Most of us have arranged marriages, you see, and we quickly grow tired of our spouses."

"You'd be surprised what goes on in the country, milady."

Dorilde laughed. "Speaking of interesting men," she said, "did I hear you say you know Mathewar?"

"No," Angarred said. What in the name of all the Godkings did this woman have to do with Mathewar? "I don't know why people think that—I never met the man."

"Ah, well. I hear his wife died. I do wish he'd come back from wherever he's got to."

This time Angarred could not contain her outrage. "Whoever he is, I'm sure he's still in mourning for his wife."

"She was very common, I hear. A washerwoman—Emme or Embre Washer, something like that. Still, magicians don't have arranged marriages—perhaps he truly loved her. Perhaps he's in mourning, as you say. What a pity."

She had to change the subject, Angarred thought, or she would do irreparable harm to this woman. She remembered Jerret's and Mathewar's suspicion that Enlandin was a Hollow One and asked, "Have you spoken to Lord Enlandin lately?"

"Oh, no—the man's so terribly boring. All he talks about is the council—who said what, who sided with whom. Why—are you interested in him? You certainly have my permission."

"No. No, I thought—well, he seemed a little strange the last time I saw him."

"Oh, he's always strange. I wouldn't worry about him. Well, I should go. If you do hear from Mathewar please let me know."

Angarred left the Great Hall, her fists clenched within the folds of her skirt. So many people had wounded her in precisely the places she was vulnerable—Tezue and his lack of interest in her cause, Norue and his threats, Dorilde and her disturbing hints about Mathewar . . .

As she went to her apartments she isolated one worry, one phrase running over and over through her mind: "a provincial from Lake Sar." How in the name of the Navigator did Norue know where she came from? She knew he had been keeping watch on her, but she hadn't realized how far he had delved into her life.

She knew only one remedy for fear, and that was anger. How dare he threaten her like that! She had important friends, important knowledge—she would show him how well a provincial could play the game. She thought of something Mathewar had said, and an idea came to her. She grinned.

The next morning she entered the secret corridors and went directly to the spyhole overlooking the council chamber. The council was meeting that day, but without Jerret they had degenerated into quarrels and bickering. Norue's faction now held the majority, three members to two, but the two in the minority refused to accept any changes without a full complement of the council.

After long argument they decided to elect someone to replace Jerret. Angarred smiled grimly in satisfaction. They would never be able to agree on a candidate; they would stay in the council chamber for the rest of the day.

She went back out the secret entrance and headed toward Norue's apartments. No one she knew passed her in the hallways; there were only servants, going quietly about their tasks. A while ago she had gotten a master key from Gedren, and now she unlocked the door to Norue's rooms.

"I suppose I could always search through Norue's papers," Mathewar had said at the College. Perhaps he had been joking, but to Angarred, barred at every turn by hints and secrets, forced to live within the rotting glitter of the court, his suggestion seemed to be the only means left to her.

She had not brought a lantern; she knew from watching the prince that his apartments were lit by great mullioned windows facing east. Once inside, though, she could see more of the rooms than the spyhole had shown her. They were full of beautiful things: tapestries and carved chairs and a bed canopied in Emindal cloth. In one room she found shelves displaying golden plates and goblets made of alabaster inlaid with silver.

Everything shone as if freshly cleaned, sparkling in the golden sunlight. And yet it seemed as if no one ever used these rooms, as if no one lived there. She could see no trace of Prince Norue at all.

Perhaps that was why he wanted to be king, she thought. He seemed not to know who he was; perhaps he thought that if he were king he would be someone, would become visible, would have a crown and a robe.

She dismissed her thoughts; she was not here to enter the mind of someone as distasteful as Norue. A table stood in one corner, with shelves filled with paper above it, and she headed toward it.

She took down a pile and began to read. Expenses, lists of income from his lands, letters in an unfamiliar language, Takekek, probably. The next pile held a letter from Norue's tailor asking for payment, more lists of expenses and, at the bottom, a goodly number of petitions from workers on his estates.

She brushed her hair from her eyes and reached for more. At this rate she would be here reading for the rest of the day, and she couldn't be certain when the council meeting would end. Suppose Norue got angry and stormed out? Suppose—the Godkings forbid—the councillors actually reached a compromise?

Time passed as she brought down pile after pile; she had no idea how much. Finally she stopped, startled at discovering a sheet of paper covered with familiar handwriting. Her father's.

Someone spoke outside, and someone else laughed in response. The first voice was Enlandin's, she realized—the council must have ended. She looked around fearfully, as if Norue were already in the room with her, then grabbed a handful of papers and stuffed them down the front of her dress.

The voices passed. She waited a moment and then opened the door to the corridor and peered out cautiously. Two men turned a corner to the hallway, too far down to see who they were. She slipped out the door and walked toward them, her mind racing.

It was Norue and another man, Lord Tarkenin she thought, heading toward the prince's rooms. She moved slowly, trying to appear unconcerned. As she neared them she nodded politely.

"What are you doing here?" Norue asked.

"I—I'm afraid I got lost," Angarred said.

"You got lost. By the Navigator, where were you headed that you ended up here?"

"To the menagerie, milord."

"The door to the menagerie," Norue said, drawing out his words as if speaking to an idiot, "is at the end of a corridor a good distance to your left."

"Yes, milord. As I said, I got lost."

"Permit me to doubt that. And I had better not find anything missing from my rooms."

"There's nothing I'd want in your rooms."

Norue studied her closely, his suspicions evident. For a moment she thought she had gone too far. Then the prince continued down the hall without another word.

"Good day, milord," Angarred whispered when he was too far to hear her. Her knees shook, and she began to walk briskly to drive away her tremors.

Every instinct told her to run. She headed toward her apartments as slowly as she could, alert for guards or any unusual movement. Finally she reached her door. She closed it behind her and dragged one of the chairs in front of it to make certain no one could interrupt her. Then she went to the hearth and, by the light of her small windows, she struck a flint to make a fire. Her fingers were trembling so badly it took her three or four tries before she managed it.

She lit a candle from the fire and took out the pages she had stolen, riffling through them until she found the letter from her father.

"My dear Prince Norue," it said, "I am writing to tell you that a magician has joined my household, a man by the name of Mathewar Tobrin. I am assured by those who know these things that he is one of the greatest in the realm. It is time to invite me back to court or, with the help of my household magician and some information you and I both know, I will confront King Tezue and the council. Most sincerely, Lord Challo Hashan."

She sank into the chair, closing her eyes. So that was it, she thought. It had been Norue all along. He had not bothered with Hashan for fourteen years, had not thought Hashan strong enough to worry about—until the lord claimed to have a magician. Then Hashan had become dangerous, very much so.

But had Norue been after her father or Mathewar? Her father, she thought, both the Hashans, because Norue had tried to kill her next. His spies must have told him that Mathewar had left—though the message must not have reached him in time to prevent the attack on the stairs. And when she had come to court Norue had seen how harmless she was, how ignorant, and had decided to leave her alone.

To leave her alone but to watch her, she thought. She would have to be very careful with what she said to the prince; she could not make the slightest mistake. She prayed to all the Godkings that he wouldn't notice the papers missing from his room.

That afternoon she changed into her riding clothes and headed toward the Snoppishes for supper. No one spoke to Lord and Lady Snoppish any longer; they were tainted by Jerret's actions, his supposed treachery. No one but Angarred, who still considered them her only friends in Pergodi now that Chelenin was dead. She had to be very careful when she visited them, though; she had seen blue-cloaks watching their house more than once.

As she rode she saw long lines of people snaking back from some of the stores. Very little of that year's harvest had come through the gates; at the Snoppishes' they ate bread and fish and the few canned vegetables that had somehow remained untouched over the spring and summer. For the most part the people stood in their places quietly, but here and there fights broke out over something as small as a loaf of bread.

A beggar ran alongside her horse. "Money, milady?" he said. "I was a butcher, but there's no meat in the city . . ."

"I'm sorry," she said.

"Miserable Two-names," the butcher said and spat after her, no doubt thinking that someone who rode a horse must also have untold wealth.

Only Lord and Lady Snoppish were at supper, and she told them what she had discovered after they had eaten. "You went into the prince's rooms?" Lady Snoppish said, pleasantly horrified. "I could never have done that."

"I doubt that, Lady Snoppish," Angarred said. "Jerret told me how you hid the Stone from Alkarren's soldiers. That certainly took courage."

Lady Snoppish blushed with pleasure. "Your father must have been desperate, claiming to have a household magician," Lord Snoppish said. "Surely he knew Prince Norue would act, given a challenge like that."

"I don't know," Angarred said. "I don't know what he thought. He'd become stranger and crazier over the years."

"Well, as you say, you have to be careful," Lord Snoppish said. "Don't give Norue the slightest hint that you know Mathewar. It's fortunate Mathewar's gone away—that should make it easier." He frowned; Angarred knew he worried about Jerret, and wished that his son had stayed home.

"Though it's too bad he took the Stone with him," Lady Snoppish said. "Perhaps it could have protected you."

"Princess Rodarren needs it far more than I do," Angarred said. "Anyway, only a magician can use the Stone, I think. I wouldn't know what to do with it."

"Are you certain of that?" Lord Snoppish said. "We were able to use it a little. It showed us pictures . . ."

"Yes, Jerret told us," Angarred said. "Wait. Jerret said there was a parchment wrapped around the Stone. Do you still have that?"

"Do we, dear?" Lord Snoppish asked his wife.

"Of course we do. Somewhere. Oh, dear . . . I think I remember."

She left the table and went upstairs. "That *was* odd, now that you mention it," Lord Snoppish said. "The parchment said a number of things I didn't understand. Something about a bridge . . ."

"One of Pergodi's bridges?"

"I think so."

"Do you remember which one?"

Lord Snoppish shook his head. A few minutes later his wife came clattering down the stairs, holding a piece of paper.

"Found it!" she said. "It was with my underclothes, as I thought."

She spread it out on the table and they all bent to look at it. The top edge was frayed and jagged; a piece had been torn off, long ago, from the look of it. The handwriting curled and looped back on itself in the manner popular hundreds of years ago.

". . . the Stone of Tobrin," it said. "Keep the Commandments of Magic. Climb the Giant's Bridge to seek the Answers to your Questions, at the Place where Live Stone calls to Dead Stone in the south of the City. All Peace to the Possessor of this Stone."

"The Giant's Bridge?" Angarred said. "I never heard of that one."

"Neither have I," Lord Snoppish said. "There are only six bridges in Pergodi, you know, an even number for good luck. No one knows why it's called the City of Seven Bridges. There's the

Bridge of the Summer Stars, the Waning Moon Bridge, the Two Sisters Bridge . . ."

"The Spiderweb Bridge," Angarred said.

"The Crying Madwoman," Lady Snoppish said. "Oh, and the Leaping Dog Bridge. There you are. Six."

"Could the Giant's Bridge be the seventh?" Angarred asked.

"It certainly could be," Lord Snoppish said. "But if it is, where is it?"

"Live Stone calls to Dead Stone," Lady Snoppish said. "That reminds me of something, but I can't think what it is. Well, I'll sleep on it—maybe it will come to me in the morning."

Angarred stayed at the Snoppishes' that night, after carefully watching for blue-cloaks. By breakfast Lady Snoppish had remembered her errant thought. "There's a cemetery in the south of the city," she said. "The only one left in Pergodi—all the others were moved outside the walls as the city grew. That could be the dead stones—the tombstones—and the live stone could be, well, the Stone of Tobrin."

"Or the bridge, if it's made of stone," Angarred said.

"Yes. It seems unlikely, now that I've said it out loud. But it's the only thing I could think of."

"I can visit the cemetery, I suppose," Angarred said. "We could certainly use answers to our questions."

"Wouldn't you need the Stone? The Live Stone?"

"Maybe. Unless the Live Stone is the bridge, as I said. Well, I could have a look—I can't lose anything by trying."

"Today?"

"Why not?"

After breakfast Lady Snoppish insisted on giving her a generous portion of her homemade wheat cakes for the journey. "The Navigator travel with you and guide you," Lady Snoppish said as she left.

I can't impose much longer on their hospitality, Angarred thought miserably, going to the stables and getting her horse. They're stretched to the limit as it is.

The day was dull and overcast. Despite that, the journey south reminded her of the last time she had come this way, with Mathe-war. Well, everything reminded her of Mathewar. She wondered what he was doing. She had thought—had hoped—that when he left her desire for him would fade away, would heal like a fever, but it remained as strong as ever. She felt as if she had been struck by lightning, every part of her on fire; and yet the lightning had gone on, unconcerned, leaving its damage behind.

She passed the Craftsman's Quarter, and then the Godwife House. This time she saw more long lines of people waiting patiently for food, and more beggars. And, alarmingly, she noticed fewer stray cats and dogs on the streets; people had already started using them for meat.

She reached the southern walls without finding the cemetery, though she spotted the house she and Mathewar had gone through when they left the city. She got directions from a passerby and con-tinued along the wall.

The booming noise of the catapult sounded. She looked at the parapet, hoping to see archers shooting down at the Takekek sol-diers. Only a few women stood there, pouring boiling water from cooking pots, and they fled when a rain of arrows came toward them.

A while later she found the cemetery. She dismounted and looked around. There was no bridge anywhere in sight, though the cemetery sloped down to a rocky, swift-flowing tributary of the Pergodi River. Tombstones covered an area about the size of her father's manor: ancient-looking lumpish stones, eroded by rain and covered with copper-green moss. Some leaned dangerously or had fallen to the ground.

She bent to examine one of them. The writing was too faded to read, though she could make out the same archaic, looping strokes as in the Snoppishes' parchment. She straightened. No help there, she thought. Well, she hadn't expected much to begin with.

She caught a glimpse of something as she moved, a darkness over the river against the gray of the sky. She looked directly at it but it was gone, if it had ever been there at all. She glanced away. Yes—there it was again, a smudged black line arching out over the river.

She walked toward it, her eyes carefully fixed on a group of tombstones. The line grew broader, more solid. Without thinking she looked at it again, and it disappeared.

Once again she advanced toward it, keeping it at the edge of her vision, and once again it appeared over the river. It was definitely a bridge, made of black stone and stretching out high above her, as befitted a structure built by giants. Surely other people had seen it over the years; why had the Snoppishes never heard of it?

She reached the edge of the river and the base of the bridge. Then she stopped, unable to move. She couldn't climb it; it would never hold her. The bridge wavered and began to fray into air.

That was the trick, then. She had to believe that a real bridge stood before her; if she thought for an instant that it was an illusion it would collapse. Now she realized why no one had ever spoken of the bridge; they had given up, unable to climb it. And perhaps they were right; perhaps it wasn't a bridge at all. She had to admit that the idea of walking out above the water terrified her. She would never be able to do it; she would doubt, and fall to the river to die on the rocks.

She had to, though. And others had done far braver things; at this very moment, perhaps, Jerret and Mathewar and the rest were fighting off Norue's forces. She took a deep breath and stepped onto the bridge, steadfastly looking at the houses on the other shore.

The bridge held. She continued to climb. Halfway up she saw something at the top of the arch: two black statues, she thought, sitting back to back. Her eyes remained fixed on them a moment too long; the bridge seemed to disappear, and she caught a glimpse of running water beneath her. She wrenched her eyes away and set her foot down on nothingness—and felt solid stone. Her heart shaking like a leaf, she continued on.

She became aware of the sound of the river, rushing below her. She remembered the rocks she had seen, the terrible rapids, and could barely move one foot in front of the other. Finally she dropped to all fours and began to crawl.

As she went she stole glimpses of the statues at the top of the bridge. Her first impression had been correct: two great figures sat there, one facing her, the other looking away toward the opposite shore. They loomed above her, growing larger as she drew closer.

"What questions have you?" a booming voice said.

Shocked, she looked straight ahead. The statue facing her had moved; it was now staring directly at her. The bridge seemed to soften, to give way, and she hurriedly glanced to the side, away from the statues.

"I have many questions," she said. Her voice trembled. "I would like to know—"

"Come, don't waste our time," a different voice said. "Quickly, quickly."

"Why are there two Stones?" she asked, the words tumbling out as fast as she could speak them.

"There are three Stones," the first voice said. Now she could hear that the first was male, the second female.

"Three? But why—" Faster, faster, she thought desperately. "Why are there three Stones?"

"The Stone of Tobrin broke into three pieces," the female voice said—they seemed to take turns.

"When—" No, she didn't care when it had happened. "Who has the third Stone?"

"The giants."

"When did the giants get the third Stone?"

"Fourteen years ago."

The Others take it—she didn't care about that either. She had to think. "Why did Alkarren open the gates of Pergodi to Takeke?"

"He wants to create chaos."

"Why?"

"He is forced to. He is becoming a Hollow One."

Alkarren, a Hollow One? "Who made him a Hollow One?"

There was a long pause. Finally the statue—it was the male's turn now—said, "We do not know. We cannot see."

"But why does his—his master want chaos?"

"They want to conquer all the realms. They want country to fight against country, and the people to exhaust themselves, so that they can step in when everyone is defenseless and rule all."

"Why do they want to rule?"

"We told you—we do not know who they are. We cannot tell you that."

Did she hear impatience in the male's voice? She felt she could not bear to stay on the bridge any longer. In her confusion she could not think of another question, though she knew she must have many more.

"Thank you," she said. She stood quickly and ran back down the bridge.

EIGHTEEN

Mathewar woke to a knock on his door. A voice called, "We're meeting in the main cottage in an hour," and then footsteps went on down the hall.

An hour later he walked into the meeting hall in the largest cottage. Rodarren and Jerret were already there, along with a number of the Emindalek he had met yesterday, all of them seated at a great table in the center. A woman entered, her dress, a complex pattern of red-and-orange squares and triangles, sweeping out behind her.

"I'm afraid Pentethe's duties are keeping her busy," the woman said, her Karedek softly accented. "She'll be here soon."

Windows opened out on three sides of the room; from the one facing west he could see the slope of the mountain and the sea beyond. Pieces of cloth draped the opposite wall.

He went over to look at them. They showed brightly colored complex patterns of stripes or triangles or stars or odd shapes that had no name. "Each of these pieces has a meaning," the woman who had spoken before said, coming over to him. "We're a solitary people—most weavers live in cottages far from others, and we need a way to speak to our neighbors, to signal up and down the mountain. This one for example—" She pointed to the closest piece. "It means 'come and visit—I'd like company.'"

Jerret and Rodarren and a few of the others left the table to join them. "And here's the answer," the woman said, indicating another piece of cloth. At first Mathewar thought it looked the same as the first one; then he noticed there were actually a good many differences in color and pattern. "It says, 'I will—expect me soon.' And this one here—this says, 'Danger coming, watch out.'"

She pointed out a few of the other meanings—"Illness, keep away," "I'm hurt, please help"—and then Pentethe and her women came into the room and the meeting started.

Mathewar's attention soon wandered. Only Rodarren and Pentethe spoke, setting up protocol, laying the basis for some sort of agreement between them. The creeping petty diplomacy bored him; he wondered why he had been invited.

At the end the two women looked pleased with their progress, though no decisions had been made. Everyone stood up; Pentethe and her women left first. "Mathewar," Rodarren said. "Stay a minute—I'd like to talk to you."

Jerret frowned. Rodarren nodded to him and he went outside. When only she and Mathewar were left she said, "None of this interests you, does it?"

Very little interested him these days, but it wouldn't do to say so. "I'm sorry, milady."

"I didn't expect it to, to be honest. I have a chore for you, if you like. And in exchange you'll never have to attend another meeting again."

Mathewar smiled. "What is it?"

"One of my men—Correg—stayed out most of last night. Normally I wouldn't care, as long as he didn't do anything to offend our hosts. But when I asked him where he was he said he had been in bed all night."

"Are you certain he left?"

"The man sharing the room with him noticed he had gone, and came to tell me." She saw his expression and said, "I know—I don't like my men spying on each other either. But Correg could be meeting someone from Norue, or trying to sell information. I wonder if you could gain his trust, see where he goes. His room is in your cottage, which should make it easier."

"I'll try, milady."

"I hear magicians have something called the Clear Sight . . ."

"The Clear Sight isn't very predictable, unfortunately. But as I said, I'll try."

She smiled at him, a dazzling, lovely smile. "Thank you," she said.

Mathewar joined Rodarren and her company for the midday meal and then went back to the cottage. A group of men sat by the fire in the common room, playing a card game. One roared loudly, thumped his cards to the table, and raked in all the coins in the center.

"Do you play?" one of the men asked Mathewar.

"I'll watch for a while," he said, leaning against a wall and crossing his arms.

"If you watch you can't talk," the man said, gathering the cards together and shuffling them.

A while later Mathewar heard Correg's name; he was a short man who sat hunched over his cards, saying little to his fellow players. One look at him and Mathewar knew immediately where he had spent the night. Sattery drinkers learned to identify each other; they recognized a certain pallor of the skin, a brightness in the eyes. Correg had probably gone in search of more drink.

After the game Mathewar moved to Correg's side. "Have you found any?" he asked softly.

"Any what?" Correg said, his eyes distrustful. He had a pockmarked face, small squinting gray eyes and colorless hair.

"The inexhaustible jewel."

Correg relaxed, seeming only then to notice Mathewar's own pale skin. Sattery was not difficult to obtain—any apothecary would have some—but Correg showed no suspicion at Mathewar's question. "I did better than that, my friend. I found a drinking room, in a village down the mountain. Would you like to come with me tonight?"

Mathewar hated drinking rooms; he preferred to drink by himself, without interruptions. But the princess had made a request of him. "Very much," he said.

"Meet me at the front door at moonrise, then."

That evening Mathewar did not take sattery. He would have to drink with others later, to be convivial, and he didn't want to drink too much. He stayed awake, moving restlessly through his room, feeling the dull ache in his stomach and his joints, the dryness of his throat. And worse than that, the terrible yearning, the desire that threatened to overwhelm him and send him back to his own sattery and his own fire.

Finally, after what seemed like a night of waiting, he saw the moon begin to rise. He wrapped himself in his cloak and went outside.

No one stood by the front door. He paced quickly, his nerves stretched. The moon rose fully, blossoming in the sky. "Hey!" someone called. "Over here!"

He whirled around and saw Correg coming out of the cottage. "Let's go," Correg said, his words slurred. His eyes on Mathewar, he tripped over a stone in his path and nearly fell, then laughed wildly. "Great night, isn't it?

"Hush," Mathewar said, looking anxiously toward the cottage. There's another reason I don't like drinking rooms, he thought. I don't want to see what I've become.

"What's the matter, man? Haven't drunk your sattery yet?"

"No."

"Stupid. Stupid, stupid man. Very, very stupid."

They started down the path. Clouds rolled in, hiding the moon. The path grew darker, and Correg stumbled again. Mathewar made a small light and set it above them.

"Stupid, stupid," Correg repeated every so often, whispering now.

Finally Correg headed off the main path. They were skirting the mountain now, the summit rising sheer above them on one side, a cliff plunging to the base below on the other.

A short time later they came to a cluster of cottages. Correg took the path between them and continued on, into a wood of dark looming firs. A light burned in the distance.

It was a solitary cottage, all its windows lit, welcoming them. As they came closer Mathewar extinguished his light. A man opened the door and motioned them inside.

Smoke clouded the room. Other things were sold here as well

as sattery—drinks, rare herbs, food—and the place smelled of a combination of spices, earth and rope. People, mostly men, sat on the floor or leaned against the walls, talking softly or laughing at nothing.

A great red-brick hearth stood in the center, with a brick shelf stretching around it. Mathewar moved toward it, through the crowd. A woman gave him a silver cup and poured sattery from a flagon. He paid her, then sat by the hearth, shrugged his cloak off and set the cup on the brick shelf.

When the sattery had heated enough he took the cup and drank, his hand trembling so hard he spilled some on the floor. Immediately several men sitting near him rubbed at the drops and then put their fingers to their mouth.

He stayed seated, feeling the familiar warmth spread through him. He looked around the room, detached now, seeing it as if it were a picture or tapestry. A man near him ate a flower from the Forest of Tiranon, one Mathewar knew to be poisonous in large quantities. Another man puffed from a pipe and then coughed for a long time.

Emindal cloth hung on the walls. He studied the wavering patterns through the smoke, wondering what they meant. "I have taken sattery and am completely incapable," maybe. He laughed softly.

He couldn't see Correg anywhere. It didn't matter; he could find his way back without him, and presumably the other man could take care of himself. Someone near him said, "Prince Norue," and laughed.

Mathewar looked around for the speaker and found him on the other side of the flower-eater. "Excuse me, did I hear you talking about Prince Norue?" Mathewar asked, trying to concentrate. The smoke stung his eyes. "I know him. I'm from Karededin."

The flower-eater moved away. "We were talking about the siege of Karededin, nothing more," the man said in unaccented Karedek. He was tall, with long blond hair and a blond beard. "Nothing more, nothing more."

He didn't look like a sattery drinker, though he sounded like one. Well, perhaps it was his first time. The man turned away and looked into the fire. In drinking rooms this was not considered rude or impolite; people who didn't want to talk simply said nothing, and no one bothered them.

Mathewar stared into the flames as well, keeping the other man in the corner of his eye. A short while later the man stood and left the room.

For a moment Mathewar wondered if he should follow. But a chance mention of Prince Norue meant nothing, especially if they were only discussing the siege. Anyway, he did not want to leave the room and go out into the cold night.

Tiredness overcame him. He wrapped himself in his cloak, lay down on the hard floor and went to sleep, oblivious to the muted life around him: the clink of coins, the muttered conversations, the laughter.

When he woke his back felt tied into knots. Nothing seemed to have changed; people still moved around him, conducting their quiet transactions. Now he noticed that several people had brought blankets with them, and he decided to do the same when he came back. If he came back. Would Rodarren want him to follow this lout a second time?

A woman approached him with a tray, then said something in Emindalek that Mathewar did not understand, though he caught the word "sattery" and knew she was asking him if he wanted more drink.

He sat and rubbed the back of his head, feeling his tangled hair. "No," he said, though his craving had returned. But he knew people who drank sattery more than once a day, had seen how it meant the end of any normal life, and he had resolved to put that off for another few years. "Do you know what time it is?"

The woman looked puzzled. "Almost morning, I think," she said in a heavy Emindalek accent.

Of course—time did not exist in this room. He stood and searched for Correg, but there was no sign of him. He left and began the climb up the mountain.

The sun had not yet risen fully by the time he reached the summit. Only one person seemed awake, a woman sitting on a bench in the middle of the cottages. As he came closer he saw through the gray light that it was Rodarren.

"Good morning, milady," he said, dropping to the bench beside her. He wondered briefly how he appeared to her, tired and disheveled and smelling of strange vices.

"Good morning," she said. "Have you discovered what Correg has been doing?"

"I have, and I don't think you need to worry about him. He goes to a drinking room down the mountain."

Rodarren looked at him keenly but said nothing. "You knew that I drink sattery," he said, suddenly aware of her thoughts. "That's why you sent me after him."

"Yes."

"Not much escapes you, milady."

"No. Well, I've had a lifetime of watching."

"There is one thing that concerns me. A man at the drinking room mentioned Prince Norue. He claimed to be talking about the siege, though."

Rodarren frowned. "What did he look like?"

"Tall. Blond hair, blond beard."

"Do you think you can describe him to an artist? They have some very good people here designing cloth patterns—maybe one of them could sketch him."

"I'll try."

"And can you go back to the drinking room and see if he returns?"

He rubbed his forehead. The morning light was dull and gray, but it seemed to pierce his eyes like swords. He wanted nothing more than to go to his room and sleep forever.

"Well, maybe not right away," Rodarren said. She smiled at his surprised expression. "As you said, not much escapes me."

Jerret left his cottage and saw Rodarren and Mathewar sitting together on a bench. He headed toward them, frowning. What did those two have to talk about?

Rodarren was saying good-bye to Mathewar as he reached them. He sat next to her. "Good morning, milady," he said, watching Mathewar walk to his cottage. "Where was he all night? He looks drunk."

Rodarren said nothing.

"I'm afraid I don't trust that man," Jerret said. "What do we know about him, after all? Only that Angarred recommended him."

"I knew him years ago, when he was King Tezue's magician. Well, I didn't know him, of course—I didn't really know anyone. But I loved to watch him work."

"I don't remember him. I suppose we moved in different circles."

"He was brilliant then. He walked all the way around the city, placing spells on the walls and gates to strengthen them—they've withstood the siege this long because of him. I can certainly use someone like that among my followers."

"But look at him now. And speaking of Tezue—he doesn't even know whether he freed the king from Alkarren's spell. Whatever he was like in his glory days, he's certainly changed a great deal."

"He had a wife and child, I remember. Something happened to them, I think."

"He probably left them. And if that's the case I don't like it that he spends so much time with Angarred. The Godkings know why she thinks so highly of him."

She turned to him and laughed. "She spends time with him because she loves him."

"She—what? How do you know?"

"You only have to look at her."

"I don't see it."

She laughed again. "You have to know how to look."

"I hope you're wrong. She came to court an innocent—she knows very little about the world. Does he know how she feels about him?"

"That's a harder question to answer. He does and he doesn't, if you know what I mean."

"Well, let's hope he won't try to take advantage of her, to corrupt her in some way."

"Oh, he's not as bad as that."

"Do you truly think so?"

"I do."

"Well, then, milady, I will try not to be so distrustful."

"Thank you. We need to be careful with one another here. We may be in Emindal for a very long time. Maybe forever."

"I'm content to be wherever you are."

For the first time he saw her flustered. "I—I thank you, milord. Thank you for your loyalty."

Jerret took a deep breath. He had realized long ago that some of his dislike of Mathewar sprang from jealousy, realized also that the only way he could go on was to act with complete honesty toward Rodarren. "It's not only loyalty. I mean it—I'll follow you always, even to imprisonment. Even to death. I love you, milady."

She put her hand to her mouth. "No one has ever loved me before."

"That's because they never truly saw you. They never saw your intelligence, your beauty, they were never moved by your tremendous bravery."

Her hand traced the scar on her cheek. He had never seen her make that gesture before. "Not beauty, milord, certainly. My face is ruined."

"Your face is beautiful."

"No—I—"

He took her hand and kissed her softly on the cheek, then drew her toward him and kissed her lips. A look of great surprise came into her face, surprise and wonder. She moved closer, responding to his kiss, answering his urgency.

Suddenly she pulled away. He leaned toward her again, but she put her hand to his lips. "I can't do this," she said. "I need to be a princess—my people can't see me like this." She hesitated, shy as a young girl. "And this is my first—I've never—"

"Of course, milady," Jerret said.

Several weeks passed. The autumn rains came; the pines and firs on the mountainside stayed a dark green but the other trees turned as gold as coins or fiery red, and then lost their leaves one by one. Jerret trained Rodarren's soldiers in the mud, and frequently he noticed the princess watching him from the side, an unreadable expression on her face. Other soldiers began to arrive from Karededin in ones and twos, men fearful of what Norue would do if he took the king-ship. Everyone went armed now, worried about sudden attacks from the mainland. Mathewar recited Spells of Strengthening over the swords and armor to keep them sharp and free of rust, and every so often he headed down paths slick with rain to the drinking room, but the man who had mentioned Norue never returned.

No one knew what Norue would do next, whether he would try to wrest the kingship from Tezue or attack Rodarren while she was still weak. Jerret questioned the men who had escaped Karededin, but none of them had been privy to the prince's plans.

Jerret and Rodarren were often together, talking about the troops, or Karededin, or their childhoods—anything that came to mind.

"You once said that people couldn't see you with me, that you had to act the princess—" Jerret said. They were in the meeting room, sitting at the large table after everyone had gone.

"I didn't mean I was ashamed of you," Rodarren said quickly. "But the people expect certain things of their princess, of their queen, a certain morality—"

"What if I were to marry you?" he asked. "Could people see us together then?"

She put her hand to her mouth; he had come to know that the gesture meant she was uncertain. "I—I hardly ever think of mar-riage," she said slowly. "I don't even know if my mad gamble will succeed, if I can take Karededin from my cousin. Most days I don't think I can. And if I do—well, I will probably marry for reasons of state, to ally myself with one lord or another."

"Is that what you want? To marry for political reasons?"

"No. No, of course not. But if I were queen, my person would not be my own. I would belong to the country. I've known that since I was very young."

"But would you be a good queen if you were unhappy?"

"I don't know. I don't know. Do you think the people would accept you?"

"Why wouldn't they?"

"I don't know," she said again. She looked at him for a moment, and even Jerret, who had come to know her moods, could not tell what she was thinking. Then she moved toward him, a quick jerky motion as if she was afraid she might change her mind, and kissed him.

He kissed her back, gently, so she wouldn't move away. She pressed him closer, her kisses hungrier.

After a long while she pulled away. His desire turned to frustration, and he had to remind himself of his promises to her.

"Can we go somewhere else?" she asked softly. "My people—"

"—can't see you like this. I know," he said, suddenly filled with joy. "What about my rooms?"

They left the meeting room and walked between the cottages, watching carefully for observers. He didn't touch her but he was aware of her by his side at every moment, feeling her every motion somewhere within him.

At his rooms they unbuckled their belts and dropped their swords to the floor. Then they stood for a time, studying each other shyly. He moved toward her and undid the lacings of her dress slowly, remembering her confession to him, that it was her first time. But after an initial hesitation her excitement matched his own, and they hurried into bed, eager to discover everything they could about the other.

Afterward she fell asleep for a while and he watched her, his eyes tracing the curve of her waist to her hip; her skin there was as brown as her face. He had never been so happy, he thought. He must not forget this; he must fix it in his mind, recall every detail.

She opened her eyes, coming awake immediately. "I have to go," she said. "I have to meet people, to plan . . ."

"I'm sorry," he said.

"So am I." She began to speak quickly; once again she seemed afraid she might change her mind. "Listen. I could come to love you, I think, if I had time. But we can't marry here—the people will only accept a wedding performed by a religious, sacred to the Godkings. If we get to Karededin, and if we still feel the same way about each other, we'll marry then."

Had he thought he could never be happier? Hearing her say she could love him, that she would marry him, even with conditions— now he understood what true happiness was.

"We'll get there," he said. "I swear it by all the Godkings."

On a night without rain Mathewar donned his cloak and went down to the drinking room. The sky was overcast, with no moon, and he created a light to show him the path.

In the drinking room Correg sat by the hearth, talking in a low voice to the blond man. Mathewar took a cup of sattery and cast an illusion to make himself uninteresting, a man who looked like anyone else, and then sat down next to them.

Correg mentioned Norue's name. "Yes," the other man said. His voice was so soft Mathewar had to strain to listen. He missed several words and then heard, ". . . coming soon."

Mathewar's sattery had heated, and he drank it quickly. The two men said nothing for a long time. He dropped the spell that cloaked him and turned to Correg. "I haven't seen you here for a good while," he said. "And who's your friend?"

"Mathewar," Correg said. He blinked several times and rubbed his eyes, though the room was less smoky than usual. "I didn't see you there. This is Vorrek." He turned to the other man. "And this is Mathewar Tobrin."

"Ah," the man said.

"What were you saying about Norue?" Mathewar said.

"Just that it's fortunate the prince is still in Pergodi," Vorrek said. "The king is very ill, and the people need someone to lead them."

"Were you saying anything else?" Mathewar said, using his commanding voice.

Correg opened his mouth. The other man shoved him back with an elbow. Correg fell, then struggled to sit up. "What—" he said.

Vorrek held out a clay mug to Mathewar; it smelled sharply and unpleasantly of herbs. "Here, have some of this."

"No, thank you," Mathewar said. He lifted his own silver cup. "Sattery is my drink."

"Ah, but this does wonderful things when combined with sattery, doesn't it, Correg?" Correg nodded. "And why should we talk with those who refuse to drink with us?"

Why indeed? Mathewar thought. Vorrek would never let him talk to Correg, and Vorrek's will was too strong to respond to his commanding voice; Mathewar's only hope lay in gaining the blond man's trust. He took the cup and drank it down. It tasted as bad as it smelled, like the paint women put on their faces, or very powerful drink.

"Good man!" Vorrek reached around Correg to slap Mathewar on the shoulder. "Come, let's go down the mountain—we can't get what we want here."

Mathewar never truly remembered the rest of that night, or sorted out what was real and what a result of Vorrek's drink. Vorrek led them to drinking rooms and taverns, dance halls and gaming houses. People swirled around him, dancing or playing cards or rattling dice in cups like bones. He lost long stretches of time, talking to one man and coming awake to find he was talking to another.

In one room a man turned over cards and he saw the faces of Rodarren and Jerret, Angarred and Norue. The final face was Alkarren's; the magician reached out to him from the card and he jerked back in alarm.

In another he saw men and women bent over huge vats, dyeing the Emindal cloth they traded throughout the realms. Piles of color were scattered everywhere, and as he focused he saw that they contained flowers and tree bark and nettles, and even dead insects and spiral shells, though perhaps he only imagined those.

Vorrek led them tirelessly through narrow passages and alleyways. Days seemed to fall away like leaves. Stars burned beneath his feet. Women in black sat around a fire, then rose into the air and turned into birds. Vorrek urged him on, showing him more strange delicacies in more strange rooms; he could not remember if he sampled them or not.

In all the confusion he struggled to hold onto several thoughts—that he had to keep Vorrek in sight, that he must not mention Rodarren, that he must listen for any talk of Norue and remember it to tell Rodarren.

He knew that Vorrek was playing with him, that the other man wanted to confound him so badly he lost his way on the mountain. But he thought it was a game he could win; he had a good deal of practice in keeping his balance amid chaos. Though if Vorrek knew that he spied for Rodarren the game was forfeit before it even began.

He lost the two men several times in the darkness, and called out or created a light or listened for them blundering through the trees and laughing. Then after a blank period he found himself on a narrow path skirting the mountain, a sheer cliff falling away nearly beneath his feet.

He staggered back from the cliff and stumbled against the mountain on the other side of the path. His heart shook, the beats loud and irregular.

He was heading down the mountain, he saw. Vorrek and Correg walked somewhere ahead of him, deep in conversation.

He continued on for a few more minutes. The voices grew softer, then fell silent. He stood still and listened. Had they fallen? But surely he would have heard something.

Then he understood, and he cursed himself for being so slow. They had climbed off the path and up the mountain, doubling back; they planned to throw him down the cliff. He tried a spell, fumbled with the words, frantically tried again. Now he could hear their footsteps above him, coming closer.

Finally he managed to take on the illusion of a tree. Vorrek and Correg slid to the path behind him. "The Others take him and rend him into pieces!" Vorrek said. "He's used a spell, turned invisible or flown away. We'll never find him now."

"Do you think he heard much?" Correg asked.

"I don't know, by the Orator. You were supposed to watch out for him. What happened? He could have been there for hours, listening to us."

"He was probably invisible, like you said," Correg said sullenly.

If Mathewar hadn't been a tree he would have laughed. Thank the Godkings these men did not know the limits of magic.

"Well, let's go," Vorrek said. "We just have to hope he didn't hear anything important."

The two men headed up the path. Mathewar waited a long while and then broke the illusion, this time succeeding on his first try. He laughed softly, though without any reason for it; he had not managed to hear whatever the two men thought was so important. Still laughing, he began to climb the mountain.

Dawn was breaking when he reached the summit. Someone headed toward him; as he came closer he saw it was Jerret. The Others take it, he thought, the very last man I want to see.

"Where have you been?" Jerret asked.

"Out," Mathewar said. He leaned against one of the cottages to steady himself and crossed his arms.

"All night?"

"Yes."

"Are you drunk?"

"Probably."

"Listen," Jerret said. "We were invited here by Pentethe herself. We can't afford to antagonize the people here, to do anything that goes against their customs. We have to—"

"The only person I've antagonized is you."

"We have to be civil to them at all times."

"Civil? What—are we to tiptoe around and couch our words in whispers? A sniveling sort of civility. A silly civility, if you like."

"Very well, you can talk rings around me. But we have to make sure that the Emindalek don't—"

"Mathewar!" Rodarren called. He turned; the movement made him dizzy, and he braced himself against the cottage wall. "We're going to meet in my rooms. Why don't you join us? You look as if you have something to say."

He wanted nothing more than to go to his cottage and sleep; he had been awake all night. But the idea of riling Jerret appealed to him. Jerret, he knew, would be waiting for him to prove his incompetence in some way, probably by falling over drunkenly. He would have to be very careful, though; at the moment the prospect of falling over was all too real.

"Certainly, milady," he said. He followed them to Rodarren's cottage, trying not to laugh at Jerret's obvious discomfiture.

Rodarren had a room very much like the meeting hall in the largest cottage. He saw immediately why she hadn't used the hall, though; this was a private meeting, with none of the Emindalek present.

The princess sat at the table and the meeting started. People talked about weapon stores, food, spies that had been sent to Karededin. Mathewar stared out a window at some nearby cottages. At one point he lost some time again, and when he came to a different person was speaking.

Finally Rodarren nodded to him. "Milady," he began, and went on to tell her about Vorrek and Correg, about Vorrek's mention of Norue and his reference to something "coming soon."

"And you couldn't hear what it was?" she asked.

"No, I'm sorry. I'm nearly certain that he was talking about Norue, that it's Norue who will do something soon."

"What is it, I wonder? Will he invade Emindal, do you think?"

Mathewar shrugged. "I wish I could say, milady."

Other people spoke, and then Jerret talked about training Rodarren's men. If they could hold out until spring, he said, and if others joined them from Karededin, they would have a fighting force that might stand against Norue. Two people walked past the window, one a woman in patterned Emindal cloth.

Something about the cloth looked familiar. Mathewar blinked hard, trying to make certain the people weren't another hallucination. The woman came closer. He stood. "That pattern!" he said.

Jerret glanced at him, annoyed at the interruption. "That pattern means 'Danger coming—watch out,'" Mathewar said.

Jerret and Rodarren and some others joined him at the window. "No, you're mistaken," Jerret said. "All those patterns look alike—I'm sure this is something else. Anyway, you only saw that pattern once."

"Yes, and I remember it," Mathewar said. "That's most of what being a magician is—memory, memorizing spells. Get the Stone."

"What?"

"Get the Stone. Perhaps it's Norue—perhaps Norue has landed and has sent that man as a scout, using the woman as a guide. She's warning us in the only way she can that we're about to be attacked."

"Nonsense. You're drunk—you don't know what you're saying."

"Get the Stone," Mathewar said in a commanding voice.

Jerret moved toward the door, then seemed to summon his will and stopped halfway. "Jerret," Rodarren said. "You'd better do what he says. If he's right we'll need it, and if he's wrong we haven't lost anything. I'll summon the troops."

"Very well, milady," Jerret said.

Jerret ran to his cottage. Rodarren was right; he might as well humor Mathewar and bring him the Stone. And when Mathewar proved to be mistaken she would see him as he really was, she would forget her romantic delusions and realize how much he had changed.

He reached the door and opened it, then went to a chest and threw out clothes until he came to the bottom. There was the Stone, still in its wooden box. He picked it up and felt the familiar nausea it caused, then headed back, moving slower now.

He was still a long way from the meeting room when he saw Norue's army come over the summit of the mountain.

NINETEEN

*A*ngarred rode back slowly from the cemetery, her mind whirling with what she had heard. Some force was behind everything that happened, all the wars and plots and intrigues, working secretly to create chaos. There was no reason to suppose they would stop with the war between Karededin and Takeke; the statues had said they wanted every realm defenseless and exhausted. And in the end, when everything had been destroyed in the fighting, they would simply come in and take over.

But who could it be? Who had made Alkarren a Hollow One? Whoever it was, she thought, they couldn't be involved in the current war; they were biding their time, pitting country against country.

She had not had a formal education, but her father had taught her to read and write and she had gone through the books in his library. Now she tried to remember the history she had read. It couldn't be the Takekek, engaged in a war with Karededin, or the Emindalek, who had sided with Rodarren. Countries lay to the east of Takeke, but the inhabitants there would have to travel a long way west if they wanted to reach Karededin, through a desert left from the Sorcerers' Wars called Endless Desolation.

She wished she had paid more attention to the ancient maps.

There were places to the north, she knew, Goss and Ou and others she couldn't remember, and a scattering of islands out past Emindal. The Gardeners, people called the folk who lived there, strange-looking men and women with dark skin and blue eyes. They had come long ago from a place even farther west, but Angarred had never met anyone from that country, could not even recall its name.

Suddenly she remembered the giant they had seen in the forest, his huge hands, the easy way he had brought down the deer. The giants were massing, the masters at the College said, and the statues had told her that they had a third Stone.

She spurred her horse toward the Snoppishes' house. She had to go to Emindal, find Mathewar and Rodarren, tell them that they were not fighting their own war but playing into the hands of a subtle enemy. The war would have to stop, somehow; they would all have to turn against the real adversary, the giants. She thought again of the giant's huge hands on the deer, and she shuddered.

She had wanted to be a power at court. She had wanted to be the one manipulating the strings, like the puppet-master in Pergodi, making others dance to her desires. She had had no idea how complex it all was, how far back the strings went. Alkarren held Tezue's strings, but someone held Alkarren's in his turn.

What she had heard did not change her mind, though; it only increased her desire for power. It was far better to hold the strings than to be bound by them.

For the first time she understood her father's terrible need for mastery. People in authority did not have to fear those below them; the power they wielded over them saw to that. And it was important to be as safe as possible, especially in a snake pit like Pergodi.

When she reached the Snoppishes' she told them what she had learned, and the plans she had made. "That's—I'm sorry, my dear, but I think that's a terrible idea," Lord Snoppish said. "How will you possibly get out of Pergodi, for one thing?"

"Mathewar showed me a way through the walls," she said.

"Yes, but what will you do once you're out?" Lady Snoppish asked. "You'll have to find a ship somehow, and get to Emindal safely, avoiding the Takekek ships in the harbor . . . And even if you do make it, I doubt anyone will listen to you. People won't stop fighting a war just because you tell them to."

"Mathewar will listen. And he'll know I'm telling the truth. He'll go to Rodarren, and she'll . . ."

"Yes, what then?" Lady Snoppish said. "If she does talk to Norue he'll just think it's a trick. Anyway, he doesn't care about some giants in some forest—he wants the kingship, and he'll do anything to get it."

"But even if he becomes king he'll still have the giants as enemies, and by then they'll be stronger than ever. Wouldn't it be better—"

"Norue isn't sane, dear. You and I might think that way, but he won't."

"Well—well, I have to do something. I have to tell someone. We're going to destroy ourselves fighting—I have to make people see . . . And what about Jerret? What will happen to him? The giants won't stop here—they're going to create more chaos, bring more people into the war."

Lord Snoppish winced, and she immediately regretted mentioning Jerret. "There must be someone you can talk to here, though," he said. "It's far too dangerous to go to Emindal."

"Who? King Tezue and Alkarren are Hollow Ones, Norue is a madman, the council seems to be under Alkarren's control . . . No, I'm going to Emindal. That's where the only sane people are." She smiled at the Snoppishes. "Except for you, of course, and your family."

The next day she returned to the castle to pack and rode south once again. As she went she thought of the one argument the Snoppishes had not made, that she wanted to go to Emindal only because Mathewar was there. Perhaps they didn't know how she felt about him; she hoped so, anyway.

She reached the house Mathewar had shown her, dismounted and knocked. The door opened slightly, enough for her to see Mathewar's friend, the man from the Forest of Tiranon. "Yes, milady?" he said.

"Please, can I come in? I'd like to go through the wall."

"Through the wall?" the man said.

The Others take it—he didn't remember her. She would have to say something to gain his trust. "I was here with Mathewar, remember? We left Pergodi together."

He nodded, his face showing recognition now. He stepped back and pulled the door open.

"Stop there, both of you!" someone said from the street.

She turned. The doorkeeper slammed the door shut behind her. Five armed men on horseback surrounded her, their swords drawn. They wore purple and gold, Norue's colors.

One of them dismounted, headed for the door and slammed into it with his shoulder. The old doorkeeper was no match for him and it burst open. The soldier went through.

"A door to the outside, just as we thought," the man said when he returned, one arm tight around the doorkeeper's neck.

The others came closer to her, making a half circle, pressing her toward the wall at her back. Her horse, terrified, broke from her hold and forced its way between them, then galloped off down the street, its reins dangling.

"What do you want with me?" she asked. "Surely I should be allowed to ride through Pergodi."

One of the men laughed. "Through Pergodi? Through the walls of Pergodi, I'd say. And what did you plan to do once you got outside? Sell information to the Takekek?"

"No, of course not. I don't have any information to sell."

"We'll see. Prince Norue has had his eye on you for a long time, you know. That's why we followed you, and a good thing we did, too. It isn't every day we capture a traitor."

"I'm not—"

"That's not for us to decide. Our orders are to take you to prison. Prince Norue will talk to you there. Intimate conversations, you may be sure."

Her mouth went dry at the suggestion of torture. She glanced around desperately, seeking a way out. The soldiers moved closer; one of them held a sword to her throat.

She shrugged, trying to look unafraid. The man with the sword motioned to her to mount in front of him, and she rode with them back to Pergodi Castle, her heart beating fast and hard in her chest.

Rodarren had managed to summon some of her troops, Jerret saw, but they seemed vastly outnumbered by Norue's men. He drew his sword and hurried, cursing himself for his delay.

When he reached the fighting he looked around frantically for Mathewar. Mathewar stood in the midst of the battle; he seemed taller and broader, and sparks flew from his sword as it clashed with his opponent's. Light shone from him as he fought. Jerret had heard of this magical style of fighting and knew that they taught it at the College, but he had never seen it.

Mathewar's opponent ran off. "Mathewar!" Jerret called, trying to make himself heard over the shouts and the ringing of swords. The magician turned. "The Stone!"

Jerret threw the Stone. Then, to his horror, he saw a big man from Norue's army run out in front of Mathewar and catch it.

They both pursued the man, but he disappeared in the press of fighting. Jerret nearly reached Mathewar. "The Others take it!" he said.

"I think they already have!" Mathewar shouted, but he grinned as if to show he didn't blame Jerret.

Someone engaged Mathewar and he turned toward him, raising his sword. Another soldier challenged Jerret, but the man was easily parried and Jerret kept his eyes on Mathewar, feeling guilty. A sword flashed; it looked as if Mathewar's opponent had managed to wound him in the thigh. Jerret gasped but Mathewar continued fighting, ignoring the wound. Perhaps nothing had happened after all.

A group of men came between them and they were forced to separate, and the battle continued.

Some hours later Mathewar made his way to a tree and leaned against it. He took several deep breaths and listened cautiously, but he heard only a muted clash of arms and horses neighing; the battle seemed to have gone elsewhere for the moment.

An arrow jutted from his side, just below his ribs. When it had slammed into him he had stumbled away from the fighting. Now he looked at it, still more startled than hurt, and noticed for the first time the other wound on his thigh, saw the dried reddish blood around it. The arrow had gone all the way through his body; he tried to break it but it was somehow positioned wrong, and he had to bite his lip to keep from screaming.

A man headed toward the stand of trees. Mathewar reached out with the Clear Sight and saw to his relief that the man was one of Rodarren's. "Hey!" he called out.

The man turned quickly. "Don't worry—we're on the same side," Mathewar said. "Do you think you can break this arrow off for me?"

The man stared at him. Mathewar continued to see him with the Clear Sight. This was his first battle and he was terrified, wanting nothing more than to be back in Pergodi with the woman he loved, a seamstress. His feet hurt; his shoes had never fit right and he had been running all day. And he didn't think he could help Mathewar; the idea of breaking the arrow seemed almost as frightening as the battle itself.

He showed none of this, though. He was tall and strong, and he had adopted a look of toughness, hoping that Mathewar would back down. "It isn't very difficult," Mathewar said, using a little of his commanding voice. "Just break it here. I'd do it myself but I can't reach it."

The man came closer. He grasped the arrow in both hands and closed his eyes, then snapped it. The sickening pain came back, turning everything dark, but Mathewar knew he could not show any of it or he would frighten the man away.

Mathewar pulled the arrow out slowly. Blood welled from the wound, and the other man's tough expression changed to horror. Mathewar pressed his hand against his side to stem the blood.

"It's all right," Mathewar said, speaking through the haze around him. "Thank you."

The darkness subsided in waves. His Clear Sight, always unpredictable, now began to show him others nearby. A soldier marched along, exultant, thinking about the people he had captured. The prisoners themselves were roped together and forced to walk behind him, surrounded by guards. Mathewar touched Jerret's mind among the prisoners, then Rodarren's. It's over, then, he thought bleakly. So ends the inglorious reign of Queen Rodarren the First.

"Run," he said to the other man. "There are people coming, Norue's men. Hurry!"

The man stood still, listening. "I don't hear anything."

"Just do as I tell you."

"What will you do?"

"Never mind that."

The man fled. Mathewar slid to the ground, his back against the tree. He tried to summon an illusion that would hide him but he was too weak for magic, and the soldiers came upon him before he could finish.

"You!" one of them said. With one quick motion he took Mathewar's sword. "Get up and join the rest of them."

Mathewar stood and walked to the end of the coffle of prisoners, nodding grimly to Rodarren and Jerret as he passed. Someone tied his arm to the arm of the man in front of him and they set off.

A great weariness came over him. He had been awake for a day and a half; he wanted nothing more than to slip to the ground and sleep. There was something wrong with his leg, his thigh, he could not seem to walk properly . . . If they killed him for sleeping here at least he could rest; he would be in the Celestial Court, he would see Embre and Atte again . . .

He looked up. He had fallen without being aware of it. The man in front of him pulled him to his feet, not roughly. "Come along," the man said. "We all have to walk together, see?" He slung Mathewar's free arm over his shoulder and they continued.

After that Mathewar remembered only bits and pieces of the journey. They were walking down the side of the mountain, and then they were thrown into the hold of a ship. He slept for a long time. He woke to see someone handing out food and drink, but he was too weak to fight his way through the crowd for it. He woke again and felt water at his lips; someone sat next to him, trying to make him drink, the soldier who had practically carried him down the mountain. Perhaps the man had decided to take responsibility for him, Mathewar thought gratefully, and fell into sleep again.

His craving for sattery woke him the next time, and he realized he had gone without it for several days, how many he did not know. He felt all the familiar reminders—pain in his stomach, in his joints, a pounding in his head—but this time they were stronger than ever before, drowning out even his wounds.

Once he saw, or dreamed he saw, Correg walking through the hold. Correg came and stood over him, gloating. "Ah, it's Mathewar Tobrin," he said.

"Ah, it's Correg Traitor," Mathewar said.

Correg swung his leg, ready to kick him, but someone pulled him away.

He woke again when he felt the ship shuddering beneath him. They had docked, one of the prisoners said, and soon after the soldiers came into the hold and ordered them off the ship.

Outside on the dock he blinked at the bright light, though the day was gray and cloudy. Someone grabbed hold of him and thrust him into a cart. He lay back, his eyes closed, feeling the jolt of the cobblestones. A long time later he raised himself to look out; he saw the silhouette of Pergodi Castle and then fell back.

For the first time he wondered what would happen to him. He would probably be interrogated by Prince Norue and then sentenced to death. Or he might die before that; he knew of addicts who had died when they were deprived of sattery.

Death, then. Well, he had wanted to die, hadn't he? But he had imagined himself borne off on a river of sattery dreams, not helplessness and torture.

The cart stopped. A soldier ordered him out. They had reached Pergodi Castle, he saw. The soldier gestured to him to go ahead. He walked unsteadily down some stairs and along a damp corridor, pain shooting through his leg at every step.

Finally they came to a barred gate, with a man standing guard before it. The soldier spoke to the guard, who took a ring of keys from his belt and unlocked the gate. The soldier pushed Mathewar into a cold, brightly lit room beyond. He fell to the floor, grateful not to be moving.

"Not there," the soldier said, motioning him to the opposite wall. Somehow he managed to go the remaining few feet. The guard fastened a shackle to his arm and turned the key in the lock, then left with the soldier, laughing at something the other man said.

The shackle was attached by a short chain to the wall, a foot off the floor. He would be able to lie down, maybe even to sleep. He huddled against the wall. A cage stood across from him, and there was someone in it, someone familiar . . . Angarred?

No—it must be a dream, he thought, and fell asleep.

The bright light woke him. Lamps and torches stood in sconces all around the room, shining mercilessly, making his head pound. The heavy scent of lamp-oil overlaid other, worse smells: mold and stale bodies and urine.

Now that he was lying still the pain from his injuries felt agonizing: they all seemed to be shouting out at once, demanding his attention. His left side seemed to be on fire from the wounds he had taken. He had a terrible thirst for sattery; his joints ached and he felt sick to his stomach. And the room seemed icy cold; either that or he had a fever.

He remembered his last thought before sleeping. He sat up cautiously and looked at the cage across the room. It was Angarred. She leaned against the far wall, her gaze unfocused. She no longer looked like one of the standing queens: her regal, indifferent expression had gone. Or perhaps she was a queen fallen from the Celestial Court, enmeshed in earthly things, her face dirty and her hair tangled.

All at once, despite everything, he felt extraordinary happy, a wild happiness. The religious had been right: one was broken, but two were whole. "Angarred!" he called.

She looked up. "Who—"

"Over here. It's me."

"Who are you?"

"It's me. Mathewar."

"Mathewar?" She sounded shocked, disbelieving.

"Do I look that bad?"

She hesitated. "No," she said finally.

"You've never lied to me before."

"But—well, what happened to you?"

"We lost. Rodarren and Jerret, all of us. Norue captured us."

"No. Oh no. He said he was going to find out where Rodarren went, but I never dreamed . . . How are you? Are you all right?"

"I'm fine."

"You've never lied to me before," she said, smiling.

Mathewar laughed, then winced at the pain in his side. "How did you get here?"

"I tried to go through the wall, and Norue's men followed me. I had to find you—I have to tell you something, something important—"

Mathewar held up his hand. "Wait," he said. "Don't tell me anything you don't want Norue to know. He's going to question me, and I might not be able to hold out against him."

"To question—" Her eyes widened as she understood. "But this is important, this is something everyone should know—"

"Are you certain? Is there anything in your story that Norue could use to his advantage?"

"Oh. Oh, I see. Yes, you're right."

"Why don't we talk about safe subjects? How are Lord and Lady Snoppish? And what are the people at court doing?"

"The court isn't a very safe subject these days. Or the Snoppishes, for that matter."

"No, I see that."

They talked for a while, trading harmless stories, until they heard footsteps outside in the corridor. Angarred did not need to be told to pretend she didn't know Mathewar; she stopped in the middle of a sentence and hurried to sit back against the wall.

It was only a jailer, bringing each of them a plate and mug. The plate held a piece of bread that looked as if it had been dipped in grease. Mathewar pushed it away. He had no appetite, anyway; he never did when he needed sattery.

The mug contained water. He lifted it, his hand trembling. He was very cold; the air in the dungeon chilled him to the bone.

He felt a little better after he drank. He sat back and looked at the shackle on his arm, then reached out with his mind for the locking mechanism. He saw nothing, nothing at all.

He tried again. Nothing happened. One more try, this time

forcing himself to go slowly, to make no mistakes. It was no good. Panicked now, he spoke the words to create a small light, but even that, the first spell he had ever learned, proved to be beyond him.

His shivering grew stronger. He understood what was about to happen, and it was worse than Norue, much worse.

"Hello, Mathewar."

Angarred had slipped into a light doze. She woke to see someone standing in front of Mathewar, his back to her, several guards at his side. It wasn't Norue, but who . . . ?

"Hello, Alkarren," Mathewar said.

Alkarren moved and she saw Mathewar sitting on the floor of the prison, his knees drawn up against him, his free arm around his legs. She hurried back to her blanket and hid herself within it; Alkarren would surely separate them if he saw her. But Alkarren was intent on Mathewar.

"I thought you'd be more surprised than that," Alkarren said. "Weren't you expecting Norue?"

"No."

"No? Come, stop playing the clever scholar for once—you don't have to impress me. Of course you thought Norue would be here to question you—he was the one who captured you, wasn't he?"

"I can't do magic, Alkarren," Mathewar said. He sounded weary. "Someone must be keeping me from it, someone stronger than I am. Someone, probably, who has the Stone. And we both know that's you."

"Ah, of course. It's obvious once you say it like that. Do you want to know why I'm here instead of Norue?"

"No."

Alkarren laughed, though without amusement. "He mentioned at court that he had some prisoners from Emindal, you among them. I asked if I could question you and he gave me permission immediately. Apparently he doesn't think you're terribly important in the scheme of things."

Mathewar said nothing.

"Well," Alkarren said. "You know why I'm here, of course. I need you to help me with the Stone."

"I've already told you I won't help you. Anyway, why do you think I know anything about the Stone?"

"Oh, I'm sure you don't. You're probably entirely ignorant. But you have some small talent in discovering how things work, more mechanical than anything else."

" 'Some small talent.' " Mathewar laughed. "Tell me you're almost completely baffled by the Stone, that you can only do the simplest tricks with it, barely enough to entertain a king at a banquet. Tell me you were the worst magician ever to come out of the College. I might help you then."

"You know very well I can do more," Alkarren said angrily. "You've learned that to your cost, haven't you? And right now I'm a far better magician than you are. Well, anyone would be, wouldn't they—even a raw boy learning his first spell at the College. You were right about one thing—you can't do any magic at all."

"That's what this is all about, then. You've been envious of my ability ever since I got to the College, and now you've finally found a way to keep me from doing magic. Very good—you've taken the College's most important device and used it to exact a childish revenge. Though it's too bad you haven't found a way to make yourself a better magician—you're still as incompetent as ever."

Alkarren clenched his fists, trying to hold in his anger. Finally he said, "Oh, but you're wrong. I'm not keeping you from doing magic. I've taken away your magic for good."

Angarred nearly gasped aloud. She looked at Mathewar, horrified. His expression hadn't changed; he would not give Alkarren that satisfaction. "Take away magic?" he said. "I don't think you can."

"Are you sure of that? Imagine you're sitting at home, reading something, say. It grows dark, and without thinking you try to make a light. And you can't. What would that be like? To be without magic for the rest of your life?"

"I imagine I'd be living like you, before you got the Stone."

Alkarren lunged forward, his hand raised. Mathewar stared up at him levelly, not moving. Alkarren stood still for a moment, and then dropped his hand.

"You'll have to be careful not to insult people, in your new life," Alkarren said softly. "It could be dangerous for you, very dangerous, without magic. But you were always arrogant, I remember. That was your problem, wasn't it?"

"No. My problem was that you killed my wife and child."

"Enough of this," Alkarren said impatiently. "Will you work with me, help me discover the Stone's properties? Or are you going to have to light candles when it grows dark like everyone else?"

"You heard my answer."

"You will work with me, though. When I'm done with you you will. I have any number of unpleasant things in mind for you—we haven't even started here. I'll see you tomorrow."

As soon as Alkarren left Mathewar began to shiver. "Mathewar," Angarred said.

She watched as he brought his trembling under control. "Yes," he said.

"You're cold. Let me throw you my blanket."

"Then you'll be cold. It's freezing here."

"I'll be fine."

"You're lying to me again, aren't you? We set a bad precedent that first time."

"No, really. It isn't that cold here. Truly—you can look into my mind if you don't believe me. Oh," she said, remembering.

"Oh," he said, his voice expressionless. "Anyway, if you give me your blanket Alkarren will realize we know each other, and that would be very dangerous for you. He doesn't seem to like people who are close to me."

Close to me, Angarred thought. She stored the phrase away to think about another time; at present she was too busy simply surviving. "I'll give it to you in the evening, after he leaves," she said. "And you can throw it back in the morning. Alkarren will probably come back at the same time—he said he'd see you tomorrow, remember? Anyway, I don't sleep very well here—I'll wake you up if I hear him before then."

"When's morning around here?"

"Oh, right—I didn't tell you. I made up a way of telling time, to keep me from going crazy. There are three guards, so each of them probably keeps watch for eight hours. That guard out there—I call him Smelly—he gets replaced at midnight. What I decided was midnight, anyway. And then the next man—Stupid—he leaves at eight in the morning. You can give me the blanket back then."

"All right then. If you're sure you don't mind."

For an answer she put a hand outside the bars and threw the blanket across the room as hard as she could. It skittered into a corner, one of the few places the harsh light didn't reach.

Mathewar spoke a few words to create a light. Nothing happened. "Marfan's balls and Mathona's tits!" he said savagely, jerking the chain hard several times. He took a deep breath, reached into the darkness and brought back the blanket.

He wrapped it around himself; he looked like an old man, or an invalid. "Thank you," he said, calmer now.

He lay down and huddled against the wall, pulling the blanket with him. After a while his breathing grew regular. She waited until she was certain he had fallen asleep, then returned to the work she had been doing. It was another secret she had to keep from Alkarren, and so from Mathewar: one of the bars of her cage seemed to be loose. The bars rose from the stone floor to the roof, which was little higher than the height of a man; the floor around one of them had been picked at, probably by generations of prisoners. If she could remove it she would have enough room to step outside. She jerked it back and forth, clearing out small chips of stone.

Close to me, she thought. What had he meant by that? She *had* lied to him, though, if lying meant not telling him the most important thing about her. Well, it didn't matter. Nothing would matter if they couldn't get free.

TWENTY

Jerret sat in his cage. Rodarren leaned against his shoulder, somehow able to sleep while the religious in the cage opposite them droned on through his liturgy.

The liturgy praised all the Godkings and their attributes, starting with Marfan and Mathona and ending with Queen Chelenin, then cycled around to begin again with the First King and Queen. Jerret had already yelled at the man to stop, to hold his tongue, but the religious just smiled serenely and continued on. Apparently nothing could interrupt the liturgy, not even someone desperate for sleep.

Jerret let his mind drift from the irritant in the opposite cage. He had promised to bring the princess to Karededin, but he had never imagined they would come bound in rope and then be thrown unceremoniously into prison. They had lost their gamble; they had even let the Stone slip from their hands. He would probably die with Rodarren, as he had promised. A thin hope remained that his father had enough influence with King Tezue to rescue them, but the king might still be under Alkarren's control. Anyway, his father could have no idea of what had happened to him.

He had imagined such a bright future with Rodarren. Marriage and then children, another family to add to the already overflowing

Snoppish household. And if Rodarren had become queen he would have tried to reform the court, curtailing the hypocrisy and flattery and corruption by his example if nothing else.

If only they could have married. He wouldn't mind dying so much if the world could see what they had meant to each other. She had promised to marry him when they got to Karededin, and now here they were: the Godkings had probably laughed wildly at their plans, knowing what would become of them.

Wait a minute. He was an idiot. The religious could marry them; they needed nothing else. "Hey!" he called to the man in the opposite cage.

The man continued singing. "Hey!" Jerret said. "Could you marry us?"

The religious stopped. "You and the woman wish to be married?" he asked hoarsely.

"Yes. Could you do it?"

"Of course."

"Rodarren!" Jerret said, shaking her gently. "Rodarren, wake up. We can be married after all."

Rodarren opened her eyes. Once again Jerret was impressed by her uncanny ability to come awake immediately. "How?"

"The religious, across from us. I was an idiot not to think of it sooner."

"Are you ready?" the religious asked.

Rodarren smiled. "This isn't the way I imagined marrying you," she said.

"Nor I," Jerret said. They stood and held hands, facing the religious. "Go ahead."

"The first husband and wife were Marfan and Mathona," the religious said, beginning the ancient ritual. "The sun shines by day, and the moon by night, to remind us of their constancy . . ."

Men tramped in and out of Mathewar's cell the next day: to relight the lamps, to take away the dishes, to bring bowls of soup for dinner. They made so much noise it was impossible to sleep. "You should eat what we give you," one of them said as he took Mathewar's plate. "The rats will get it if you don't."

But he couldn't eat the soup either. All his various injuries had combined into a single constant torment; he couldn't focus, couldn't think, probably couldn't fall asleep even if the guards would let him.

He had to concentrate to talk to Angarred, though. It was good to talk to her, even if they said nothing of importance; she reassured him just by her presence. And he had to stay alert enough to pretend he wasn't hurt too badly, at least; she had enough to worry about without him.

Alkarren and his guards returned at the same time, halfway through Smelly's watch. Mathewar watched as he carried in a brazier and set it down in the middle of the room, then took one of the candles and knelt to light the wood inside.

"My man here says you're a sattery-drinker," Alkarren said without turning around. "He's seen the signs on you. Terrible, to let yourself go so badly."

Mathewar knew what would happen next, even before Alkarren took a leather bottle and a silver cup from one of the guards. He drew his legs up and put his arm around them, holding back his trembling.

Alkarren poured the bloodred drink into the cup and set it close to the brazier to heat. He turned to Mathewar. "You know what you need to do for this," he said.

Mathewar shook his head, not trusting himself to speak. He swallowed hard.

"Are you certain? It's been a while since you've had sattery, isn't it? Some addicts die when they try to stop. Or their minds burn away, and they become madmen, or idiots. Which would you rather be, do you think?"

He thought of a caustic reply, bit it back. Every part of his body wanted the drink; it overwhelmed him, promised him surcease from his other wracking pains. He could smell it as it heated, a rich, promising scent.

Alkarren lifted the cup and brought it close to him. "Tell me what you know about the Stone," he said. "I really don't understand why you're being so stubborn about this. What would be the harm if I knew more about it? Just tell me and I'll let you drink this. I'll let you have all the sattery you ever wanted. Maybe I'll even give you your magic back—who knows? All this, just for a few hours' conversation."

Saliva flooded his mouth. A hard cramp in his stomach made him nearly double over. He breathed shallowly, trying not to cry out.

"What? I didn't hear you. Did you say you would help me with the Stone? We could work together, you know, making fantastic discoveries. You and I, moving from height to height, far above the common folk. We could even rule together."

"Rule?" Mathewar said.

Alkarren laughed. "Ah, now I see your difficulty. Yes, rule. What would be wrong with that? Why do you think I would be such a bad king?"

What difference would it make? Mathewar thought. It didn't matter who was king; he would have his sattery back and be able to drink himself into oblivion. And truly, who was to say that Alkarren would be worse than Norue?

Alkarren moved the cup closer, careful to stay out of Mathewar's reach. One moment longer, he thought. One moment more and I'm going to try to tear that cup from his hands.

"And you'd be beside me, the king's advisor," Alkarren said. "You'd like that, wouldn't you? Though I can't promise I'll follow your advice . . ."

He saw Angarred then, staring at them both in horror, and he realized he couldn't do it. He had a responsibility to more than just himself; he couldn't let her live under Alkarren, no matter what happened to him. And Rodarren, and Jerret . . . He shook his head weakly.

"Too bad," Alkarren said. "Well, I'll see you tomorrow." He headed toward the door, then walked back a few paces and set the cup near the brazier. "I'll leave this here to help you make up your mind."

Mathewar watched him go. For a moment he seemed to shimmer, to change into other people Mathewar had once disliked: Prince Norue, a master who had been a harsh disciplinarian . . . It wasn't magic; he was fairly certain of that. Probably his fever had grown worse. He hoped that was it, anyway; if not it meant that his mind was starting to burn away, just as Alkarren said it would.

He bent over and started to retch. He vomited again and again, for a long time, though there was nothing in his stomach to bring up. Finally he stopped and began to cough, holding his hand to his side.

This time Angarred said nothing, but simply threw him the blanket. He wrapped it around himself and lay down, and coughed for a long time.

He tried to sleep again the next day, his back against the wall and his legs stretched out in front of him, but the comings and goings in the cell made it nearly impossible. The smell of sattery tantalized him; it seemed insistent, underlying everything.

"Mathewar," Angarred said. "Mathewar, are you awake?"

"Yes," he said, his eyes closed.

"Listen, I have a question for you. Why do you think Alkarren lit the fire with a candle, and not with magic?"

He could not seem to think. "What?"

"He could have used magic to light that fire. Alkarren. You did, at my house and in the forest."

He opened his eyes. "So you *were* watching me at your house. I thought I sensed you there." He began to laugh, then coughed again, on and on. He took a long breath.

"Never mind that. This is important. Pay attention."

Pay attention. He would have to pay attention that night, when Alkarren came back—it seemed unfair to have to do it twice in one day. "I don't know. Why didn't he light the fire with magic?"

"Because he couldn't. He used the Stone to put a spell on this room—no one can do magic here, not you and not even him. He hasn't taken away your magic after all."

He said nothing. She was waiting for an answer, though. He looked for what seemed the hundredth time at the cup of sattery Alkarren had left, then made himself turn back to her. Her shape frayed and she changed into a statue of a Godqueen, tall and regal.

"That would be helpful if we could leave the room," he said finally, ignoring the hallucination. "But we can't."

"We'll get out," she said, becoming Angarred again. "We will."

He smiled tiredly, more at her cheerful optimism than at anything she said. Well, she was still young, young enough to leave home and wager her entire future on a slim hope. She had not yet learned that things did not always work out for the best, that sometimes the wrong people died, that sometimes justice wasn't done, not even if you petitioned the king for it.

"All right—here's another question," he said. "Alkarren surely knows that if I study the Stone with him I'll learn all sorts of things about it, and that sooner or later I'll be able to overcome him, to use the Stone against him. But that doesn't seem to bother him."

"Maybe he hasn't thought that far ahead."

"If I've thought of it he has. He was always able to think several steps ahead of everyone else—that's how he climbed so high in the king's favor. It worries me—he has something planned and I can't see what it is."

He closed his eyes. He began to cough again, and he drew his legs against him, wincing at the pain in his side.

Alkarren said nothing when he and his guards came into the cell that evening. He looked grim, full of purpose. Mathewar tensed, used to the other man's gibes and insults, but Alkarren didn't seem to notice.

Suddenly Alkarren invaded his mind. He felt it like a sword thrust, a great wound tearing him apart. Alkarren paused at obvious, important memories, stopping before them as though studying portraits in a manor house, seeing him at the College, with Embre, at the birth of his daughter.

He tried to pull away from the violation, but Alkarren stayed with him. He was looking for something, some knowledge, moving quicker now. While he was still distracted by his search Mathewar put up a shield in front of what he knew about the Stone, but it was flimsy, created too hastily.

Alkarren found a memory of him working a complex spell and stopped to study it. Mathewar shuddered in disgust. But he could strengthen his shield while the other man was distracted. He worked as quickly as he could, speaking strengthening spells, shoring up defenses, hoping Alkarren would stay where he was and not follow.

Suddenly he realized that he should not have been able to work his spells, that Alkarren had taken away his magic. Angarred had said something . . . He struggled to remember, careful to hide his thoughts.

Alkarren had put a spell on the room. Alkarren could do magic, though, so he must have lifted the spell. And therefore he, Mathewar, could do magic now too.

Mathewar set one last strengthening spell on his shield. He knew he should do more, should not let this opportunity pass, but he felt exhausted from the work he had done, unable to continue. He shook himself and gathered as much strength as he could, then broke through Alkarren's weak shields.

Now it was his turn to study old memories. He saw Alkarren as a young boy being teased by the others at the College, as a teacher assiduously flattering Narinye and Merren and the other masters, as a counselor slowly gaining influence over the king. He pushed on, unheeding, ripping apart Alkarren's memories, his tiredness replaced by ferocious delight at the damage he could do.

Alkarren fought back weakly, too shocked by the invasion to defend himself properly. Mathewar seized control of Alkarren's body, forced him to the ground and made him writhe there helplessly. Alkarren's head hit the stone floor over and over; Mathewar heard the loud cracks twice, once through Alkarren's ears and then through his own.

Suddenly he felt a dim pain in his stomach. One of the guards was beating him, trying to get him to stop. He raced back through Alkarren's mind.

He stopped, horrified, at one of Alkarren's memories. He understood the depths of the man's treachery then, understood how he had betrayed him over and over. Understood that he, Mathewar, would eventually have to do Alkarren's bidding, and that Alkarren had known that all along.

He returned to his own mind and found himself on the floor, the guards kicking him in his ribs and head. "Stop," he said weakly. "Stop. I've stopped."

The guards forced him to sit up. Alkarren stood, putting his hand to his head. Mathewar saw that he had drawn blood, and he grinned savagely.

"Very well," Alkarren said. "I've been enjoying all this tremendously, but I'm going to have to end it tomorrow. Tomorrow you will do whatever I ask of you, and you'll do it willingly."

Alkarren and the guards left. The new ache in his ribs joined all the others shouting for attention. He curled up against the wall, feeling hopeless.

Angarred threw him the blanket but he made no move to catch it. "That was wonderful," she said. "What did you do to him? I loved seeing him on the floor like that."

Mathewar said nothing. "Mathewar?" she said.

He did not look up. "It's over," he said. "He's won. I can't—I can't—"

"What do you mean? What can he do that's so terrible?"

He turned away without answering. Several times that night she woke to hear him coughing or tossing restlessly, the chain clanking as he moved, but when she called to him he said nothing.

He leaned against the wall the next day, his eyes closed, not speaking. For the first time she let herself see how ill he had become. He had a sparse beard now, almost black with dirt, and his once-shining hair was dull and matted. His face looked pale, haggard. And something else worried her—when she had gotten the blanket back the day before she had seen what looked like blood.

She went back to her work, jerking the loose bar against the floor. Why did he think he couldn't hold out against Alkarren? Surely he could—he had faced him bravely so far. But even she had to admit that he would die if he stayed here much longer.

One thing gave her hope, though—she had hidden her spoon after yesterday's supper, and the stupid guard hadn't thought to look for it. She dug furiously at the floor with it, prying out stones. The bar seemed looser today, though perhaps she only imagined it.

An hour later the hole had grown a good deal larger. She pulled the bar hard and it swung back, suddenly free of the floor. Something cracked loudly in the ceiling above and stone and dust pattered down on her.

She wrenched the bar from the ceiling and stepped out of the cage. She had done it. She stood for a moment, feeling triumph course through her, deciding what to do next.

The guard unlocked the gate. It creaked loudly as he pushed it open. "What's going on in here?" he asked. "What was that noise?"

She swung the bar at him. More by luck than anything else she connected with something and he went down. She dropped the bar and took the keys from his hand, then hurried to Mathewar.

Mathewar was deep in sleep; even the noise hadn't woken him. She tried several of the guard's keys in his shackle. Why were there so many of them? Suddenly the lock opened, and she cried out at the small victory.

"Mathewar," she said. She hunted around the room and picked up the blanket and a lantern. "Mathewar, get up. We're going."

"What?"

"Get up." She draped the blanket over him, then put down the lantern, grasped his hand and pulled him up. He stared at the open shackle, puzzled.

"How—"

"I'll tell you later. Let's go."

He took a step and fell against the wall. She helped him up again, this time slinging his arm over her shoulder. Then she picked up the lantern in her other hand, and moving slowly, far too slowly, they made their way across the room, past the unconscious guard, and through the gate.

There was a long corridor outside, lit by widely spaced lamps. It was not as bright as their cell, but after days of harsh illumination she welcomed the dimness. She chose a direction and they began to walk, Mathewar dragging her down. He seemed able to use his legs now, though he limped badly; she wanted to shake him and had to grit her teeth to keep to his pace.

The corridor seemed to go on forever. Surely other people must come here, she thought; at any moment they would see a guard or soldier heading toward them. She strained to hear over Mathewar's coughing and the uneven beat of their footsteps on the stone, but there were no other sounds.

A while later Mathewar sighed and fell against her. She let him slip to the floor and sat next to him, exhausted herself, then turned to study him.

He had a bruise on his cheek, just beginning to turn black, and his lips were cracked and dry. A blackish stain mottled his shirt; she bent closer and saw dried blood, her worst fears confirmed. She lifted the shirt and drew a breath at the wound: an arrow, she thought; it had gone clear through his body.

There was more blood on his thigh. She tried to peel his trousers away but the blood had crusted to the wound. Mathewar stirred and moaned and she drew her hand away quickly, feeling a horrible queasy pity.

She couldn't let him sleep very long; someone might stumble on them at any moment. She woke him reluctantly and they continued on.

A short while later she heard voices ahead of them. She stopped, terrified, and peered forward. She thought she could make out bars in the wall, more prison cells.

She went on, moving slower. They passed a few cells, some harshly lit, some so gloomy and dull that the light from the corridor did not penetrate all the way inside. Prisoners shouted to them from behind the bars, proclaiming their innocence, asking for favors. Someone called out her name.

Startled, she looked inside the next cell and nearly cried aloud. Lord Enlandin and Lady Karanin stood there. Their once-splendid clothes were filthy rags, their hair lank and uncombed, their flesh almost wasted to the bone. She had last seen them sleek and healthy, their usual imperious selves, before she had ridden south. And that had been—she thought back, amazed—only a week ago.

"Lady Karanin," she said, appalled.

"Yes, that's right, it's me. Don't just stand there jabbering—get us out of here."

"How can I? I don't have a key. But I don't understand—I saw you last week at court, and you were—how did you get—"

"Nonsense. We've been here a month, at least. Would we look like this after only a week?"

"Quiet, Karanin—we need her on our side," Enlandin said. He

turned to Angarred. "Listen, Lady—Lady Angarred, isn't it? You're a clever girl—I'm sure you can think of a way to help us. Let us out and you'll be rewarded beyond your wildest dreams. What do you want? Wealth? Power? A seat on the council, and the ear of the king?"

"I can't. I said I can't." Despite her desire for power she could not help feeling some satisfaction at her words, and at the expressions on their faces. "But I saw you just last week, truly. What happened?"

"Oh, don't listen to her—she's lost her mind, the foolish country girl," Karanin said. Mathewar coughed and Karanin peered outside the bars. "Who's that with you?"

Angarred turned and left them. Someone's lost their mind, that much is true, she thought. But she had to get out; she could think about the puzzle some other time, when they were safe.

They went past more cells set into the wall. More people called out to them for help, but she saw no one else she recognized. The corridor ended in two flights of stairs and they climbed them slowly, Mathewar holding on to her for balance at each step.

At the top Mathewar stopped, exhausted; he had used up all his strength. She helped him lie down and then sat beside him and glanced around, fearful of discovery. They had reached a hallway that went on ahead of them for several yards. A door stood at the end, carved and painted like many of the doors in the castle. The life of the castle went on beyond it, she knew; they would probably encounter servants or courtiers or guards. And how would she explain what they were doing, unwashed and ill and poorly dressed, wandering through the corridors?

A small cabinet stuck out from the wall near her. She pulled it open. Inside was a lever she had seen before, in fireplaces and as part of decorative friezes; they led to hidden corridors in the castle. She tugged at it and saw without surprise that a door opened in the wall, revealing a dark hallway beyond.

She roused Mathewar and dragged him inside. She closed the door, blocking out the light from outside; now the only illumination came from her lantern.

Suddenly Mathewar's eyes opened and he looked directly at her. "Art a celestial messenger, come to tell me of my death?" he asked.

"No. No, of course not. You know me—I'm Angarred."

"Art no earthly woman—hast an unearthly beauty, the look of a celestial messenger. Hast no wings, though. What happened to thy wings?"

His words turned her speechless. Did he truly think she was beautiful? Or was it his delirium talking? "I'm Angarred," she said finally.

"Funny—if I should die and they live. Funny."

"You're not going to die. We're going to get out of here and you'll be fine."

He dropped back to the floor. His pupils were huge, and in the light of the lantern his eyes looked black and unseeing. She touched his face; it felt far too hot. Sweat pooled in the hollow of his breastbone.

She remembered what Alkarren said about people who stopped drinking sattery and her sense of urgency returned; she had to get help before his delirium grew worse. She loosened the blanket she had placed around him, then forced herself to wait, to let him sleep a little. Finally she woke him and they continued on, leaving the blanket behind them.

Some time later Mathewar spoke again. "Stones become women, women become birds," he said, as if continuing a conversation. "Narinye said that magic is artifice and illusion, but Rone said no, that magic is real, a true thing. Dost understand this? Everything changes. It changes everything."

She barely listened, too preoccupied to try to make sense of his words, if there was any sense to be had from them. She saw nothing in the hallway for a long while, and she wondered how long they had been walking, what time it was in the world outside.

Mathewar was moving quicker now, though still limping. They nearly passed another cabinet in the uncertain light of the lantern but she recognized it in time, and opened it and pulled the lever.

The room beyond was dark. She let go of Mathewar; to her relief he stood without her help, though his eyes were still unfocused. She headed out carefully into the hallway. It looked familiar, even in the dim light of the lantern; she had explored this part of the castle before.

The hallway seemed deserted; doubtless everyone was asleep. Another piece of luck, she thought. She led Mathewar quietly through a tangle of intersecting hallways. They came to a side door she remembered; she opened it and they slipped outside.

The sheer darkness of the night surprised her; she had grown used to the continuous, oppressive light of her cell. The lantern dimmed and then went out just as they started down the path from Pergodi Castle. She cursed, straining to see the path by starlight, trying to separate the darker trees and boulders from the night around them.

Pergodi never slept, they said, and once in the city itself she saw that it was true. Carts drove over the cobblestones, making early deliveries; prostitutes headed home; drunkards staggered to the next tavern; sattery-drinkers sat propped against walls, their eyes vacant. She stopped a cart and asked for a ride to the Snoppishes' house, but the driver took one look at her and Mathewar and rode off without bothering to reply. The next two drivers shook their heads, one firmly and one with regret.

Finally her urgency must have communicated itself, because a man smoking a pipe nodded back toward his cart. "Thank you," she said, her relief making her giddy. "You'll be well rewarded for this, I promise you."

They settled themselves among odd-sized pieces of wood; no lumber had come into Pergodi since the siege and people had begun scavenging ruined houses. She wondered what this man had been doing under cover of darkness, then decided it was none of her business.

"I'd better be," the man said, and flicked his reins.

He'd better be what? she thought as they set off. Oh, rewarded. Why in the name of all the Godkings did I say that? I have no coins or jewels, and I'm sure Mathewar doesn't either. Maybe Lord Snoppish . . . But she had imposed on the Snoppishes enough; he would be well within his rights to say no, or even turn her away.

When they reached the Snoppishes' house she told the driver to wait, then knocked loudly, hoping to wake someone. The lord himself came to the door, yawning widely.

"Angarred!" he said, abruptly awake. "Are you all right? Did you get to Emindal? Is there any word of Jerret?"

She thought of Jerret, no doubt locked away in a cell much like her own, and she dreaded having to break the news to the old man. "I'll tell you later," she said. "Could you—could you pay that man in the cart, please? He brought us here, and I promised him . . . And you have to help me bring Mathewar inside—he's ill, and he has to hide—"

"You can't hide him here." It was Lady Snoppish; she had come to the door without Angarred noticing.

Of course—the blue-cloaks were watching them. She had forgotten.

"I know," Lord Snoppish said. "Lord Anfarna asked me to look after his house while he's at his estate. He won't be coming back, not during the siege. We can take Mathewar there."

"And the cart?" Angarred said.

Lord Snoppish walked out to the cart and spoke a few words, then went back into the house and returned with something he handed over to the driver. Angarred could not hear what they said, but the man seemed very satisfied.

"You go with him, Angarred," Lord Snoppish said. "We'll follow."

She went back to the cart and climbed in, then checked to make sure Mathewar was still breathing. For the first time in a long while she felt secure, protected. She hadn't cried once in the cell or the labyrinth of corridors, but she cried now, not at her ordeal but because people like the Snoppishes existed in the world.

TWENTY-ONE

Lord Anfarna's house was nearly empty; he seemed to have taken almost everything he owned to his country estate. Angarred and Snoppish and the driver of the cart carried Mathewar by lantern-light down a long echoing hallway to a room containing only a bed and a table.

"You wait here," Snoppish said. "I'll get a doctor, and you can come back to our house when he's done."

"I'll just sleep here," she said, wanting to be close to Mathewar. Snoppish gave her an odd look, but he said nothing as he went out into the city.

She found another sparsely furnished room. Early morning light came through the window; she lay on the bed and listened to the confused sounds of the city waking up: carts clattering, soldiers shouting, someone whistling. Just as she drifted off to sleep she heard a distant rending crash and a high shrill scream; the huge Takekek catapult had woken for the day.

After an unsatisfying rest she woke and went out into the hallway. Snoppish sat there, in a decaying chair he had dragged in from somewhere. "Didn't you go home?" she asked.

He shrugged. "It was nearly morning when I got up," he said. "I found a doctor, but he's making us pay dearly for the privilege—they're all busy, and feverchill has broken out in the poorer quarters . . ."

"I'm terribly sorry—you shouldn't have to pay for all of this."

Lord Snoppish waved off her concern. "How is Mathewar?" she asked.

"The doctor's with him now—you can go ask him."

She went into Mathewar's room. He lay on the bed, asleep, breathing regularly. Someone had washed him and combed out his silky hair—Angarred suspected Lady Snoppish—but he still looked sallow, ill.

"How is he?" Angarred asked the doctor, speaking softly.

"Oh, you don't have to whisper—I gave him something to make him sleep like the dead," the doctor said, laughing. Angarred scowled, but he didn't seem to notice. "His wounds are getting better, thank the Healer. But his fever comes and goes—it doesn't improve, but it doesn't get worse, either. It's not feverchill—I don't know what it is. I've never seen anything like it."

"It's not fever. He used to drink sattery, and he's been without it for a while."

"Ah, so that's it. Then it's more serious than I thought. Well, if the chills don't go away I'll give him some sattery, see if that will help."

Angarred scowled again. I thought doctors were supposed to be reassuring, she thought. She was about to say as much when she saw Mathewar stir.

"No," he said hoarsely, his eyes closed. "No sattery."

"There—you heard him," she said. "He doesn't want any sattery."

"He doesn't know what he's saying. He could die without it. Or his mind might burn away—"

"Yes, I know all about it. Why don't you leave him alone for now, see how he does?"

Mathewar opened his eyes. "Hello," he said.

"Hello," Angarred said. "Do you know who I am?"

"Of course—you're Angarred. Why . . . ?"

"You thought I was a celestial messenger, back in the tunnels."

"A celestial messenger." He laughed weakly, a whisper of a

laugh. "Yes, I can see how . . ." He closed his eyes and fell back asleep.

"There, you see," Angarred said to the doctor. "His mind is clear."

It was only now, when Mathewar was safe, that she had time to think about his delirious words in the castle. A celestial messenger, she thought. Well, it was better than being mistaken for Embre. Still, she could not help but wish that he would see her as she truly was.

Lord Snoppish came into the room and gave the doctor some coins. "Thank you for your help," he said. "And remember—you're not to tell anyone he's here."

"Oh, I'll be as silent as the grave," the doctor said, chuckling.

After the doctor left Lord Snoppish ushered Angarred out of the room. "You'd better tell me what happened to Jerret now," he said.

She told him everything she knew—Norue's attack on Emindal, the defeat of Rodarren's troops. "He's probably in the dungeons, just like Mathewar was. Rodarren too."

Snoppish frowned. "I'll have to go, then," he said.

"Go? Where?"

"To court, to get Tezue to release him."

"But they called him a traitor. Do you think you can convince Tezue to let him go?"

"Maybe. For one thing, Tezue owes me a great deal for warning him about Norue's plots. It's been fourteen years, but I've never asked him for anything since then, and he knows it. And for another, the king knows that the nobility can't be locked away in the dungeons—it goes against everything we believe."

"Norue must hate you," she said, realizing only then that Snoppish, too, was in danger from the prince. "You'll have to be careful. And what if the king's still a Hollow One?"

"I thought of that, of course," Snoppish said, shrugging. "What else can I do, though? He's my son."

"I wish I could go with you," Angarred said. She would love to see Lord Snoppish cut through the glitter and arch mannerisms of the court and confront the king, see what the courtiers made of this blunt, kindly old man.

"I'll tell you all about it," he said.

She tried to read his mood when he came back to Anfarna's house that evening. He had changed his clothes before going to court; he was dressed in what Angarred now knew were hopelessly outmoded trousers and cloak, both far too dark and heavy, and he carried a thick wooden cane. Somehow the clothes added to his presence, though, as if announcing to the world that he didn't care about such foolishness as fashion.

"Did you see the king?" she asked. "What did he say?"

"He said he'll look into it. At least he didn't refuse me outright."

"No. Did he—did he seem like a Hollow One?"

"He seemed the Tezue I used to know. Proud, uncompromising, sure of himself."

"That's good, isn't it?"

"I certainly hope so."

Angarred returned to Mathewar's room the next day. He opened his eyes and smiled when he saw her. She had been pleased when he refused the doctor's offer of sattery, and now she felt hopeful that he might recover without it.

"It's my celestial messenger, come to watch over me," he said. He sat up carefully. "Would you give me some water, please?"

"Of course." She sat on the bed next to him, then reached for the pitcher and mug on the table and poured some water. "Here you are."

He tried to grasp the mug but his hands were trembling so badly he spilled most of the contents. She took it from him and held it up to his mouth, putting her arm around his shoulders to steady him.

He drank it all; she filled the mug and held him again. As he drank his blanket fell away, and she was suddenly aware that he was naked, at least from the waist up. She had not thought anything of her nearness to him when they were escaping through the tunnels; her only concern had been to get them to safety. But now her arm seemed warm where she touched him, and waves of excitement at their closeness coursed through her. She felt as if she could barely breathe.

He finished and she took the mug with her free hand and set it on the table. She should move; she had no real reason to continue holding him. But the exquisite pleasure she felt kept her near him as surely as any enchantment.

She could smell his hair, his skin, a wonderful scent that reminded her of the pine needles in the forest. He had already rejected her once, she thought. But he had not been in his right mind then, and now he seemed awake and free of sattery. And she wanted him terribly.

She leaned toward him and kissed him. His hand cupped the back of her neck and he drew closer.

They kissed for a long time, hungrily. By a strange transformation she was the one trembling now; his hands were steady. She ran her hands down his back, feeling his smooth skin, his hard muscles. She touched cloth—a bandage—and pulled away quickly.

He moved back. "What?" she asked, breathless. "Does that hurt?"

"No." He leaned against the wall, looking uncomfortable. "No, it's not that. It's—it's that—well, I think my wife is still alive."

"Your wife! But your wife died—you saw her."

She sounded ungenerous, she knew that. But how could his wife be alive?

"Do you remember when we saw Karanin and Enlandin in the tunnels?" She nodded; she had not realized that he had been conscious enough to recognize them. "I think Alkarren is somehow able to create copies of people, shadow people. We learned something about that at the College, but only the magicians of old were able to do it—we've lost the knowledge or are no longer strong enough. But it seems to be possible with the Stone."

She remembered reading about shadow people in *The Life of Tobrin*. "And you think Alkarren created copies of your wife? And what Dalesio destroyed was the copy, a—a shadow person?"

"Copies of my wife and child, yes."

"But do you have any proof of that? Or are you just hoping it's true because you saw Karanin and Enlandin?"

"I saw them in his mind. Embre and Atte. They were in a tower in the forest, Alkarren's tower. We may have even passed it on our journey. That's why he knew I would help him with the Stone, because if I didn't he would kill them. Kill them for real, this time."

"Maybe he just wanted you to think they were alive. It was only his thought, after all . . ."

"No, it's true—I saw it clearly in his mind. Or it was true—it might be an old memory and he's moved them since." He lay back down and closed his eyes.

She saw how exhausted he was. She should stop arguing with him, stop trying to prove him wrong. He had seen them in Alkarren's mind, after all—though if it was an old memory Alkarren might have killed them since then.

She couldn't say that, of course. Still, she felt a sudden unreasoning hatred for Embre, a woman she had never met but who kept coming between them. "That's wonderful," she said. It sounded insincere, but he didn't seem to notice.

The next day a knock came at the door; she looked out and to her surprise saw Lord Jerret and Princess Rodarren standing there. "Hello!" she said, letting them in. "How did you get away? You were in the dungeons like us, weren't you? Did Lord Snoppish get you out?"

"Yes, to all of that," Jerret said, smiling. "King Tezue told my father that nobility should never be imprisoned except in cases of treason. Of course Norue argued that this *was* treason, but Tezue said that we'd only sailed to Emindal and he didn't see what was so terrible about that."

"Did he?" Angarred said. "He doesn't sound like a Hollow One at all, does he?"

"My father thinks he's fine. But we need to talk, to share information and decide what to do next."

"We'll have to go to Mathewar's room, then. I don't think he's well enough to get up."

Jerret raised an eyebrow. "But is he well enough to—to talk to us? My father said some things—"

"Oh, yes. Come on, I'll show you."

Angarred knocked on Mathewar's door and put her head inside the room. "There's some people to see you," she said.

He was sitting up in bed, leaning against the wall, a blanket around his shoulders. He wore his usual roughspun worker's clothing; she felt disappointed to see it, but relieved as well.

Rodarren came into the room. "Princess Rodarren!" he said. "I thought you were in prison!"

Angarred turned to find chairs for all of them while they caught up. Jerret hung back in the hallway, looking almost embarrassed. "What's wrong?" she whispered.

He seemed to nerve himself to go inside. Curious, she followed him. "Mathewar," he said stiffly. "I want to apologize for underestimating—for misunderstanding—"

Mathewar shrugged. "There's nothing to apologize for," he said.

An uncomfortable silence settled between them. She was not going to learn anything more. She left for the chairs and returned to find that they had somehow broken through the awkwardness and were laughing about the food in prison.

"Well," Rodarren said as they sat down. "I have a feeling we all know things that can help us, important things. And that if we put our heads together we might be able to decide what to do next."

"I certainly know something," Angarred said. She told them about the parchment Lord Snoppish had shown her, her journey to the Giant's Bridge and the questions she had asked of the statues.

Mathewar whistled when she finished. "Alkarren, a Hollow One," he said. "I did see something in his mind that made me wonder . . . And three Stones—Alkarren would have been very interested in that news. I'm certainly glad you didn't tell me this in prison. The giants have the third, is that what you're saying?"

She nodded. "And the giants are the ones behind everything, waiting to take over after we all manage to destroy ourselves. Probably they've been angry at us ever since Tobrin bound their magic into the Stone."

"I wonder," Rodarren said. "I never heard that the giants were angry with us, or even that they went in for warfare. They're said to be a very peaceful people. The statues didn't tell you the giants were controlling everything, did they?"

"No, but who else could it be? Everyone else is at war, or too far away to take advantage of the chaos. I could go back to the Giant's Bridge and ask—"

"You shouldn't leave this house," Rodarren said. "None of us should call attention to ourselves by going to the bridge, for that matter. We won't be able to get answers that way, unfortunately." She turned to Mathewar. "Did you say that Alkarren was interested in you?"

"He asked me questions in prison," Mathewar said. Angarred shook her head, amazed at how calmly he spoke of it. "He wanted my help with the Stone."

"Did he learn anything from you?"

"No. But it was far too close—if Angarred hadn't managed to get us out I probably would have told him everything."

He turned to Angarred, giving her all the credit. He no longer mocked her, or anyone; he seemed almost at peace. She should be pleased that he was happier, she thought—but in her dreams she had been the one to make him happy, not some woman locked away in a tower.

"What worries me," Mathewar said, "is that King Tezue let you out of prison. Just your presence in Pergodi could create more confusion here, divide the Pergodek further into factions. If Tezue is a Hollow One, and if his purpose is to sow chaos, he couldn't have picked a better way."

"My father said he seemed completely normal," Jerret said.

"Well, we should continue to watch him," Mathewar said. "Unfortunately Angarred and I can't go back to court—Alkarren is no doubt looking for both of us. I'll have to be very careful when I leave."

"Leave?" Rodarren and Angarred said together. "Where are you going?" Rodarren asked.

"To the Forest of Tiranon, to find my wife and child. I saw them in Alkarren's mind—he's hidden them away in his tower."

"You can't leave," Angarred said. "You just said Alkarren wants to find you—"

He looked at her; she nearly flinched away from the pain and resolve in his gaze. "Do you truly think I'm going to leave my family in Alkarren's hands one minute longer than I have to?" he asked. "They've been there for a year and a half already, because of my mistakes, my arrogance. The Godkings know what he's done to them in that time."

"How—how will you get out of Pergodi?" Angarred asked. "Norue knows about the house in the wall."

"My friends will have made another gate by this time. They need to get to Tiranon and back." He turned to Rodarren and Jerret. "What about you—what will you do?"

"We'll try to build up our forces here, and bring some of our friends over from Emindal," Rodarren said. "Quietly, of course, so Norue won't become suspicious. I'd hoped to have your counsel, but I certainly understand why you want to go. But please be careful, my friend—"

"Don't you see what you're doing?" Angarred said, unable to stand it any longer. "You're playing right into their hands, all of you. You're all going your own ways, building up your forces, leaving Pergodi—and meanwhile we weaken ourselves with these stupid wars, and when we need a magician he goes off on his own—" Mathewar tried to say something but she went on, speaking over him. "And the giants will just walk in and take what they want. They're the ones we have to fight—we have to unite, all of us, even Tezue, even Norue. We can't let them control us this way."

"We can't unite," Rodarren said softly. "Norue will never agree to it. And Mathewar has to find his family—surely you understand that."

"Very well," Angarred said. "But someone should be keeping watch on the giants, see what they're up to. See what kind of an army they've managed to create. At least that way we might be ready for them when they attack us."

"That's not a bad idea," Jerret said. "Perhaps we can spare someone . . ."

"We can't spare anyone," Rodarren said. "We need everyone we have."

"I'll go then," Angarred said.

"You?" Jerret said. "It's far too dangerous."

"Yes, me. I've been to Tiranon before and I managed to survive it. And I know how to live off the land—I practically grew up in a forest."

Rodarren looked at Jerret. Something unspoken passed between them. "These are dangerous times," Rodarren said. "She'd be just as unsafe in Pergodi—you know that." She turned to Angarred. "Are you sure you want to do this? It would be good to have some idea of the giants' strength."

Angarred nodded.

"You can come with me, at least for part of the way," Mathewar said. "We're both going to the forest, after all."

She hadn't considered that; she hadn't thought that far ahead. The very last thing she wanted was to travel with Mathewar again.

"Good idea," Rodarren said. "When do you think you'll be well enough to go?"

"In a few days," Mathewar said.

Mathewar lay back on the bed after they had gone. He felt exhausted, and his leg hurt fiercely, but he grudged every moment he had to spend healing. He should be out searching for Embre and Atte; his own pains were nothing compared to what they had had to endure.

His injuries were not the worst of it, though. Every so often he would see something shift and change: Angarred had turned into a celestial messenger from a picture he had seen once, and Rodarren had become Queen Chelenin as she had been when he had first arrived at court. He had to sort out illusion from reality very quickly, and be careful not to address any of his hallucinations; if the others knew how confused he was, how badly he needed sattery, they would never let him leave.

His impatience grew from minute to minute. He could not stand to be idle. He knew that his wife and child had been in the tower for over a year, and that a few days more would not matter; still, he felt anxious to be outside, heading through the forest.

He threw back his blanket and stood up carefully, then gritted his teeth and forced himself to walk around the room.

Labren walked toward the Craftsman's Quarter, on his first leave from the king's militia in a month. Heavy rain beat down on him and he felt hollowed out with hunger; the troops had been on reduced rations as supplies of food dwindled in the city. He hoped his brother had some spare loaves of bread at the bakery; he would eat anything, no matter how stale.

"Labren!" someone said.

He looked around, seeing no one through the gray rain. "Labren!" the voice said again. "I thought you were dead for sure."

Now Labren made out a huge man lumbering toward him. It was someone from Norue's company, the man who had been in the fight—Hallen, that was his name. He felt immediately apprehensive; would Hallen report him to Norue? But it was too late to run.

"Hello, Hallen," he said.

"What happened to you?" Hallen said. "The last we heard you'd been taken to the dungeons—we thought you were having one of those intimate conversations with Norue, or you'd been killed. How did you get out?"

"Are you going to tell Norue you saw me?"

"Nah—the Others take that. You saved my life by going for that doctor, remember? Anyway, Norue's been acting odd lately. He sent us off to Emindal, of all places, and we had to fight people from Karededin, our own countrymen. Can you believe that? I'd joined up to fight the Takekek, teach them a lesson, you know?"

Labren looked around, worried that someone might overhear Hallen's disloyalty. Norue had spies all over, everyone knew that—everyone except Hallen, it seemed. Fortunately the downpour had kept everyone inside. "Emindal? Where's that?"

"Out in the ocean somewhere. Strange place. It's good to see you, Labren. What have you been up to?"

"Let's get out of the rain first."

"Where? All the taverns are closed."

"I was just heading home—do you want to come with me?"

"Sure."

Labren led him through the Craftsman's Quarter and into the family's quarters at the back of the bakery. Sounds came from the kitchen, and he followed them to find his mother there, washing up. She turned.

"Labren! You're home!" She hugged him and made a fuss over him, much to his embarrassment. "You're far too thin," she said, stepping back to look at him. "Don't they feed you in the militia? Sit down, sit down."

She seemed too thin as well; every Pergodek he saw had a pinched, hungry look. "This is Hallen, Mother," he said.

"Sit down, Hallen," Gedren said. "Borgarrad, do you have anything to feed your brother and his friend?"

The kitchen was warm from the hearth, and condensation streaked the windows. Labren took off his sopping cloak and rubbed at the rain trickling down his neck. Gedren hung his cloak and Hallen's by the fire, then poured water into a pot and set it to boil. Borgarrad came in from the bakery carrying two loaves of fresh bread.

"Don't give me the good stuff," Labren said, sitting down at the pine table. "Don't you have anything stale?"

"Nothing stays around here long enough to get stale," Borgarrad said, going back to the bakery.

Gedren gave them mugs of hot water, apologizing for not having anything better. "This is fine, Mother," Labren said. "We're just going to sit here and talk awhile."

For once his mother seemed to understand; they wanted to talk about soldiering without interruptions from anyone who hadn't experienced it. "All right," she said, leaving. "I was going to visit Mashak, anyway."

Hallen finished his bread in three bites. "That was wonderful," he said. "Thank you. So how did you get out of the dungeons?"

"A friend found me there and helped me out. Don't tell Norue, please."

Hallen drank some water, then wiped his mouth on his sleeve. "A friend, huh? You're a sly one, Labren—you must have some friends in high places if he could get you out of there. Who was he?"

"I don't want to get him in trouble."

"Sure, I see. So what are you doing now?"

"Fighting for the king."

"The king? Not bad, I suppose. But Norue's going to be king

one day, and we'll be the king's militia then. And the ones who have stayed with him the longest will be rewarded the most."

Labren doubted it; he had never seen Norue deal fairly with anyone. "Why did he send you to Emindal?"

"Don't know. Orders. Strange place, Emindal."

"You said that before. Strange how?"

Hallen hesitated. Then he said, speaking quickly, "Listen. You know people, right? Someone got you out of the dungeons—you must know something. I got this thing in Emindal. Look."

He took a dirty piece of cloth out of his trouser pocket and unwrapped it, revealing a green-and-black stone. Labren drew a breath, feeling its oddness. "What is it?"

"I don't know. One of their men threw it to someone else, and I caught it. I don't know why. But ever since it's been, well, showing me pictures. And it's making me feel sick to my stomach, if you want to know the truth."

"What kind of pictures?"

Hallen shook his head. "Never mind about that. But what I thought was, you could give it to someone. Someone important, who would know what to do with it."

"Why don't you give it to Norue?"

"You know why. He'll be king, sure, but I don't trust him with something like this."

Labren nodded. Suddenly he remembered that he had heard about a stone before—when was it? The day the blue-cloaks had come to talk to his mother, that was it—they had said his father might have stolen a stone. He had never seen his mother so worried, not even the day he joined the militia. "Sure, I'll take it," he said.

Hallen gave him the stone. Immediately his stomach clenched with nausea; the bread he had eaten felt like a heavy weight. He put the stone down quickly and wrapped the cloth back around it. "I see what you mean," he said, catching his breath. His face must be as green as the stone, he thought. "There's something wrong with it, isn't there? Almost something missing."

Hallen shrugged. "I wouldn't know about that," he said. "Just give it to someone who'll know what to do with it."

Mashak Cobbler looked up from the piece of leather he had been working on. "Gedren," he said, a smile breaking through his sour-looking face. "It's good to see you."

"Hello, Mashak," Gedren said.

"Sit down," he said. "What's new at the castle?"

"Not very much," she said, sitting opposite him. "Everyone talks about the siege, but no one can agree on what to do next. Too many people, I suppose—Norue and Tezue and that magician of his, Alkarren . . ."

"Any news of Dalesio?"

"No. Nothing. Do you think he's dead, Mashak? I think I could bear it, if I just knew one way or the other. If I could just be certain."

"How long has it been?"

She thought a while, listening to the rain pound on Mashak's roof. "A year and a half. Holy Godkings—I hadn't realized it was that long. All the magicians are still gone too, all of them but that Alkarren. Do you think Dalesio's a magician? Dalesio Tobrin—it sounds ridiculous, doesn't it?"

"I don't know." Mashak put down the leather and his awl. "Listen, Gedren. If you—if you ever—well, if you ever think the time is right, I'd like to marry you."

"What?"

"Is it that much of a surprise? I want to marry you. You don't have to say anything now—I know if we married it would mean that Dalesio, that you think Dalesio . . . Well, it would be a sad occasion as well as a happy one. You don't have to give me an answer now—just think about it sometimes."

Marry Mashak? Well, why not? If Dalesio was truly dead . . . Mashak seemed a good man, and she was lonely, very lonely, working in the great echoing castle. And there was the question that had haunted her all the past year and a half—if Dalesio was alive, why hadn't he managed to get word to her? He could have written, or sent someone. Did he truly expect her to go on without knowing, to wait patiently until he decided to come home?

No, she couldn't make a decision in this state, still angry at Dalesio. "I'll think about it," she said, and Mashak smiled again.

She returned home in a daze, barely noticing the rain. Labren's friend Hallen stood at the door, and she nodded to him as he left.

"Mother, can I show you something?" Labren asked.

"Later, please, Labren," she said.

She went upstairs, intending to sleep. But when she lay down and closed her eyes she saw her thoughts chasing themselves round and round, never stopping.

TWENTY-TWO

aster Narinye sat next to Merren at a table in the College's great dining hall. Both had gotten their supper from Dalesio in the kitchen, salmon cooked lightly with butter and herbs. Narinye took a bite of his and blessed the fisher folk who continued to trade with the College despite all the disruptions in Karededin.

Merren sat with an open book in front of him. Other books lay scattered around his plate, some with bindings etched in gold or worked with jewels, a conqueror's hoard. Narinye had reminded him before not to bring books from the library to the dining hall; many of them were valuable, or had been acquired with great difficulty. This time, though, he kept silent; Merren certainly knew his opinion on the matter by now.

Rain drummed on the roof, loud enough that he could hear it from where he sat on the ground floor. Dalesio joined them at the table, carrying a plate of salmon. "Thank the Navigator that the fisher folk are still able to bring us their catches," he said, echoing Narinye's thought. "They've had terrible news lately—they can't get through the port at Pergodi to supply the city, and they fear the Pergodek might be running out of food."

Narinye frowned. "Is there any news about King Tezue?"

"Too much news, most of it rumor. The fisher folk have to rely on what other people tell them now, refugees and forest folk. Some Pergodek who know a little about magic are worried that Tezue's become a Hollow One, they say, but many more see nothing wrong with him and are content to follow him."

"A Hollow One," Narinye said. "I wonder if this means that Mathewar failed to free him."

"Let's hope not." Dalesio hesitated and then said, "I've been thinking that perhaps we should go to Pergodi ourselves. I've heard rumors that everything is in confusion there, that there's a great deal of fighting. It's not just Takeke any more—the giants are moving, and even Emindal seems to have taken an interest in Karededin. We might be able to do something, to help somehow."

Narinye had been having similar thoughts. He knew that this was not an odd coincidence; he had frequently had glimpses into what other magicians were thinking, and they had had the same experiences of him. Still, if they were going to head for Pergodi he wanted to make certain they had considered everything.

"Our reason for hiding has not changed, though," he said. "Have you heard anything about Alkarren?"

"He's in the city, or at least that's the last news I had of him. We'll have to steer clear of him if we go, but we can do that, I think. He won't be expecting us."

Narinye nodded. "There's something to what you say. After all, the College is sworn to protect the king. And if Tezue's a Hollow One we might be able to free him, to succeed where Mathewar failed. But I know how much you miss your wife and children—are you certain you're not making this suggestion just to be able to see them again?"

Dalesio's pleasant, open face clouded at the mention of his family. "As certain as I can be."

"What about you, Merren?" Narinye said. "What's your opinion?"

The ocean burst against the cliffs beneath them, booming loudly over the rattle of the rain. Merren looked up at last from his book. "Of course we should go to Pergodi," he said.

Narinye hadn't been sure Merren was following the conversation, still less that he had an opinion on it. Of late he had become even more taciturn; he did nothing but take books from the library and study them in his room, burning oil lamps until late, and Narinye feared that he had grown obsessed with some arcane subject. "Why do you say that?" he asked.

For an answer Merren pulled another book toward them and opened it to a marked page embellished with old-fashioned flourishes. "It says here that around the same time the Stone was stolen, four hundred years ago, various places were invaded by the Others. They broke through all semblance of normal life, and even destroyed a few towns and villages."

"But what does this have to do with King Tezue?" Narinye asked, and Dalesio said, "You can't waste time studying history while Karededin's at war, Merren."

"Everything is related," Merren said. "Tezue, the Stone, Tobrin, the history of the College."

Merren's eyes, as always, looked as if they held depths of wisdom, and for the first time Narinye wondered if the man might indeed discover something that could help them. But he was far too preoccupied with his histories to be of any use to them in Pergodi. "Perhaps you should stay here, continue your research," he said. "You can send a messenger bird to let us know what you find out."

Merren seemed to make an effort to tear his eyes from his books. "No, I think I can help," he said. "And if King Tezue is a Hollow One we have to free him."

Well, that was plain enough. Suddenly, though, Narinye had a sense that something had not been said. A feeling of wrongness, almost tangible, surrounded the three of them, and for a moment the warmth of the College turned chilly. Was it Merren's obsession with history, the way he saw connections where none existed? Or Dalesio's desire to visit his family? Mathewar had accused them of hiding something, he remembered—but Mathewar's judgment was clouded by sattery.

No, they both seemed genuinely concerned about the fate of Karededin. And Narinye had known a generation of eccentric masters; Merren and Dalesio certainly weren't the worst of them. "Very well," he said. "Let's go to Pergodi."

To her amazement Angarred found that her horse had returned to the Snoppishes' stable while she had been in prison. She stroked him and made much of him, giving him treats she denied herself. A few days later she saddled and mounted him and, once again, began riding south with Mathewar.

The siege had worsened, even in the short time she had spent in prison and Anfarna's house. Whole buildings had been torn down and looted for food or wood or fuel. Few people ventured outside, and those who did seemed bewildered by the changes or stupefied by starvation. Even the soldiers moved slowly, as if uncertain, and she saw at least one man asleep at his post.

Once she and Mathewar rode behind a group of noblemen and she heard one of them say, "It's as I've said all along—King Tezue is a Hollow One. Look around us—his decisions cannot possibly be those of a rational man."

"I fear you're right," a second man said. "Anyone else would have broken the siege and attacked Takeke by now, or at least manned the battlements and destroyed the catapult. But why don't our magicians come back from wherever they are and do something? Alkarren at least must see what is going on right under his nose."

"He can't," another man said. "I heard Rodarren stole the Stone and is directing his every move, and Tezue's moves as well. Our country is in the grip of a madwoman."

When the men turned down another street Mathewar said quietly, "I'd hoped we could avoid those kinds of rumors. The people are terrified enough without bringing in magic. If they don't trust their own king the Spinner knows what will happen."

Angarred said nothing. It was odd, she thought sourly, how they had changed places since their last journey, when he had been so silent and she eager to make conversation. And she couldn't help but think that if he wanted to help Karededin he could do more, instead of simply worrying about what might happen next. He could come with her to spy on the giants, for example. How could someone with his power decide not to use it, how could he be content to sit back and not seek to influence events? There would always be time later to free his wife and child.

The noblemen's conversation reminded her of something, and a few minutes later she asked, "Did Jerret keep the Snoppishes' Stone?"

"We—actually we lost the Stone in battle," Mathewar said.

"What!"

"These things happen," he said. He smiled at some memory. "Jerret tried to throw it to me and one of Norue's men caught it instead."

"Why are you so amused by that?"

"Am I? I suppose it's because that's when Jerret and I started to like each other. Before that he thought I was a drunken reprobate, and I thought he was a self-righteous prig. But he's a fine man, really—you could do worse than to marry him."

Marry Jerret? For a moment she had no idea what he was talking about. Then she remembered their conversation at the College, when she had jokingly suggested it. But didn't Mathewar realize that Jerret was in love with Rodarren, and that she loved him in return? It was obvious from their every movement. What a narrow focus the man had, first thinking only of sattery and then of his wife and child.

Well, if he didn't see it she was certainly not going to tell him. It was good that he hadn't realized the depths of her feelings for him, that he thought she was interested in someone else. But she could not forget the excitement in his kiss, and she knew that in some way he shared her desire, however much he wanted to deny it, however genuine his love for his family.

They passed the cemetery at the southern edge of the city. She caught a glimpse of the Giant's Bridge, a thin band like a black rainbow, but she said nothing about it to Mathewar. A steady rain began to drizzle down and she took out a heavy cloak lined with wool that Lord Snoppish had given her.

The gate in the walls had moved, as Mathewar had guessed, but their passage through it, and their transformations into Takekek soldiers, were much the same. This time she managed to keep the foreign warlike thoughts at bay, and the shift back to her own body was easier.

They mounted again and set off, their horses' hoofs churning through heavy mud. She looked around cautiously, noticing that the land here had changed as well. Takekek soldiers had marched through and destroyed a wide swath, leaving behind broken farmhouses and trampled fields. The air smelled of burning wood, and behind that was the sweetly sickening odor of animals that had been torched and left to rot. Birds flew toward distant carrion, cawing loudly. People stood dazed at their doorways and watched Angarred and Mathewar ride by with dull wonder, as if looking at illusions or ghosts. Probably they had not seen anyone from the city in months.

Once they spotted a line of soldiers marching in the distance, and they hurried behind a ruined wall in the middle of a field. On the other side were sticks of furniture and broken crockery; a hearth stood out starkly against the sky, grass and moss already growing between the stones. Angarred wondered uneasily what had happened to the people who lived there.

The night came early. They made camp under a stand of trees, their bare branches offering little protection from the rain. Gold and copper leaves lay strewn on the ground, the trees' profligate spending.

As she and Mathewar moved to gather wood for the fire she noticed for the first time that he limped slightly when he walked, and that he stopped often to knead his left leg. Oddly, it seemed that the wound from the arrow had healed almost completely; it was the other, smaller wound that had caused the most damage.

They sat to eat their sparse supper. Rain fell through the branches, making the fire hiss. "Did you learn anything more about Prince Norue?" he asked.

Once again she reflected on how strange it was that he wanted to talk. Well, she had never told him the story; she might as well start now. "Yes, I did, actually," she said. "Do you remember when you said someone should look through his papers?"

He laughed. "I hope you didn't think I was serious."

"No, of course not. But I did it anyway—I couldn't think of any other way to get information."

"Did you really? You went to his rooms?"

"Yes—and I found letters from my father to Norue. You won't

believe what he'd done. When you showed up at the manor he told
Norue he had a household magician, and that Norue had better
invite him back to court. Of course Norue had no intention of
doing that."

Mathewar laughed again, harder this time. "A household magician? I was his household magician, is that what you're telling me?
He might have let me know."

Angarred laughed too; she couldn't help it. "I told you he was
crazy. He looked at everything and everyone as a way to get back
to court—nothing else existed for him."

"And finally it killed him. A fitting end, you might say, except
that it put you in danger as well."

"Oh, I don't think he thought that far ahead. And then when I
went to court Norue saw what an innocent I was, and how little I
knew about anything." She shook her head. "Now I can't believe
how calmly I walked into that court. If I'd realized how dangerous
those people were . . . You did try to warn me, I know."

He stretched his bad leg out in front of him. "And you repaid
me a thousandfold. I never did thank you for saving me from the
dungeons, did I? Of course it would take the king's treasury itself
to thank you properly."

"Well, I had to get out myself—I thought I might as well take
you with me."

The rain came down harder. The talk reminded her of something that had puzzled her, and after a while she said, "You once
said something about Spells of Strengthening, right?" He nodded.
"Then why can't magicians heal themselves when they become ill?
Why couldn't you?"

"That's a question magicians have been asking since the estab-
lishment of the College. We don't know. Perhaps it's something
else Tobrin bound into the Stone. Or perhaps there are other limi-
tations we don't know about, other prohibitions. If we could heal
ourselves we'd live forever, after all, and that would change the balance of the world."

The fire flickered and nearly went out. They added more wood,
then wrapped themselves in their cloaks and blankets and settled
down to sleep.

Angarred lay awake a long time, staring at the shifting gold of the fire. She had enjoyed talking to Mathewar; she had loved him before, but now she liked him as well. Everything had probably happened for the best, she thought regretfully. He would find his family, and live with them, and be happy, and she would . . . she would . . . She drifted off to sleep, and dreamed of crows flying overhead.

When she woke she found the rain had stopped. They breakfasted and continued on, coming to the forest at noon the next day. Without their leaves the trees looked very different, their naked branches stretching out like hands of bone. Only the pines had retained their green. Soft leaves covered the path.

A few hours later she felt the forest begin to change. The trees were bare here too, but the woods seemed murky, suffocating, suffused with a weird darkness. She saw the little lights she remembered, and once again she found she could not look at them straight on.

"Where was it we saw a tower?" Mathewar asked. "I remember it was on our second day in the forest—is that right?"

"I think so," she said.

Crows shrieked above them. They both looked up at the same time and saw one of them come plummeting to earth. In the next instant Rone stood there before them on the path.

"I was coming to look for thee," she said. "I sensed thee in the forest."

"Us? Why?" Mathewar asked.

"Thy masters have left their College. I saw them on the path, three of them."

"The masters? Where are they going?"

"I do not know. They seemed to be heading toward Pergodi, but . . . I do not know. What brings thee to the forest?"

"I'm searching for a tower. My wife and child are imprisoned within it, sent there by Alkarren. Dost know of a tower near here? It's in a clearing, and wound about with roses."

"I think so." She frowned. "Sayest that thy family is imprisoned there?"

"Aye. Canst show us in what direction it lies?"

"I do not know. The forest changes around us from day to day."

"Canst take us there, then?"

She hesitated, then seemed to come to a decision. "Dost want me to fly ahead and look for it, or lead thee through the forest?"

"Fly ahead and come back. We'll wait for thee here. And I thank thee for thy help with all my heart."

"Wait a minute," Angarred said. "I'm not looking for a tower. I mean, I hope you find it, but I'm looking for the giants."

"The giants?" Rone asked. "Why?"

Angarred told her what she had learned at the Giant's Bridge, and what she suspected. "But the giants are from old a peaceful people," Rone said. "I have never heard of them fighting a war, or even forming an army. Anyway, Tobrin took their magic and bound it into his Stone, as he took away the magics of so many other people. Surely they cannot be very dangerous."

"Yes, but they have a Stone now. And the masters at the College warned us about them."

"Art certain they have a Stone?"

"That's what the statues told me at the Giant's Bridge. Do you know where they live?"

"Let me look for Mathewar's tower first. Then I will try to help thee."

Why is Mathewar's errand more important than mine? she thought. Why doesn't anyone believe me about this? If I'm right the giants are creating chaos even now, and preparing to march on Pergodi. And if the masters get to Pergodi and fight for one side or the other the confusion will be that much greater.

Well, it didn't seem as if she had a choice. Rone bade them farewell and shifted into a crow shape, and they watched her until she became a black speck against the cloud-filled sky.

"We might as well make camp while we wait for her," Mathewar said.

They found a fairly dry spot under a great pine and made a fire. "I learned some other things at court," Angarred said as they sat to warm themselves, remembering their conversation of the day before. "I even talked to Alkarren a few times."

"Alkarren!" Mathewar said, his face filled with disgust. "Why in the name of the Orator would you want to talk to him?"

"You told me to. I was supposed to distract him when you left for Emindal."

"So I did. What did he say? Any advice on imprisoning women and small children?"

"He seemed sad, in a way. He told me about being a student at the College, and how hard it was for him, and how he persevered despite everything. I almost felt sorry for him."

"You shouldn't. He's a man who would do anything for power. If you had something he wanted he would kill you without thinking about it. Well, you saw him in the dungeons."

She nodded. "I know that. And I realize that he did terrible things to you and your child—your wife and child." She stumbled on, hoping he hadn't noticed her slip. "But he seemed interested when I told him about my father—he might even talk to King Tezue for me."

"Why should he talk to Tezue? The king does whatever Alkarren wants anyway. Is that the kind of justice you want for your family?"

"I thought of that, of course. But when I talked to him he seemed—"

"He's a monster. That's all you need to know."

She could think of nothing to say to that. They sat in silence, watching the fire, until the early evening fell. Then they ate supper and prepared to sleep. "She won't fly back in this darkness," Mathewar said, spreading his blanket, but he stopped to gaze up at the sky anyway.

Mathewar lay awake for a long time, staring up at the sky, his hands behind his head. He remembered a story Embre had told Atte, that Mother Mathona the moon was a laundress, and that she had hung out the stars to dry.

His hallucinations came less often now, thank the Healer, but every so often Angarred would blur and shift into a celestial messenger, and he would be hard put not to comment on the change.

It made for strange pauses in the conversation, though so far he thought she hadn't noticed. And Rone had become a crow once, but a crow the size of a young woman, and the sight had been so bizarre that several times he had almost laughed. What would she do, what would either of them do if they knew how unprepared he was to go out into the world?

He thought about hallucinations, about illusion and reality, about true transformation. It was all woven together somehow; he felt certain he would have to understand something of women's magic before the end, and he tried to remember everything Rone had told him.

All of this reminded him of something else as well. At the College the older students had passed along garbled spells to the younger ones, spells not taught but somehow known to everyone like childhood rhymes. The masters ridiculed these magics, though, and whenever they caught anyone using them he was punished, so that most students forgot them in time.

Could they be women's magic, these snatches of spells: bits of song, mysterious half-phrases, ragged poetry, incomplete but somehow persisting for hundreds of years? And what would happen if they were combined with the magic he knew? Would spell simply add to spell, or would the two powers work together to create something new, something stronger than both? One is broken, but two is whole, he thought.

He found he could remember most of them; he had forgotten little from his days at the College. He turned over the scraps and tags in his mind, seeing them in this new light. He and his fellows, like all first-year students, had done experiments in the privacy of their rooms; most of them had yielded nothing, but there had been a few spectacular results . . .

It was very late by the time he finally got to sleep. He dreamed he was in a tower, stumbling in the dark, that he had been forbidden to make a light. Finally he cast a light despite the prohibition, and when it bloomed out he saw his daughter Atte, sleeping peacefully. But where was Embre? What had happened to her? He continued to look for her, but the tower had expanded into a long hallway and he walked on and on, taking turns at random, becoming more and more anxious. And how would he find his way back?

He woke abruptly, wondering if he had cried out. It was near dawn; he stood stiffly and went to gather firewood, ignoring the dull pains in his joints and his bad leg.

Angarred found him the next morning wrapped in his cloak by the fire, his knees drawn up to his chest. "Is something wrong?" she asked.

"No," he said, staring into the fire.

"You're lying again," she said.

She had expected him to laugh, or at least smile, but he said nothing and continued to gaze into the fire. Finally he spoke. "I had a strange dream last night. I dreamed I was in the tower, and Atte was there, but I couldn't find Embre . . ." He shook his head. "But it couldn't be a portent—it was only a dream, after all. And Atte was the same age as when I saw her last, still four years old, and how could that be?"

"Don't worry—I'm sure they're fine," Angarred said. She took an oatcake out of her pack and nibbled at it. "What were they like?" she asked, to take his mind off the dream. "Embre and Atte?"

"Embre was—is—she's a small woman." His mouth crooked in a smile. "But tough—you wouldn't want to quarrel with her when she gets angry. She worked in the laundry at the castle. I met her just after I had gotten out of some—some court entanglements."

"Entanglements?" Angarred said, suddenly unreasonably jealous. She remembered Dorilde, and the familiar way she had spoken of Mathewar. "Who were you entangled with?"

He shook his head. "It's not a time I'm proud of. I was twenty years old, the youngest magician ever to come to Tezue's court— they didn't know what to make of me. And I didn't know what to make of them either. I did some very foolish things. And then when I met Embre I thought that the Godkings were rewarding me for giving up court pastimes. She laughed when I told her that— she said, 'And what are the Godkings rewarding me for, then?'

"Atte's a lot like her mother—small but tough, completely fear-less," he went on. "I was terrified for her life a good deal of the time. She climbed a tree higher than our house once, and wouldn't come down because she knew I'd be angry with her."

Angarred had never heard him so talkative. She hurried to take advantage of it, hoping Rone would not return soon. "You know, I don't know anything about your family, and yet you know all about mine," she said. "What are your parents like? Do you have any brothers or sisters?"

"One of each," Mathewar said.

"Older or younger?"

He said nothing for long moment. Angarred had the idea that he was seeing something other than her, something in the far dis-tance. Then he shook his head. "I'm sorry. I've gotten out of the habit of conversation. My brother Galawar is two years older, and very envious of all the attention I got when we were growing up, and of the fact that I was sent to the College. My sister is two years younger, and for a while I could do no wrong in her eyes. I don't know what she's like now—I haven't been to visit in a while. And my parents are ordinary, hard-working farmers who always seemed to be wondering how I ended up as their son—there have never been any magicians in the family, as far as I know."

"I thought magic was inherited."

"No one understands where it comes from. You look a great deal like your father, speaking of inheritance." Angarred scowled. He hurried on, clearly realizing he had insulted her. "But at the same time you look nothing like him—it's as if a horse and a, well, a celestial messenger shared some similarities. And you act nothing like him, or he like you. No one knows at all how any of this hap-pens."

"My father told me once that I don't look anything like my mother, that I take after him completely. I hate it—sometimes I see him when I look in the mirror. I wish I'd had a larger family."

"You wouldn't if your brother wanted to kill you."

Angarred laughed. Mathewar looked solemn, though; he hadn't been joking. Then he smiled wryly, as if he saw the humor in what he'd said.

"Could we end up at your parents' farm?" Angarred said. "If the forest shifts the way you say it does?"

"We could, I suppose, but it's not likely. The farm's all the way on the other side of the forest."

"Do you think you'll ever go home?"

He hesitated again. "It's not home, not really," he said finally. "And I don't know what I'll do. Everything depends on if—on what happens next."

He broke off and looked into the sky. Angarred followed his gaze. A crow flew toward them, its glossy wings outstretched. Angarred blessed Rone for coming when she did; Mathewar had probably reached the end of his sudden talkativeness. Still, she was amazed that she had gotten as much as she had from him.

The crow landed on the ground in front of them, shifted and became Rone. "I found a tower that matches thy description," she said, breathing hard from her journey. "Old gray stone, covered in roses. But I flew all the way around it, and there are no doors to it anywhere."

"Good," Mathewar said. "Canst take us to it?"

"Aye."

She waited while Mathewar and Angarred rolled up their blankets and put out the fire. "No doors?" Angarred said softly. "How are you going to get in?"

"There's an enchantment on the tower, no doubt," Mathewar said. "I just have to discover what it is, and how to break it."

Angarred said nothing. Once again Mathewar seemed to have forgotten that Alkarren had the Stone, that he could no longer defeat the other man as easily.

They mounted their horses. Rone changed back into a crow and they followed her as she flew from tree to tree.

After a while they came to a scene of great destruction: trees felled and rotting, mud churned up, a few animals lying dead, trampled into the ground. "What happened here?" Angarred asked.

"Your giants, it looks like," Mathewar said. To her surprise he untied his pack and took out a sword, then buckled it on. Where had he gotten it? And did he think he would need to use it? "No one else could have caused this much devastation. Look—you can see their footprints over here."

She reined in her horse and looked around. "I thought the giants are a peaceful people," she said. "That's what everyone tells me, anyway."

Rone had stopped as well, and shifted into her human form. "I have never seen them do anything like this," she said.

"They have a king now," Angarred said. "And they're marching on Pergodi."

"No sense worrying about it now," Mathewar said. He glanced up, no doubt checking the time until nightfall. Thick gray-black clouds blanketed the sky, hiding the sun; it would rain soon, Angarred thought. "How much farther to the tower?" he asked.

"I cannot tell thee," Rone said. "It all looks different from the air."

Mathewar rode ahead without waiting for them. Rone became a crow again and they continued on.

They picked their way carefully through the swath of destruction, avoiding roots and branches and deep mud. Mathewar grew more and more impatient; he glanced often into the trees on either side as if looking for an easier path.

As they rode Angarred kept an eye out for the giants. She would leave the others if she saw any; she had no reason to go to Mathewar's tower. But there was no sign of them; if they had created this devastation they were long gone.

After a while the giants' path branched off from theirs. The trail became narrow, the trees pressing closely around them. The forest here did not look familiar at all; once again it had changed since the last time they had come this way.

Suddenly the path opened out in front of them. Angarred gasped, and stopped without thinking. A wasteland the size of the College stood before them, a flat plain covered with dull gray ash. The trees around it looked stunted, bent over as if in thrall to whatever had caused the destruction. There was no wind, but every so often plumes and spires of ash drifted upward or blew along the ground.

"What is it?" Angarred asked, feeling compelled to whisper. She could taste the ashes, dry and bitter and metallic. "Is it magic?"

"Something from the Sorcerers' Wars, I think," Mathewar said, his voice low as well. The swirling ash seemed to take on the semblance of fantastic creatures, coiling serpents or people with wings. "We should go."

Rone flew out over the dead land. She cawed and turned away from it, following a new trail, doubtless sensing its strong magic. Angarred and Mathewar urged their horses after her.

"There's a place in Takeke called Endless Desolation," Angarred said. She could still feel the grit of the ashes in her mouth. "I wonder if it's like this."

Mathewar said nothing. Perhaps he saw it as another bad sign, Angarred thought. She shook her head; she didn't place much stock in omens.

Trees arched above them, shadowing the path. Mathewar created a light and sent it on ahead.

A long time later Angarred saw a dull glow through the darkness. Mathewar spurred his horse forward. They came to a clearing; a tower stood in the center, pointing upward into the sky. Red roses twined around it, choking it, their curving thorns as sharp as claws.

Rone came to rest on the ground. Mathewar circled the tower. "It's true, there are no doors," he said when he returned. "Still, there has to be a way in."

He dismounted and studied the tower, rubbing his bad leg absently. He spoke a few words, but nothing happened. He shook his head and tried again, then walked a few paces and recited another spell.

Angarred sat next to Rone and watched him. She marveled at how meticulous he was, how careful, how tightly he reined in his impatience.

"Hast thought about thine animal?" Rone asked her.

"What?"

"Thine animal. What thou art. Hast thought about it?"

"No, of course not," Angarred said absently, still watching Mathewar. "I don't have an animal."

"Thy magic is very strong—I can feel it. Hast an animal like all other magicians."

Angarred turned to Rone, startled. The other woman's coal-bright eyes were studying her sharply. "A magician?" Angarred said. "What makes you think I'm a magician?"

"Dost believe that only men can be magicians?"

"No. No, of course not. But—"

"I heard thee in the forest, arguing about this with Mathewar."

Angarred scowled. She had not realized how much the forest folk had overheard of their conversation. She remembered telling Mathewar about dropping back in the forest before the arrow hit her father, and suggesting that that might be magic. But did she believe it?

"A woman from our village wants to talk to thee. Hast met her already—her name is Perren."

What if she was a magician? What if she could change into an animal, could fly like Rone? She didn't think she could, of course, but it would do no harm to talk to this Perren—though she had an uneasy feeling that Perren was the woman with the strong features, the one who had made her so uncomfortable at the forest people's supper.

"All right," Angarred said. To her surprise she felt excited, as if something might actually come of this meeting.

Mathewar had stopped walking around the tower. He put his hand against the stones and closed his eyes, standing there for a long moment.

The clearing grew darker. The ground turned cold; Angarred stood and began to pace for warmth. Mathewar circled the tower again, reciting more words.

"Look," Angarred said when he had stopped. "There's something at the very top, hidden by the roses. A small window, it looks like."

Mathewar turned to her, annoyed. "Yes, I've seen it."

Fine, she thought. I won't try to help you again.

Rone changed into crow shape and flew up to look at it. With her beak she pulled aside some brambles, then grasped a branch with her talons and turned her head to peer inside with one eye.

She flew back and shifted instantly. "Didst see anything?" Mathewar asked.

"Nay—it was far too dusty. Canst create a fire to burn the roses away?"

For an answer he spoke a few words. Fire bloomed at the top of the tower. The roses flickered within it, red within red like another flame, but did not burn. "He thought of everything, didn't he?" Mathewar said. "There's even a spell on the roses."

"Aye, but it's a spell of men's magic," Rone said.

"Men's magic," Mathewar said thoughtfully. "I wonder . . ."

He said something else, harsh, angular words. The fire blazed out so brightly Angarred had to avert her eyes; she felt the heat of it on her skin. When she looked back the top of the tower seemed engulfed in flames.

"What—" Rone said. For the first time she sounded surprised, even admiring.

"I've been thinking about women's magic since I met thee," Mathewar said. "I remembered some things, and I combined them with—" He looked up at the burning tower. "Let's discuss this another time, shall we?"

He recited another spell. The fire dwindled and finally guttered out. Thick black marks scorched the stones where it had been.

Rone flew halfway up the tower and rested on a branch, waiting for the burnt stones to cool. Then she returned to the window and caught at something with her beak. She pulled and the window came open, a little at a time. When she had pried an opening wide enough she forced her small crow's body inside.

"Rone!" Mathewar shouted. "Rone, come back!"

She stayed in the tower. "She has no idea what she's doing," Mathewar said, pacing. "She could be trapped by a spell inside the tower, or lost in the darkness—she doesn't even know how to make a light . . ."

A crack appeared at the base of the tower. The crack widened, became the outline of a door. Mathewar pulled at the brambles clinging to the doorway. Angarred moved to help him. As soon as enough of the door showed he grasped it and wrenched it outward, scratching his hands and bloodying them on the thorns.

He went inside, brushing past Rone at the door. Angarred followed. He spoke the words to create a light, his voice shaking.

A small child lay on a nest of leaves and blankets, her eyes closed. Mathewar lifted her carefully. "Atte," he said, his voice soft. "Atte, sweet, wake up."

The child did not move. Mathewar said something in the sharp, grating language he had used before. The child stirred.

"Matte," she said, opening her eyes. "Matte! You're here! I had such a bad dream."

"It's all right. It's all right, sweetling. You're safe now. Where's your mother?"

Atte looked around her, only now taking in the gray stones, the unfamiliar people. She began to cry. "She's dead, Matte! He killed her. It wasn't a dream. I tried to help but I couldn't do anything, and he killed her!"

"Shhh. I'm here for you now. It's all right."

"No, it isn't! He was a horrible man, with a long white hair and awful black eyes. She tried to escape and he killed her, and then he said he was going to put me to sleep for a long time. And that I would only wake up if you came and helped him. Did you help him, Matte? He's horrible—you can't help him!"

"No, I didn't. I'd never help him. Don't worry—he can't hurt you now." He put his hand over her eyes and, with great tenderness, he closed them and whispered a few words. She fell back asleep, murmuring. He studied the sleeping child, then kissed her on the forehead.

When he looked up his expression was harsh with hatred. "Could you carry her outside, please, Angarred?" he said. "I want to look around in here."

Angarred took Atte from him and went outside, then laid her on the ground and tucked her inside her blankets. The child shivered in the cold and Angarred got another blanket from her pack to put around her.

Atte turned on her side, settling down to sleep. With her short brown hair and small delicate features she looked nothing like Mathewar. This must be what Embre had looked like, Angarred thought, the last reminder of Embre on earth. She shook her head and, to her surprise, began to cry.

Mathewar came out of the tower and she wiped her tears away quickly. "Did you find anything?" she asked.

"No," he said. He collected wood and built a fire near the tower, his movements neat and methodical, then carried Atte over by the fire and adjusted her blankets.

He sat near his child, leaning against the tower and staring into the fire. Finally he stood and got his pack, then brought out the familiar leather bottle and silver cup.

"No," Angarred said as he sat by the fire again. "You don't need that."

"Yes, I do," he said.

"No, you don't. Mathewar, listen to me. You're not addicted to it anymore. If you start now it'll be just as hard to stop as it was the last time."

"You're wrong. I still want it, more that I ever wanted anything, even Embre. And I don't plan to stop, so it doesn't matter how hard it will be."

"What about Atte? You're the one taking care of her now, the only parent she's got." She heard the cruelty in her words but continued on, wanting to shock him. "And you have to help Rodarren, and King Tezue . . ."

"I don't care," he said. He dropped the bottle and cup and leaned back against the tower, his eyes closed.

He was so still that Angarred thought he might have gone to sleep. Then she noticed a tear near one closed eye. She sat next to him and put her arm around him.

"She's dead, Angarred," he said. She had never seen a man cry; her father's response to any reversal was more anger. Still, she knew enough to look away from him, to let him pretend to privacy. "She's truly dead. I looked into Atte's mind and I saw her die. She tried to get away from him—she was so brave . . ."

"It's all right," she said, much as he had said to Atte. "Hush. It's all right."

"I can't mourn her a second time. I can't do it all again. I have to—have to . . ."

He laid his head on her shoulder. She could feel his grief shudder through him, though he made no sound. "Yes, you can," she said.

She picked up the bottle of sattery. He opened his eyes in alarm but said nothing. She pulled the clay stopper and handed him the bottle. "Pour it out," she said.

"I can't. You do it."

"No. Take it. Narinye said you were the best magician he'd ever taught—surely you have some part to play in this, and you'll need to be clear-headed . . ."

"Someone else can be the best magician for a while—I'm tired of the responsibility." He tried to laugh; it sounded like a sob.

"Someone is—Alkarren."

That seemed to rouse him. He reached for the bottle and put the stopper back with shaking hands, then returned it to his bag. "I won't drink it tonight," he said. "That's the best I can do."

They ate their supper and spread their blankets on the ground. Mathewar lay down close to Atte.

"Where's Rone, I wonder?" Angarred said.

"Probably left us alone," Mathewar said. "Very tactful of her."

TWENTY-THREE

Atte seemed thoughtful the next morning, too quiet for a child her age. Finally she roused herself to say, "I'm hungry, Matte."

"Are you now?" Mathewar smiled and took something from his pack. "What about this?"

He held out an orange. Angarred marveled, wondering where he had found an orange at the beginning of winter; it must have cost a small fortune. He threw it in the air. It became an apple at the top of its flight, and at the next cast turned into a pear, then a plum.

"Which one do you want?" he asked, still tossing and changing the orange. "You can have any one you like as long as it's the orange—that's the only one that's real."

Atte giggled. She had the same changeable blue-gray eyes as her father, Angarred saw now. "The orange, please," she said.

Mathewar tossed the orange to her and she caught it, still laughing. In that one exchange Angarred caught a glimpse of what his family had been like, and how much Alkarren had destroyed.

Atte peeled the orange solemnly. "What are you going to do now?" Angarred said, speaking softly so that Atte wouldn't hear.

"Go to the giants with you, I think," Mathewar said.

"What? Why? I mean, I thought—"

"I want a Stone. I'm going to confront Alkarren, make him pay for what he did."

"How will you get their Stone?"

"I don't know. I'll think of something when we get there."

"What about Atte? She can't travel with us—"

"I'll see if I can leave her with Rone's people for a while. I hate to do it—too many people have left her already, and I know she'll worry that I won't come back. But you're right—I can't take her with us, and I don't know what else to do."

"You could put her to sleep the way Alkarren did."

"No!" He spoke sharply, and Atte looked up in alarm. He smiled at her and she went back to her orange. "I won't interfere with her mind like that. I felt guilty just sending her to sleep last night. Don't you see what he did? He took a year and a half from her life."

"She still looks four years old. Maybe he didn't take anything, just stopped her growth."

"Maybe. I hope so. But we're trained not to harm people unless it's necessary, and that includes their minds, their very beings." He sighed. "I wish I didn't have to leave her."

Suddenly he looked up. A crow hurtled downward, nearly upon them; they had been so caught up in their talk they hadn't noticed it. It landed at their feet and become Rone.

"Hello," Mathewar said. "We need thy help again, I'm afraid. We want to find the giants—"

"Canst wait here for a moment?" Rone said. "Angarred, didst promise to meet Perren."

She had forgotten Perren; Atte's rescue and the news of Embre's death had driven everything else from her mind. Suddenly she felt terrified, for no reason she could see; her palms were wet with sweat. "All right," she said.

"Wilt want to meet her, I promise thee," Rone said.

Mathewar seemed anxious to leave. Angarred looked helplessly at him. "I don't see any way out of it," she said. "I did promise." He shrugged and went to talk to Atte.

"So where—" Angarred said.

"Hush," Rone said.

A great eagle flew toward them and dropped to the ground, then shifted into the shape of a woman. She had the strong features and long black hair streaked with gray that Angarred remembered. "Angarred, this is Perren," Rone said.

"Hello," Angarred said.

Rone joined Mathewar, leaving her alone with Perren. The other woman studied her in silence for several moments. Finally she said, "Have you thought about your animal?"

"No," Angarred said.

"You should. You have a good deal of talent—I see it in you." She did not speak with the strange archaic dialect of the forest people but sounded like a Pergodek, her speech fast and clipped.

"All right."

The woman fell silent again; she seemed uncomfortable about something. "How—how is your father?" she asked. "Lord Challo Hashan?"

"My father? How do you know my father?"

"Tell me how he is first."

Perren's gaze was compelling. "He died, I'm afraid," Angarred said. She told the story of his death once again, wondering as she did how many times and to how many people she had repeated it so far. She did not mention Norue's part, though—she did not know this woman and had no reason to trust her.

Perren's expression did not change; Angarred saw neither grief nor horror nor even interest at a minor piece of gossip. "How do you know him?" she asked again.

"We—I knew him in the city, a long time ago. Before I came to the forest. He was—"

Suddenly everything came clear. Angarred gasped. "You're my mother!" she said.

Perren bowed her head and said nothing.

"Are you really Lady Verret? My mother? But what happened? Why did you leave me?"

"Challo told me you'd died. Of a fever, he said."

"And you believed him? You knew what he was like. And

because of you I had to grow up with a foolish, selfish, power-mad father, someone who ignored me unless he could use me in some plot or other—"

"Well, then, why didn't you come looking for me?" Perren asked.

"He told me the same thing, that you were dead," Angarred admitted. She felt strongly that Perren was to blame, though; mothers should not leave their children to the likes of Lord Hashan. "But I was just a child—surely you don't think I could have guessed that he was lying. But you—you didn't even make an effort—"

"Angarred. Listen. I was caught up in Norue's plots. I joined those who wanted to overthrow the king and put Norue in his place. Like your father, but I did worse than your father. I—I had an affair with Norue. Challo encouraged me—he thought it would make Norue more generous with us when he came to the throne. But I have to say I enjoyed it as well—it was exciting being so close to the center of power. I even saw myself divorcing Challo and becoming queen.

"And then the plot came to light, and Challo was exiled. I was under the protection of the prince, and so Tezue allowed me to stay in Pergodi. Then Challo wrote me from his estate to say you'd died, and I realized how much I had sacrificed for power, how little power really meant when compared with the important things, family and friends and love. I changed my name and retired to a Godwife House, and after a few years I met a woman there who told me about the forest people and women's magic. And so I came here."

"But why didn't you come back for me?"

"I would have rescued you if I'd known. Truly. I was amazed when I saw you in the forest and realized you were alive after all."

"You knew who I was then? Why didn't you say anything? Did you think it wasn't important enough?"

"I didn't know how to tell you. I was ashamed. Then when Rone said she saw you again . . ."

"I don't believe you. You're as selfish as he was. It was inconvenient to carry a daughter around with you, so you left me with my father, then didn't even acknowledge me when you saw me."

"That's not true!"

"No? Then why did you do it? Because you didn't care about me? I remember you, you know. Just a little, but I know what you were like. Always rushing around, going to one feast or ceremony after another, leaving me with different servants—"

"Angarred." Perren's tone was commanding, nearly as forceful as Mathewar's. "I thought you were dead. I couldn't possibly have known that Challo lied to me. It was terrible that you had to grow up with him, but I don't see how it can be called my fault, except that I was wrong to get mixed up with Prince Norue."

Angarred said nothing.

"I wonder why he told me you died," Perren said.

"You know him. If he could do anything hurtful he would."

"No—I think he always had reasons for what he did. Bad reasons, but reasons nonetheless. Perhaps he resented me after the plot came to light, resented the fact that I could stay in Pergodi while he was forced to leave. Or perhaps he realized somehow that I'd thought of marrying Norue and wanted to punish me for that."

Angarred fell silent again. She thought of the times she had dressed up in her mother's clothing and she burned with shame and embarrassment.

"I thought I might teach you women's magic," Perren said. "Though I understand if you don't want to speak to me."

White light cracked across the sky, and thunder boomed out. The sky had turned a deep, unearthly blue; even the clouds seemed blue. "Get inside!" Angarred said. She caught up the horses' reins and hurried for the shelter of the tower. "It's going to rain any minute."

Mathewar picked up Atte, and he and Perren and Rone followed her inside. Atte began to struggle; she was clearly terrified of the storm but at the same time did not want to return to her prison. Mathewar and Angarred ran outside again to retrieve their packs.

From the shelter of the tower she peered cautiously through the open door. Lightning snaked from end to end of the sky. Water poured down, looking as solid as glass.

She turned back to the round room and saw Mathewar gathering sticks of wood. She bent to help him; when they had piled enough he spoke some words to start a fire and they set their packs near it to dry. Smoke streamed upward and poured through the open window. Atte moved closer to the warmth and Mathewar sat next to her, talking softly.

Rone glanced outside. "We'll have a few hours here," she said. Angarred wondered how she knew. "Dost want Perren to start thy lessons?"

Did she? She might as well, if they were forced to stay in the tower. She could take lessons from the woman without forgiving her, after all. "All right," she said.

Someone shrieked, a terrible cry of pain and loss. She turned quickly. "No!" Atte shouted. She clung to Mathewar. "No, you can't go, you can't go!"

Mathewar said something to her. She sobbed loudly, the sound drowned by the beats of the thunder. He moved to hold her, but she pushed him away as if punishing him.

Gradually she stopped crying, and finally fell asleep on the dirt floor. At the same time the lightning and thunder subsided, but the water fell as strongly as ever. Angarred looked at Perren, indicating that she was ready to begin.

Perren took some dried leaves from a pouch at her belt. "The lessons go easier if you pick these yourself," she said. "Unfortunately we don't have time for that."

The leaves had a powerful smell, something like pepper and other strong spices, and Angarred realized that she had seen them before. She had been out picking herbs and flowers and berries with Worrige and had stopped, caught by a strong scent in the middle of nothing but low scrub and dirt. Finally she looked down and saw a small, ragged bush, half its leaves crumpled like paper and the other half dry and dead.

"That's mirrorleaf, love," Worrige said. "We don't pick that one."

"Why not?" Angarred asked.

"Magicians pick it. It's powerful, very powerful."

Angarred studied it doubtfully. "Then why don't you use it? If it's that powerful?"

Worrige looked horrified. "I wouldn't dare. I don't know the words, and anyway it's far too dangerous for me . . ." And she had walked away, muttering, her small form even smaller as she bent over the ground; she looked a bit like a withered shrub herself in her dark tattered clothing.

Now Angarred said, "Oh, yes. Mirrorleaf."

Perren looked at her, startled and impressed. She clearly wanted to ask Angarred where she had learned the name. Angarred had no intention of telling her anything about herself; if her mother hadn't been interested enough in her while she was growing up then she didn't deserve to learn anything now.

"Do you have a bowl?" Perren asked.

For an answer Angarred took a small tin bowl from her pack.

"Go outside and fill it with water," Perren said. "Then bring it back and crush these leaves and drop them in the water."

Angarred did as she had been told. "Now," Perren said. "Stare into the bowl and recite the words I will tell you. Then concentrate, go deep within your mind. There is an animal there, inside you, part of you, waiting for you. Think about what it might be, what it is your body wants to become. When you find it the water will show you its picture."

Suddenly she saw Mathewar watching Perren through the flames of the fire; he seemed amused at something. "Should he be here, listening to all this?" Angarred asked. "Didn't you tell me this is women's magic?"

"Aye," Rone said. "But he has a part to play here—I feel it. He should know what it is that women do."

"I thank thee," Mathewar said. Now Angarred saw that he wasn't amused at all but listening closely to Perren's words. She didn't like it; he seemed to understand things very quickly, and she would hate it if he mastered women's magic, her magic, before she did.

"Ignore him," Perren said. "Concentrate. Close your eyes if that helps. Go deep within. Your animal is there, waiting for you in the lair of your mind." She spoke the words of the spell and then fell silent.

Angarred repeated Perren's words and looked into the water. The leaves, to her surprise, disappeared completely as she spoke, turning the water pale silver. She stared into the water and thought about animals, but she found only ordinary thoughts: when will the rain let up, where are the giants, how will Mathewar get their Stone away from them? "Concentrate," Perren said.

She closed her eyes, then opened them, certain Mathewar was watching her. But his eyes seemed to take in everything: her and Perren, Atte, the tower around them.

She tried to ignore him. She thought of animals she would like to be—a cat, a wolf, an otter—but they all seemed wrong somehow, and no picture appeared in the bowl of water. Gradually the fire warmed the small room; steam rose from the horses' flanks and the place smelled of their sweat.

It was too bad Worrige could not have learned this, Angarred thought. The old woman's magic was strong; she would have enjoyed changing into a bat, or whatever her shape turned out to be. But Perren had not seen fit to visit Hashan Hall, and so Worrige had learned only scraps of magic, had remained powerless and ignored all her life.

Well, if I learn this I can go back and teach her. Is Hashan Hall still standing, or has it turned into a home for owls and badgers? She forced her disorganized thoughts away and fixed her attention on the bowl of water. Owls, badgers, bats, she thought, but no picture appeared in the bowl.

An hour later she still had not understood what Perren meant by finding her animal. She felt hot and extremely tired, as if she had put in a full day's work in the fields. "Let's stop now," she said.

"The children in the forest work at their transformations for hours," Perren said. "A good many of them are able to change after only one lesson—sometimes they don't even need the mirror, though that's very rare."

"Well, I don't live in the forest," Angarred said, angry once again. "And I'm not a child. And maybe I can't do this, did you ever think of that?"

"I think you can," Perren said. "Your magic is strong—I can feel it. You knew who I was before I told you, for example."

And I knew other things too, she thought. She summoned up the strength from somewhere and returned to the bowl.

By the time the rain stopped, another hour later, she was still no closer to her goal. Mathewar stood. "We should go now," he said.

"Very well," Perren said. She turned to Angarred. "You must say the words to end the lesson—otherwise you will continue to concentrate on your animal, even when you need to do other things. But I do want you to think about what it might be every so often, when you have some time. We'll work with the mirror again when next we meet."

"Are we going to meet again?" Angarred said.

"Oh, yes." Perren hesitated. "I haven't found my daughter only to lose her once more."

Angarred realized, surprised, that it was hard for Perren to talk about personal things, that she was far more comfortable as they had been, teacher and student. And yet somehow, from just that one sentence, Angarred knew that she had been glad to find her daughter still alive.

Perhaps she had been wrong about Perren, then. She dismissed the thought; after a lifetime of loss and emptiness she was not yet ready to forgive her.

Perren spoke the words to end the lesson and she repeated them, then poured the water out and packed away her bowl. She and Mathewar led the horses back outside and tied on their packs.

Mathewar crouched by Atte. "Rone will take care of you, my heart," he said. "I'll come back for you soon."

Angarred prepared for another bout of weeping but Atte looked resigned, her eyes dull gray, almost as if she never expected to see her father again. Mathewar kissed her gently on the forehead and then mounted his horse. "That's one promise I'd better keep," he said quietly to Angarred.

Rone pointed to a path that led out of the clearing. "I saw the giants in that direction," she said. "But as I told thee, when I am in the air it is difficult to judge distances on foot. It might take thee another day, perhaps."

They said good-bye to Rone and Perren. Perren shifted into an eagle and flew off. Angarred thought she turned her head once to look back at them, but the eagle might have been studying any number of things, the sun or the trees or the position of the shadows.

Angarred and Mathewar set off down the path, riding in silence. Water dripped from the naked branches above them. She could not help but think of Mathewar's parting from his daughter, and how different it had been from her own farewell to Perren. She sighed. "You're lucky to have a family," she said. "Oh. I'm sorry, I wasn't thinking—"

"No, you're right," Mathewar said. "I'm very lucky to have my daughter back, luckier than I had any right to expect. I wish I could give wholehearted thanks for my good fortune, and be satisfied . . . So many things worked in my favor—that Alkarren didn't visit his tower, for one—"

"Yes, I wondered about that. Why doesn't he?"

"He has to stay in Pergodi, has to keep watch on all his Hollow Ones and shadow people. I sensed in the tower that he hadn't been there for months, maybe a year. I suppose he thought that it was safe, that no one could break in, that Atte would sleep until he woke her . . ."

He shook his head. Angarred guessed he was thinking of Embre again, and her death. "I liked your daughter," she said to distract him.

"Did you?" His mouth quirked in a smile. "You didn't exactly see her at her best."

"No, but I could tell what kind of person she is. Just as I could tell that my mother—"

"Your mother, yes. How did you know who she was?"

"I don't know. I realized it all at once—somehow I knew that she had been married to my father, and that she felt some terrible guilt about it—"

"That was the Clear Sight, I think. And I think it was no coincidence that you were talking about her just before you met her."

"The Clear Sight? Really?"

He smiled again. "Yes. When you receive the Clear Sight you learn a great many things about another person, all at once, as you said. And some of them are things you don't want to know."

She grinned. "Will I be able to attend the College then?"

"Stranger things have happened," he said. "One thing is for certain—I will have to have a long talk with the masters, when all of this is over."

A few hours later the light began to fade. They lit no fire, for fear the giants might see it; they ate a cold supper, then spread their cloaks and blankets on the wet ground. Suddenly Mathewar said, "You don't have to watch over me, you know. I'm not going to drink sattery tonight."

"I wasn't watching you," Angarred said, furious.

"I'm sorry then. I thought you were."

She got under her blankets and said nothing more. She *had* been watching him, she knew, though she hadn't been aware of how closely. And it wasn't only to see if he would drink sattery. How did matters stand between them now that he knew his wife was dead? Did he ever think about their kiss in Anfarna's house? Though of course it was too soon for him to think of anything but Embre; as he said, he had to mourn her a second time. She tried to read him with the Clear Sight, but as she expected she could see nothing.

They set out again the next morning. At about noon they came to a track through the forest, as wide as the giants' path they had seen earlier but without the evidence of destruction, the dead animals and rotted trees. It was nearly as difficult to follow, though; the giants had churned up huge ruts in the mud, forcing Mathewar and Angarred to guide their horses carefully.

A slow dreary rain began. They pulled their hoods up and continued on. Finally the woods before them opened up. They stood at the edge of the trees and saw a sight that made Angarred gasp: a neat row of cottages, with flower beds and gables and colorful paint, each the height of a three-story building.

"Holy Godkings," Angarred said.

Mathewar turned to answer her. A net fell over them from the tree above. The horses shied in panic. Angarred and Mathewar fought against the tangled net to dismount, and Mathewar tried to reach his sword, but the net held them too tightly. Angarred spoke soft words to her horse to calm him.

A giant came out of one of the houses and studied them for a while. "Well," he said, kneeling down to talk to them. "What have we caught here?" His voice sounded like an avalanche of boulders, deep and rolling.

"Two people who have as much right to visit the forest as you do," Mathewar said. "Let us go."

"Indeed," the giant said. "And what brings you to the forest?"

"I had to rescue my child, who was imprisoned in a tower."

"And where is your child now?"

"I left her with the forest people, with Rone's people. It's too dangerous to take her back to Pergodi."

The giant's eyebrows, each the size of a baby squirrel, lifted in interest when he mentioned Rone. "Why are you going back to Pergodi, then? Why don't you stay here with Rone?"

"I'm not answering any more of your questions," Mathewar said. "It's none of your concern. Let us go and we won't trouble you again."

"It is our concern, though. Strange things are moving in the forest, things none of us have seen in our lifetimes. Magicians and crows, and those which cannot be mentioned—"

The Others, Angarred thought. "Are you the king of the giants?" she asked.

"The king?" The giant laughed. Angarred felt the gust of his breath, a pleasant smell, like baking bread. Deeply rutted crevices formed on his face, making it looked like a worn boulder. "No. We don't have a king—there are not enough of us for a king to rule over. Why do you ask?"

"I heard the giants had a king, and that they're massing under him."

Mathewar frowned, clearly unhappy at her openness. But she felt that this man would not hurt them, that the giants were as peaceful as everyone said. Was this the Clear Sight? Or was it an opinion based only on wishful thinking, one that could easily be wrong? How did you tell?

"One of our people—" the giant began. "No. I'll get you out of this net, and then I will tell you what happened."

He pulled out a dinner knife as large as a sword and cut the net open. "Let's go to my house, out of this rain," the giant said. "My name is Tok, by the way."

They dismounted with relief and introduced themselves. The giant straightened. He was about three times their height, something like the relation Mathewar stood to Atte. For a moment Angarred worried that he would want to carry them. Then he turned and strode away.

They tied the horses to a tree. The giant made no concession to their smaller legs and they had to hurry after him, nearly running. He walked up the stairs to one of the cottages and opened the door, and they climbed the steps with difficulty after him.

He led them into a kitchen with a huge table, a huge hearth, a cupboard displaying dishes that looked as if they could be used as sleds. He sat at the table, then frowned and lifted them carefully to the edge, where they sat with their legs dangling. High overhead they could hear the rain pattering on the roof.

"Now," he said. "You're right—one of our people has declared himself king, and attracted followers. Dolk, his name is. He says that our magic was stolen from us long ago and bound into Tobrin's Stone, but that now our Stone has been returned to us. And that this is a sign that we should rise up and take whatever is ours, what was our right from old." The giant shook his head. "I have to say I don't understand it. We don't have kings, as I told you, and we move cautiously over the earth, because we know that our passage can cause great harm. We certainly do not *march*." He pronounced the word with disdain. "In fact, we have not been to war in over a thousand years, since before Tobrin created the Stone."

Another giant came into the kitchen, a woman wearing a voluminous skirt and shawl. She took out a pot the size of a cauldron from an ancient legend and filled it with some water, an enormous amount of vegetables and an entire chicken. Then she hung the pot over the hearth and sat nearby, watching it.

"This is my wife, Kav," Tok said. "Kav, these little people want to know about the Stone."

Kav studied them and nodded, then returned to her cooking.

"How did you get the Stone?" Mathewar asked.

The giant frowned; the squirrels that were his eyebrows moved closer. "That was strange. A man stepped out of the forest and gave it to me fourteen years ago. No, it must be fifteen years by now."

"What did he look like?"

"I don't remember. He was a little man, like yourselves. And he had gray hair, I think, but he wasn't terribly old."

"Did he have a beard? And a staff?"

"I don't think so. But as I said, I don't really remember. He asked only one favor of us in exchange, and that was the oddest thing of all—he wanted me and some others to go to Pergodi and walk up and down a roof."

"The Snoppishes!" Angarred said. "You walked on the Snoppishes' roof!"

"What?" Mathewar said. "Why? Oh—so that the roof would collapse, and they would discover their Stone."

"Jerret even said it sounded like giants walking, remember?" She turned to Tok. "Was this during a storm?" she asked.

"Yes, it was. Odder and odder. And you say you know the people who live there?"

The giant woman ground some pepper and scattered handfuls into the pot, so much of it that Angarred's eyes started to burn. She added an entire sprig of some herb, then sat again and stirred the stew. "Yes," Angarred said. "And they have a Stone like yours. But why would this man, whoever he was, give you a Stone? And why did he want the Snoppishes to find theirs?"

"I think he's the one your statues referred to," Mathewar said. "He's behind all this, or he works for someone who is. He wants to cause chaos, and giving inexperienced people Stones is a good way to do it. Look what Alkarren's done, and this giant, the one who calls himself king."

"Oh, Dolk doesn't have the Stone," Tok said. "I would never give it to someone so irresponsible. He wanted it, of course, but I hid it away where he couldn't find it. He worked on me for fifteen long years, or perhaps he was waiting for me to fall ill and show someone else my hiding place. And then finally he heard there was a Stone in Pergodi and decided to march his people there. He said that Stone is rightfully ours. His, he means."

"You mean—you still have the Stone?" Mathewar said.

"Yes."

"Can we have it?" Angarred said. "We need it to—"

"Angarred!" Mathewar said.

"Well, he's not using it—he probably doesn't even know how to. And we need it, to stop whoever is behind all this confusion. You'd know how to use it, wouldn't you?"

Mathewar nodded slowly, thinking no doubt of what he had learned from Alkarren in the dungeons.

"Mathewar Tobrin, you said your name was?" Tok said. "A magician?"

"Yes."

"I'll show it to you—I'd like to know what you make of it. It seems wrong somehow, odd. Just holding it makes me feel ill. You stay here—if I decide not to give it to you I don't want you knowing my hiding place."

He stood and left the room by a back door Angarred hadn't noticed. He walked with slow care; undoubtedly, as he said, he would cause a good deal of destruction if he hurried.

He returned a few minutes later. Like Jerret, he had tried to isolate his Stone inside a box. He handed it to Mathewar, who took out the Stone and held it for a moment.

"It's the Stone of Tobrin, certainly," he said. "A part of it, anyway. The Stone broke into three pieces—we don't know when, or if it was a deliberate breaking or an accident. I think that's why it feels so unnatural—because it's incomplete, not whole. Perhaps in some way it's seeking the missing pieces." He put it back in the box.

"Hmmm," Tok said. "And what would you do with it if I gave it to you?"

"Stop the fighting," Angarred said.

Tok looked at her, puzzled.

"We've discovered that someone is trying to cause war and confusion," Mathewar said. "Your gray-haired man, maybe, the one who's handing out Stones to people who lack the knowledge to use them. I'm sure he knew exactly how much harm the giants could do if you chose. We want to stop him before the land lies in ruins."

"Hmmm," the giant said again. "You say you know Rone?"

"Yes," Mathewar said.

"My mother lives with the forest people," Angarred said. "Perren. You could ask them to vouch for us."

"We keep to ourselves, mostly, in the forest," Tok said. "Anyway, I wouldn't know how to go about finding them, things change so much here. But Rone's a sensible woman." He sighed. "Would you like to stay for supper?"

Angarred foresaw an evening of mishaps—fumblings with outsized knives and spoons, attempts to carve mountains of food into manageable pieces. Still, there seemed no other way to get the Stone. And steam was beginning to rise from the cauldron, bringing with it tantalizing smells of chicken and vegetables.

"We'd love to," Mathewar said.

The giant-woman came over to the table. She set down two vast plates for her and her husband, then gave Angarred and Mathewar what looked like saucers. Mathewar sat cross-legged on the table and held his in his lap, and after some experimenting with hers Angarred did the same.

Kav ladled food into their plates. Everything, Angarred saw with relief, seemed small enough to eat. The spoons Kav gave them were huge, but not as awkward to use as she had feared.

They ate a while in silence. "How do you know Rone?" Tok said finally.

"We met her on our last journey through the forest," Mathewar said. "We had some interesting discussions on magic."

Tok asked more questions and they answered, careful to show themselves as people who would be worthy of the Stone. Angarred noticed that Mathewar did not mention his arguments with Rone, and for her part she managed not to tell Tok that she hadn't seen her mother since she was a child, and that she had felt hatred when they had finally met.

By the time the supper ended, though, they were talking easily, freely. "Who is this gray-haired man you mentioned?" Tok asked. "The one with the beard and the staff?"

"An evil magician named Alkarren," Mathewar said. "The man who imprisoned my daughter. He couldn't have been the one to give you the Stone, though—I see that now. He spent years looking for a Stone himself."

Angarred, who had already realized that, wondered now if Mathewar would start to see Alkarren behind every plot. He certainly had good reason to hate the man, she knew, but she hoped his hatred would not affect his judgment.

"Very well, then, I'll give you the Stone," Tok said.

Angarred, startled, spilled stew down the front of her shirt. Kav handed her a napkin the size of a small blanket. Of all the answers they had given, why had that one made up the giant's mind?

"Why?" she asked. Mathewar gave her a warning glance, but she ignored him.

"There's too much here I don't understand," Tok said. "Why would a magician confine a child in a tower? Why would a man I don't know give me a valuable Stone—or, even stranger, only a third of a Stone? Why are our people on the move now, after a thousand years? There are too many people fighting for too many things, and it's beyond my wit to untangle it all. And the Stone's given me no peace for fifteen years, and at least this way I'll know that addle-head Dolk won't get it."

"I thank you," Mathewar said. "Very much."

Angarred wiped the last of the stew from her shirt. "Yes," she said. "Thank you."

The giants invited them to sleep by the hearth, and they brought their things in gratefully. Angarred watched Mathewar as inconspicuously as she could while they prepared for bed. But he made no move to take out the familiar leather bottle, and if he noticed her scrutiny he said nothing.

It was only as she began to fall asleep that she remembered her reason for seeking out the giants: she had thought they were the force behind everything, the cause of all the confusion. Now she realized that they couldn't be; the powers had used them just as they had used everyone else. Someone was playing a vast game, with all the world as their playing field; giving the giants the Stone had been only one move in that game. They had hoped the giants would lay waste to everything around them, and it was only because of Tok's common sense that they had failed.

But then who were the manipulators? Perhaps Mathewar could find out, using the Stone. And she could use the Stone too, to rise at court, to thwart her enemies. Though Mathewar would no doubt want it to destroy Alkarren . . .

She dreamed she was watching the Pergodek puppet-master, but that this time it was people she knew who were dangling from his strings—Tezue and Jerret and Rodarren and Norue. At the very bottom, unnoticed by anyone else, two tiny dolls were dancing wildly to their master's tune. She looked closer, and saw herself and Mathewar.

Mathewar woke several times in the night from stomach cramps and aches in his joints, but the pain was so much less than it had been that he felt almost grateful. Once he turned and saw Angarred sleeping peacefully, her face nearly hidden in her long tangled hair. For the first time he seemed to see her truly, not as a celestial messenger or some other hallucination. He remembered how she had urged him to stop drinking sattery, and suddenly he understood that it had been concern and not disapproval that had moved her.

Without stopping to think he searched his pack for the leather bottle and walked barefoot over cold wooden planks to the front door. The latch was just low enough to reach; he opened the door, went out onto the steps and poured the thick liquid on the ground.

He stayed there a moment despite the cold. The air tasted like wine, chill and crisp and sweet. The sky for once was clear; he looked up and saw a myriad of stars, and Mother Mathona the moon. My life starts now, he thought. I have mourned her too long.

He waited for the guilt he felt sure would come at abandoning her, but there was only the usual sadness that he had been unable to save her. I'm not abandoning her, he thought fiercely. I'll keep her with me always, in my memories.

He went inside and settled back into the warmth of his blankets, staring up at the distant ceiling. The clarity he had felt looking up at the sky had already left him. What do I do with this new life I seem to have, he thought, a life without sattery, without Embre?

He looked at Angarred again, imagining her married to Jerret, happy, surrounded by children . . . There was something wrong with that thought and he chased it for a while, until finally he fell into an uneasy sleep.

sh
piec

The next morning, as they prepared to leave, they learned that the giants' village was not in a clearing as they had thought but outside the wood, that they had come to the very edge of the forest. Mathewar glanced at the sun and decided to skirt the forest on their way back to Pergodi. They would have to cover more ground that way, he said, but they could go faster, and they would avoid the dangers and enchantments of Tiranon.

They noticed more burned villages and destroyed fields on their way back, but saw almost no people. Once they passed a huge muddy trail leading through cropland, more evidence of the giants' destruction. "I wonder where all the soldiers are," Mathewar said.

"Well, they aren't around here," Angarred said. "That's all I need to know."

"Yes, but they could be at Pergodi. They might have broken the siege."

"You're very cheerful this morning."

Mathewar smiled without mirth. "I didn't get much sleep," he said.

When they neared Pergodi a few days later Angarred saw, shocked, that Mathewar had been right: the wooden gate lay in es, and large sections of the walls had been thrown down. The catapult had done its work all too well. Soldiers clashed outside the city, a massed confusion of colors and weapons. Muted sounds of battle came toward them, and the smell of smoke coiled in the air.

"Who's fighting who, can you tell?" Angarred asked.

"Everyone, it looks like," Mathewar said. "I can see Norue's colors, and Rodarren's—"

"And Tezue's. And look, over there—there's a band of giants."

"You were right, then. Someone wants all this to happen. I can't imagine there will be much of Pergodi left standing after this."

"What do we do now?"

"We get some idea of what's going on first. And we look for Alkarren's Stone, and perhaps the one that was stolen from us in Emindal. I can sense at least one Stone inside the city."

"You want to go through the gate? How in the name of the Navigator are we going to do that?"

"There are a good many unguarded places along the walls, it looks like, and people are going in and out. I'll make us look inconspicuous. We'll have to set the horses free, though—if we go in with them we'll seem too important."

She looked down at her horse. He had been the one constant in all her adventures, had brought her all the way from her father's house and carried her twice through the Forest of Tiranon; and he had returned unexpectedly when she thought him lost for good. "What—what will happen to him?" she asked. "Do you think he can make his way back to the Snoppishes' a second time?"

She expected him to mock her sentimentality. Instead he said, "It's possible. Or perhaps they'll come to a pasture and be taken in by some farmer. But it's possible the soldiers will find them. I'm sorry."

They dismounted and untied their packs. Mathewar slapped both horses on the rump and they ran off. Angarred watched them until they were nearly out of sight.

He recited some words over himself and Angarred. She felt herself dwindling, becoming unimportant. So strong was the spell that she had to fight to hold on to her sense of herself.

"Come," he said. He drew his sword and led them up toward the walls, and they entered Pergodi.

Labren fought through a press of people, struggling to reach the Takekek soldier ahead of him. Too many armies crowded the narrow streets of Pergodi; he felt lost in the tangle of shouts and colors, unable to separate ally from foe. His commander had ordered them to attack the Takekek but to leave Norue's troops alone— Labren had been unable to convince him of the prince's treachery. Likewise they were to avoid anyone with Rodarren's colors. But around midday soldiers carrying a standard of Emindal cloth took the field, seeming to come from nowhere, causing a great deal of confusion. Weren't the Emindalek a peaceful people? And the giants continued to wreak destruction, trampling soldiers from every army before them.

Labren turned his head clumsily to follow the Takekek. He had taken a Takekek helmet from a dead soldier, grateful for its protection; the clothing he wore, he thought, would be enough to identify him to his fellow Karedek. He was still not used to the helmet's weight, though, or its narrow field of vision. The other man slipped between two horsemen and disappeared.

Labren chased him, feeling tired and hungry and dirty. It had been a frustrating day, plagued by difficulties. Several times the company had raced toward a skirmish only to find they were a few minutes too late, or that there was no fighting at all. The soldiers murmured about the king, whispering that he received bad advice, that he had become a Hollow One, that whoever controlled him didn't want to win the war at all. Others said that these mistakes happened in war, that King Tezue knew what he was doing. Still, everyone felt dissatisfied and ill-tempered, ready to lash out against friend and enemy alike.

The early winter sun was beginning to set, lighting the western turrets and rooftops on fire. The Karedek trumpeter played the signal to regroup. Labren abandoned the Takekek soldier with relief and returned to their camp, a narrow field at the juncture of three streets.

When his company gathered together they discovered that they had sustained no deaths and only a few serious injuries. The wounded were sent or carried to the infirmary. The rest removed their ragtag stolen armor and ate a meager supper, then settled down to sleep in makeshift tents or on the hard ground.

Labren had another reason for wanting to leave the battle-ground. He lay on a blanket, listening to the men around him grow quiet as they dropped off to sleep. A picture of the Stone formed in his mind. It seemed to call to him from the bottom of his pack where he had placed it. He felt powerless to stop his thoughts; his mind returned to the Stone again and again, as though seeking out a rotting tooth, urging him to study it.

Finally he gave in and reached for the pack. He took it out and turned it in his hand. In the dark it glowed with a strange green-and-black light. The pictures he had seen before returned, battle sounds, horses rearing, people shouting orders.

Suddenly he saw his father's face. He gasped; he had not seen Dalesio for so long that he had almost forgotten what he looked like. His mother was there too, tears running down her face. Was it grief, or happiness at seeing Dalesio again?

So his father would return. He wished he could tell Gedren. Maybe he could slip away and see her; the fighting had neared the Craftsman's Quarter a few times.

The Stone showed him another picture. He saw that he could kill using the power of the Stone, and he bent forward attentively. Obediently, the Stone repeated the image, as if to make certain he understood it.

Mathewar and Angarred headed down a quiet street, their hoods pulled up against the cold. He motioned her to stop and removed his spell; they no longer needed it, he said, hidden as they were inside their cloaks. Still, she felt strange for a while afterward, insignificant, a tiny mote in a world that swarmed with far more important people.

She was shocked at the destruction all around her; Pergodi looked like a different city from the one she had left. The streets were deserted, though several times they noticed people watching them anxiously from the windows. Fire had burned through parts of the city, leaving shells of ruined buildings. Lots stood empty where wooden houses had been torn down for firewood. Windows had been broken and not boarded up; that wood, too, had been burned for warmth. Filth layered the unswept streets, and rats nosed in one pile of garbage and then moved on to another.

A man lay in the street, shivering violently. "Feverchill," Angarred said, remembering Worrige's lessons. "It happens a lot during sieges, when people are cold and hungry. Don't go near him or you might catch it yourself. There's nothing we can do— it's almost always fatal." Despite her words they both looked at the man in horror as they passed.

They searched through the streets, seeing no one outside except that one man. They heard the distant sounds of battle, and the wind brought them an unpleasant smell, something noxious burning.

"Is it close?" Angarred said. "The Stone?"

Mathewar shook his head. "I don't know. It's here somewhere, but I'm not sure . . ." He looked up at the sky. "It'll get dark soon, and the corpse-robbers will be out. Let's see if the inn I stayed in is still there."

They walked through the twisting streets to the inn, coming there as evening started to give way to night. In the dim light it looked much the same, though the wooden sign with the ruddy king's face was gone. They went inside.

The innkeeper came out of a back room, looking delighted to see them. "Hello, hello!" he said. "You can have your choice of rooms, any one I have, all the same low price." He studied them with open curiosity. Did he remember Angarred's visits? "Or any two, if you like."

"In that case we'll take your two best," Mathewar said.

"Wonderful," the innkeeper said, leading them toward the stairs and on up to the next floor. "I'm afraid I can't provide supper, or breakfast either, for that matter."

He turned down a corridor at the top, opened a door and motioned them inside. It *was* a good room, Angarred saw, very spacious, with a hearth, a large, comfortable-looking bed and a painted chest. Odd, to live in luxury in the midst of a siege.

Mathewar continued down the hall to his room, turning back for a moment to say, "I'll join you for supper later." She watched

him as he walked away. Why two rooms, she wondered, after they
had spent countless nights sleeping only inches apart?

The fighting in the streets the next day was much the same, bewildering and frustrating. No one seemed to know what to do or
where to go; only the giants made any inroads, toppling houses and
carts, cutting down everyone before them with their great clubs
and axes. The fire in one of the poor sections of the city continued
unchecked, and an unpleasant burning smell reached Labren's
company as they fought, making it difficult to breathe.

Labren clutched his Stone in his left hand, using his sword with
his right. The Stone made him dizzy and sick, and its pictures confused him; several times he had lashed out only to find nothing at
the end of his blade but illusion. And he was still not yet used to his
helmet; twice so far men had come within a sword's distance before
he spotted them.

Around noon a heavy, drenching rain began to fall. Labren listened for the trumpeter's signal to regroup, but it did not come. He
pulled his jacket closer against the chill and looked around him.

Suddenly he saw Prince Norue's standard-bearer. He fought his
way toward him. Soldiers with Norue's colors blocked his path but
he cut them down unheeding, only half-aware that the power of
the Stone was helping him.

He reached the standard-bearer. He used the Stone as he had
learned; black-and-green light flared out in front of him. The
other man dropped to the ground like a puppet with its strings cut.
The standard fell, ringing out against the cobbles. Labren jumped
back, startled, horrified at the power he wielded.

But he had to keep going. He saw Norue ahead of him, the
visor of his helmet raised. The prince wore ceremonial armor; the
plate metal shone silver in the heavy rain, like an exotic fish
glimpsed through a rushing stream. The outfit was never intended
for fighting, though, and Labren thought scornfully that he could
see half a dozen places to attack.

He had a clear path to Norue now. The prince was facing the
other way, bidding farewell to an officer dressed in similar foppery.

Labren moved forward, seeing no one but the prince, remembering the man's treachery and his own imprisonment in the dungeons. The sword for this one, he thought.

A soldier cried out to Norue. Labren heard him faintly over the storm and the sounds of battle: "Prince Norue! Sir! Guard yourself on the right!" In the rain no one else saw Labren and the green-black light that blazed out in front of him.

Prince Norue ignored the man and continued to talk to his officer, who was walking away from him. Labren moved around Norue quietly and, remembering Jerret's training, slipped his blade between Norue's helmet and breast plate. He felt the strike go home, and he knew with elation that he had killed him. Blood welled up from the prince's neck and he fell to the ground.

The officer shouted; so did the common soldier who had called out to Norue. They converged on Labren. He struck out with his sword, keeping them at bay while he used the Stone. The officer fell but the other soldier continued to attack; apparently the Stone had only limited power.

The two fought in earnest now, thrusting, parrying, struggling to keep their footing on the wet, slippery cobbles. Suddenly the other man moved forward and sliced open Labren's arm; Labren had been defending his body and had forgotten for a moment the hand holding the Stone. Shocked, Labren dropped the Stone to the ground.

The two men dove for it; the soldier had seen enough to know it was valuable. They fought on the slick cobbles, kicking, rolling, twisting, looking for an opening. The Stone skittered across the street, knocked there by a chance blow. The other soldier spared a moment to glance at it and Labren struck out blindly with his sword. He felt something solid; he had hit the man's leg. The soldier froze, staring at his gushing blood. Labren scrabbled to his knees and thrust down at the man's chest to deliver the final blow.

But now someone else had seen the Stone and was bending over it. Labren got to his feet, gasping for breath, and hurried toward this new threat. The other man picked up the Stone. Labren braced himself for a burst of green-and-black light but the man did not seem to know how to use it. The two raised their swords and engaged.

This man fought better than the last one, Labren noticed. He was hard put to hold his own; he seemed to be led first in one direction and then in another, almost as if the man was dancing with him. And he felt the pain from his wounded arm now; it distracted him, making him miss several opportunities.

There was no opening at the other man's neck; Labren could not use the move that had served him so well thus far. He thrust at the man's chest but the sword skittered off to the side; the shirt was padded with chain mail.

Suddenly Labren slipped on the wet cobblestones and dropped to his knees. Desperate, he stabbed up under the other man's mail shirt. The man put his free hand to his abdomen, surprised; it came away red with blood. He swung his sword downward and, as Jerret had taught them, delivered a blow to Labren's neck below the helmet.

Labren cursed the Godkings and dropped to the ground, kneeling, bent over, his hand tight against his neck. For a moment he felt nothing; then the pain hit him, horribly sharp. "Who—" the other man said, hearing his voice. "Labren?"

The man lifted his helmet and Labren saw Lord Jerret. Jerret's face contorted in pain but he also looked terribly confused, as if he could not understand how he had come to this pass. His lifeblood spilled out onto his mail-shirt, pulsing slower and slower.

Labren pulled off his own helmet with difficulty. "I thought you were Norue's," Jerret said, gasping. "You had the Stone . . ."

"And I thought . . ." Labren said. "I wanted to fight for the right side. I wanted . . . and I killed you instead. I thought everything was so clear . . . All wrong . . ."

Jerret slipped to the ground. ". . . wrong . . ." he said.

Labren took a deep breath, wanting to say one more thing before he died. "I got Norue, though. He ignored a commoner and he died. The Balance served justice there . . ."

Jerret's eyes were closed now, and he lay unmoving. Then with a great effort he smiled at Labren's last words.

Labren coughed and tasted something metallic. He wiped his mouth; his hand came away covered with blood. He lay down next to Jerret. The sounds of the battle faded around him, and then disappeared.

Mathewar hurried through the streets with Angarred close behind him, tracking a power he had felt earlier. The rain had slackened; for the first time since noon they were able to move quickly.

Suddenly he stopped. Two men lay close together and he knelt, bending over one of them.

He looked up at Angarred. "It's Jerret, I'm afraid," he said softly. "What? No! No, it can't be—"

She knelt next to the fallen man. Mathewar put his hand near Jerret's face. "He's not breathing," he said.

It *was* Jerret, Angarred saw—the same high forehead, the same straight brown hair. The first man who had been kind to her in Pergodi.

"Can you—can you do something?" she asked Mathewar, knowing it for a forlorn hope even as she said it.

Mathewar shook his head. "I'm sorry," he said. "The Bearer bring him safely home."

He opened Jerret's hand. A Stone lay in his palm, a twin to his own. He lifted it gently and put it in his box.

Angarred glanced up and noticed three men walking toward them. Mathewar got to his feet hastily and she did the same. "Hello, Mathewar," one of them said. "Angarred." It was Master Narinye.

Now she could see Dalesio and Merren with him. "Hello," Mathewar said. "Why did you leave the College?"

"We had to," Narinye said. "We heard about the fighting and decided we couldn't stay away. Have you found Alkarren?"

Dalesio dropped to the ground near the other fallen man. "It's—it's Labren," he said. "It's my son. No. Oh, no."

"I'm sorry, Dalesio," Mathewar said. He put his hand on Dalesio's shoulder but the other man shrugged him off. "No!" Dalesio said, standing and shouting into the thin rain. "Godkings, no!"

"What happened here, do you know?" Merren asked.

"This man here is Lord Jerret Snoppish," Mathewar said. "It

looks as if the two fought and killed each other, but we don't know why."

Dalesio looked at him. There were tears in his eyes, not yet fallen. "I don't understand," he said, his voice hoarse. "Lord Jerret is from Pergodi, the same as my son. Why would they fight?"

"I don't know," Mathewar said. "This war—everyone seems to be fighting everyone else."

Mathewar motioned to two soldiers. As they came closer Angarred saw that one of them wore Emindal cloth. "Could you take this man to Princess Rodarren?" he asked. "It's Lord Jerret Snoppish."

The two men nodded. Mathewar studied them a moment and then added, "Be careful when you tell her. This man was very important to her."

More soldiers passed, men looking for their own dead. Dalesio called to two others, Karedek soldiers, and asked them to carry his son to King Tezue. He wiped his eyes roughly with his sleeve. "I have to find Gedren," he said, but he stood unmoving.

"Gedren?" Angarred asked. "Are you—you're Gedren's husband! She said you were missing, but she never told me your name. So you're—you're a magician after all."

Dalesio looked at her, his face tired. "I'm sorry," she said. "You have more than enough to think about . . . Please, go find your wife. You might look in the castle—she works there as a cleaning woman."

"It's getting late," Narinye said. "The corpse-robbers will be out soon."

"Come stay at our inn," Mathewar said. "The King's Head. The innkeeper says there's plenty of room."

Dalesio bade them farewell. The rest of them headed through the darkening streets toward the inn. Jerret dead, Angarred thought. It was too huge to believe, too impossible to take in. She remembered their talks together, his attempts to guide her through the strangeness of the court, his generosity. She thought of Lord and Lady Snoppish, of Jerret's sisters, of Gedren, all of them still thinking of Jerret and Labren as alive somewhere, talking, eating, laughing. And Rodarren. Poor woman, she had only just found him.

Dalesio walked slowly toward the Craftsman's Quarter. Why would Gedren work as a cleaning woman when she had a good livelihood at the bakery? And how did Angarred know? He shook his head. It was all too confusing—he had understood nothing since finding Labren.

Night had fallen by the time he reached the quarter. No candles or lamps shone in any of the windows, and no smoke curled from the chimneys; wood and wax and oil had no doubt run out a while ago. He found his way to his house by habit and knocked on the door.

No one answered. He knocked again. Gedren came to the door and peered out cautiously. "Oh," she said, swinging the door open. "Oh, holy Godkings, it's you—you're home."

They held each other tightly. "Come in, come in," she said finally. "Get out of the cold. Though it's not much warmer in here, to tell you the truth."

They moved into the kitchen, where the business of the household had always taken place. "I'm afraid have bad news for you, Gedren," he said.

"Bad—what do you mean?"

"Labren is dead."

She stared at him without understanding. "What? Labren?"

"Our son is dead. I saw him on the battlefield."

Suddenly, with no warning, she hit him. He made no move to defend himself. "You—you bastard!" she said. "You Other-loving bastard! You leave me for a year and a half with no word, leave me to struggle alone in the middle of a war, and then you come home to tell me my son is dead! He joined the army while you were gone, did you know that? Do you even care? And it's all because you left, because you weren't here to talk him out of it! And the blue-cloaks came, and they told me you were a magician, and Borgarrad has no wood for the ovens . . ."

She lashed out at him again, a hard slap on the face. "I'm sorry," he said. "I'm sorry. I couldn't—"

"Sorry! I nearly married Mashak, did you know that?"

"I—Mashak? No. No, I didn't know. Come, sit down—I'll tell

you why I left. Do you have any food? I could make you some-thing to eat."

"Food," she said scornfully. "You think food solves everything." But she sat down at the kitchen table and watched while he bustled around the kitchen, collecting rotting carrots, withered lettuce, ancient dried-out herbs.

"The blue-cloaks were right—I am a magician," he said. "I—"

"Then why didn't you tell me? Here I've been married to you for twenty years, and you never said a word. I thought married folk shared everything."

"I couldn't tell you. My master at the College, Narinye, he sent me out into the world after my studies were done. He had a pre-monition that danger was coming, that everything was about to change, and he needed someone to keep watch in Pergodi, some-one no one would suspect of being a magician. My family had been bakers, and I found I liked baking more than magic, so he chose me. Here, what's so funny?"

Gedren was laughing and crying at the same time. "Your master. The College. You say it all so matter-of-factly."

Dalesio took out a knife and began to chop the vegetables. "Well, anyway, twenty years later Alkarren stole the Stone of Tobrin."

"Yes, I know. I saw him use it."

"You saw—what do you mean?"

"Never mind. Go on with your story—I'll tell you later. You're not the only one with secrets."

"I knew then that he wanted power for himself, that he would use the Stone to further his own ambitions. And I knew also that I couldn't stand against him if he wielded the Stone. I had to disap-pear, just like all the other magicians, had to make certain he couldn't follow me to get to you and the children, threaten you in some way." Gedren began to say something; Dalesio raised his hand to stop her. "Believe me, the danger to you was real. As it turned out, he needed someone to help him master the Stone. He moved against the family of a friend of mine, Mathewar, first ensorceling his wife and child to gain his help and then destroying them when Mathewar still defied him. I had to help Mathewar, had to con-

vince him that his family was truly gone . . . It was horrible. He
still hates me for it, I think. And then I ran away to the College to
hide."

"And never sent me a letter, or a simple message . . ."

"I couldn't, don't you see? He might have gone after you next. I
couldn't risk putting you in danger."

He placed a wilted-looking salad in front of her and watched
anxiously while she took a bite. "Good," she said, surprised. "Is
that why you're such a great cook? Magic?"

He laughed shortly. "No."

They sat in silence while she ate. "And Labren?" she asked when
she had finished.

"Labren. I saw him on the battlefield, as I said. He had apparently fought with someone named Lord Jerret, and they killed each
other."

"Lord Jerret? But that's impossible. He served under Lord Jerret
for a while, thought nothing but good of the man. Why would he
have killed—"

She began to cry again. Dalesio moved around the table and
drew her into his arms, holding her while she wept. "Oh, this
war," she said. "This terrible war. Everyone's confused, no one
knows what's going on . . ."

"Come, sweetling," Dalesio said. "Let's go to sleep. We can talk
some more in the morning."

"Are you back, then?"

Was he? Nothing had changed; Alkarren still had the Stone, still
wanted power, might still harm his family. But he could not leave
Gedren like this; she had suffered enough. "For good," he said.

At the King's Head the innkeeper, delighted at two more paying
guests, welcomed Narinye and Merren and showed them to their
rooms. The four of them agreed to bring what food they had and
meet in the common room for supper.

Over hard sausage and week-old bread Mathewar told the other
magicians about his wife and child, and how he and Angarred had
found the two Stones. "What are you going to do with them?"
Merren asked.

"Find Alkarren and make him pay for what he did," Mathewar said.

"Don't you think——" Narinye said cautiously. "Well, the Stone belongs to the College."

"And the College will get it back, just as soon as I'm finished."

"But shouldn't you put an end to the fighting first?" Narinye asked. "If this keeps up there won't be anything left of Pergodi. Karededin will fall, and this lunacy will spread to other countries. And then if Lady Angarred is right someone will simply step in and rule us all, whatever is left to be ruled."

"No, I think he's right," Merren said. "Alkarren killed his wife, after all—surely he's entitled to justice." He turned to Mathewar. "You've stopped drinking sattery, haven't you? You must have thought this through, then, decided there was good reason to go after Alkarren first."

Angarred did not think Mathewar had considered anything but his own hot revenge. But Mathewar was nodding calmly, agreeing with Merren.

"Do you think you can stand against Alkarren?" Merren asked.

"Yes. I have two pieces to his one. And I learned a good deal about the Stone on my travels."

"Very well, then," Merren said. "And you have to admit, Narinye, that it would be good to be rid of this man once and for all."

A short while later they said good night and climbed the stairs to their rooms. "So you knew about Jerret and Rodarren," Angarred said to Mathewar.

"What?" Mathewar said.

"You knew all along that Jerret and Rodarren were lovers. You told the men carrying him to be careful with what they said to her. So why did you tell me I could do worse than marrying Jerret?"

Mathewar looked at her. His face showed confusion, but so briefly Angarred thought she might have imagined it. "I have no idea," he said.

When he got to his room Mathewar took out the two Stones. He had tried to fit them together before supper, but their edges did not match up no matter which way he positioned them. Probably Alkarren's Stone belonged between them.

He tried once again to put the Stones together, though he knew he had been thorough the first time. The sickly feeling he got from handling them was stronger now, as if the two felt the loss of their missing piece more intensely.

He set them back in the box and went to bed. He woke sometime in the night, his throat parched. Still half asleep, he realized he hadn't drunk any sattery that evening. He sat up, heading for the hearth, before he remembered that he had given it up, at least for now.

He lay back and stared at the ceiling. Why had he thought Angarred would marry Jerret? He had seen the affection between Jerret and Rodarren, and the passion for each other they had never managed to hide completely in Emindal.

Because, he thought slowly, Angarred unmarried was dangerous. He was starting to notice women again, the way they moved and spoke and laughed, now that he was breaking free of the spell of sattery. But he had to keep some distance from her—and not just from her, but from everyone. Better to stay aloof, to rely on no one but yourself. People could leave, or disappear.

He smiled crookedly. Things had been much easier when he had expected nothing ahead of him but death. Life was far more complicated.

Mathewar, Narinye and Merren were already in the common room when Angarred came down for breakfast. Dalesio entered as she sat down.

"Good morning, Dalesio," Narinye said. "How is Gedren?"

He sat heavily. "Not good," he said.

"No, of course not," Narinye said. "I'm very sorry about your son."

Dalesio nodded. "She told me some of the rumors she had heard. Norue is dead, people say. And Rodarren is ill, of feverchill perhaps, or perhaps she has returned to madness after the death of Lord Jerret."

"She never was mad, not really," Angarred said. "But I hope it's not feverchill—if it's true that Norue's dead she's the last of the king's family. And I have to say I hope he is dead."

"We should pray for her," Narinye said.

"Oh, and Gedren said a strange thing last night," Dalesio went on. "She said that Labren would never have killed Lord Jerret, that he had served under him and admired him more than any of the other commanders."

"It's this war," Angarred said. "We were talking about it last night. Someone is trying to sow confusion throughout Karededin."

Someone said something, but Angarred barely heard him. She understood something suddenly, all at once, the way the lightning had flashed across the sky. They were all puppets, all of them dancing to someone's tune. Alkarren held Tezue's strings, but someone else held Alkarren's, and even that person might be controlled by someone in his turn.

You could never gain power, never be safe. There was always someone higher, someone who held your strings. Look at Jerret and Labren, friends who had been made to kill one another by the unseen forces controlling them.

"Listen," she said to Mathewar urgently. "Alkarren isn't important. You have to go after whoever is behind him, whoever made him a Hollow One, or to the person behind that. You have to stop all this or friends will kill friends until it's over. Look at Jerret and Labren. Both of them were good men, both thought they were fighting for the right side, and all they managed to do was die by each other's hand."

"I told you," Mathewar said. "I'll stop using the Stone as soon as I kill Alkarren. The masters can do whatever they want with it after that."

"But don't you see? You're just creating more confusion. You're playing their game, and it's a game you can't win. The only way to win is to refuse to play."

"But you're playing a game as well, aren't you? Or did you decide you don't want to rise at court after all?"

She hadn't thought of that. She remembered her resolve, her strong desire to gain power over all of them, Norue and Enlandin, Karanin and Dorilde. She saw herself at the king's side, watching as he stripped land and rank from her enemies and sent them disgraced from court. Oh, she would like that, after all they had done to her!

But she understood now that her court battles were as petty and divisive as everything else. She would have to unite with the courtiers, distasteful as it might seem, and turn against the true enemy.

"The Others take the court," she said. "We have to stop this. Listen to me."

"There's something to what she says, Mathewar," Narinye said. "Maybe we should wait a bit, study the Stones . . ."

"I want justice for my family," Mathewar said. "Even Merren thinks I'm doing the right thing."

"Of course you are," Merren said. "No one wants to deny you justice. Perhaps you should take Dalesio with you—he can revenge himself on those who killed his son."

"What!" Angarred said. Merren turned his gaze on her, and for the first time she felt the strength in his dark gray eyes. His scrutiny seemed to strip her naked, but she would not let him stop her from speaking. "Revenge himself? How can Dalesio revenge himself? His son's death was an accident! Or do you want him to go to Lord Jerret's house and kill his old mother and father and all his sisters?"

"Are you certain it was accidental?" Merren said. "You just said that a good many people in the war are controlled by those above them, and that these in turn are controlled by others. Someone may have wanted Labren dead."

"That's nonsense," Angarred said.

"Leave it, Merren," Dalesio said heavily. "It's enough that he's dead—I'm not going to kill someone for it."

"Well, at least Mathewar can see justice done," Merren said.

"Be careful, though," Narinye said. "Remember what Angarred said—there are hidden players in this game. We don't know everything that's going on."

Merren turned to talk to Narinye. "Since when do you listen to Merren?" Angarred said to Mathewar, quietly so Merren wouldn't hear.

"When he agrees with me. No, I'm going to look for Alkarren today. You can't talk me out of this—don't even try."

"Very well. But give me the Stones when you're done. I'll see they're put to good use, for a change."

"I can't think of a better use than killing that evil man," Mathewar said. He looked straight at her, and she flinched away from the terrible determination on his face.

athewar moved quickly through Pergodi, barely seeing the carnage around him. Angarred hurried after him. Men and women lay in the streets, dead of battle wounds or fever-chill, which was spreading outward from the poor quarters of the city. Fire scorched the horizon, running wild with no one left to put it out. Once he caught a glimpse through broken walls of the Takekek camp and was startled at how large it was; with all its booths and tents it looked like a market day in Pergodi.

He was holding the Stones and felt their presence at every moment, the strange wrongness that emanated from them. And he felt something else, the answering call of another Stone. Alkarren was somewhere in the city.

Around noon his sense of the other Stone grew stronger. He walked through twisted alleyways and up flights of stairs, nearly running, past a tavern, a butcher's, a Godhouse. The twinge from his bad leg had grown to a fiery ache.

They turned another corner and were in time to see a man duck down and rip open a horse's belly. The rider jumped to the street before his horse fell, then raised his sword against the first man. More men soon joined them and they began to tear at each other savagely, using stones and axes and ancient farm implements. Judging from the uniforms they were all from different armies, or no army at all, but none of them seemed interested in looking for their allies; instead they fought as if some madness had descended on them.

Mathewar backed away and saw a man on horseback riding down another alley. Alkarren. Mathewar held out his pieces of the Stone, gritting his teeth against the sense of something horribly amiss. "Alkarren!" he called, using his commanding voice. "Come here!"

Alkarren started to turn, then stopped. "Come here, you coward!" Mathewar said.

The horse veered around and headed toward him. "Good day, Mathewar," Alkarren said. He sounded calm, as if he had intended to face Mathewar all along. "The blue-cloaks are looking for you—they don't take kindly to their prisoners escaping—"

"Give me the Stone," Mathewar said.

Alkarren reached into his saddlebag, then pulled his hand out with difficulty. "No," he said. "You don't want to do this. I have your wife and child, you know."

"No, you don't." Mathewar called on the power of the Stones and thrust into Alkarren's mind, showing him the tower and Atte's rescue. "Give me the Stone."

Alkarren stared at him fiercely, trying to break into his mind. Mathewar resisted. He felt a wild triumph, the certainty of knowing that he could best his enemy, that compared to him Alkarren was weak, nearly powerless. "Give me the Stone," he said again.

Alkarren did not move, though the painful struggle to break away showed on his face. His saddlebag opened; his Stone flew toward its fellows in Mathewar's hand.

Mathewar pieced them together quickly. They merged seamlessly into one. The sense of sick wrongness vanished; instead Mathewar felt that something had been put right, that everything was as it should be. His feeling of exultation grew.

He looked up to see Alkarren fleeing away, already halfway down the street. Alkarren kicked frantically at his horse, urging it onward as fast as he could among the close-packed houses. Mathewar raised the Stone.

"*No,*" Angarred said.

Green-black light shot from his hand, but Alkarren was already far beyond its reach. He tensed to run, knowing he would never overtake him. An instant before he moved Angarred put her hand on his arm, recalling him to his senses.

"No," Angarred said again. "You'll never catch him. Listen to me. We have to stop this."

"The Others take it!" Mathewar said. If he hadn't been so intent on piecing the Stone together he could have had him. The Stone had called to him somehow, had used him for its own purposes.

"Give me the Stone," Angarred said. "You said you would."

"He's not dead yet," Mathewar said.

"We don't have time. Everything's falling apart. Anyway, you don't want him—you want whoever's controlling him, the power that made him a Hollow One. Stop them and you'll stop Alkarren."

He looked down at the Stone. He thought of the men he had seen, hacking away at one another until they were all dead. Who had caused all that chaos, all those deaths? He held within his hand the most potent magic the world had ever known; he had to do something.

"Who is responsible for all these wars?" he asked the Stone. "Who is behind all the confusion?"

The Stone's light grew brighter. It glowed all around him, hemming him within green-black walls. The walls spun, circling faster and faster, like a whirlwind. He felt as if he were moving, but his eyes told him he had gone nowhere. Sounds from the outside faded away.

The spinning slowed, then stopped. The walls grew paler, gauze-like, and began to fade away. He grasped the Stone, wondering what he would face on the other side, and how he could possibly defend against it.

Two rows of trees stood like pillars in front of him, forming a path. Far down wonderful colors danced and played, brightening even as he watched. "Holy Godkings," he breathed. He had come somehow to the realm of the Others.

Suddenly he understood a good deal. Who would benefit from the collapse of the realms, and with them the destruction of reason, of the settled places of men the Others feared so much? And as people grew crazier and more desperate the Others would use them to come and go as they pleased, until all the world became mad, and the Others controlled it all.

He set off down the path. The trees on either side seemed made of gold, with golden leaves and fruit; he touched one and felt cold metal. The path beneath him was marble, inlaid with gold. The sky overhead was a deep midnight blue, with a huge moon and a great spread of golden stars as large as coins. Lights waited at the end: sea-green, brick red, silver.

The lights pulsed faster. They seemed to offer all he could desire: excitement, enchantment, a release from dull, painful life. It was like sattery, he thought, an abdication, a setting down of burdens.

He thought he was done with sattery. But he found himself hurrying down the path, hungry for whatever experience lay at the end among those tantalizing colors.

The colors had seemed close, but he walked a long time, as though the end of the path receded before him. He called to mind several spells that could be used to break through illusion and saw how they could be changed to fit his circumstances, and using the power of the Stone he spoke some words.

Nothing happened; the colors remained as distant as before. He tried the other spells but managed to come no closer. Very well, he would have to call to them, ask them to invite him. Though if he did that he did not know how he would ever come home again.

"Others," he said. He shuddered; all his training warned him never to speak their name in their presence. "Let me in. I want to come to you."

It was easier than he thought. Well, he had asked for enchantment every night for the last year and a half; he had in some sense been preparing for this. The path widened out and the colors enveloped him: deep blue, pale gray, the purple of plums.

He did not feel disoriented, though; rather, he felt he had come to a place he had known long ago, a place where he had been happy. He understood everything now: the reason for Embre's death and his long mourning, and the deaths of Jerret and Dalesio's son, and why everyone in the world had to fight an impossible war they could never win. And he understood why the Others needed to enchant the people of his world, and why it was right for them to do so. He felt not lost, but found.

He stood unmoving for long moments, as his newfound certainty flowed through him. He found himself grinning—it was all so simple. Why hadn't he seen it before?

Someone headed toward him through the mists of colors. Angarred, he thought, and felt a small prick of guilt and alarm. Had she traveled with him?

The person came closer. It seemed as if he doffed robe after robe of color—sun-yellow, dark green, pale blue—becoming clearer and more substantial as he went. It was a man, he realized, taller than Angarred, with a cap of nearly white hair . . .

"Master Merren?" he said, fighting against the great elation he felt. "What are you doing here?"

"Oh, I've been here a long time," Merren said. "Ever since I discovered the spell that would let me come and go freely. There are a good many things in the College library that have been lost or forgotten, don't you find?"

"But why? Why do you want to come here?" But even as he asked it he knew the answer. Why would anyone not come here?

Merren grinned. "I don't need to answer that, I see. Anyway knowledge for its own sake is always a good thing."

Mathewar struggled to concentrate. And here, too, his experiences in the past year and a half aided him; he had learned how to think with his mind drowned in sattery. "Why didn't you tell the other masters?" he asked.

"Because they would have stopped me, of course," Merren said.

Of course. He understood now. Find out who is behind everything, Angarred had said. "You hypocrite," he said, trying to summon anger. "You pretended to work with the masters, but all the time you were letting these—these creatures into the world, helping them destroy our homes, our lives—"

"But why should we hold on to our dull, unhappy lives? The Others will bring us enchantment, wonder, amazement. That's what you wanted from sattery, after all."

"No wonder you urged me to go after Alkarren. Angarred was right—you'd divided us all—"

"Yes, and you played your part well. And I was very pleased when you gave up sattery—I wanted your mind clear for your struggle against Alkarren. In fact I didn't realize you'd accomplish quite so much."

"You're the man who gave the Stone to the giants, then. And you told them to destroy the Snoppishes' roof, so Lord Snoppish would find his own Stone. And you made Alkarren a Hollow One, so he'd steal the Stone from Takeke. But how did it get broken in the first place?"

Merren smiled. "The Others were able to influence the world through men before, of course, mostly through dreams and madness. They broke the Stone trying to destroy its power. And they caused petty wars, scattering the pieces as far as they could. One Stone became lost in the forest—the Others showed me where it was and I gave it to the giants. One piece stayed at the College, where the masters studied it endlessly and wrote down everything they'd learned on a parchment. That one came to an ancestor of old Snoppish in another war. And the third, the Takekek Stone— that had a complicated history, four hundred years of battles and conspiracies, but finally it landed in Takeke."

Eddies of color parted behind Merren. Mathewar saw a small grass-covered hill near a river. A man and a woman sat on the ground, surrounded by their court. They wore gold and jewels in their hair; their robes were the color of clouds touched by the sun. Light shone from them, sparking from their hands and eyes and jewels.

They were more beautiful than anyone Mathewar had ever seen, unearthly, dazzling. Merren followed his gaze and the man and woman—surely the king and queen of this realm—saluted him.

Even Merren wasn't behind everything, then. The strings didn't end with him but extended even further. "You're working for them, is that it?" Mathewar asked.

"Yes. They promised me sovereignty over our world and a seat at their court at the end."

Mathewar doubted it. Someone like Merren, a gross man of his world, had no place in this enchanted court.

He thought quickly. The Others fashioned dreams; they gave men and women their deepest desires. Merren wanted a seat in this fantastic court, wanted to feel worthy of such creatures. But the king and queen did not exist outside Merren's mind: what use had the land of dreams for a ruler? The Others controlled him, just as surely as Merren controlled the Hollow Ones he created.

"Listen, Merren," he said. "Those are creatures of your fantasies, of your own mind, don't you see? They're not real."

"Of course they're real. They welcomed me to this land, when I finally found a way through to it. You're envious, aren't you? I could find a place for you in their court, something worthy of your talents."

"A dream office in a dream court? No, thank you."

Suddenly Merren flashed a sword toward him. Almost without thinking Mathewar created a shield to block it, and felt a violent shock as it hit.

Their dream-contest began in earnest. Now it was Mathewar's turn to fashion a sword, and Merren a shield. They fought back and forth, but Mathewar had the advantage of youth and strength, and Merren soon began to give ground.

Merren grew to twice his height, three times, became a giant. He raised his club. Mathewar hurled his sword at Merren's head. Merren shrunk quickly, and the sword sailed harmlessly over him.

This was not illusion, Mathewar realized, hurrying to create another sword. Or perhaps it was, but in the realm of the Others illusion and truth were two sides of the same coin, equally capable of doing harm. Whatever the mind could think of became real here.

Merren shaped himself into a lion breathing fire. Mathewar imagined a great jug of water instead of the sword, and as quick as thought he held it in his hands and doused the fire.

Think, he told himself. He had never learned this kind of fighting, had never even guessed it existed. He knew how to find a real thing hidden within skeins of illusion, but here he had to break through one truth into another, and another after that.

Merren became a squat spitting toad. Mathewar raised an iron shield. The toad's poison burnt through the shield and Mathewar dropped it quickly, then shaped another sword and flung it at Merren.

Merren disappeared. Mathewar searched wildly through the coiling colors but saw nothing. No, there he was, a scorpion with his tail raised, crawling toward him.

There were infinite possibilities here, Mathewar thought. He made himself invisible, the dream of every magician since Tobrin. Merren became a whirlwind of sand and gusted around him; he heard the scream of the wind and felt the grit blown in his eyes and mouth. The sand outlined him, made him visible. He cursed, and flung himself into the shape of a bird.

He flew high over the realm of the Others. He saw little but the colors swirling around him, but sometimes they parted and he could make out trees and streams and fields. And there were strange sights: an ancient panoply of glittering kings, winding through the forest like gold through a tapestry; a stag with the moon caught in its antlers; a feast that looked as if it had lasted days, or years; a great fountain of wine, its white stone stained red where the wine had purled down to the bowl below.

Exhilaration coursed through him; wind blew through his feathers. There was nothing like this, nothing in the world. He would have to tell Rone . . .

He had made himself a crow, he realized, probably because of some memory of Rone. He cried out and heard a harsh rusty caw; but to that part of him that was a crow it sounded like a call of triumph.

Another bird followed him, an eagle. He flew faster but the eagle, stronger and larger, gained on him. He would have to land before he could change into another shape—or could he fall from a height safely in this world?

The eagle began to drop back. Mathewar tried to grin but the crow's beak made it impossible, and he cried out in exultation instead. His plan had worked.

He had remembered Merren giving way before his sword, and he realized that one thing did not seem to change in this shifting world: Merren was older and weaker. Or perhaps Merren could only imagine himself as an older man; but either way the result was the same.

He soared on, feeling the first strain on the muscles in his wings and back. The eagle slowed further and began to glide toward the earth, until finally Mathewar lost sight of him amid the trees.

Mathewar wheeled around, heading back. He had to return to the place where he had first seen Merren; he didn't know why but he sensed that it was important. Perhaps when he was in his human shape again he would understand.

On and on he went, his wings burning, his back feeling like knots tightening. Finally he peered between the flowing colors and saw a river, then the fantastic court arrayed beside it on a grass-covered hill.

He dropped toward the earth and landed, then took on his human shape. He felt exhausted. He sat on a rock, breathing heavily. Why had he wanted to come back to this place? It was a barren plot of ground, nothing special or interesting about it. He would have to think of the answer quickly, though, or Merren might return, guessing where he had gone.

Music sounded from the court beside the river, a haunting song that reminded him of his childhood. Two of the court played pipes, another a harp, a third a steady insistent beat on a drum. The court stood and began to move, seeming to barely trouble the grass as they went. Gold and silver shimmered around them.

They headed toward a domed castle made of alabaster, the pipers in the lead. Moonlight shone on it, white upon white, so bright that Mathewar could see the lacy towers, the fretwork windows, a glimpse of the marble halls inside. It was beautiful beyond imagining.

It had not been there a moment ago. He felt a strong desire to explore it, to taste the wonders inside.

The Others wanted him, he thought frantically. He had called to them, he belonged to them now . . . He had to get out.

But how? And where was the Stone? He stood quickly. That was what he needed to remember; he had dropped the Stone in the heat of the battle with Merren. A feeling of dread, almost of despair, came over him; he had lost the one thing that could help him.

He looked around wildly. The moon had gone, and a pale sun lit the land; then they succeeded each other quickly, scudding across the sky like clouds. He saw stones everywhere; his desire for them had conjured them up. He forced himself to take a deep breath and sense the land around him.

He felt no magic but that of the Others. The colors grew stronger, wrapping him in enchantment. They parted like a curtained doorway to show him what he might have if he stayed; he saw Embre, and himself on a golden throne, and Angarred . . . Haunted, fantastic shapes called to him.

The colors darkened, became blood red, twilight gray, deep forest green. They flowed sluggishly around him, forcing him to move carefully. Something dropped to the ground in front of him, and through a break in the colors he caught a quick glimpse of an eagle, and then Merren.

"I thought . . . that you would come here," Merren said, breathing hard.

In the next instant Embre stood before him. "No!" Mathewar said, the word breaking from him without his realizing.

Embre grinned. Her shape wavered and frayed, and she became Merren again, still grinning.

Merren was tired, he saw, exhausted from his flight and the long fight between them. The shape continued to change, shifting between Merren and Embre and horrible combinations of both, Merren's old man's face with Embre's long brown hair.

"I know you, you see," Merren said. "I know what will . . . make you stay. Stay with me."

He lost control of his shape, became Merren again. Mathewar fashioned a sword and thrust it to Merren's heart.

"No," Merren said. "Wait . . ."

Would it work? Could an illusory sword cause a real death? Merren spat blood; it looked black amid the darkening colors.

"We could . . . we could have . . ." Merren said. He braced himself to say something else. An apology? Some knowledge about the Others? "It was so lovely here," he said, and then his knees gave way and he fell to the ground.

Mathewar knelt to make certain that he was dead, that death was not merely another of his transformations. He stood. He had to concentrate, had to put Merren's treachery, and Merren's death at his hand, behind him, at least for now. He had to find the Stone; and the colors, the music, the smells, all the exotic blandishments of the Others had grown even stronger.

He was the only one left to them now that Merren was gone. They would do anything they could to keep him. He glanced around quickly, trying not to panic. Stones multiplied in front of him, each one identical to the true Stone.

He closed his eyes and tried to sense the Stone, but he could feel nothing. No, wait. He touched someone else nearby, someone human, thank the Godkings. He opened his eyes and began to walk slowly through the featureless land.

He stopped at the place where he had felt the person, whoever he was. He saw no one. The sense grew sharper, though; he could tell that it was a man, and very old . . .

He looked down. A stone lay on the ground; he knew it for the true Stone as soon as he saw it. He picked it up and studied it, turning it over and over in his fingers, feeling the familiar strength emanating from it. He had not lost it after all. Relief washed over him.

But the sense of another presence had not left him. He probed the land around him, coming back always to the Stone. Something else flowed from it now that it was whole, something he had not noticed in the heat of battle.

Everything changes, he thought. He set the Stone down. "Show yourself!" he said.

In the next instant a man stood before him. He was thin and short, yet he radiated an authority Mathewar had seen nowhere else. He had black penetrating eyes, and white hair that flew about his head as if his body could not contain all the power within him. Mathewar knew him immediately; he had seen his portrait in the place of honor during all his years at the College. "Tobrin!" he said, astonished.

"Tobrin," the man said slowly. "Yes."

"You—you turned yourself into the Stone, then. But no one—you said yourself no one could work a real transformation, and yet the Stone was a true stone . . ."

"Yes, all that is true," Tobrin said. He looked around him. "But where have you brought me? This is the realm of the Others, isn't it? We must leave—this is not the place to discuss truth and falsehood. Even I could not bind the Others completely to the Stone."

Mathewar nearly asked him how they were to escape, but he discovered he knew the answer; he had only to ask the Stone. And Tobrin was somehow both Stone and man; when he concentrated on that part that was the Stone he saw the path clearly in front of him.

They headed back through the pillars of trees. The elation he had felt, the sense that everything had a purpose and worked for the best, was nearly gone. A longing to return to the Others overcame him, and he had to force himself to continue walking, to place one foot in front of the other.

More than anything the presence of Tobrin kept him going—the desire to get answers to his questions at long last, to learn from the greatest magician in the history of the realms. "Spells of Transformation are possible, then," he said. "Why did you mislead generations of magicians?"

"You know why," Tobrin said. He looked closely at Mathewar for the first time. "You summoned me—no one has ever done that in all the long years I spent as the Stone. You tell me."

"Because—because of the wars. You didn't want any magician to learn true transformation because he would wreak more ruin, and the lands had suffered damage enough."

"Yes, exactly. And I did not allow women into the College, and I wrote that women's magic was weak, so that no student there would ever see a transformation and learn how to do it."

"But we continued to study your books hundreds of years after the war. You led us down the wrong path."

"No. I showed you many right paths—there was only one I kept hidden." He turned to Mathewar again. "And you would have done the same, if you had seen the ugly legacy of the wars. The Spells of Transformation are too dangerous. I don't regret my decision."

"Why—" Mathewar began, then realized that Tobrin would only tell him to work out the answers to his questions himself. "You changed yourself into the Stone because that was the only way you could bind so much magic together. A Stone could never hold so much power, but a man could. The masters at the College always wondered how you had made such a small thing hold so much."

Tobrin smiled. "Well, they weren't supposed to know."

"Will you teach us Spells of Transformation now?"

"No."

"No? But we need them—we need to put an end to this war—"

"Haven't you been listening to me? These spells are too dangerous. You would begin by ending the war, but sooner or later you would use them for your own purposes, or someone else would. Anyway, how do I know that you have the right of it? I understand very little about the quarrels of your time. Why did you go into the realm of the Others, for example?"

Mathewar told him briefly what had happened within the various lands. "Ah," Tobrin said finally. "I could not see much around me when I was the Stone, and even less when the Stone broke into pieces."

"But are the stories true then? Have you come back to aid us? Because the lands need you more than ever now."

"No. These are not my battles—I fought my own war years ago. And sooner or later someone would demand the secrets of transformation from me, and I would refuse to give them."

"But—"

Tobrin held up his hand. "I see that you want knowledge from me, more for its own sake than for any advantage in battle. But you will have to solve the problems of your own time by yourself."

The colors around them began to fade. They walked in silence for a while. Mathewar's arm brushed the hilt of his sword, and he realized that he had not thought to use it once in the Others' realm. But would it have been as effective as a dream sword? He didn't think so.

The dark streets of Pergodi appeared in front of them. Mathewar heard shouts and smelled smoke, and he felt more than a little sorry to leave the enchantments of the Others and return to such a harsh and difficult place.

Tobrin walked off quickly into the city. Mathewar thought of spells to keep him, to change him back into the Stone, but he knew with certainty that he could not best Tobrin, a man who could work the secrets of transformation. He watched him go, thinking of all the things he could have done with the Stone, all he might have learned.

"Mathewar!" someone said. He turned; it was Angarred. "What happened? You disappeared for a moment. And who was that man?"

"Only a moment?" he asked, knowing that his lack of a direct answer would infuriate her.

"Why can't you ever give a simple answer, by the Orator?"

"Well, it's not a simple question. I'll explain everything later, I promise you. Right now I have to see what I can do here."

He looked around him, feeling cold after the warm air of the Others' realm. People were stepping back from their battles, staring at their opponents as if dazed. Someone called a command to halt, and more and more folks sheathed their swords. A man nearby stopped hitting a soldier's head with a stick of wood, and then, surprisingly, he apologized.

"What is it?" Angarred said. "What's happening?"

"The Others have lost control of their Hollow Ones," Mathewar said. "It was the Others who were behind everything, and Merren who did their will outside their realm. And now Merren is dead."

"Merren? He's—he was a master, wasn't he?"

"That's right. Do you remember when I told you that one of the masters was hiding something? He had discovered a way to go to the land of the Others and come back safely, or so he thought. Only of course it wasn't safe—he had fallen under their spell."

Some Takekek soldiers continued to fight the Pergodek—no doubt they still suspected Karededin of stealing their Stone—but most of the fighting had stopped. Soldiers hurried past carrying buckets, heading toward the fires in the poorer quarters. People no longer looked dazed but ashamed, as if they could not imagine how such madness had overcome them.

Suddenly everyone around them was bowing or curtsying. Mathewar turned to see King Tezue riding toward them, five archers in blue cloaks riding at his back.

"Ah, one of my magicians," Tezue said. He wore brightly colored clothing and jewels hung from his neck and ear; he looked out of place, almost ridiculous, among the dirt of the battle. "I wondered what happened to you. You and all the others haven't been to court for over a year, isn't that right? You've been derelict, gravely derelict. We've had only one loyal friend in all this trying time—our servant Alkarren."

He held out his arm, his full sleeve billowing in the wind. Alkarren walked up and took his place at the king's side.

Angarred nearly stopped breathing. As far as she knew Mathewar still wanted to kill Alkarren; now he would probably do it in the sight of the king, and be killed himself for an act of treason. And she would not be able to stop him; she had tried, and had seen how obstinate he was.

"Alkarren," Mathewar said, nodding to him instead of bowing. "You remember Angarred."

"Of course." Alkarren studied her with his dark piercing eyes. "You told me you didn't know Mathewar, didn't you?"

Angarred said nothing. Mathewar turned to the king. "My lord, King Tezue," he said. "Alkarren killed my wife and tried to kill me. He imprisoned my daughter. He imprisoned and tortured me. He stole your Stone and used it for his own gain. He attempted to take control of Karededin, and to create chaos within your realm. I demand justice—I demand that you shut him up in the dungeons as he shut me up, and that the king's court decide if he is to live or die."

Tezue blinked at him. His mind's gone, Angarred thought in despair. He doesn't understand anything Mathewar's said.

Tezue looked at Alkarren, then back at Mathewar. "You are not in a position to demand anything," he said finally. "As I said, you've been missing from our court for a good long while."

"I was afraid Alkarren would kill me, milord."

"You will not interrupt us. And the idea of Alkarren killing anyone is ludicrous. He has been the only magician loyal to us this past year—the others turned tail and scampered, just as you did."

"They feared him as well. I told you—he stole the Stone."

"Another baseless and ridiculous charge. Tell me, did you steal the Stone, Alkarren?"

"No, milord," Alkarren said, smiling.

"Would you open your pockets to me, Alkarren?"

"Of course, milord." The smile grew wider, became a sneer.

"He doesn't have the Stone now," Mathewar said, less forcefully than before. "He—"

"No?" Tezue asked. "Then where is it?"

"He had it, milord," Alkarren said. "He has it now, or knows where it is."

Tezue motioned to his men, who readied their bows and advanced on Mathewar. Mathewar could do nothing, neither draw a sword nor call upon a spell; attacking the king or his servants was treason, and he would be killed before he finished. He stood unmoving, gazing up at the king without expression.

A great many things went through Angarred's mind, all in the time it took to blink. Mathewar saying that Tezue was still a Hollow One, and Perren's training, and Alkarren talking to her in the menagerie, and a conversation in Chelenin's bedroom . . .

Her bones and muscles flowed, lengthening or contracting. She changed. She was a leopard: as a leopard she leapt toward Alkarren and slashed him from his throat to his stomach with her claws; she knocked him easily to the ground; she placed her great paw on his chest; she nuzzled at his neck, working toward that delicious place on the spine where she could crack his bones.

"Angarred!" someone called. "Angarred, stop!"

She glanced up. Everything looked amazingly bright, though some colors were missing. Sounds had sharpened as well, and scents collected in great pools, so strong she could almost see them. She smelled the tang of fear from a horse nearby, and more complex odors from two men, one drenched in horrid perfume, the other familiar, with a scent that carried associations of warmth and closeness. And strongest of all, the tantalizing, urgent smell of blood on the ground, demanding all her attention.

"Stop!" the familiar-smelling one said again. "He's dead! Angarred, stop! Remember!"

She could trust this one, she knew. She struggled to understand him, to remember. She had been a Takekek soldier once, and with this man's help she had come back from that.

She went deep inside herself again. Her bones and muscles shifted, and the smells faded. She found herself on all fours, sniffing a welling pool of blood, and she made a sound of disgust and stood.

"Oh, holy Godkings," she said. She pressed her hand to her mouth, looked at the clawed and bleeding body on the ground, looked away.

"It's all right," the man said. "You're back—it's all right."

Who was he? Bits and pieces returned—sleeping on the ground, looking up at the stars through the trees; leading him down a long bright hallway; sitting on a table and talking to giants—and then suddenly everything rushed back. Mathewar. Of course.

"Oh," King Tezue said. He shuddered violently. "I'm back. I'm back, and that horrible *thing* is gone. Thank all my holy ancestors in the Celestial Court."

"Do you mean Alkarren?" Angarred asked.

Tezue turned toward her. "You're that girl who asked for justice," he said. "I saw and heard everything, but I could do nothing. Nothing, all this time. For ridding me of that monster I'll grant you anything in my court, anything at all. But right now we have to—" He looked around, more alert than she had ever seen him, seeming to take everything in at once. "—we have to finish this war, once and for all. And with Alkarren gone, and those he controlled free again, I daresay it won't take very long."

"And now that Norue's dead, his Takekek army seems to be coming apart," Mathewar said.

"Norue made an alliance with Takeke?" Tezue asked. "Everyone turned against me, seemingly, and I could do nothing. But that changes now. You," he said, pointing to three of his guards. "Look for Karedek soldiers, all you can find, and order them back here."

The guards rode off. "One more thing," Tezue said to Angarred and Mathewar. "I call upon you both as witnesses. I hereby appoint

Rodarren as my heir—and the Godkings grant that she doesn't have the feverchill."

"I heard she was ill—" Angarred said.

"No time for that," Tezue said. "We'll see her later. Right now we fight one final battle."

T W E N T Y · S I X

Angarred spent the rest of the day looking for soldiers and directing them to King Tezue. Occasionally she felt again the strangeness of changing into another shape, how her feet had shortened, her spine lengthened, the way the blood tasted, but she put those memories away to think about some other time.

Perren would be proud of her, she thought. She had found her animal without the help of mirrorleaf, like those well-disciplined children in the forest.

But did she care what Perren thought? She would think about that later too. Still, it seemed fitting that it was her mother who had shown her her birthright.

Once she saw Mathewar, fighting for the king. He seemed taller and broader, and light clashed around him, and she stopped to look at him for a moment before she recalled herself to her errand.

She returned at evening and found a spot out of the way to watch the battle. Tezue's orders were sharp and precise, and he displayed great skill as a commander. With Norue's troops gone and the Hollow Ones freed he had a clear advantage by the end of the day.

The Takekek captains surrendered to Tezue with the nightfall. The rest of the soldiers, confused and tired, turned and headed for home.

Tezue motioned to Angarred and Mathewar. "Come along with us," he said to them. "We're going to the castle to parley. You can look in on Rodarren." He ordered the guards to find mounts for them, and they rode behind him and his train and the Takekek captains through the city.

They passed a gap in the wall, and for the first time Angarred saw the great Takekek encampment, laid out like a small city with its own streets and even a marketplace. A deserted city—the tents and cookhouses and timber yards were empty, the soldiers all fled. A few carts still struggled through the mud, axle deep, the drivers desperate to set out for home before the Karedek soldiers began looting.

Once at the castle Angarred led Mathewar quickly to Rodarren's apartments. She had worried about the princess all day, and not only because she liked her. If Rodarren died the great procession in the Hall of the Standing Kings would come to an end, and what would happen to Karededin then?

They reached Rodarren's rooms. The door was slightly open; no doctors clustered around it, though, and Angarred feared the worst.

She pushed the door and looked inside, but saw nothing but an empty room. "Princess Rodarren!" she called.

She went farther in. Rodarren's apartments, like Norue's, stretched out a long way. She went from room to room, calling. Finally she saw her, sitting by herself on a chair, unmoving.

She's dead, Angarred thought. No, she was smiling; no dead person had ever looked like that. "Princess Rodarren?" she asked.

"Come in, come in," Rodarren said. "It's good to see you."

"We heard you were ill," Angarred said.

"I was. I am. I haven't been able to eat in three days." The princess burst out laughing. "Oh, don't look like that! It's the most amazing news. I'm pregnant."

"Oh!" Angarred said. "Oh, holy Mother Mathona. But—"

"But how, you want to say. Isn't that right?"

"It's Lord Jerret's child," Mathewar said, speaking for the first time. "Congratulations."

"Yes." Rodarren's smile grew broader. "The line of kings will continue—I will have an heir. Jerret's child. And if I don't marry—and I don't intend to—it will be Jerret's statue in the Hall of the Standing Kings opposite mine, and Jerret ruling with me in the Celestial Court. He'll gain immortality through me. Of course," she said, quieter now, "I would have preferred him alive."

"But will the people accept him?" Mathewar said. "And will they accept your child as a legitimate heir?"

"They'll have to. Jerret and I were married in the dungeons— there was a religious in the cell across from ours."

"You'll have to find him, then," Mathewar said. "Get him to write down his account of the wedding and have it witnessed. You know what people are like—there are factions that won't believe you without evidence. Do you remember where you were in the dungeons?"

"I should have thought of that myself," Rodarren said. She called for a servant and gave him precise orders, then wrote a letter for the guard at the prison, freeing the religious.

Sounds came from the corridor. Angarred went to the door and looked out. An unplanned gathering seemed to be taking place as people learned that the war was over. And when the religious was led down the hallway to Rodarren's rooms, skeletally thin and leaning on the arm of the servant, rumors of Rodarren's wedding spread through the gathering, and the noise of celebration grew louder.

After Angarred and Mathewar and the servant witnessed the religious' account Rodarren said, "I'm afraid I have to sleep now— I'm very tired. Thank you both for everything."

The servant ushered them out. A swirl of merrymakers moved past Angarred, some of them people she had met at court, but no one stopped to talk.

When they reached the main part of the castle the crowd had grown so thick they had to push their way through. Some of them had taken out their costumes for the New Year; the festival of the year's turning, Angarred realized, was less than a week away. They wore masks, ribbons, feathers, jewels, and clothing more splendid than anything Angarred had ever seen. She passed bodices and coats sewn with pearls and golden thread, necklaces hung with rare emeralds, glittering silver-and-ruby tiaras. A great mask of Mother Mathona the moon loomed out of the crowd and then disappeared.

Narinye came toward them, looking as drab as a religious next to the merrymakers. "There you are," he said to Mathewar. "Come—King Tezue wants to talk to us about the Stone." He took hold of Mathewar and opened a path for them through the crowd.

Angarred watched them go, feeling strangely bereft. The celebration continued around her but she recognized no one. Suddenly she realized how tired she was. She went to her apartments in the castle.

She couldn't sleep. The noises of celebration came up to her rooms, but that wasn't why she lay awake. She felt odd, dissatisfied, as if the story had ended for everyone but her.

She would have to talk to Tezue about his promise to her. Perhaps with what he gave her she could return to Hashan Hall and re-create it as it was in the days of its greatness. She could hire Rushlag and Elenin again, reclaim her fields and lands, set an army of craftsmen to work inside the house and out.

But was that what she wanted? Now that she finally had it she felt unsure. She heard bells ringing in the city below, and between the peals the distant sound of singing. She turned on the bed and tried to sleep through the long night of revelry.

Narinye beckoned Mathewar into a quiet place beneath an arch. "Takeke wants the Stone back," he said. "They've sworn not to sign any treaty until they get it. When I saw you last you had two pieces—we could give them one and keep the other at the College."

"I found all three pieces," Mathewar said. "And they fit together and made the Stone whole again."

Narinye was silent a moment. "This is both good and bad," he said finally. "We have the complete Stone, but we will have to return it to Takeke to make peace."

"The Stone isn't ours to give."

"What do you mean?"

"The Stone of Tobrin," Mathewar said. "The name explains everything, but we never saw it."

"Stop talking in riddles. What—"

"The Stone *is* Tobrin," he said. He told Narinye what he had seen and learned in the land of the Others.

"Holy Godkings," the master said. He looked confused for the first time since Mathewar had known him. "Merren . . . and Tobrin . . . and Spells of Transformation . . . And he just walked away, you say? Why didn't you try to convince him to stay?"

"I did. He didn't want to. And you know, I think he may have been right. The Stone is too powerful—too many people would be tempted by it. I was, certainly—I would dearly love to learn Spells of Transformation. And it seems that even the might of the College can't protect it—the Others managed to get at it once, and they would almost surely try again."

He didn't tell Narinye what he suspected, that he had not seen the last of Tobrin. The magician would wander the realms as he had done before, learning and teaching, perhaps even visiting the College. And if Mathewar encountered him again he would be ready for him, with new theories and questions. He had not given up trying to discover the secrets of transformation.

"What do we say to the king?" Narinye asked.

"Let me talk to him," Mathewar said.

Narinye said nothing but led him down several corridors. The sounds of celebration dropped behind them the farther they went from the main part of the castle. Narinye stopped at one of the doors, and the guards in front ushered them inside immediately.

Tezue sat at a large table. He had changed his clothes since Mathewar had seen him last; he looked even more magnificent than he had in the streets of Pergodi. He was surrounded by advisors, and several Takekek captains sat across from him.

"Ah, Master Narinye, Mathewar," he said, standing. He motioned them into a smaller room off the larger one and carefully closed the door behind them. "Mathewar, I'm told you have the Stone."

"I'm afraid that isn't true, milord," Mathewar said. "The Stone has gone its own way."

"What! Well, get it back, man."

"I can't. It has its own will, and its own destiny."

"Where is it now?"

"I don't know."

The king's ruddy face grew even redder. "What if I threaten to imprison you until you bring it to me?"

"Even then, milord."

Tezue sighed. His anger seemed to leave him. "I have to have it. The Takekek won't make peace without it."

"With all respect, milord—you've won the war already. If you tell them you don't have the Stone there's very little they can do about it."

"I know that, of course. But I'd hoped to conclude this meeting amicably, and not end it by threatening them. They're sitting across our border, after all—I want them as friends, not enemies."

"Yes, but you want the magicians as friends as well. And the Takekek will be our allies once again."

"But when? This year? Ten years from now?"

"I'm sorry to have caused you so much trouble, milord."

Tezue studied him, his blue eyes sharp and bright. "Not as sorry as you should be." He sighed again. "Well, it seems there's nothing I can do, not unless I want war with the College. And no king has ever been foolish enough for that."

He waved his hand in dismissal. "Go, go," he said. "You've already given me several more days of work, until I can get these pig-headed Takekek to sign a treaty. And Mathewar—"

Mathewar turned on his way to the door.

"I'll remember this," the king said.

Mathewar and Narinye went out past the large meeting table and into the corridor, walking together silently for a long time. Finally, when they were certain they could not be overheard, Narinye turned to Mathewar and said, "I always knew you were reckless—I just never knew *how* reckless. Why in the name of the Godkings didn't you tell him what you told me?"

"I didn't think he should meddle in this," Mathewar said. "It's a matter for magicians, not kings."

———

Angarred woke to a loud knock. Bright sunlight came in through her window; she had stayed awake most of the night and then apparently slept a good deal of the morning.

The knock sounded again. She walked on bare feet toward the door and opened it. A young woman dressed in some sort of livery stood there. "Lady Angarred Hashan?" the woman asked.

"Yes?"

"Princess Rodarren sends you this," she said, handing her a small package. She bowed and left.

There was a letter inside, closed by a seal, and a small velvet purse. "My dear Angarred," the letter said. "There will be a celebration tonight at the castle, more formal than the one last night. Both King Tezue and I would like you to come. Our present today is a token of much more to come, though we know we can never repay you for all you did for us. Please buy yourself something splendid for the festivities. Your servant, Princess Rodarren."

She opened the purse and saw a mix of coins, silver and gold, great and small, more, it seemed, than she had gotten for the entire contents of Hashan Hall. She caught her breath. Her first impulse was to hoard it all away, to save it and parcel it out for necessities. She had never trusted promises; her father had veered from one crazy scheme to another, putting down one to pick up another, so that she had learned not to believe in any of his plans for the future.

She poured the cold coins, clinking, into her hand. Rodarren had sent the letter, though, and she had never known the princess to be anything less than honest. And she would dearly love to wear something beautiful, something of her own, to show off at last for the court.

She dressed and went out into the city. People were still celebrating, whole neighborhoods of them. Grocers took down the last of their food and passed it out to the crowds; vintners brought out kegs of wine; musicians played while other revelers danced in the streets. Bonfires smoldered out; folks had kindled them as soon as they heard the news of victory and had gathered around them all night, exchanging news, reliving battles. Workers were already repairing the breaches in the city walls. She found the nearest

Craftsman's Quarter and spent the rest of the day there, then returned to her apartments.

When evening came she left her rooms. She wore a pale rose dress set with pearls, and her hair was bound in a circlet of pearl and gold. Five petticoats rustled underneath her dress as she walked.

People thronged the corridors of the castle. Light shone from the walls, falling on moonstone and amethyst, garnet and emerald, lace and ivory.

As soon as she stepped downstairs she was caught up in a flowing tide of people, carried unwillingly from one group to another. Once again she saw no one she knew, and she began to wonder why she had come; whether, after all she had seen and done, she still sought the approval of the court. And several times she caught herself looking for Jerret, thinking with pleasure of all the gossip she had to tell him.

"Make way, make way," a voice said, and the crowds parted before her. Guards came through, leading a line of gaunt men and women with tattered clothes and thickly matted hair. Some of them could barely stand, and had to be helped along by the guards. "Prisoners," someone murmured. "Freed prisoners."

Angarred saw Lady Karanin among them. She looked like the poorest Pergodek beggar but she held her head high, wearing her rags as if they were the latest fashion. She nodded to the right and left as she went, like a queen reviewing her subjects, her expression almost haughty.

First one and then another of the courtiers began to applaud, and finally the whole crowd cheered her as she passed by. Angarred found herself joining in. You had to admire her poise, she thought, if nothing else.

Before the crowd closed up again she caught a glimpse of someone who looked like Mathewar. It couldn't be, though; the man was dressed in courtier's clothes, black trousers and a tight-fitting black jacket worked in silver thread, the cuffs and neck edged with silver. But he had Mathewar's height, and he wore his hair tied back. He had been talking to someone, someone she thought she knew . . .

She pushed her way through the crush of people toward where she had seen him last. Lady Dorilde stood there, talking to another courtier. No, it was Mathewar.

He looked so splendid she could hardly breathe for a moment. She had never seen him in such finery; on their travels he had always worn simple shirts and trousers. She moved closer, keeping the crowd between them. He had a silver-and-pearl earring.

Dorilde put her hand on his arm and smiled. "It's good to see you, Matte," she said. "Everyone's talking about you—listening to them it sounds as if you won the war single-handedly."

Matte? Angarred thought.

As if he had heard her thought Mathewar turned. "Angarred," he said. She could not read his expression. "Hello."

"You told me you didn't know Mathewar," Dorilde said to her.

"I lied," Angarred said.

Dorilde smiled uncertainly. "I was just telling Matte how glad we are to have him back. You've been away—how long? A year?"

"I didn't mean to interrupt," Angarred said. "I'll see you later. Matte," she added, feeling spiteful.

"No, stay," Mathewar said. "If you'll excuse me, Lady Dorilde . . ."

He bowed and left her. For a brief moment Angarred saw a look of disappointment cross her face; then she put on her courtier's face and disappeared into the crowd.

They found an alcove nearly empty of people. They stood awkwardly for a while, saying nothing. Finally Angarred said, "I thought only your daughter called you Matte."

"Embre called me that," he said. "Dorilde must have heard her say it."

"Oh. Sorry."

"For what?"

"For bringing up bad memories. For taking you away from Dorilde—clearly she had plans for you tonight."

"What do you mean? I was about to bed her, is that what you think?"

"Well, you've done it before. Her or someone else. You told me so in the forest."

"You remember that, do you? Then you'll remember that I also said I gave up court pastimes. I never looked at her after I met Embre."

"That's right," Angarred said. "Embre."

"What about her?" Mathewar said.

She had never seen the expression he showed her now: not anger, but anger held closely in check, a warning. His eyes were gray, the color of old swords. She nearly stopped speaking, but something pushed her to go on. "Well, she's the perfect woman, isn't she? You don't have to worry about caring for anyone or feeling anything ever again—she'll always be there to stand between you and someone else."

He said nothing.

"Well, it's not my business, thank the Godkings," Angarred said. "I just thought someone should tell you. Though I suppose it doesn't matter—you probably want to spend the rest of your life alone."

He was silent a long time. She thought she had gone too far, made a terrible error, that he would never speak to her again.

"You've always had the Clear Sight with me, haven't you?" he said finally. "You've always been able to see clear through me, and then tell me the truth about myself. I used to think it was just bluntness . . . But no, I don't want to spend the rest of my life alone. And I do care about other people. I think—I care about you."

She felt suspended between apprehension and deep delight. What did he mean by "care about"? She cursed herself for using such an ambiguous phase.

"Say something," he said. "Please. My life is in your hands."

She looked at him in surprise, hearing a tone in his voice that had never been there before. "But—well, I thought you knew. I've loved you for a long time, ever since we traveled back from the College, that first time in the forest."

"I think I've loved you longer than that. Since the first time I saw you, wild and barefoot and freezing in your father's house. But everything then was second to my craving for sattery, and after that there was my quest for Embre . . ."

They had moved closer without realizing it. All her senses were heightened; she felt the velvet nap of his clothes, heard the harsh rasp of his breath. They kissed; it was softer and less urgent than their last time, more of a question. "Do you want to leave?" he asked. "I'm sure the festivities can go on without us. I have a room in the castle."

"Yes," she said. "Oh, yes."

At his room their desire had grown so strong they could not be bothered to take off their clothes. They fumbled in the darkness; she got rid of her underclothes, and two or three of the petticoats, and he slipped out of one leg of the trousers, and they fell upon each other in the bed.

Afterward he had time to create a light, and to speak words to lock the door against visitors. They began again more slowly, taking turns undressing each other, she parting his jacket, he unlacing her dress. "How many petticoats does this cursed thing have?" he asked, and she laughed and helped him with the ones that remained.

Finally they lay naked to each other, exclaiming over their discoveries. "Ah," she said, running her hands over his broad chest and corded muscles. "Ah," he said, kissing her full breasts and rounded stomach. Their urgency kindled again, and he moved into her, and she felt a vast pleasure start deep within her, carrying her upward like a wave. She cried out as the wave broke, and heard his cry answering her.

Then they lay on their sides, gazing at each other. "How could I have known?" he asked, smiling. He traced the line of her face, plucked a pearl from her hair. "You were either friendly to me or very distant, distant and regal. What was I to make of that?"

"Well, you were always mocking me," she said.

"Was I?" He was still smiling.

"All right, not always. Sometimes. And you would never explain anything."

"I had to learn secrecy this past year—learned it too well, maybe. I'm sorry."

"Oh, it doesn't matter now. Though you might tell me how you disappeared after you fit all the pieces of the Stone together."

She listened, amazed and more than a little terrified for him, as he told her about his visit to the land of the Others and his magical contest with Merren, and what he had discovered about the Stone.

"So that man you saw, the one you asked about—that was Tobrin," he said.

"Tobrin," she said, marveling. A man out of legend had walked into the streets of Pergodi, had passed within a few feet of her.

"And now both Narinye and the king are angry with me—they wanted to give the Stone back to Takeke."

"Didn't you tell Narinye what you told me?"

"Most of it. Oh, the Others take it!"

"What's wrong?"

"I promised Narinye I'd talk to him tonight. He said he had something important to tell me."

She put her hand on his arm. "Don't go."

"I don't intend to. I can see him tomorrow."

She ran her hand over his arm and up to his shoulder, and they moved together again.

They found Narinye in the castle the next day. If he felt surprised to see them together, he said nothing.

"You wanted to talk to me," Mathewar said.

"Yes," Narinye said. He paused, perhaps thinking how to begin. "We've lost two masters recently. Merren, of course, and yesterday Dalesio told me he's renouncing magic and going back to his family, that Gedren and his other son need him. And I'm getting older, and I would like very much to retire soon. I'd like to offer you a position in the College, if you're interested."

Mathewar moved to speak, but Narinye held up his hand. "Hear me out. You would not be a master only, but First Master. You would have my position when I retire. You'd be the youngest First Master in history, but seeing what you did here I believe that my trust in you is not misplaced."

Mathewar looked at Angarred. Since the night before they had been open to each other, their minds nearly as naked as their bodies. They had finished each other's sentences, or had not needed to speak at all. He knew without asking that she wanted to stay with him, though it was too early to discuss the details. Would she go back to her estate, or stay in Pergodi, or join her mother and the forest people?

Suddenly he saw the solution. "Angarred," he said. "Would you like to come study at the College? To study and to teach?"

"Teach?" Angarred said, and a moment later Narinye said, "What? You would bring women into the College?"

"Yes, I would. I told you that Spells of Transformation exist, that Tobrin understands them. And so does Angarred, and so do the women in the forest—I've seen it. Tobrin won't teach us, but she might. And I'll bring in some of the forest people, and in exchange for their knowledge we can teach them our magic."

"But Tobrin said—"

"Tobrin lied to us. Women can do magic. We can't ignore that fact any longer—we need their magic and they need ours, the two joined as one. That's my offer. If I can't run the College as I want then I'll stay here in Pergodi as one of the king's magicians." He crossed his arms and leaned against a wall, waiting for Narinye's answer.

"But you know the king's angry at you. He said he wouldn't forget what you did."

"And you know he desires my service, and will probably forget his anger the minute the Takekek sign the treaty."

Narinye said nothing for a while. "I'll have to discuss this with the other masters," he said finally.

"Angarred," Mathewar said, turning to her. "Of course all this depends on your plans. If you want to return—"

She answered him before he had a chance to finish the question. "There's nothing for me at Hashan Hall, nothing but empty stone and unhappy memories. But—but I don't know nearly enough to teach at the College, though I'd love to go there. We could invite Perren, and Rone, and—and even Worrige. And I could study with them and with the masters, and then when I'm ready I could start to teach. And when we travel to the College we can visit the forest people and get Atte, and bring her along with us."

He smiled at the way she had read his thoughts again: she knew how worried he was about his daughter.

"Don't be so quick with your plans," Narinye said. "The other masters—"

"They'll agree," Mathewar said, suddenly seeing pieces of the future, one picture after another. He left the wall and faced Narinye, feeling full of purpose. "The two types of magic contradict each other—either you can change into something else or you can't. And yet they both exist. There's a mystery here, but if we can teach people to do both we can solve it. We can make discoveries no one has ever made before." No one but Tobrin, he thought, and I'll find out his secrets, with or without him. "We're on the verge of something utterly new, something exciting."

Narinye repeated what he had said about the other masters, but Mathewar barely heard him. He saw himself and Angarred living at the College with Atte, teaching and working together. He saw Tobrin stopping for a visit, staying in a room high under the eaves; saw the two of them talking, playing a game that would become familiar to both over the years, one trying to gain knowledge and the other trying to hide it. And for a moment he saw other children besides Atte, though the details were unclear. He felt something he had never thought to experience again—happiness.

He took Angarred's hand, and they left to pack for another journey together.